THE BLACK BARONESS

*

The Black Baroness is the third of seven volumes
incorporating all the principal events which
occurred between September, 1939, and May,
1945, covering the activities of Gregory Sallust,
one of the most famous Secret Agents ever created
in fiction about the Second World War.

Set in Norway in 1940, Gregory is sent on a
mission to that country in order to thwart plans
for the capture of the King. His adversary on
this occasion is the Black Baroness, the French
associate of his old enemy Gruppenführer
Grauber, and as events move from Scandinavia
to the Low Countries and then on to France, it
soon becomes a matter of life-and-death importance to frustrate the might of the German war
machine . . .

Dennis Wheatley

The Black Baroness

ARROW BOOKS

ARROW BOOKS LTD

178–202 Great Portland Street, London W1

AN IMPRINT OF THE HUTCHINSON GROUP

London Melbourne Sydney
Auckland Bombay Toronto
Johannesburg New York

∗

First published by
Hutchinson & Co (*Publishers*) Ltd 1940
Arrow edition 1960
Second impression 1964
Third impression 1965
This new edition 1969

*This book is published at a net price and
supplied subject to the Publishers Association
Standard Condition of Sale registered under
the Restrictive Trade Practices Act 1956*

*Made and printed in Great Britain
by The Anchor Press Ltd.,
Tiptree, Essex*

09 002550 4

For

the earliest Readers of my unpublished work

CAPTAIN HUBERT STRINGER ,

COLONEL CHARLES BALFOUR-DAVEY, M.C.

WING-COMMANDER SIR LOUIS GREIG,

K.B.E., C.V.O., R.A.F.

WING-COMMANDER L. C. DARVALL, M.C., R.A.F.

and

CAPTAIN PEVRIL WILLIAMS-PAWLETT, R.N.

in order of their appearance on my war horizon.

Author's Note

The sequence of the seven books which recount the war adventures of Gregory Sallust is as follows: *The Scarlet Impostor*, *Faked Passports*, *The Black Baroness*, *V for Vengeance*, *Come Into My Parlour*, *Traitors' Gate* and *They Used Dark Forces*. Each volume is a complete story in itself, but the series covers Gregory's activities from September, 1939, to May, 1945, against an unbroken background incorporating all the principal events of the Second World War.

Gregory Sallust also appears in three other books: *Black August*, a story set in an undated future; *Contraband*, an international smuggling story of 1937; and *The Island Where Time Stands Still*, an adventure set in the South Seas and Communist China during the year 1954.

Contents

1

Hitler's Secret Weapon

Although it was mid-March snow still capped the tops of the Norwegian mountains which stood out white and clear against a pale, frosty sky. But the sun shone in the valleys and dappled the wavelets of the greenish sea as the little Baltic tramp steamer puffed its way into Oslo Fjord.

On the tramp's foredeck a man and a woman sat in a pair of rickety old basket chairs that they had carried out from the tiny saloon. The woman was golden-haired and very beautiful. Her proud profile and the lazy grace with which she half-reclined in the easy chair marked her at once as an aristocrat. The man was a loose-limbed fellow in the late thirties; dark, lean-faced, and sinewy by nature, a recent bout of fever had given him an almost wolfish look, but it was relieved by a pair of smiling eyes and a cynical twist to his firm, strong mouth.

The woman was the Countess von Osterberg or, since she preferred to be known by her maiden name, Erika von Epp. The man was Gregory Sallust or, as he preferred to be known by the name under which he was travelling, the Colonel-Baron von Lutz. It was March the 19th—six days since the Russo-Finnish War had ended and five days since they had escaped across the ice, which was beginning to break up in the Gulf of Finland, to the little tramp that was now just completing the first journey of the year south to her home port.

For the first two days of the voyage they had lain in their narrow quarters almost comatose, gradually recovering from utter nervous and physical exhaustion; the result of the ten days' ordeal through which they had passed before escaping from *Herr Gruppenführer Grauber,* the chief of the Gestapo Foreign Department, U.A.—I.

From the third day they had staggered out on deck to continue their convalescence in the fresh air and wintry sunshine. Gradually they were getting back to normal, but they still spoke little and slept from dusk to dawn each night, just content to be in each other's company.

Had it not been for their third companion, the Bolshevik General, Stefan Kuporovitch, who had decided to shake the dust of the Soviet Union off his feet with them, they would have talked even less, but the Russian was a talkative person and he had passed through no such ordeal as theirs.

It was he who had made arrangements for the three of them with the captain of the little tramp, but as they had approached the coast of Norway they had realised that he could not enter another country without a passport. In consequence, he had been landed from the ship's boat, in the early hours of that morning, on a desolate stretch of the Norwegian shore, with the understanding that if he could evade the police he was to meet the others in Oslo. So Erika and Gregory were at last alone.

While the tramp chopped its way down the Baltic, they had avoided any discussion about the future. The war had reached a stalemate; for many months the British had appeared satisfied to blockade Germany, while the French accepted the Siegfried Line as impregnable and did not even attempt to test it by attacks in force, and Hitler seemed content to remain blockaded indefinitely, only playing upon the nerves of his opponents and neighbours by threatening a *Blitzkrieg* on the Balkans, the Low Countries and Scandinavia from week to week in rotation. It looked as though things might go on in that way for years; which was not a happy prospect for the two lovers in view of the fact that she was a German girl and he an Englishman.

If Erika returned to Germany the Nazis would promptly execute her, but she refused to seek sanctuary in Britain or France, so her only course was to live in a neutral country where she might still work for Hitler's overthrow. Gregory, on the other hand, was perfectly free to return to England although, as a lone wolf, working entirely outside the Secret Service, there was no compulsion for him to do so. But Erika knew her man; he would never be content to settle down with her in Norway or Sweden while his country was still fighting for its existence.

With every mile that the tramp came nearer to its destination that thought had troubled them both more and more. They had been in love for over six months and when Erika could get a divorce from her husband they intended to get married. It seemed utterly tragic that now that they were free and together again they must part so soon.

He had tried desperately hard to persuade himself that he

was entitled to remain in Norway with her for a few weeks at least. Old Sir Pellinore Gwaine-Cust, who had sent him out on his strange mission, already knew the results of his wanderings, so there was no one to whom he felt bound to report. Even when he got home he might be kept kicking his heels for months before he was offered another job which really suited his unusual capabilities. Yet he knew that it was no good. Britain was at war and it was up to him to find a way of taking a new hand in the game without an hour's unnecessary delay.

'We should be in by about three o'clock,' he murmured.

She nodded. 'Yes; but they may keep us hanging about for hours before they allow us ashore.'

'That depends on how soon we can get hold of your friend at the German Legation, and how long it takes him to secure entry permits for us.'

'Yes, it's a bore our passports not having Norwegian visas but I'm sure Uli von Einem will soon fix matters up.'

'I only hope to goodness he doesn't happen to know that you're wanted by the Gestapo or that the real Colonel Baron von Lutz was killed while resisting arrest by the Nazis last November.'

Erika shrugged. 'As I said last night, it's not easy for any legation to keep track of what has happened to eighty million Germans while a war is going on and, even if they do know, they can't do anything to us while we're on a neutral ship. We'll just have to think up some other method of getting ashore or transfer to a ship that will take us round to a Swedish port and try our luck there.'

'I can always get in touch with the British Legation,' Gregory said slowly, 'and I might be able to wangle some way of getting you into Norway; but if I can continue to pose as a German it will prevent a lot of unwelcome speculation as to why we're always together while we are in Oslo.'

She turned suddenly and looked him full in the face. 'For how long is that to be, Gregory?'

'Not very long, darling—worse luck,' he replied quietly. 'You know how things are, so we needn't go over it all and add to what we're feeling. As soon as we land I must find out when there's a plane that will take me home, so we've now got only a few days together at the most.'

Erika could have screamed with the frightful injustice of it all. Through his crazy ambition this mountebank, Hitler, had

11

sown the seeds of misery, poverty and death broadcast throughout half the world. The foul crop was barely visible as yet, but in time it would strangle innumerable beautiful things, and already the shoots of the filthy weed were forcing apart the roots of countless loves and friendships. But she was a splendidly courageous person so she did not seek by a single word to dissuade Gregory from his decision, and her intense distress was shown only by a slight moistening of her very beautiful blue eyes.

An hour later the tramp had berthed and by six o'clock Uli von Einem had joined them with papers enabling them to go ashore. He was a thin, fair man, who in the past had been one of Erika's innumerable admirers, and he possessed all the tact of a born diplomat. Privately, he thought it a queer business that his lovely friend should arrive, without even a beauty-box for baggage, on a tramp steamer that had come from Leningrad, but the one lesson that *Freiherr* von Einem had learnt since the Nazis had come to power was that the less one knew officially about anything the less likelihood there was of finding oneself carted off, without warning, to a concentration-camp. The passports of both Erika and her friend were in perfect order except that they lacked Norwegian visas, and Erika had intimated that they were both on urgent secret business connected with the prosecution of the war, so von Einem had accepted her statement without comment.

Gregory had thrown overboard the Gestapo uniform that he had stolen from Grauber so he was dressed in a ready-made suit which he had bought off the first Mate of the tramp, but its poor quality was concealed under his rich furs. Erika also was still in her furs, and their only belongings were contained in a single handbag that Gregory had brought out of Russia with him, so they were not long delayed by the Customs. Von Einem drove them to the Grand Hotel in the Karl Johansgt and, having accepted an invitation to lunch with them on the following day, left them there.

On going into the lounge they saw, to their delight, that Kuporovitch had succeeded in evading the Norwegian coastguards. He was sitting with a long-stemmed glass in front of him but as soon as he caught sight of them he disposed of its contents and came hurrying over with a gay wave of his hand.

The Russian was a clean-shaven man in his early fifties. His grey hair was brushed smoothly back and, strangely contrasting with it, his eyebrows, which were still black, ran thin and pointed towards the temples of his smooth white forehead. Under them were a pair of rather lazy blue eyes, but their glance was apt to be deceptive as behind them lay an extremely shrewd intelligence. Up to the age of twenty-nine he had been an officer of the Imperial Russian Army, but when the Revolution had broken out a strange set of circumstances had resulted in his joining the Bolsheviks. After the Civil War he had come to loathe and despise his new masters, yet with the laudable desire to keep his head on his shoulders he had concealed his antipathy for many years with superlative skill. For a long time past he had been hoarding foreign currency with the idea of escaping from the dreary, depressing land of the Union of Soviet Socialist Republics so that he might spend his old age among civilised people, and his great ambition was to see the Paris of his youth again.

Greeting his friends in French—which was their common language—he said with a smile: 'I've booked rooms for you—two bedrooms with a bathroom in between, so that you can preserve the proprieties of this charming old world into which I am so delighted to have returned. Come upstairs and I will show you.'

Upstairs, perched on Erika's bed and smoking a long cheroot, he told them, with many chuckles, of his adventures that day. It had all been too easy. He had walked to the nearest village, found its school and routed out the village schoolmaster, to whom he had said: 'I am a member of the French Legation in Oslo and was returning there after a visit to Kristiansand. When the train halted in the station here I got out to get some hot coffee in the buffet and the train went on without me. Unfortunately, too, it carried on my baggage and a small attaché-case in which I had some papers and my ticket. Would you oblige me by acting as interpreter at the station so that I can buy another ticket and take the next train on?' The Norwegian had been most polite and helpful, so Kuporovitch had arrived in Oslo without the least difficulty.

Having washed and tidied themselves they went down to the grill-room. The head waiter was nearly guilty of raising an eyebrow when he saw them approaching, for Kuporovitch was in shoddy 'ready-mades' that he had bought at an old-clothes shop in Leningrad, Gregory was in the first Mate's second-best suit and Erika's tweeds showed obvious signs of the hard wear they had sustained; but as the man's glance swept across their faces he noted Erika's regal beauty and that in spite of their shabby clothes both her escorts had the air of men who were used to being obeyed. With a swift bow he led them to a sofa-table.

The under-waiter who took their order brought the *maître d'hôtel* scurrying back again, his face now wreathed in smiles. The strangely-dressed trio had ordered a superb meal and some of the best wines that his cellar boasted. He did not know that the broad-shouldered, middle-aged man with the black, pointed eyebrows had been cooped up in Russia for nearly a quarter of a century and that it was many months since the others had had a meal in a good restaurant. They were speaking French but he put them down as rich Germans who had been suffering from the Nazis' impoverished larder and had somehow managed to get away to Norway.

Although they had spared no pains or expense in ordering their favourite dishes, the meal was not the success that it should have been, because the black cloud of war and the coming separation weighed heavily upon the spirits of the little party. The tables were widely spaced so they were able to talk freely without risk of being overheard, and when they had reached the coffee and brandy stage Gregory turned to the Russian.

'The time has come, Stefan, when we must discuss plans. I shall have to leave here in a day or two—as soon as I can get a plane—for England. What do you intend to do?'

Kuporovitch smiled. 'Now that I am a free man once more I can hardly wait until I get to Paris; but the devil of it is that I have no passport. What are the intentions of *Madame la Comtesse*?'

'It would be unwise for her to remain here long. The Germans are so thorough that solely as a matter of routine von Einem will have reported our arrival in Oslo. It may take a week or two passing through the files of petty officials, but sooner or later the Gestapo will learn where she's got to.'

'Does that matter now that she is in a neutral country?'

Gregory grinned. 'You don't know the Gestapo, my friend. They're quite capable of kidnapping Erika or arranging one of their jolly little motor-car accidents in which she would be knocked down and killed. Besides, as we told you on the tramp, by the merest fluke we happened to come into possession of the German war plan. They've followed it step by step so far, and

Norway is the next on their list. Her life would not be worth a moment's purchase if she were still here when they staged an invasion.'

Erika drew slowly on her cigarette. 'What d'you suggest then?'

'Stage 7 of the plan lays it down that Sweden is strong enough to require a separate operation, so she should be left for the time being, but that Norway and Denmark can be taken over together. Sweden would then be entirely isolated and so in no position to resist whenever the Germans consider it convenient to take control there. The plan then passes to Stage 8, which concerns Holland and Belgium, and no further mention of Sweden is made at all. As it's quite on the cards that the Germans will be content to absorb Sweden's entire exports without actually walking into the place for some considerable time, I suggest that Erika should move there.'

The Russian raised his dark eyebrows. 'But surely she will be just as liable to secret attacks from the Gestapo in Sweden as she would be here?'

'No. Here she had to disclose her true identity to get into the country. My suggestion is that she should quietly slip away from Oslo and cross the border at some place up-country; then she could settle in Sweden, under an assumed name, until I can make arrangements for her to sail to America.'

'America!' Erika exclaimed. 'But, darling, once there I may not be able to get back, and I just can't live unless I'm to have some hope of seeing you again before many months are past.'

Gregory sighed. 'We'll talk of that later, my sweet. Your immediate safety is the most important thing. It shouldn't be difficult for you to keep out of trouble in some small Swedish town, even without a passport, for the next few weeks, and my idea was that Stefan could go with you.'

'But I have no wish at all to go to Sweden,' the Russian protested. 'It is to see Paris again . . .'

'I know.' Gregory interrupted swiftly; 'but you didn't let me finish. Without a passport you haven't got a hope in hell of getting to France, but the British Government owes me a bit for services rendered so I mean to try to get you a passport and entry permit to France at the same time as I get them for Erika to the United States. In the meantime you can take care of each other.'

'Ah, in that case'—Kuporovitch waved his cigar—'I shall

be delighted to place myself at the disposal of *Madame la Comtesse.*'

'That's settled, then,' said Gregory. 'Let's pay the bill and go up to bed.'

Kuporovitch accompanied them only as far as the lift, since now that he was back in civilisation he had other ideas as to how he meant to spend his evening.

Very reluctantly the following morning Gregory and Erika got up at eleven o'clock and went out into the clear, frosty air of the Norwegian capital. Since he was staying at the hotel as a German, they went to Cook's, where he was able to produce his British passport, and he managed to secure a seat on the air liner which would be leaving for London two days later—Friday the 22nd; after which they bought a number of things that would add to their comfort and some new clothes to make themselves more presentable.

Uli von Einem lunched with them and, preserving the same discretion as on the day before, forbore to inquire into their private concerns but gave them the latest war news that had come through the German Legation. The Finns were submitting peaceably to the terms which the Russians had imposed upon them. The uncaptured portion of the Mannerheim Line was being rapidly evacuated and Soviet troops had already taken over Finland's 'Gibraltar' on the island of Hangoe, so Russia was now the unchallenged mistress of the Northern Baltic. That was the price that Germany had had to pay to keep her eastern neighbour quiet while she dealt with her enemies in the West. On the other hand, Hitler and Mussolini had met on the Brenner Pass the previous Sunday. No details had been allowed to leak out about the matters discussed there, but it was understood that the meeting had proved highly satisfactory. One presumable result had been the withdrawal of Italy's support from Rumania so that King Carol had been compelled to lift the ban on the Rumanian Iron Guard, which was definitely a victory for the Nazis. Gregory took it all in with the glib appreciation which might have been expected from a German officer, and it did not add to his satisfaction about the way in which the war was going.

He had already scanned the latest English papers to reach Oslo so was more or less *au fait* with the situation. The big news item was that an Indian fanatic had assassinated Sir Michael O'Dwyer and succeeded in wounding Lord Zetland, Sir Louis

Dane and Lord Lamington before he was overpowered, but otherwise old England seemed to be jogging along as though the war were just a rather remote and tiresome business. The British Union, the Nordic League, the Peace Pledge people, and all sorts of other dangerous bodies composed of rogues, cranks, half-wits and actual traitors were still allowed complete liberty to publish as much subversive literature as they liked and to advise cowards how to evade military service on the plea that they were conscientious objectors.

One had only to glance at the small news items in the National Press to see how a weak-kneed government was being intimidated by a handful of irresponsible M.P.s into permitting Hitler's Fifth Column in England absolute freedom to contaminate thousands of misguided idealists and so immensely weaken Britain's war effort. Gregory would have liked to have been given Gestapo powers in the Home Office for half a day. He would have signed the death warrant of every spy caught red-handed since the beginning of the war, had them shot in the courtyard and published photographs of their bodies to intimidate the others. He would then have made both the Fascist and Communist Parties illegal, locked the Home Secretary up in one of his own asylums, retired every permanent Civil Servant over the age of fifty and departed with reasonable confidence that the younger men who remained would have got their bearings in a week and settled down to the job of making Britain safe from her internal enemies.

When lunch was over Erika went off to have a permanent wave, and Gregory spent the afternoon in a state of gloomy depression. It was bad enough that he would so shortly have to leave her, without this awful feeling that a gang of woolly old men were letting Britain drift into the gravest danger.

That night they dined alone and went to Oslo's best musical show, where in spite of the fact that they did not understand Norwegian, they were able to forget for a few hours the separation which so soon was to render them even more miserable.

On the Thursday they did not get up until lunch-time; their last lunch together until neither knew when. In the afternoon, in a desperate effort to forget themselves again, they hired a car and a guide and drove round the principal sights of the Norwegian capital, but by cocktail-time they were gazing forlornly at each other over their glasses, with hardly a word to say.

For dinner Kuporovitch joined them. They had seen little of

17

him during the past two days. Perhaps he would really have done them better service if he had remained with them as much as possible to cheer them up, but realising how little time they had together he had tactfully left them to themselves and amused himself with a glamorous blonde whom he had acquired in a dance-club on his first night in Oslo. But it was necessary that their final arrangements should be made, as Gregory's plane left early on Friday morning.

To Gregorys' relief he found that the Russian was a much more capable companion than the stout-hearted but unimaginative young airman, Freddie Charlton, who had accompanied him on his travels through Germany, Finland and Russia. Kuporovitch had spent such time as had not been occupied in playful dalliance with the glamorous blonde in thinking out the details of the plan that Gregory had outlined two nights before.

He proposed to accompany Erika as her deaf-and-dumb uncle and had already booked accommodation for them at a hotel in Flisen, a small town about seventy miles north-east of Oslo and only about fifteen miles from the Swedish border. After Gregory's departure they would leave Oslo by the eleven-fifty train, sleep at Flisen and hire a car for a week. During the next few days they would make several motoring expeditions as though seeing the sights of the country, in order to carry out a careful reconnaissance of the frontier, which, as Norway and Sweden were on the most friendly terms, must be very lightly guarded; then it should not prove difficult to drive to an unfrequented spot one night, abandon the car and slip over the border. Having arrived in Sweden he suggested that they should make their way to the university town of Uppsala, where they were not likely to run into any foreign diplomats who might know Erika by sight, but which, owing to the nature of the town, included in its inhabitants many foreign teachers and students whose presence would render them inconspicuous while living there quietly. As soon as they were settled in they would send Gregory their address by air mail and await his further instructions. He then handed Gregory a slip of paper with the names under which he proposed they should travel, and three copies of a passport photograph of himself that he had had taken.

'Bless you,' smiled Gregory. 'It's great that you should have thought all this out already. Erika had a passport photograph taken yesterday, so all that remains is the question of money.

18

You had most of mine off me in Kandalaksha and Erika hasn't got any, so by the time I've settled the bill here we shall be pretty well stony.'

Kuporovitch shrugged. 'I have plenty; all my savings in foreign currency that I brought out of Russia as well as the six thousand marks which I changed for you. I'll see to that side of it.'

'Thanks. Whatever you pay out on Erika's behalf I'll refund when you get to France. If they won't let me send cash from England, I've got quite enough pull to fix a trip to Paris and meet you with it there.'

Erika sighed. 'Oh, Stefan, how lucky you are. If only I could go to Paris, too. As it is, I suppose when you two meet I'll be on my way to America.'

Gregory looked across at her with sudden intentness. 'There's time to reconsider your decision yet, darling. Why the hell can't you be sensible and let me get you a permit to enter England as a refugee from Nazi persecution?'

She swallowed hard but shook her head. 'No, dearest, it's no good. Because my country has fallen into the hands of a set of unscrupulous blackguards that doesn't make me any the less a German. I can't accept the hospitality of England or France while your friends and mine are killing one another.'

For a long time they were silent. The fine wine remained almost untasted in the glasses and they ate perfunctorily, hardly noticing the rich dishes which were placed before them. Kuporovitch did his best, but after one or two false starts even the jovial Russian gave up any attempt to make it a jolly party.

Gregory could have coped with most situations but this was beyond him. He and Erika were perfectly free; nothing compelled her to remain in Norway or him to leave it; they could both change their minds at the last moment, but he felt certain now that she would not change hers and he knew quite well that he would not change his. The very fact that their coming separation was self-imposed seemed to make it ten times harder, but a force that was stronger than either of them had them firmly in its grip and was tearing them apart just as surely as diverging currents would carry two pieces of driftwood in different directions.

This was their last night together, perhaps for years, perhaps, in the uncertainties of war, for ever; yet instead of savouring every moment of it they were sitting there tongue-tied and speechless. He felt that he was letting Erika down appallingly badly—after all, it was always up to the man to make the running—yet for the life of him he could not bring himself to be even normally cheerful—let alone gay and entertaining.

Erika knew just what he was feeling and her heart went out to him. Like him, she would have done anything to be able to recall their mood of the night on which they had first abandoned themselves to their wild passion for each other; but she was wise enough to know why that was impossible. *Then* they had just been a very beautiful woman and a damnably attractive man, both of whom were highly experienced in the art of love; two born pagans, who openly boasted that they had always taken with greedy hands all the joys that the gods had given them; but they had hardly known each other. Two brief meetings, with an interval of a few weeks between, had lit the flame of desire in both of them; each knew that the other was courageous, unscrupulous and clever, but no more, and after that night, but for a far deeper attraction, their interest in each other might soon have exhausted itself. *That* had been passion; *this* was love. And where Passion is given to those whom the gods love as a glorious plaything, Love is a harsh taskmaster. They could have parted after that night with no regrets and a lovely memory; they could only part now, after they had come to know each other so well, with an actual physical pain that seemed to grip them in the pit of the stomach and rend each separate heart-string. To have pretended anything else would only have been a hideous attempt at play-acting which Erika could not have borne. She was terribly glad that Gregory did not attempt it.

From a glance at the clock she saw that it was already half-past nine. In less than twelve hours Gregory would have left her. She was not greedy for the caresses he had lavished on her in the previous nights, because her passion was temporarily numbed by her acute despair, but she wanted desperately to lie in his arms while he comforted her, to cling close to him in every moment that was left to her and gather all the strength she could for their separation. So she thrust back her chair and said:

'You've got to make an early start tomorrow, darling. I'm sure Stefan will forgive us if we desert him.'

Kuporovitch smiled sympathetically. 'Please. I can take care of myself, and I'll settle the bill. I shall see you both in the morning.'

Gregory nodded his thanks and followed her out into the lounge. At one table a little group of people were sitting drinking coffee and liqueurs. There was a very handsome dark girl of about twenty-three among them. She had a well-modelled, full-lipped mouth, fine, regular features, a strong, determined chin and large, lustrous brown eyes. On seeing Erika her eyes widened and she stood up.

Erika smothered an exclamation of annoyance as the dark girl hurriedly left the table and came towards them. This was the last moment she would have chosen to exchange meaningless gossip with her best friend—let alone a woman who was only a casual acquaintance—but there was no escape. The girl seized both her hands impulsively and exclaimed:

'My dear! How absolutely marvellous to see you! I thought —I thought . . .' Her voice tailed off as she glanced uncertainly towards Gregory.

Erika introduced them, *'Oberst-Baron* von Lutz—*Fräulein* Paula von Steinmetz,' and asked: 'What did you think Paula? You can speak quite freely in front of the Colonel-Baron.'

Paula extended her hand to Gregory with a gracious smile, upon which he clicked his heels, bowed from the waist and kissed it in the approved manner of the Prussian officer; then she turned back to Erika.

'I thought that after the Army revolt last November the Nazis had passed a sentence of execution on you.'

'They did,' smiled Erika; 'but, as you see, they haven't carried it out yet.'

'The swine gave me ten years because I hid my brother Oscar, the one who is a Captain of Uhlans; and they're holding him as a hostage for my good behaviour,' Paula said quickly. 'They've done the same sort of thing with any number of girls I know. There are at least forty of us here in Oslo; but as they passed the death penalty on you I was afraid that you had been pig-headed and refused to play.'

'How are you finding life here?' asked Gregory amiably.

She shrugged. 'Naturally, I hated the idea at first, but it's much more fun being here than in Germany now there's a war on, and they give me plenty of money. I'm rather sorry for the poor Norwegians, but, after all, in the long run it's going to be much better for them that they should succumb to Hitler's secret weapon instead of having a long war in which lots of the poor dears would get killed—isn't it?'

21

'Of course it is,' smiled Gregory. 'That's a very sensible way to regard matters. You and Erika could do more damage between you than an armoured division, any day.'

'What a charming way of putting things.' Paula's lovely dark eyes swept over Gregory's lean face with approval. 'Will you both lunch with me tomorrow? You *must*—I insist. I've got the sweetest apartment—No. 97 Universitesgaten.'

Erika hesitated for a second, then she said quickly: 'May I telephone you in the morning?'

'Of course.' Paula squeezed her arm, flashed another dazzling smile at Gregory and added: 'I must fly now; I've got a little Major man in tow who is in command of one of the forts outside the harbour. But I shall expect you both at one o'clock so don't dare to telephone and say that you're not coming.'

Having smiled 'Goodnight' Gregory and Erika walked in silence towards the lift, and it was only as they were going down their corridor upstairs that she said bitterly: 'I never knew Paula intimately, but she comes of a decent family, and it makes me almost physically sick to think that a girl who is really one of us should have sold out to the Nazis.'

Gregory shrugged. 'Don't be too hard on her, darling: It isn't everyone who has your strength of character; and remember, those devils have got her brother. From what she said, it's clear that they gave her the choice of death for him and ten years—the best ten years of her life—in some God-awful concentration-camp, or to come here as one of their agents. One can hardly blame her, and from that "come hither" eye of hers I shouldn't think she finds the job they've put her on by any means distasteful. Naturally, on seeing you she jumped to the conclusion that you had bought your liberty on the same terms.'

At their respective doors they parted, but a quarter of an hour later Gregory entered Erika's room through the bathroom they were sharing. He was wearing a brightly-hued silk dressing-gown which he had bought two days before; in one hand he was carrying a fat Turkish cigarette and in the other a magnum of champagne.

She looked across at him from her bed as he set the magnum down and walked over to a side-table to collect some glasses that were standing with a half-empty bottle of Madeira which they had opened that morning.

'Darling,' she murmured a little hesitantly, 'would you mind very much if we didn't make a night of it?—I mean—not a magnum-of-champagne sort of night—because all I want now is to hold you very close to me for every moment that's left to us, and we've got so little time—so desperately little time.'

'Have we?' he said, turning suddenly, and she saw that his whole face had altered. 'Don't you believe it, sweetheart!'

'Oh, Gregory! You mean . . .' Her face suddenly lit up but the rest of her sentence was never uttered. With one great, panther-like spring he landed right on her bed and seizing her face between his hands he forced it back on the pillow, pressing his mouth to hers.

When he released her he was laughing like a genial devil as he cried: 'I mean, my angel, why should I go home now there's work to be done here in Norway? Tomorrow we are lunching with Hitler's secret weapon.'

2

Fifth Column at Home

Before they had been in Paula von Steinmetz's flat for ten minutes, Gregory knew that his decision to stay in Norway had been thoroughly justified. Either she already had a luncheon party arranged for that day or else she had quickly got a number of people together after Erika had telephoned to her that morning. Her guests and their attitude were both a shock and a revelation.

The men consisted of a high Balkan diplomat and four Norwegians, one of whom was a member of the *Storting* and one the editor of a leading paper; the two others were the Major with whom Paula had been the night before and another Army officer. All the women were German born, although one of them was the diplomat's wife and so nominally of his nationality, and another had married the Norwegian M.P. only a fortnight before. The women accepted Erika as one of themselves, and paid a special deference to Gregory in his role of a Prussian aristocrat who had served with distinction upon their own General Staff.

They talked with complete freedom about the hopeless plight of the Democracies under their aged and effete leaders and with supreme confidence about everything going according

23

to plan and Hitler's becoming the first World *Fuehrer* in 1944. The Norwegians and the diplomat obviously accepted this forecast as quite inevitable and, far from showing any distress at the thought of their own countries becoming vassal states to a foreign power, appeared to consider themselves as the chosen vessels for carrying the Light of the new world order to their countrymen. In fact, Gregory had to keep on reminding himself that he really *was* in Norway and not attending a luncheon with a number of Nazi Party chiefs and their women in Berlin.

He had always realised that the Scandinavian countries were strongly pro-German, however greatly the majority of English people liked to believe the contrary. During the last world-war they had seriously hampered the Allied blockade not only by selling most of their own produce to Germany but also by re-selling to her a very large proportion of the raw materials which the Allies had allowed through for neutral consumption. Moreover, when the Allies had at last had the sense to tighten up their blockade, and Germany was beginning to feel the pinch, the Scandinavians had done their utmost to relieve the pressure by taking enormous numbers of German women and children as refugees for the remainder of the war. That was a work of humanity, but Gregory believed in facing facts. The Germans were waging unrestricted submarine warfare at that time; they were also bombing Paris and London on every possible opportunity, thus sending considerable numbers of our women and children to their deaths. As Germany was eventually brought to her knees through the pressure of the blockade, the fact that the Scandinavians were feeding a considerable section of her population during the latter part of the war simply meant that the war had gone on several months longer than it need have done, during which many thousands of our soldiers, sailors, airmen and civilians owed their deaths entirely to this humanitarian gesture which had been made by the pro-German neutrals.

Knowing all that, and having no reason to suppose that the attitude of the Scandinavians had materially altered in the past twenty years, Gregory had not expected to find the bulk of the people in Norway waving Union Jacks, but he had supposed that they at least had every intention of preserving their tradition of independence and he was utterly horrified at this revelation that such prominent and influential Norwegians as those at Paula's luncheon-party had obviously sold out to Hitler.

24

At luncheon he was given the place of honour on Paula's right and she lost no opportunity of seeking to attract him. With her young, dark beauty and full-lipped smile she was a fascinating person but she got little chance to talk to him alone until the end of the meal, when the others all became involved in a general discussion on the eternal question as to where the *Fuehrer* would really strike first now that spring was here. She then inquired about the reason for his visit to Norway, upon which he became intriguingly mysterious, but she only laughed at him and began to pull his leg.

'Of course you mustn't *tell* me,' she mocked him. 'Still it's obvious that arrangements have to be made for the troops to land when the country is actually taken over and all the details must be seen to with the thoroughness for which our General Staff is so justly famous. But really you are to be congratulated upon having a delightfully "cushy" job, because there won't be any fighting—or hardly any. With Hitler's new technique you Army men will have to take a back seat for a change, and it's girls like Erika and myself who will reap the real honours of the new war.'

'You certainly seem to be getting a great deal of fun out of your baptism of fire,' Gregory smiled.

As the others were not listening she shrugged and went on in a low voice: 'It's quite true that most of us acted from compulsion to begin with, but once one gets into the game it becomes frightfully thrilling. After all, whatever we may have said about the Nazis in the past, Hitler himself is an amazing man, you know. One must confess that. And although we may not agree with all his methods he *is* showing us Germans how to conquer the world. One must admire him for that. So, quite honestly, I'm all for him now and I'm not a bit shamefaced about this business any more.'

Gregory could only agree that she was perfectly right and that for Germany to be supreme above all nations was the only thing that really mattered; then he laughingly expressed the hope that he might be present to applaud when the *Fuehrer* decorated her with the Iron Cross for her services to the Third Reich.

Her wicked eyes crinkled at the corners. 'Wouldn't it be more appropriate if he instituted a new Order called Ladies of the Golden Garter?'

'Grand!' laughed Gregory. 'Grand! Yet somehow I don't

think he's quite the right fellow to bestow the decoration personally. It would be much more fun for the girls if he selected certain stalwarts among his Black Guards to put the garters on.'

She shook her head. 'No. They are so dull—great, stupid animals. I think each girl should be allowed to choose her own man to deputise for the *Fuehrer,* and the installation should take place at night to soft music and in candle-light. One might even adopt the procedure of the Ancient Orders of Chivalry, where squires who were to receive the accolade spent the night on their knees, in prayer, before the high altar of a church.'

'I get you,' Gregory grinned. 'The night would not be spent in prayer, but the lady would receive her decoration in the morning.'

'That's it.' Paula's hand brushed his as she reached out for a chocolate. 'Now, what sort of man d'you think I should choose for my initiation?'

Her question was an open invitation for Gregory to describe himself, and in other circumstances he would have done so without hesitation, but now he had Erika to consider. Quite apart from the fact that, being in love with her, he was not in the least interested in any other woman, he had to make allowance for her possible reactions to any signs of Paula and himself becoming somewhat more than friendly. Erika would, of course, say that she trusted him completely and did not at all mind his entering on a flirtation with Paula for the sake of the interests they served, but Gregory owed much of his success with women to the fact that experience had taught him a great deal about the workings of the female brain. Erika would quite honestly mean it when she said that she trusted him, but that would not affect the fact that it would make her extremely unhappy if he played up to Paula very far and that was bound to have an adverse effect upon their own happiness.

Fortunately his acquaintance with Paula was still so slight that she had had no time or opportunity to develop a real interest in him. It was just that she was a gregarious young woman who was obviously prepared to have an affair with any attractive man whom she might meet and, having put Gregory down as a desirable property, she had evidently decided that it would be rather fun to try to take him away from such a handsome rival as Erika. He therefore made up his mind at once that before he was drawn further on to this extremely dangerous ground he must side-track Paula by conveying to her that

26

he was not really a very desirable property at all.

After a moment he looked up at her and smiled a little weakly. 'I must say I'd envy the chap who got the job and I'd apply for it myself if I thought that I had the least chance.'

'Nothing venture—nothing win,' she murmured, lowering her long lashes.

'The trouble is,' he admitted slowly, 'that I'm always a damned sight too honest with myself, and knowing my limitations so well I'm quite certain that when it came to the point I should let you down.'

'Why?' she asked in an astonished voice. 'Whatever makes you think that?'

'Well, the sort of man you want is a chap who'd treat you rough and give you a beating if you played him up.'

Mein Gott, nein! Paula protested quickly.

'Oh yes, you do,' Gregory assured her. 'Every woman does. I don't mean a drunken blackguard or anything of that kind, but a chap with a will of his own who wouldn't stand any nonsense and if he saw you flashing those lovely eyes of yours at anybody else would take you home and give you a good spanking.'

Paula's colour deepened a little under her make-up and Gregory knew that he had judged her rightly. She was a strong, highly-sexed young woman who would thoroughly enjoy occasional rows with her lovers and derive tremendous kick from a mild beating-up in which she was finally possessed forcibly, so that her sobs of anger gave way almost imperceptibly to gasps of passionate emotion.

'Well,' she admitted slowly, 'if one loves a man one naturally expects him to assert himself at times, otherwise how can one possibly respect him?'

'That's just it,' Gregory nodded, 'and although I don't think I'm really a weak character—certainly not as far as my job is concerned—once I fall for a woman I find it utterly impossible to say "no" to her. I just follow her around saying, "Yes, darling," "Of course, darling," and give way to her in every single thing. I suppose you'll think me an awful fool to have told you that, but it's just a stupid weakness that I can't get over.'

'I see,' said Paula with a tinge of disappointment in her tone.

'Still,' Gregory went on more hopefully, 'some women prefer a quiet life and having their own way in everything without any trouble.' He lowered his voice to a murmur. 'Of course, I'd have to be careful about Erika, but if you think I wouldn't bore you too much—couldn't we—er—meet somewhere just for—er—a quiet meal?'

Paula stiffened slightly. 'I'm afraid you've rather misunderstood me, *Herr Oberst-Baron*; but perhaps that is owing to the turn our conversation took. We were only talking nonsense, and, in any case, it's one of my rules never to pinch my girlfriends' men, so let's say no more about it.'

'I'm so sorry,' Gregory murmured awkwardly, and as he spoke his face wore such a hang-dog look that Paula almost laughed. She would have been livid with rage if she had known the real Gregory and how inside himself he was laughing at her and the thought that he had got her just where he wanted her.

He was, however, very far from laughing when he and Erika had returned to their hotel and were discussing matters together.

'It's incredible!' he exclaimed. 'D'you realise that if what Paula said last night is true, about her knowing at least forty German girls of her own class who have been sent over here on this job, there must be scores of them having affairs with half the leading men in Norway. They're undermining the whole political structure of the country and if we can't do something to stop it the place will fall into Hitlers' hands without a shot being fired.'

She nodded. 'It's rather amazing that we should so quickly have tumbled to what is going on. I don't suppose the real Norwegian people have any idea of it at all, and we shouldn't have, either, if we hadn't happened to run into Paula last night; but, naturally, she assumed that I was just one more of the lovelies whom the Nazis had sent to do their dirty work and opened up the whole business to us. What's our next move?'

'We must stick close to the von Steinmetz, then she'll lead us to the other women who are playing the same game and we can find out which Norwegian leaders are still trustworthy and which have succumbed to Hitler's fascinating secret weapon.'

'That shouldn't be difficult. I saw her making a play for you at the end of lunch.'

He grinned. 'She cooled off when I intimated that, although I'd love to play, I'm really a bit of a weakling when it comes down to brass tacks.'

'Oh, darling,' Erika roared with laughter and flung her arms round his neck, 'what delicious nonsense! And she really took that in?'

'You bet she did! And she promptly changed her tactics, becoming one of those high-principled girls who never snatches her friends' men. She even declined a stolen meeting on the first occasion that I could get you safely out of the way, but as I paid her the compliment of appearing to get all hot-and-bothered about her, honour is satisfied. She now has no use for me at all in the role of prospective lover but will continue to play ball. It is a case of no offence given—and none taken, I'm sure.'

'You adorable swine. Then we can tell her that we know hardly anybody here and suggest throwing a dinner-party to which we'll ask her to bring her friends.'

'I think we should go further than that. I'm certain that Paula is the type who thoroughly enjoys a playful beating, and since I disappointed her by deliberately labelling myself "tame cat" we must arrange for the lady's requirements to be satisfied elsewhere.'

'Stefan!' said Erika.

'Exactly,' grinned Gregory. 'Paula can't be getting much fun with that old Norwegian Major, who is obviously her duty boy-friend at the moment, and Kuporovitch is like a dog with two tails to wag, he's so full of beans after his escape from the Soviets. These Russians have the hell of a reputation with the girls so I don't think Stefan should find much difficulty in making the running. The question is, though, would he be prepared to play a hand with us against the Gestapo?'

'True. He's a neutral, and there's no earthly reason why he should involve himself in our affairs, but I'm sure that we can trust him not to give us away, and he'd be splendid bait for Paula. Let's tackle him this evening and see how far he is prepared to go.'

That night after dinner, in a quiet corner of the lounge, Gregory explained to the Russian the reason why he had cancelled his departure for England at the last moment, and as Paula was really a very attractive young woman he was able to describe her without unduly overpainting the picture, which might have led to Kuporovitch's being disappointed when he later saw her in the flesh.

'She sounds a most delightful person,' the Russian remarked, 'and although my blonde is a nice little thing she is exceedingly stupid so I should much prefer a mistress of my own class. It was most charming of you to think of me, but'—his blue eyes narrowed slightly—'what is the catch in it?'

'There is no catch in it at all,' Gregory assured him. 'If you can get her, Stefan, it will be all for love and should be excellent fun for you, but while we are on the matter I'd like to know what you really feel about the war.'

'What has that to do with it?'

'Just this. We've told you how we met *Fräulein* von Steinmetz and what she's up to here. Erika and I are two of the considerable number of people in this world who have made up their minds that Hitler has got to be slogged for ten and counted out for keeps, and we don't particularly mind if we lose our own lives in helping along the process. You probably don't feel so strongly that way—or you may even admire the Nazis, for all I know, although I suppose the real fact is that you don't give a hoot for any of us. What I really want to get at is if you would be prepared to pass on to us any information you may be able to get out of Paula should you succeed in making the running with her.'

Kuporovitch showed his even white teeth in a wide smile. 'You are right; I am now a man of no country and no allegiances. My own poor land is ruined beyond repair and I have no interest in Germany or Britain. All the same, I have certain convictions about how people should be governed. I did not like living under an Autocracy where some rascally favourite of the Tsar might say "Off with his head!" about any person he didn't like, at any minute, and promotion could be achieved only by influence or bribery. Equally, I should not like to live under a Democracy. I despise leaders who are afraid to lead because they must pander to every whim of an ill-informed mob for fear that if they do not they will be thrown out of office at the next election; but even under these two muddle-headed systems something of man's independence and creative spirit is allowed to survive.

'On the other hand, in a Totalitarian state that is not so. People lose all their individuality and become only pieces of the state machine which they are compelled to serve from birth to death. I know that, because I have lived under such a régime for nearly a quarter of a century. There is no more colour in life, no more joy; only one eternal fear of being reported, which forces one to curb every ambition or desire to express oneself and, instead, to take the protective colouring of the great illiterate mass.

'I am an old-fashioned person animated by entirely selfish

30

motives. Quite frankly, I am not in the least interested in the betterment of the masses, but I am extremely interested in gratifying the tastes which I acquired when I was young. I like good food and good wine, beautiful women to make love to, fine horses to ride, freedom to travel and meet many people, music, painting and books which will enable me to explore every type of mind and discuss it without restraint. No Totalitarian world-order would permit me to enjoy more than a fraction of these things—and then only surreptitiously. Since, therefore, this is not a war of nations but a world-wide civil war, I am neither for the British nor for the Germans but I am one hundred per cent against the Nazis.'

'Good man!' cried Gregory. 'We can rely on you, then, to secure all the dope you possibly can through the beautiful Paula?'

Kuporovitch nodded and his lazy blue eyes took on a thoughtful look. 'Leave her to me. Unless I have lost my cunning I have rather a way with young women and, if you have described her type accurately, she will take like a duck to water to some of the little Russian tricks that I can show her. What is it that you particularly want me to find out?'

Gregory's reply came without hesitation. 'The date on which Hitler proposes to invade Norway.'

3

The Rats of Norway

Paula's French was not excellent but adequate, and love—if you can call it love in such a case—has its own language. At the dinner-party that Erika gave the following night she did not place Kuporovitch next to Paula but next to herself, and she quite obviously cold-shouldered Gregory for him. Erika and Gregory had given out that they had spent the last few months in Finland but nothing had been said of their having been in Russia with Kuporovitch, so the impression was created that he was a new acquaintance who happened to be staying in the same hotel.

When at last, in the lounge afterwards, he did get a word alone with Paula, Erika gave them only a few minutes together, then, feigning ill-concealed jealousy, intervened to reclaim him. Paula was, therefore, all the more tickled the following morning when he rang her up to say that he had succeeded in obtaining her address from one of the other guests at the party and that he was so impatient to see her again that he absolutely demanded that she should lunch with him.

From that point matters developed rapidly. Erika pretended to be peeved and Paula became all the nicer to her as she could not resist the temptation to patronise the lovely rival over whom it had given her such a kick to triumph. In consequence, she showered Erika with gifts and secured invitations for her and Gregory to every party that any member of her set was giving.

Inside a week they knew a hundred people, all of whom appeared entirely unconcerned with the grim struggle that was being waged outside Norway's borders. They lunched and chattered; cocktailed and flirted; dined, danced and drank far into each night. Oslo was throwing off its winter furs and coming out to enjoy the spring sunshine. All Paula's friends seemed to have plenty of money and nearly all of them were indulging in some illicit love-affair which provided gossip and speculation for the rest. It was a grand life for those who liked it, and the Norwegians, who formed far the greatest proportion of the men in this interesting set, were quite obviously having the time of their lives. Norway is not a rich country and her official classes cannot normally afford the same extravagances as their opposite numbers in London, Paris or New York, but Gregory noted with cynical interest that this group of soldiers, politicians, diplomats and Civil Servants always had ample funds and nice new cars in which to take their little German girl-friends about.

Since many of them were middle-aged men, heavily married and in responsible positions, a certain amount of circumspection was observed, but, as Erika and Gregory soon discovered, the 'goings-on' in the apartments of the *Fräuleins, Gnädigefraus, Baronins* and *Gräfins* concerned were just nobody's business.

'It's just the age of the men that makes the whole thing so simple,' Gregory said to Erika one day. 'If they were handsome young fellow-me-lads they would be wrapped up in girl-friends of their own nationality or their young wives, and Hitler's secret weapon might find it a bit difficult to muscle in; but it's a dozen years or more since these middle-aged gentry have had the chance of a cut at a good-looking young woman except by picking something up late at night, on the sly, and paying for it. Paula and Co. are giving them back their lost youth; without any risk of blackmail, no nasty scares about divorce, and a good time to be had by all.'

Although Kuporovitch was no younger than the average Norwegian in whom Paula and her friends were compelled to interest themselves he was infinitely more virile. Moreover, never having been burdened with a conscience or a wife, and the ethics of the Soviet Union being extremely elastic, he had kept his hand in with the prettiest young women he could find in every town where he had been stationed, so his advances had none of the nervous fumbling of the Norwegians who had lived as respectable married men for a number of years. He just bit Paula hard on the first occasion that they were alone together— so hard, in fact, that she had to wear a chiffon scarf round her neck for some days afterwards. She had, of course, hit him and flown into a fearful rage but he had flung himself on his knees and, embracing her in a bear-like hug, vowed that he had been driven crazy by her beauty; upon which her anger had given place to bewildered curiosity and a violent urge to discover what other excitements this tempestuous wooer would provide for her. In consequence, a few days later Erika remarked to Gregory, not very kindly, that to see Paula with Stefan was like watching a bird fascinated by a snake.

He was clever enough not to interfere with her 'duty' affair with the elderly Norwegian Major, neither did he overdo it and make a nuisance of himself, but he saw to it that she never had a moment of spare time and thoroughly enjoyed himself in the process. Apparently he had no other object whatever in life and while he never showed the least curiosity about the course of the war he appeared to delight in scandal as much as any old woman, so Paula produced every titbit she had for his amusement and in this way he was able to secure a mass of data about her girl-friends and the occupations of the various Norwegians they had in tow.

Gregory was delighted with Stefan's success, and although he knew that by remaining in Oslo he and Erika were as good as sitting on a powder barrel which might blow up at any moment, he felt that they were doing really useful work. Except for those forebodings of trouble to come they were able to abandon themselves to the joys of what amounted to an unofficial honey-moon while gathering much important information about the machinations of the enemy and transmitting it to Sir Pellinore Gwaine-Cust in London.

Gregory dared not go near the British Legation or be seen with any of its officials, for fear of arousing suspicion among Paula's set, so he could not put anything through in the Legation Bag, but as Norway was still at peace there was no censorship of mail leaving the country and he was able to communicate by the ordinary post. There was the risk that his letters might be opened or stopped by people in the Norwegian post-office who were in the pay of the Nazis, but that had to be taken, and in order to minimise such a risk he sent a duplicate of each letter that he wrote, on the following day, and used the utmost discretion in his communications.

His first effort was to buy an English edition of Ibsen's play, *The Rats*, on the blank front page of which he wrote: *With best wishes for a happy birthday, from Gregory.* Underneath his signature he put *Oslo* and the date. That would be quite sufficient to inform Sir Pellinore that he had got safely out of Russia and had arrived in Norway, but the astute old gentleman would naturally speculate on the meaning of this strange present, and, having looked through it to see that no passages were specially marked, he would undoubtedly concentrate upon the title.

By the same air-mail Gregory sent a postcard to his faithful henchman, Rudd, on which he wrote the laconic message: *Having a grand time here, except for the fact that the whole place is overrun with vermin,* knowing quite well that Rudd would immediately take the postcard to Sir Pellinore, who, linking rats and vermin, would guess that Gregory referred to the human variety.

A few days later he wrote a long, chatty letter to his non-existent half-brother, Otto Mentzendorff, an entirely bogus personality who was supposed to be Sir Pellinore's foreign valet. In it he said that he had succeeded in obtaining a situation as butler to a German Countess, although he omitted to mention the Countess's name. He then went on to describe life as the Countess's servant and the parties she gave, disclosing the fact that all her German women acquaintances had Norwegian men-friends who held positions of some importance. There was not a word of harm or slander in the letter; it was just the sort of screed that one gossip-minded servant with a sense of

34

humour might have sent to another, and a good half of it was devoted to a description of a mythical young woman who was supposed to be the Countess's lady's-maid upon whose virtue the writer had very definite designs.

By the time he had been in Norway a fortnight the details about his commerce with this buxom young Norwegian had reached such heights of both temperament and temperature that if anyone was following the correspondence the reader would have paid scant attention to the rest of the letter but waited for the next instalment with the utmost anxiety.

Had the writer's plan for getting into the girl's room succeeded or not? *No time for more; they're calling for drinks.*

Yes, it had, but he feared that their mistress had seen him slip through the door. Was he discovered? *No time for more. That accursed front-door bell again!*

No, he had not been discovered, but the girl had been so scared that she had turned him out immediately and forced him to leave by the window. There followed the night on which they had had the house to themselves—a godsent opportunity; supper; the girl well primed with cherry brandy. Then: *No time for more. The Countess will wear the legs off me! I am late in taking her filthy poodle for its evening outing.*

So the hectic saga continued, and Sir Pellinore was kept well posted as to who was taking an interest in whom in Oslo. The man who featured most prominently in these reports was the Air Attaché at the German Legation, a Captain Kurt von Ziegler. He was a lean, fair-haired man with a long, pointed nose and rather a pleasant smile, and he played a considerable part in directing the activities of the women; so he was evidently a secret member of the Gestapo. There was a distinct dash of the adventurer about him which appealed to Gregory, and he would have liked to cultivate the Captain further, but he did not dare to do so as every time he met him he feared that his assumed name of *Oberst-Baron* von Lutz might feature in one of the Captain's reports to Berlin. However casually the mention was made it would be quite enough to imperil the lives of Erika and himself.

The war was still meandering on, but Gregory was conscious of a growing tension. In Oslo he was able to listen to the English, French and German broadcasts as well as seeing the more detailed accounts of events in the newspapers of the three countries a few days later. It had been strongly suggested that the real reason for the Hitler-Mussolini meeting on the Brenner had been to persuade the Italians to adopt a less antagonistic attitude towards Russia and consent to a three-power Axis; but that had been offset by Molotov's making a speech which was equally offensive to Germany and the Allies.

A few days after Gregory's arrival in Oslo the R.A.F. had bombed Sylt; that being the first attack on a land-target. The British Press loudly proclaimed that the operation had been a huge success while the Germans declared with equal force that no damage of any consequence had been done and that a number of the raiders had been shot down. As Gregory was in a situation to hear neutral reports of the affair he knew the truth, and it made him almost sick with rage.

Sylt was probably the best-defended military zone in all Germany, and instead of being directed to attack any of the innumerable vulnerable points in the German economic system, which were comparatively lightly defended, our wretched pilots had been ordered to go for this base which positively bristled with anti-aircraft guns. In consequence, twelve British bombers had been shot down, with hardly a thing to show for it.

Dissatisfaction in France had led to the fall of the Daladier Government, and *Monsieur* Reynaud had been chosen as the new Premier; so it seemed that public opinion there was at last pressing for a more vigorous prosecution of the war. In Britain, too, there was evident discontent. Churchill was the only outstanding figure who really possessed the confidence of the public, and the broadcast that he made on March the 30th, in which he warned neutrals that it was quite time they took their ostrich heads out of the sand and, facing facts, united against Hitler before they were gobbled up piecemeal, was a joy to listen to. But he seemed to be carrying the whole burden while the remainder of the War Cabinet concerned themselves with fostering Britain's trade prospects after the war before they had even started to think about how they were going to win it.

By April the 2nd, even with the knowledge that he had conducted himself as warily as possible, Gregory was becoming intensely anxious. They had now been in Norway for a fortnight. At any moment some little cog in the vast German system might turn over and *Herr Gruppenführer* Grauber learn that the pseudo *Oberst-Baron* von Lutz and the beautiful Erika von Epp, his two most inveterate enemies, were hobnobbing with all his best agents in Oslo and informing themselves of exactly what was going on.

After that it needed only one brief radiogram to blow the whole party sky-high. The people at the German Legation would warn Paula and her friends to make no apparent difference in their attitude to these enemies who had crept into their midst, but to report their every movement; the Gestapo murder-squad in Oslo would be instructed and, like a bolt from the blue, the blow would fall. The steering-gear of the car that Gregory had hired would suddenly go wrong when he was driving along one of the mountain roads around the city, so that they crashed over a precipice; or one night at a party poison would be put into some sandwiches specially prepared for them, then a doctor who was in the Nazis' pay would make it his business to see that they did not recover.

There were so many things which he had no means of guarding against, and he knew that they were running a frightful risk every day that they now remained in Oslo. Although they had not secured even a hint of the invasion date the material he was getting through was of considerable value, so he was determined to stay on himself, but the work could be continued without Erika's assistance and he became desperately anxious to have her safely out of it.

At first when he tackled her on the subject she flatly refused to go, but he managed to bring her to a more reasonable frame of mind by pointing out that if trouble broke he would be in a much better situation to cope with it if he had not her to look after; and over breakfast in bed on the morning of Wednesday, April the 3rd, they reopened the project of Erika's flitting into Sweden, with the proviso that in the event of an emergency he should join her there.

An hour or so later when Gregory was dressing in his own room, Kuporovitch came in looking extremely glum and, on Gregory's asking him what was wrong, he said:

'Paula has been ordered to leave Norway; she received fresh instructions last night from *La Baronne Noire*.'

'The Black Baroness,' Gregory murmured with a puzzled look. 'And who may she be?'

The Russian shrugged. 'I have no idea. It is just a *nom-de-guerre* by which they sometimes refer to one of their key agents. Anyway, Paula is being sent to Holland.'

He then went on to say that it seemed as if Hitler's secret

37

weapon had done its work in Norway and Himmler did not want the pick of his young women murdered by the infuriated Norwegian populace when they realised that their leaders had sold them out to the Nazis. In consequence, Paula and her friends were methodically receiving instructions to tell their Norwegian *chers amis* that they were returning home for a short holiday or that they had to leave Norway for a week or so on urgent business affairs but that they would return as soon as they could to continue the gay life, and in the meantime the Norwegians were to be good boys and carry out all the things that they had promised.

Erika joined them at that moment and, on discussing that matter further, they then recalled that several of Paula's friends had disappeared in the last few days and that others had talked vaguely of ailing relatives or of husbands who were coming on leave to their homes in Germany, which would necessitate their leaving the delightful Norwegian capital for a brief spell.

'How does Paula take the idea of going to Holland?' Gregory asked.

Kuporovitch grimaced. 'Not at all well. She says that the Dutch are even duller than the Norwegians and that she will be broken-hearted unless I agree to go with her.'

'But you have no passport.'

'That, apparently, can be arranged. Major Quisling could fix it with the Norwegian Foreign Office.'

'What, *that* conceited little poop?' exclaimed Erika.

Kuporovitch half-closed his eyes. 'It is a mistake to under-rate that Quisling man because he appears to be only an empty-headed swaggerer. He has a finger in every pie.'

'Yes,' Gregory added. 'He's a nasty piece of work if ever there was one, but he's up to the neck in this thing. I can hardly recall a party at which he hasn't been present and I'm quite convinced that he's the fellow who produces some new Norwegian general or statesman every time another blonde arrives from Germany. What have you decided to do?'

'I should like to go to Holland, as it is no great distance from France, and once I am in possession of a Norwegian passport I could easily get to Paris; but I would not say anything definite without consulting you, so I told Paula that I would think matters over and let her know.'

'That's fine. Now, d'you think that you could get Erika a passport in another name and take her with you?'

38

'That sounds an extremely tricky proposition. How d'you suggest that I should set about it?'

Gregory lit a Turkish cigarette and replied quietly: 'The story that you will tell is this: Erika has also been ordered to Holland, but she's afraid to go there in her own name because a young Dutchman fell in love with her when she was there about eighteen months ago and as she refused to have anything to do with him he practically went off his rocker and threatened to kill her. Even if he doesn't attempt to do that, he may make an appalling nuisance of himself and seriously interfere with her duties should he learn that she has returned to the country. In consequence, it would make things ever so much easier if she could go there as a Norwegian. The Gestapo people here could, of course, fake a passport for her, but it would be much simpler and sounder if the Norwegian Foreign Office could be persuaded to grant her one instead. Naturally, she's in no position to apply for this officially, but if Major Quisling can get *you* a passport I see no reason why he shouldn't wangle one for Erika at the same time.'

'So far, so good,' Kuporovitch nodded. 'But you seem to forget that this business has to be negotiated through Paula, and I hardly imagine that she will look kindly upon my proposal to take another woman to Holland with us.'

Gregory grinned. 'That, my friend, is where your devastating sex-appeal comes in. As you have known Paula barely a fortnight you are still in the first hectic flush of your love-affair with her. That gives you the whip-hand, and it is pretty certain that although she may treat you to a pretty scene she will give in and do what you wish when you make it clear that it is conditional upon your going to Holland with her. To still her jealousy you can say that Erika once did you a great service and that you wish to repay her in this way, but that otherwise you have no interest in her at all and not the least objection to her travelling in a different ship from Paula and yourself. That, I think, should put matters right.'

Kuporovitch stubbed out his cigar and stood up. 'Very well; I'm seeing her this afternoon and I will let you know tonight what happens.'

When the Russian had gone Erika smiled rather wanly at Gregory. 'So you're determined to get rid of me?'

'Yes, darling. If only Stefan can do his stuff this opportunity is much too good to miss. Apart from the risk you're running

here already, Oslo is such a small place that Grauber would be
certain to spot you when he turned up—as he always does
wherever the Nazis mean to make a kill.'

'You're convinced that it will be soon, then?'

He nodded. 'The rats are leaving the sinking ship, so these
stupid Norwegians who have been playing with fire will, very
soon now, find their flirting and dancing replaced by bloodshed
and famine.'

4

Up Goes the Curtain

Paula pouted, wept and swore—but she had fallen completely
under the spell of the sardonic Russian, who treated her with
the utmost brutality but made love to her with more vigour
than any man she had ever known; so eventually she agreed to
put up to Major Quisling the matter of obtaining a Norwegian
passport for Erika. Stefan left her with the conviction that she
was really frightened of him and so would do as he said, but it
was an anxious time waiting to hear the result of her endeavours.

On the Wednesday night that she was to tackle Major
Quisling news came through that there had been a reshuffle in
the British Cabinet, but its results were disappointing. The only
definitely good thing which came out of it was the appointment
of Lord Woolton as Food Minister. The other leeches clung on
to their jobs in spite of the fact that both Press and public
obviously considered them incompetent to fill them.

On the Thursday morning Paula telephoned to say that she
thought that things would be all right, and that if Erika had any
preparations to make she had better get on with them, as, subject to the arrangements going through, they were to sail in a
boat which left two days later—Saturday, April the 6th.

On Friday they learned definitely that the matter had been
settled. That afternoon Erika received her passport in the name
of Yonnie Rostedal, and Kuporovitch his in the name of Odo
Assburg. Both passports had been duly visaed by the Dutch
Legation and each was accompanied by a note to say that
special accommodation had been reserved in the ship which

was sailing for Rotterdam on the following day.

'Such,' remarked Gregory cynically, 'is the power of the Nazis in this so-called neutral country.'

Ever since their discussion with Kuporovitch on Paula's projected departure Gregory and Erika had realised that the possibility of their own separation was once again imminent, but they did not take the thought by any means so hardly as they had done before. *Then* it had been their own affair and a voluntary act which might result in their not seeing each other again as long as the war lasted; *now* it was dictated by policy and they could part with a reasonable hope of being reunited in the comparatively near future. There was no longer any question of Erika's leaving for the United States, as in Holland she would now be able, under a new identity, to continue her work against the Nazis with some degree of safety.

The plan was that she should live there very quietly, so as to run as little risk as possible of meeting any Germans who might know her as Erika von Epp, but keep in touch with Paula through Kuporovitch and transmit, by carefully-worded letters to Sir Pellinore in London, all the particulars that could be obtained about the operations of Hitler's secret weapon in Holland. Gregory, meanwhile, would remain in Norway and continue his endeavours to ascertain the date of the projected invasion until either he was found out or the balloon went up; but he meant to join her in Holland as soon as his work permitted.

On the Thursday evening Paula was giving a farewell party to which they were all invited. When they arrived about half-past nine they found her big apartment already crammed to capacity. The women were nearly all Germans, Austrians or Hungarians who came from good families and had been specially picked for their looks. The men were Norwegians or pro-Axis members of the Diplomatic Corps in Oslo. No secret was made of the fact that Hitler was regarded as the master of them all and they laughingly '*heiled*' one another as though the party were being given in Germany. But although Gregory cautiously sounded everyone there to whom he talked about the date of the anticipated German take-over he drew a complete blank; none of them seemed to know anything definite.

Major Quisling was there; an arrogant-looking man with fair hair that was turning grey, and heavily-lidded eyes. He quite obviously considered himself cock of the walk and many of the

41

Norwegian officers who were his senior in rank openly deferred to him.

At one period of the evening, when Gregory was exchanging playful badinage with a plump, dark-haired, bright-eyed little Hungarian girl, Quisling was standing just behind him talking to the dashing German Air Attaché, Captain von Ziegler. Straining his ears Gregory endeavoured to listen to their conversation but he could catch only scraps of it. They were planning something for which Quisling said that the airman would receive the personal thanks of Hitler, but what, was by no means clear. Then Quisling said, 'If you succeed you must fly him straight to Germany,' which gave Gregory the cue that a kidnapping was on foot.

Von Ziegler had a sense of humour, and he replied with a laugh: 'I shall need an outsize plane for that, because he's six-foot-two in height, you know.' But immediately afterwards they moved away towards the buffet so Gregory heard no more, and there were so many people in Norway on whom the Nazis had designs that he knew he might puzzle his wits indefinitely without getting any farther, so he dismissed the episode from his mind.

As it was their last night together in Oslo he and Erika left the party early and were back at the hotel shortly after midnight. For a long time they talked quietly together while she lay in his arms, but at last he managed to soothe her fears that they might never meet again and she dropped off to sleep.

Next morning he took her down to the dock, but they had already made their farewells as both had decided that for him to hang about until the ship sailed would only prolong the agony. During the time that he had been with them Kuporovitch had grown extremely attached to them both, but the Russian was such a cynical devil that Gregory was both surprised and touched when, just before Erika went up the gangway, he drew him aside, and said:

'Keep in good heart, my friend. I will postpone my trip to Paris until you can join us in Holland, and you may sleep soundly with the knowledge that I will tear the throat out of any man who attempts to lay a finger on her.'

Gregory knew that the Russian had a lion's courage and a serpent's cunning, and that when he said a thing he meant it, so he could not have asked a better protector for Erika. For once he was almost at a loss for words and could only murmur:

'That's good of you, Stefan—damned good of you.'

That week-end of April the 6th and 7th proved a trying one. He was not unduly worried about Erika as, although her change of name was only a comparatively slight protection against her being traced sooner or later by the Gestapo, her new Norwegian *nom-de-guerre* coupled with her removal to another country would almost certainly secure for her a fresh period of immunity from their unwelcome attentions; but he was restless and uneasy.

He now had many acquaintances in Oslo but that Saturday none of them seemed to be available. They had left the city without warning or were busy arranging to depart on all sorts of different excuses. Even the Norwegian officers whom he had met no longer seemed to have time to spare to amuse themselves; they either had urgent duties or had gone up-country to various military stations, so Gregory decided that zero hour must now be very near.

Having sent to Sir Pellinore all the information that he could secure there was no more that he could do about it, but he was hoping that the Allies would forestall Hitler by a sudden coup. It was common knowledge in Oslo that the Germans had an armada of troopships all ready to sail from their Baltic ports and British Intelligence must be aware of that. In addition, there were his own reports which conveyed the fact that a large section of the ruling caste in Norway had been so seriously undermined that the country would almost certainly capitulate after only a show of resistance. It seemed, therefore, the obvious thing for the Allies to act first and invade Norway before Hitler could get there.

By evening the curious quietness of the city had affected him so strongly that he decided to risk sending an almost open telegram direct to Sir Pellinor. It read:

RATS HAVE ALMOST UNDERMINED FOUNDATIONS OF ENTIRE HOUSE STOP SEND RAT POISON BY AIR AND DISPATCH PESTOLOGIST BY FIRST SHIP STOP MOST URGENT.

He had no idea what, if any, plans the War Office had made for the invasion of Norway in such an emergency, but he hoped that due notice had been taken of the entirely new tactics which the Germans had used with such success in their conquest of Poland and that the Allies would first seize the Norwegian airfields then follow up as swiftly as possible with troop-landings.

On the Sunday he spent his time out and about in the city, mixing with the crowd and entering into casual conversation with as many people as possible wherever he found that they could speak English, French or German. He talked to a girl in a tobacconist shop, a professional guide, a taxi-man, several barmen and quite a number of people who were having drinks in bars, and by the end of the day he was beginning to think that he had drawn too black a picture of the situation through having mixed entirely with pro-Nazis during his stay in Oslo.

Quite a large proportion of the ordinary Norwegians were sympathetic to Germany but very few of them were pro-Hitler and none at all thought that it would be a good thing if Norway were incorporated into a German-led federation under him. They had heard too much about the concentration-camps, the forced labour, the suppression of the Press and of free speech, which all went with the Nazi régime, to have the least wish to surrender themselves to it. Their one desire was to preserve their independence and they were prepared to fight for it if they had to; but when Gregory asked why, in that case, they did not take Mr. Churchill's tip and come in with the Allies in defence of their liberties while the going was good they seemed to think that that was a crazy idea, because Germany was so much nearer to them and so much stronger than Britain. Their success in keeping out of every war for the past hundred years had convinced them that if they kept quiet and gave no offence to their powerful neighbour they would be able to keep out of this one, and some of them even showed definite ill-feeling towards Britain for what they considered her unreasonable attitude in making it difficult for them to maintain good relations with Germany.

In reconsidering the whole situation that evening Gregory came to the conclusion that the Norwegians would fight if they were given a chance, but he was extremely dubious as to what sort of show they would be able to put up in view of his private knowledge that so many of their leaders had already succumbed to Hitler's secret weapon.

On the Monday the quiet tension of the city suddenly gave way to intense excitement. The British Navy had appeared in force off certain points along the coast and was laying mine-fields in Norwegian territorial waters. The official reason given for this was that the Allies had at last decided to take a strong

44

line and close the winter route by which Germany secured her supplies of iron ore from Narvik.

With huge satisfaction Gregory bought himself a bottle of champagne and sat down to drink it. He was a clever fellow— a monstrous clever fellow—and he was used to reading the news which lies behind the headlines; the story about blocking the iron-ore route was all 'my eye and Betty Martin'. Now that spring was here and the Baltic open again the Nazis could get all the iron ore they wanted without bringing it down the coast of Norway, so why should the Allies suddenly decide to block the winter route of the iron-ore ships when they had left it open until summer was almost here? The thing did not make sense, but was perfectly obvious to anyone. The Navy was really laying minefields to protect lanes through which troopships, bearing the British Army, could come to take over the country. Good old Winston had managed to kick some of his colleagues in the pants and Britain was at last stepping out to fight a war.

Having finished his bottle he went out to the Oslo air-port confidently expecting to see the R.A.F. sail in. There might be a little mild fighting but he doubted if the Norwegians would put up any serious resistance and thought that if he could establish contact with the British landing-force he might prove useful to them as he now had a thorough knowledge of Oslo and its environs.

Although he waited there until an hour after sunset the British planes did not appear, so he assumed that they meant to make an early-morning landing on the following day, at the same time as the troopships appeared off the Norwegian coast. Back at his hotel he found plenty of people who were only too ready to air their views over rounds of drinks in the bar, and through them he learnt that the Norwegian Press had suddenly turned intensely anti-British. In spite of the number of their ships that had been torpedoed by the Germans they appeared to resent most strongly any suggestion that the British should protect them from the people who were murdering their sailors. Then a Norwegian naval officer came in with the startling news that German battle cruisers and destroyers convoying over one hundred troop and supply ships were reported to have left their ports.

Gregory promptly ordered another bottle of champagne. Such tidings were all that was needed to crown his happiness. The British Fleet was also either in or approaching Norwegian waters. They would catch the Germans and there would be a lovely battle in which they, with their superior numbers, would put paid to Germany's capital ships and sink or capture those hundred transports. Allied transports and aircraft carriers were evidently lying out at sea, just out of sight of the Norwegian coast. The intention was to let the Germans make the first open act of war against Norway so that world opinion and the Norwegian public should quite definitely be swayed on to the Allied side. The Germans were to be given a chance to land a few hundred men, then the balloon would go up; the Navy would sail in and shell their ships to blazes while British forces landed farther up the coast.

He went to bed about one o'clock in a high good humour and full of impatience for the momentous events which he felt certain this Tuesday, April the 9th, would bring. At four o'clock he was wakened by the crash of guns.

He had already made his preparations the night before, so within seven minutes he was dressed and downstairs in the hall, where a little group of people—mostly in their night attire— was assembled. Nobody knew what was happening and most of the Norwegians seemed pathetically surprised—even stunned --at the thought that their policy of so-called neutrality had not saved them after all. They were as shocked and indignant at this unprovoked attack as an ostrich, considering itself hidden by burying its head in the sand, might have been upon receiving a sharp stone in the backside, aimed by a small boy with a catapult.

Police whistles were blowing, the guns continued to thunder and people were exchanging the wildest rumours, but no shells or bombs fell in the centre of Oslo and it seemed that the fighting was confined to the harbour district.

Within twenty minutes of the first alarm it was definitely established that the Germans were the attackers. Apparently, considerable numbers of Nazi troops had been concealed in cargo ships in the harbour. Under cover of darkness they had landed and were now shooting down anyone who attempted to oppose them, while their warships were engaging the shore-batteries along the Fjord.

This news perturbed Gregory considerably. It was all in order that Germany should be branded as the aggressor by being allowed to land troops before the Allies arrived on the scene, but what had happened to the British Navy? Why hadn't it intercepted the German Fleet that was bombarding the forts? But perhaps the German battle squadron had been deliberately allowed to reach its destination with the idea that it would be more certainly destroyed if the British sailed in behind it so that it was caught between two fires.

By 5 a.m. the invasion was reported to be in full swing by land, sea and air and Gregory began to plan what he had better do if Oslo fell to the Germans before the British put in an appearance. As the British had command of the seas it seemed reasonable to suppose that the Germans would not venture to send troopships out into the open ocean beyond the waters of the Skagerrak, whereas the Allies could land their troops anywhere along the Atlantic coast. Bergen, being the nearest large Norwegian port to Scotland, was the obvious choice for a British landing in force, so Gregory decided that he had better go there. However, he felt that there was ample time to have breakfast first and run from the Germans afterwards.

As the hotel staff was completely disorganised there was little prospect of getting proper service, so he walked downstairs to the kitchens and just shouldered his way past the stunned-looking people who had gathered there from fear of air-raids. In the larder he found that day's selection for the restaurant's cold table and while the other people sat or stood about in gloomy foreboding he made an extra large meal of some of his favourite foods because he had no idea at all when he would get another.

After his admirable breakfast he learnt that simultaneously with their invasion of Norway the Germans had invaded Denmark. The news did not surprise him and he felt that there was nothing very much that could be done for the unfortunate Danes. If Hitler had succeeded in forcing their frontier, which should not have proved a very difficult task, he could bring such a mass of men and metal to bear that no Allied expeditionary force could have hoped to hold Denmark for the Democracies. Norway, however, was a very different proposition, and he remained convinced that at any time now news would come through of landings by British troops who would oust the Germans because they could not be supported by sea-borne reinforcements from their bases.

On going upstairs again he heard that the *Gneisenau* had been sunk by one of the shore-batteries in the Fjord, which cheered him up a little. The place was thick with rumours that

47

every sort of treachery was on foot and that certain commanders of forts on the Fjord had deliberately refrained from
shelling the Germans; but there was evidence that at least one
officer had had the courage to use his guns before a 'cease fire'
order had been telephoned to him.

Soon after 7 a.m. word flew from mouth to mouth that a
somewhat belated German ultimatum had been received in
Oslo. The Nazis demanded the unconditional surrender of
Norway's armed forces, the reception of German garrisons, the
resignation of the Norwegian Government and the setting-up
of a new one under Major Quisling. During his three weeks
there Gregory had received good reason to conclude that the
pompous Major was a big cog in the German Fifth Column
machine, but it now seemed that he was an even bigger fish than
he had appeared. The Norwegian Parliament was said to be
already in session and Gregory waited with growing anxiety to
hear what reply they would give to the high-handed ultimatum.

At 7.45 the Government's decision came through. They had
rejected the ultimatum and had resolved to fight. Gregory was
considerably relieved, as although he naturally assumed that
they already had a promise of full Allied support, and that that
support was close at hand, he had begun to fear that Hitler's
secret weapon had done its work so effectively that the Norwegian Government might betray their trust and the Norwegian people. Feeling that Norway's entry into the war as an
ally thoroughly justified a bottle, and that there was still no
urgent reason for leaving the capital, he went downstairs to the
cellar.

Many of the hotel guests were gathered there and several of
them, who had sought out the cellar hours before, were sitting
on the floor drunk to the world. He helped himself to a bottle
of Krug Private Cuvé 1928 and proceeded to drink it to the
damnation of the Nazis.

He had only just finished the bottle when bombs began to
fall. Evidently the Germans were demonstrating their displeasure at the rejection of their ultimatum by letting their
airmen loose on the virtually defenceless city. The attack, by
comparison with the Russians' first air-raid on Helsinki, was like
the performance of a village dramatic society compared with a
first night in a famous theatre of a great capital. It was little
more than a demonstration; but it was enough to rattle the Norwegians, who had no experience of air-raids.

Everyone in the hotel crowded down to the basement so that it became a jam of angry men and hysterical women. In consequence, Gregory went up to the lounge again. The hotel was solidly built and by sitting on the floor behind the hall-porter's desk he was quite safe from bomb-splinters or the flying glass of shattered windows, and if the place received a direct hit from a really heavy bomb the people in the basement would just as certainly be crushed to death as those on the ground floor. As a result of his move he heard the Norwegian Foreign Minister, Professor Koht, make the first Government broadcast, via a radio-set which had been left turned full on in the manager's office nearby.

He could not understand Norwegian but the head hall-porter, who had also remained upstairs, gave him the gist of the speech in English. Apparently the Minister, who only the day before had been protesting most violently about the British mine-laying as an infringement of Norway's neutrality, was now calling upon all loyal Norwegians to resist the German invasion by every means in their power. He also stated that the Norwegian Government had asked for aid from the Allies, who had agreed to send the Norwegians armed support as soon as possible.

With some alarm, Gregory questioned the head porter upon the last phrase, but the man was quite definite about it, which gave him furiously to think. The statement should have been to the effect that, in anticipation of German aggression, the Allies had had troopships waiting off the coast which were *now landing* forces in support of the Norwegian Army, but apparently all that the Allies had said was that they *would send* troops; which might mean this year, next year, some time or never. Even if they were leaving now—at this very moment—by the time they reached Norway they would find that the Germans had secured a solid foothold and were well dug-in there. Evidently somebody had slipped up pretty badly.

It was now after nine o'clock and Gregory decided that the time had come for him to make a move. The bombing had ceased some twenty minutes before, and it seemed that comparatively little damage had been done except that the Nazis had put one down plumb on the American Legation. The Minister and his staff had escaped, but Gregory felt that by destroying their papers and belongings Hitler had done his good deed for the day; nothing could be better calculated to arouse the fury of the people in the United States than this wanton desruction of their property, and since we still had no propaganda there worth talking about it was just the sort of thing that we wanted.

Out in the street he found people now hurrying about and many cars stacked high with baggage, so evidently the unfortunate folk of Oslo who had the means to do so were already in flight from the city. That would jam the roads and make his trip to Bergen longer and more difficult, but he was well-fed and well-clothed so he had no doubts at all about his ability to arrive there without suffering any great discomfort.

Round at the garage, however, he received a nasty shock. The man who filled his hired car with petrol told him that the Germans were in Bergen. Gregory gaped at him, amazed, angry, helpless; he could only suppose that a convoy of German troopships had slipped past the British naval patrols in the night. Anyhow, the presence of the Germans in Bergen put any question of going there now right out of the picture, so he decided to head north, for Trondheim.

As he drove slowly through the crowded streets he once more reviewed the situation. By allowing the Germans to get into both Oslo and Bergen the Allies had landed themselves in a pretty mess. With their usual amazingly efficient staff-work the Nazis would now be able to seize all the strong points in southern Norway and, the power of defence being so vastly superior to that of attack, they would sit there—perhaps for weeks—wiping out any Allied forces that were sent against them. With such a lead they might even succeed in putting Norway right out of the war before Allied help could reach her.

From this he began to speculate on what measures the Germans would take in an endeavour rapidly to subdue the whole country. Obviously they would make every effort to get control of the Government machinery so that an official announcement could be made calling upon the Norwegians to lay down their arms. Paula and her friends had put in so much useful work with Norway's official classes that the way was already prepared for such a move. But it could be done only by exerting pressure on King Haakon.

The Ministers who had remained uncontaminated by Hitler's secret weapon would advise him to fight on and to put his trust in the eventual victory of the Allies; the others would urge him to spare his people the horrors of war and continue to rule over his kingdom by the gracious permission of the Nazis. What would the King decide to do?

As Gregory was pondering the point he caught sight of a man driving a car a little way ahead of him. It was the German Air Attaché, Captain von Ziegler. Instantly the snatches of conversation that he had overheard at Paula's farewell party, between von Ziegler and Major Quisling, flashed back to him. They had been planning for von Ziegler to kidnap somebody and fly him into Germany, and it was somebody who had the unusual height of six-foot-two. King Haakon had that unusual height.

Gregory's brain began to race. Could it be? It *must* be. It was the King whom they intended to kidnap and torture into surrender. At that moment von Ziegler turned his car out of the main stream of traffic and shot up a side-turning. Instantly abandoning all thoughts of Trondheim, Gregory jerked round his wheel, narrowly missing a lamp standard, and roared after him.

5

Gregory Sallust Makes His Will

A few hundred yards farther on, von Ziegler's car entered the *Stor-Tory,* the great square which is Oslo's principal market; but no market was being held there this morning. The German attack had opened before the vegetable and flower growers had left the suburbs so the square was innocent of stalls and its permanent booths were shut. Only a few knots of people stood there, gazing skyward at the German planes which were still circling overhead. Passing the massive red-brick tower of the *Vor Frelser's Kirke,* which dominates the square, the German Air Attaché turned again and Gregory saw that he was heading for the Palace. Jamming his foot down on the accelerator he put on a spurt and drew level with the car ahead. Von Ziegler, catching sight of him, recognised him at once and smilingly waved him on, but Gregory signalled to him to slow down and with a frown of annoyance the German pulled up.

'What is it, *Herr Oberst-Baron*—what is it?' he called. 'I am in a hurry—I have urgent work to do.'

'I know,' nodded Gregory, getting out of his car and stepping over to von Ziegler, who was leaning from the driving-seat of his. 'I've been sent to help you.'

Before the airman had a chance to express surprise, Gregory hurried on: 'I've done my job already, so Quisling said that the most useful thing I could do now was to lend you a hand.'

'I see.' Von Ziegler's bright-blue eyes remained quite expressionless for a moment, then he asked: 'Do you know what I'm about to do?'

'No,' grinned Gregory, 'not officially; but I have a pretty shrewd idea, as Quisling said that I should find you somewhere in the neighbourhood of the Palace. It was by sheer luck that I caught sight of you driving through the *Stor-Tory* just now.'

Von Ziegler suddenly smiled. 'You must have a pretty useful imagination, Baron, if you've guessed what I mean to attempt when I reach the Palace.'

'I don't hold down a job on the General Staff for my good looks, *Herr Hauptmann,* and I assume that you've got a number of our Fifth Column people reporting to you. It would be fine work if we could surround the Palace so that the King can't communicate with his Government.'

'It's a much more hazardous enterprise than that.' Von Ziegler's smile widened.

'Whatever it is, I'm game, and naturally in this affair I shall consider myself entirely under your orders.'

'*Danke Schön, Herr Oberst-Baron.* If I'm any judge, you're just the sort of man that I should like to have with me in this business. It needs quick wits and courage and I'm sure that you have plenty of both. But we mustn't waste time talking. Jump into your car and follow me; I'll tell you what the scheme is when we get there.'

Still grinning, Gregory got back into his car and drove after the Air Attaché through a number of narrow side-turnings by which he was avoiding, as far as possible, the main thoroughfares of the city which were now choked with refugees. The two cars pulled up one behind the other outside the Palace and their occupants met on the pavement.

Von Ziegler just nodded to the sentry on the gate and walked through into an inner courtyard with Gregory beside him. As they crossed the courtyard he said in a low voice: 'We're going to arrest the King.'

'*Donnerwetter!*' exclaimed Gregory, simulating thunderstruck astonishment.

'I don't wonder you're a bit taken aback,' murmured the air-man, who was obviously enjoying his momentous disclosure, 'and it *is* a pretty risky undertaking. That's why I'm not sorry to have you with me. But if we keep our heads I think we'll be able to pull it off all right.'

'What, in his own palace, surrounded by his guards? That's taking on a packet, isn't it?'

'It would be if his guards were all loyal to him, but if Quisling has done his stuff properly none of them will lift a finger. If he hasn't, we shall probably be dead in about five minutes; but you said that you were game for anything. Of course you've got your gun on you?'

Gregory nodded. Evidently he had been right about von Ziegler; anyone who would attempt to carry out such a desper-ate business was a man after his own heart. For the moment he was almost sorry that he was on the other side, but war was war, and if he found it necessary to do so he knew that, without hesi-tation, he would shoot the blonde, lanky airman.

Von Ziegler went on softly: 'This is my plan. There is a Major Heering in attendance on the King this morning—you've prob-ably met him at Magda von Krims'—she's been looking after him for us—and it will be his job to take us up to the King without our being formally announced. He'll tell the King beforehand that two members of the Russian Legation are ask-ing urgently for a private audience but that they don't wish to be seen going in to him. Russia has not declared her policy yet, and as Norway has rejected our ultimatum the King will natur-ally be incredibly anxious to know what Russia intends to do. Is she going to come in with us and attack him across his northern frontier, or can she be kept out so that he has a chance to form a solid front against us in the south? In consequence, it's certain that he will consent to see us and agree to our coming up by way of the back stairs.

'Directly we get into his room we simply hold him up at the point of the pistol. He is just as liable to die in agony from a couple of bullets in the stomach as any of his subjects, so I very much doubt if the old boy will have the courage to call our bluff. We shall be very polite but quite firm about it and offer him the choice of a sticky death or of coming quietly down-stairs with us to my car, with Heering in attendance, so that, for his own protection, we can remove him to a safer place than his Palace is at the moment.'

'That's all very well,' Gregory protested, 'but, besides this chap Heering, there may be other people with him when we get up to his room, and he must know you by sight as you're a member of the Diplomatic Corps here. Directly he sees your face he'll realise that Heering has lied to him about the Russians.'

'No; we shall be all right on that score, because Heering will tell him beforehand that we have insisted that nobody else shall be present at the interview, and once we are in his room it's just a toss-up as to whether he notices my face first or the automatic I shall be holding in my hand.'

At that moment they passed another sentry and reached a covered entrance. On going inside, von Ziegler asked the uniformed porter there to tell Major Heering that the gentleman whom he was expecting had arrived. While the message was being sent up a liveried footman showed them into an empty waiting-room and closed the door behind them.

Gregory produced his cigarettes and inquired in a low voice: 'What happens if the King tells us to go to blazes?'

'Thanks.' Von Ziegler took one and went on: 'Then things may prove a bit tricky, but I think we'll still manage to pull it off. According to Quisling, two-thirds of the officers of the Royal Guard have been fixed and the men are not likely to attempt anything without orders. We shall keep the King covered, and, if necessary, use physical force to restrain him from leaving the room. In any case he could not get out of the Palace now, as every entrance is specially guarded and a pro-German Norwegian officer posted at each with orders to stop him. While we are holding up the King, Heering will leave us and collect his friends. They will then proceed to arrest any Ministers, secretaries and other people who are in the Palace and might cause trouble, while we sit tight with the King until some of the troops who have landed in the harbour district have managed to fight their way up here. If we can prevent the King's communicating with anyone for two or three hours we should be all right, as by that time our Storm-Troopers will have artillery trained on the Palace and the loyal portion of the guard won't be able to offer any resistance even if they want to.'

'That's fine,' murmured Gregory, 'fine. But what happens if the King pulls a gun on us? He might, you know, and it only needs the sound of one shot to bring everybody running; then the men would probably start shooting at Major Heering and his friends and it might be anybody's day out.'

Von Ziegler shot a supercilious glance at Gregory. 'If by any chance you don't like the idea, Baron, there's still plenty of time for you to quit. I was rather under the impression, though, that you said you were game for anything.'

'I am, *Herr Hauptmann,*' Gregory replied quietly; 'but if anything *does* go wrong it looks as though you and I are going to be in the forefront of the battle. I've been under fire quite a number of times before, but nothing about my own job led me to suppose that I should be again this morning; and I haven't made my Will.'

'Made your Will?' echoed von Ziegler.

'Yes. It's a queer habit of mine; I always make a new Will before going into action. It's rather like taking an umbrella out when you're anxious that it shouldn't rain—at least, that is how it has always been with me—and, being a superstitious person, I have no intention of neglecting the custom.'

As he spoke, Gregory moved over to the other side of the room, drew a blank sheet of paper from a desk-set and began writing on it, while von Ziegler eyed him with amusement. Having completed the document, Gregory folded it neatly in two, leaving only the lowest inch of the face of the sheet visible, and called over his shoulder:

'D'you mind witnessing this for me?'

'With pleasure,' von Ziegler laughed. He seemed greatly tickled by the whole episode, but appended his signature at the bottom without comment.

'Thanks,' nodded Gregory, and folding the sheet again he slipped it into his pocket.

For a further five minutes they sat smoking in silence while Gregory badgered his wits wondering what on earth he was going to do next. If von Ziegler was correct, Major Quisling had planned the whole coup very efficiently. Even now the King's faithful friends and retainers were doubtless being got out of the way. As they would almost certainly remain close at hand, a pistol-shot in the King's room would bring them rushing to it, but traitor Heering's men would be posted in the corridors to prevent them from reaching the King's apartment. If Gregory let off his own pistol with the idea of giving an alarm it was unlikely that it would do the King any good, but would probably result in von Ziegler's realising that the shot had been fired deliberately and in his shooting the alarmist.

He could, of course, shoot von Ziegler, but it did not look as though that would do very much good either. If he did so now it would prevent the projected interview ever taking place, but it was quite clear that the conspirators had no intention of allowing the King to leave the Palace, so they would simply report to Major Quisling what had happened and wait until he sent another German officer to confront their Sovereign and carry out the arrest which they themselves were apparently ashamed to make.

If he waited until they got upstairs before shooting von Ziegler that would hardly improve matters. There would still be Major Heering to tackle and, even if he succeeded in outing him too, Heering's friends would still control the corridors and overcome any resistance which might break out at the sound of the shooting. Meanwhile he would be trapped with the King in his apartments and would have to wait there until the German troops arrived and they were both arrested. Those seemed the only alternatives to the germ of a plan which Gregory had conceived soon after entering the Palace, but that seemed so wild that he feared it would be quite impossible to carry it through without arousing von Ziegler's suspicion.

He was still racking his brains over the problem when the door opened and Major Heering came in. He was a short, stocky man with bulbous eyes and a red face which suggested that he lived too well.

The Major showed no surprise at Gregory's presence, as they had met casually at two or three parties, and since he was posing as a German Staff-Colonel there was nothing surprising about his having accompanied the German Air Attaché upon this unusual occasion. Having closed the door behind him, Heering shot a nervous glance at von Ziegler and said:

'You may have to wait some time; the whole place has been in a pandemonium ever since the guns opened at four o'clock this morning. I've been trying to get him on his own for the last quarter of an hour but it's next to impossible.'

'You'll have to manage it somehow,' replied von Ziegler with brusque authority, and Gregory noted grimly that now that the German troops were in the country their representative no longer troubled to conceal the iron hand beneath the velvet glove; things were obviously going to go badly for the red-faced Norwegian if he failed to fulfil the German Air Attaché's wishes.

'I've been doing my best,' protested the Major huffily.

'Then you must do better, my friend,' was the smooth reply.

'All right. Wait here; but you *must* be patient, otherwise we may ruin the whole thing.' The flustered Major disappeared.

Gregory prayed that the Major might still find it impossible to get a word alone with the King for a considerable time to come, since if they were detained long enough in the waiting-room it might give him just a chance to pull a fast one over the German.

He was a little chary of discussing the invasion, as in his role of a German staff-officer he would naturally be expected to know the main outlines of the operation and if he slipped up and showed ignorance upon any essential point in the plan he would immediately arouse von Zieglers' suspicions, but he began to talk of Norway in a general way and of the benefits that Germany would derive from its occupation.

Von Ziegler agreed that it was a clever stroke as, apart from the produce that could be looted from the country, it would give them many hundreds of miles of tortuous sea-coast where submarine bases could be established for attacks on Britain. 'Of course,' he added with a laugh, 'the whole thing would have been impossible if the British had proper leaders. One must not underrate them as a people, because they're tough as blazes when it comes to a real show-down, but the old gentlemen who are running the country now have simply played into our hands. If they hadn't been dead from the neck up we should never have been able to land our troops in Bergen, Trondheim and Narvik.'

It was all Gregory could do to suppress an exclamation of astonishment and fury. He could hardly believe that the Germans had been allowed to land as far north as Trondheim—let alone Narvik—without any attempt being made to intercept them, but he knew that von Ziegler would never have made such a statement if it were not true. However, the German went on in a way which revealed that the Nazis had had their men hidden in barges and other vessels all ready to come ashore in these ports, which to some extent explained what had happened. Naturally, the British could not have known that they would do that, so they had had no chance to sink these Nazi contingents before they reached their destination. Evidently it was the Intelligence, and not the Navy, who were to blame, and Gregory endeavoured to comfort himself with the thought that in this way the Germans could not have landed any considerable forces with tanks and modern war equipment. They would be unable to reinforce their landing-parties and when the British arrived they would mop them up at their leisure.

As they talked Gregory kept his eye on the clock and as the minute-hand circled the dial his hopes gradually rose. When it touched half-past ten they had been in the Palace for over an hour, so he felt that he might attempt to put his wild scheme into operation with a reasonable chance that von Ziegler would not suspect what he was up to.

First he began to fidget, then he stood up and started to pace up and down. Von Ziegler glanced at him after a few moments and murmured: 'What's the matter?'

Gregory walked over and pressed the bell as he replied: 'I've been on the go ever since one o'clock this morning so I'm going to leave you for a moment.'

In response to his ring the liveried footman appeared and Gregory, guessing that all the Palace servants would understand German, said quietly: 'Show me the way to the toilet, will you?' Then he walked calmly out of the room with the man behind him.

While it had appeared that at any moment they were about to arrest the King he had not dared to pull that old bluff to get a few moments out of sight and earshot of von Ziegler; but once it seemed that their time of waiting had become indefinite his decision to absent himself temporarily could not be taken as unnatural. Everything hung upon von Ziegler's remaining unsuspicious of him, and it was for that reason that he had felt it absolutely vital to remain there talking for so long before playing this risky card.

Even now it was only a long shot that his plan would come off, but it was better to try it than to do nothing. He allowed the footman to lead him down a long corridor and when the man threw open the door of a tiled wash-room he turned and faced him.

'How d'you feel about this morning's events?' he asked tonelessly.

The man remained standing in the half-open doorway and looked uncomfortably at his feet. 'Your soldiers are killing my countrymen down at the docks, sir,' he muttered. 'You cannot expect me to feel happy about that.'

Gregory's face twisted into an ugly sneer. 'If they are fools enough to resist, that is their own fault. But they won't resist for long; you Norwegians are too soft and pampered for that;

it's time you had a lesson.'

The footman suddenly looked up and his brown eyes were flashing. 'You're wrong there; my people are a hardy folk. You wait until you get up into the mountains—some of us Norwegians will teach you lousy Nazis a thing or two then!'

Gregory's face suddenly relaxed into a smile. Producing his 'last Will and Testament' he held it out to the astonished footman and said: 'You're a loyal Norwegian—thank God for that! Now listen. The King is in the utmost danger. Never mind who I am or how I know. Never mind about etiquette—if necessary, push past anybody who tries to stop you—but you've got to go upstairs at once and give this piece of paper into the King's own hand. If you can do that you will have the right to be the proudest man in Norway, because you will have saved your King from being kidnapped by the Nazis.'

His tone was so earnest that it never even occurred to the man to doubt him. With a swift nod he took the paper and put it in his pocket. 'Very well, sir; I'll do that. It was lucky, though, that you spoke to me and not some of these chaps in service at the Palace—half of them have gone pro-Hitler.'

Two minutes later Gregory was back with von Ziegler and he sat down to await the outcome of his plan. Knowing that the King spoke English, he had written his 'Will' in that language and it read:

Get out—get out—get out—instantly! Your guards have arranged to betray you to the enemy and German officers are already waiting downstairs to arrest you. Tear off the bottom strip of this paper and leave by one of the back entrances to the Palace. If anyone tries to stop you, present the slip and it may get you through. I urge Your Majesty not to lose a moment.

Then, underneath, he had written another three lines in German, French and English, each of which ran:

TO WHOM IT MAY CONCERN. New factors have necessitated a change of plan. It is of the utmost importance that His Majesty should be got away from the Palace as quickly as possible. Your co-operation in this is required most urgently.

Below it, little knowing what he had signed, Captain Kurt von Ziegler had appended his signature.

Gregory was far from being optimistic about the success of his stratagem. Luck had served him in that the footman had proved a loyal Norwegian and he felt confident that the man would manage to get the paper to King Haakon, but that was only the first step in this desperate attempt to save the King from capture.

As Gregory had never been presented his name would have conveyed nothing to the Monarch, so there had been no point in signing his message. The King might therefore suspect that the instructions were designed to lead him into a trap where he would be assassinated by Gestapo agents outside the back door of his Palace, if he came out of it unaccompanied. It was almost certain that he would consult his entourage before acting on it, and if anyone to whom he showed it was among the conspirators steps would at once be taken to prevent his leaving.

Again, even if he got as far as one of the back gates, what would happen then? Gregory knew that at each of them a pro-Nazi officer was stationed, and as all educated Norwegians could read German, French or English the officer would be able to understand the message which purported to come from von Ziegler. But would he act upon it?

Kings do not normally present passes to their guards when they wish to leave their own palaces. If the officer had any intelligence at all it would immediately occur to him that if his German paymasters really wanted the King out of the Palace there was no earthly reason why he should not have left by his own front door, in his own car and with his Equerries in attendance. At the first suspicion that the order had been faked he would hold the King until he had had the instructions verified. In a very short space of time one of Major Heering's colleagues would pass the slip to him and he would come pelting downstairs with it to inquire if von Ziegler had gone crazy. The second the German saw it he would realise how Gregory had obtained his signature by a trick, and then the fat would be in the fire.

Outwardly Gregory appeared perfectly calm but he knew that, except for the most extraordinary luck, in getting von Ziegler to sign that paper he had signed his own death-warrant.

6

Caught Red-handed

The clock in the waiting-room ticked on with interminable slowness. It was barely five minutes since Gregory had given the warning message to the footman. The Palace was not a big one as palaces go but, all the same, it was quite a sizable building. The King's private apartments were probably quite a distance from the waiting-room. It might have taken the footman the best part of those five minutes to reach them.

The King was in perpetual conference with his advisers and during the last two hours even Major Heering had found it impossible to get him on his own for a moment, so what chance did an ordinary footman stand of managing that? Having acquired the habit of deference from being in the service of the Crown, would the man screw up the courage to force his way into the King's presence or would he waste invaluable time hanging about the corridor until the King came out?

If he did force his way in, the King would certainly not be alone, and it was almost certain that he would show the warning to whoever was with him. Even if he kept it to himself, and decided to act upon it, how was he going to get out of the Palace without Major Heering and his fellow-conspirators realising what was on foot? Gregory realised that although he had attempted to throw a spanner into the works he had actually thrown only a straw which had very little chance of wrecking the Nazi machine.

As he sat there he was considering what he should do when his little plot was discovered and the balloon went up. The automatic that he was carrying already had a bullet in the barrel so he had only to slip back the safety-catch. If he were first on the draw there was a chance that he could hold up von Ziegler and Heering while he got out of the room. But directly he was out of sight they would begin to shout; the sentry on the outer door would come charging in with his rifle, and the other two, having drawn their pistols, would come dashing after him, so he would be caught between two fires and shot down in the passage. The waiting-room was on the ground floor but its window had stout, old-fashioned, iron bars strongly embedded in the wall, so there was no escape that way, and the room had only one door. By and large, it was about as tricky a situation as even Gregory had been in for some considerable time.

On reconsidering the matter he decided that his only chance lay in shooting von Ziegler and Major Heering before they could draw their weapons. His shots would raise the alarm so he would still have to face the sentry on the outer door, but it was time enough to worry about that when he had succeeded in killing the other two.

At a quarter to eleven Gregory stood up and walked to the window in order to get behind von Ziegler, took out his gun, pressed up the safety-catch and slipped it into his right-hand overcoat pocket where he could hold it by the butt all ready to be whipped out at a second's notice.

At six minutes past eleven he caught the faint sounds of hurrying footsteps. Someone was running down the stairs outside three at a time. A moment later the footsteps were pounding along the passage; the door was flung violently open. Major Heering stood in the entrance, red-faced, pop-eyed, panting.

Von Ziegler had sprung to his feet. Gregory remained absolutely motionless, his eyes fixed on the Major, as von Ziegler still had his back turned to him and was therefore completely at his mercy.

'The King's gone—gone—disappeared!' gasped Heering.

'*Teufel nochmal!*' shouted von Ziegler. 'When? How did this happen?'

'I don't know,' panted the Major. 'Nobody knows. Apparently he just told the members of the Council that he was going to the safe in his bedroom to get some papers and that he would be back in a moment. The Crown Prince was with him and he asked him to come and help him fetch them. The Council waited for ten minutes and there were so many urgent things to settle that his Equerry was sent in to look for him. When they got there they found that the safe was empty and both the King and the Crown Prince had disappeared.'

Von Ziegler's face had gone pale with anger; his long nose seemed to stand out more sharply than ever and his bright-blue eyes were blazing. Stepping forward he seized the Norwegian by the shoulder and began to shake him.

'You fool!' he almost screamed. 'You miserable fool! You will pay for this mess-up before you're much older.'

'It wasn't my fault.' The Major cringed away. 'I wasn't in the

Council Chamber—and, even if I had been, I couldn't have stopped him going into his bedroom.'

'No, imbecile! But someone must have warned him.'

'I know—I know.'

'And it was your job to prevent such a thing happening. Who was it? Who *was* it, eh?'

Gregory tensed his muscles and his hand tightened on his gun. Now for it! The footman could not possibly have got into the Council Chamber without Major Heering seeing him, and once the footman was exposed von Ziegler's swift mind would link the man with Gregory's absence from the room three-quarters of an hour before. He watched the Major's thick lips begin to move again so that he might act the very instant that a single syllable fell from them which would give away the part that he had played.

'No one said anything to the King,' muttered the Major. 'I'm certain of that, because our friends who were with him say so. He must have been warned by a written message.'

'Who entered the Council Chamber last?'

As Gregory saw the Major's mouth form the words 'a footman' he drew his gun.

But von Ziegler's back was still towards him and the Major's eyes were riveted upon the stern face of the German airman, as he hurried on:

'He only brought in the King's morning coffee. I saw him, through the doorway, set it down at the King's elbow and walk straight out again, so it couldn't have been the footman. One of the members of the Council must have found out something earlier, but had to wait for an opportunity, when he was un-observed, to pass a scribbled note.'

Gregory turned his gun over sideways and began to examine it as though he were just making certain that the mechanism was all in order. The footman had turned out a trump. Evidently, on realising that to give the King the paper openly might arouse the suspicions of any members of the Council who were traitors, he had conceived the brilliant idea of waylaying his colleague who was on duty upstairs and by some means or other arranging to take the King's coffee-tray in himself; after which it had been a simple matter to slip the folded message under the King's cup, where he would be bound to see it and could remove it without much chance that anyone else would notice what he was doing.

But Gregory knew that he was by no means out of the wood yet. The infuriated conspirators would immediately institute an inquiry among the guards at the various entrances of the Palace and the damning bottom strip of the paper which von Ziegler had signed would come to light. He might almost have put the thought into von Ziegler's mind by mental telepathy as the German snapped at Heering:

'Anyhow, what in thunder were your people on the gates doing to let the King through? Who was responsible for that?'

'Have patience,' the Major snapped back in a sudden spurt of rebellion against the airman's bullying. 'Colonel Ketch is now visiting the posts to find out. He will be here at any moment; then we shall know.'

Von Ziegler turned angrily away and began to pace impatiently up and down the room while Gregory, in his role of sympathetic co-conspirator, proceeded to ignore Heering's presence and began a slashing attack upon the inefficiency of the Norwegians who had bungled the job so badly.

Some moments later a broad-shouldered officer with a fine flowing moustache arrived. Von Ziegler evidently knew him already and Gregory rightly assumed that this was the Colonel Ketch whom Heering had just mentioned. Having stamped into the room the Colonel said with a worried frown:

'The King must have known that the gates were being watched, as he didn't go out by any of them. He and the Prince climbed over the wall of the tennis-court and dropped down into the street. One of the sentries saw them, but by the time the fool had gone inside and reported to his officer the King and the Prince had made off and were out of sight.'

'*Donnerwetter!*' roared von Ziegler. 'The lot of you shall answer to the Gestapo for this!'

Gregory snapped down the safety-catch of his automatic, drew out the magazine and began to toss it playfully up and down.

'Well, that's that,' he murmured with a sigh. 'We're out of luck this morning, and I suppose it's not much good our waiting here any longer.'

Von Ziegler looked round at him. 'There's no such thing as luck, Baron; only brains and organisation—as I propose to show this afternoon. Come on.' Without another word to the two Norwegians he shouldered his way past them and strode out of the room.

Gregory followed more slowly and, pausing in the doorway, said to the other two conspirators: 'I'm afraid you've made rather a mess of things, gentlemen, and in Germany such mistakes are not readily overlooked. Your only chance is to get out of the country while the going is good. There are still some neutral ships in the harbour and if I were you I should get on to one of them without an hour's delay.' Having clicked his heels and bowed sharply from the waist he turned and left them.

His advice sounded like that of a sympathetic German who was not whole-heartedly with the Nazis and was sorry for two officers who had bungled a very important operation. Actually, it was a Machiavellian piece of cunning by which he hoped to ensure that those two traitors would get their just deserts.

If they fled up-country—as they probably would have done had he not spoken to them—it was highly probable that they would have evaded capture, for the Germans had only just landed in the capital; but if they followed his advice and went down to the harbour their capture was quite certain. No neutral ship would now be allowed to leave Oslo without German permission and if they were caught trying to get out of Norway the assumption would be that they had made up their minds to go over to the Allies; so what had only been a blunder in the first place would, in German eyes, be aggravated to deliberate treachery, and they would be dealt with accordingly.

Von Ziegler was already half-way across the courtyard when Gregory reached the door. As he followed the German he blessed King Haakon and the Crown Prince. Evidently they had had the wit to see that to present any kind of pass to a sentry on their own doorstep was certain to excite comment, so they had decided not to use the pass but to go out over the wall; and that, Gregory felt, had probably saved his life.

When he caught von Ziegler up the German was climbing in to his car. 'What d'you propose to do now?' Gregory asked.

'Go after them, of course. They can't have got far. Would you like to come with me, or would you prefer to go and let Quisling know how the Norwegians have ruined our admirable plan?'

Nothing was further from Gregory's wishes than to go and see Quisling at that moment, but he hesitated artistically before he said: 'I think perhaps I'd better go with you. It will now be a matter of a hold-up in the open, and as there are two of them you may need my help if they happen to be armed.'

'Right. Are you taking your own car or will you come in mine?'

'If I leave mine here somebody may pinch it, so I think I'll go under my own steam. I'll be close behind you.'

With a nod von Ziegler let in the clutch and his car streaked away. Gregory jumped into his and ran smoothly along behind him, knowing that with the roads now so choked with refugees the adventurous airman would not get very far at the pace at which he had set off. For ten minutes they wound in and out of the slow-moving traffic until they reached the Oslo Police Headquarters, outside which von Ziegler pulled up.

'What now?' thought Gregory. 'Surely the Nazi organisation can't have managed to get the Norwegian police force under its thumb.' But he was mistaken. After he had waited outside in his car for nearly forty minutes von Ziegler came out again and hurried up to him. His blue eyes were shining and a satisfied smile curved his strong mouth.

'We're on to them,' he said. 'Oslo is such a little place that everyone here knows the King and the Crown Prince by sight. I felt certain they'd be recognised by scores of people before they had gone ten miles. We had to wait until we could get reports of them from well outside the town so as to make certain in which direction they were heading. They've taken the road to Eidsvold, a small town about forty-five miles north from here.'

Two minutes later they had joined the stream of traffic heading north and Gregory settled down to what he knew would be a dreary chase. Had he been von Ziegler he would almost have wept with frustration at the impossibility of getting every ounce out of his car, but, as it was, he was quite content to loiter. In fact, he knew that the longer they were held up by the refugees the more chance the King would have of getting away, for even crowds who had been panicked from their homes would make way at the sight of their King, whereas they would certainly not give way to anyone who had the appearance of an ordinary civilian; but in this he had counted without von Ziegler.

Directly they were outside the town and the traffic was a little less congested the German pulled up at the roadside and took two large squares of paper out of his pocket, one of which he proceeded to paste on his own windscreen and the other on Gregory's. Both bore large printed inscriptions in Norwegian, which Gregory could not understand, but the airman said Swiftly: 'No good putting them on before we were out of that crush, but they'll help us a lot now. These notices say: "POLICE—URGENT!" and the small lettering underneath means 'Offence to obstruct".'

'Grand!' said Gregory. 'You think of everything; I couldn't have tackled the job better myself.' And as they went on again he noticed with dismay how the law-abiding Norwegians paid due deference to the placards. Each time that von Ziegler sounded his Klaxon they turned to stare and immediately gave him room to pass.

Even with these aids-to-travel their going was miserably slow, as the way curved and twisted through the mountains, where it was much too dangerous to shoot ahead for any distance with one solid line of traffic blocking half the road, and Gregory reckoned that they could not be making much more than fifteen miles an hour. But the King could not be doing any better, so he had no more than his original lead, which, allowing for their long wait at the police-station, was just about an hour.

Now that spring had come, southern Norway was gradually divesting herself of her winter robe of snow. All the mountains were still white-capped but the thaw was climbing out of the deep valleys day after day and every stream and river was in spate. The road lay well below the snowline, but it was very chilly and Gregory thanked his stars that he was warmly clad. He pitied the poor wretches they were passing as he felt certain that many of them would not be able to find accommodation for the night, but conditions were nothing like so appalling for them as they had been for the Finns whom he had seen driven out of Helsinki, in the depths of winter, by Russian bombers.

At a quarter to four they entered Eidsvold, a little town that had only one hotel of any size, in its market square. Von Ziegler drew up in front of it and marched into the crowded lounge. As Gregory had not had anything to eat or drink for over eleven hours he got out too, but his hopes were disappointed. Von Ziegler simply produced a Norwegian police-pass, buttonholed the porter and, addressing him in fluent Norwegian, asked if the King was there.

For Gregory's benefit he translated the man's answer. 'No; he's not here, but he passed through about an hour ago on the way to Tangen.' And while he was speaking von Ziegler was already leading the way back to the cars.

It was about another twenty miles to Tangen and for most of the way the road lay along the east shore of the beautiful Mjose Lake, which is not very broad but extends for over forty miles, like a great inland fjord. They had ample time to admire the scenery, as the road was still choked with Norwegian families moving north, who had left Oslo early that morning; but the going along the lake-shore was distinctly better and they reached Tangen by five o'clock.

There, once more, von Ziegler produced his police-pass at the only hotel of any size, and they learnt that the King was still an hour ahead of them on the road to Hamar, a considerably larger town which lay some fifteen miles farther along the lake.

At Hamar von Ziegler had better luck. The King and the Crown Prince had halted there and were now in the private house of a rich Norwegian. When the place was pointed out to them they saw that it stood on a small promontory where it had a beautiful view over the pine-fringed lake and was cut off from the mainland by a high wall enclosing its own grounds.

Immediately they had left their informant von Ziegler said: 'Now, the question is—does the King mean to spend the night here or has he stopped only for a meal?'

'I could do with a sandwich and a drink myself,' murmured Gregory.

'Plenty of time for that, Baron,' replied the single-minded German. 'Come on; we must find out,' and getting into the cars again they drove along to the house at which the King had decided to make a break in his journey.

On the gate there was a squad of half a dozen armed police and others were standing about in the grounds, so evidently the best part of Hamar's police force had been mobilised to protect the King. But there were no military, as Norway has only a very small regular army and Hamar was not a garrison town. Quite unperturbed by this considerable body of police, von Ziegler jumped out of his car and yelled in Norwegian for their inspector. Gregory could not help admiring his tactics as he would have employed the same self-confident manner himself.

The inspector was brought; an elderly, grizzled man with a drooping walrus moustache, who did not look too happy at the great responsibility which had suddenly been thrust upon him. His normal life in this little country town was, Gregory felt sure, as placid as the surface of the lake below them, and it could be no joke for such a man to learn, on top of the news that his country had been invaded, that his King was in flight from the enemy and looked to him for protection.

Gregory wished that he could have understood the conversation that followed, as he was anxious to know if von Ziegler's swashbuckling audacity would carry him to the lengths of endeavouring to get into the house and attempting to secure the person of the King in the face of the bulk of the Hamar police force. He sincerely hoped that the airman had no such intention, for it was one thing to plan the arrest of the King in his Palace, where a considerable body of traitors had already agreed to render their assistance, and quite another to try to pull off such a coup here in the country where the King was surrounded by men who were almost certainly loyal to him. If von Ziegler started anything there was going to be bad trouble, and Gregory, as his companion, felt that half that trouble would be coming his way.

To his relief, von Ziegler came back after a few moments. Evidently the special pass that he had illegally secured from some traitor in the Oslo Police Headquarters conferred considerable powers on him, as he said in a low voice: 'I made them tell me what we want to know. He has telephoned for his Ministers to join him here, so evidently he means to stay—anyhow, for the night.'

'Good. How about a meal, then?' replied Gregory, who was now distinctly hungry.

'Yes. Let's get back to the hotel, then after we've fed I'll make a few arrangements.'

The hotel was packed with people. Consequently the meal that they secured was a far from satisfactory one. Had it been summer-time they might have fared better, as the place was a favourite holiday resort, famed for its boating, fishing and excursions into the mountains, in addition to which many of the wealthier people in Oslo often motored up there for the week-end, so in the season the hotel kitchen might have coped with this unusual rush of business. But as it was early April, with snow still on the mountains, the management was catering only for the handful of guests—mostly retired people and invalids—who lived there through the winter, and the dinner to which Gregory had looked forward with pleasurable anticipation boiled down to a couple of salted herrings on half-rolls, eaten standing up. However, the cellar was well stocked so they managed to get a bottle of passable hock.

While among the crowd Gregory was very careful to refrain from talking. He made it a rule never to disclose to anybody that he spoke several languages, unless he had good reason to do so, and he had no reason at all to inform von Ziegler of that fact; while, as feeling against the Germans was running extremely high, he preferred to remain silent rather than run the risk of being lynched.

Von Ziegler, on the other hand, conversed fluently in Norwegian with a number of people, and later, having acquired a bottle of Loitens Norwegian Punch from the barman and found a quiet corner where they could not be overheard, was able to pass on to Gregory the latest news.

General Count von Falkenhorst, who was commanding the German forces, had outlawed King Haakon and his Government on their flight from the capital and had set up a puppet Government under Major Quisling instead. Oslo had then surrendered at four o'clock that afternoon and the German troops were already taking possession of the capital. Two German cruisers, in addition to the powerful battle-cruiser *Gneisenau,* were reported to have been sunk in the operations and fighting was still going on outside the city; but the Danish Government had capitulated that morning, so the whole of Denmark had fallen to the Nazis almost without a blow.

There were no beds to be had in the hotel, but when Gregory raised the question von Ziegler said casually that they could, if necessary, sleep quite well in their cars; a hearty attitude of which Gregory did not at all approve, but as this was not his party he forbore to argue.

At ten o'clock von Ziegler said: 'I've got a little job to do before we get some sleep, Baron, and you had better come with me. It may mean that we'll have to wait about for some time, but we can always talk of this and that together.'

'Certainly,' said Gregory obligingly, and he tactfully refrained from asking any questions as they walked round to the garage to get out von Ziegler's car.

In it they drove off the main road and along a side-turning that wound its way up into the mountains to the east, for about three miles. There was no traffic on the road at all and there were as yet no anti-aircraft regulations in force in Norway about motor-car headlamps, so von Ziegler's spotlight showed the winding way ahead in its full glare, and they were able to proceed at a good pace without difficulty.

70

At a point where the road curved sharply round a great rock von Ziegler drew up, ran the car backwards and forwards several times until he had got it placed absolutely to his satisfaction, and got out. Then he turned off the spotlight and dimmed the other lamps with covers which he took from a pocket of the car.

Gregory wondered if von Ziegler had come there for a secret meeting with another Nazi agent, but he asked no questions, and when von Ziegler got back into the car they proceeded to talk. The airman was a pleasant and amusing person when he was in a good temper and Gregory could not help liking him for his dash and devil-may-care courage but, unfortunately he possessed all the true Prussian ruthlessness as well as having been tarred by the Nazi brush so Gregory was troubled by no scruples about the fact that he was there to sabotage his plans.

It was bitterly cold up on the bleak mountainside, but Gregory had filled his flask with the Norwegian Punch when he was down at the hotel and the airman had another which was two-thirds full of *Brandtwein,* so they were able to stall off the chill by swapping pulls at each other's flasks.

They had been there for over an hour when von Ziegler said, 'Hush!' and, sitting forward, began to listen intently. Gregory, too, listened, and the low note of a distant aircraft became increasingly distinct.

'That's one of ours,' said von Ziegler, and he switched on the spotlight again.

From the second Gregory had caught the sound of the plane he had tumbled to the idea. They were in the dark phase of the moon, so it was black as pitch all round them, but down in the valley he could just make out the distant lights of Hamar, some of which shimmered on the waters of the lake. That gave him his direction and he realised that von Ziegler had carefully oriented his car so that it was pointing due south down the valley, and that from their position high up in the mountains a light would have a clear field for many miles in the direction of Oslo. With swift, well-practised fingers von Ziegler began to flash the spotlight rapidly on and off, and Gregory knew that he was signalling to the German plane somewhere up there in the dark skies to southward.

For a split second it occurred to Gregory to pull his gun and stop the German, but an instant's reflection convinced him that he would be crazy to do so. If he killed von Ziegler some other Nazi would be sent in pursuit of King Haakon—someone whose

71

intentions he would not know and so would have no chance of frustrating. It was sounder to let von Zeigler go ahead, learn his plans and then take every possible measure to wreck them.

Almost at once a pinpoint of light showed in the sky. Von Ziegler's signal had been seen and acknowledged. For several moments his fingers pressed the switch swiftly up and down. Gregory knew Morse and he tried to read the message, but soon found that it was in code so it was quite useless for him to follow it any further. The plane was much nearer now as it winked again several times before roaring high overhead. It then turned and sped back towards Oslo.

'Well, that's that,' said von Ziegler cheerfully. 'Now for some sleep. We'll find a sheltered spot somewhere down in the valley outside the town,' and he proceeded to get his engine running.

'You told them that we've located the King?' Gregory said.

'Yes. And since he's too closely guarded for us to get at him I've given them instructions to . . .' Von Ziegler's sentence was never finished. While he had been backing his car to turn it down the narrow road another car had come hurtling around the corner behind them. It pulled up with a scream of brakes.

Next second there was a blinding flash in the darkness. A bullet whistled over their heads and angry orders were shouted in Norwegian. Several men had sprung out of the other car and were running towards them brandishing revolvers. One man yelled in German as he ran:

'We saw you ruddy Nazis signalling to that plane when we were three miles away. Hands up, both of you! Hands up!'

The appearance of the newcomers had been so startlingly swift that neither von Ziegler nor Gregory had had time to draw their guns. As they raised their hands above their heads the horrid thought flashed into Gregory's mind that the next few moments might see him shot—as a German spy.

7

'Think Fast, *Herr Oberst-Baron*'

The running figures flung themselves at the car. Two of them tackled von Ziegler, a third thrust an old-fashioned revolver into Gregory's face and the fourth dragged him out into the roadway. The light from the dashboard and the shaded head-lamps was sufficient to show that they were Norwegian police.

The man who seized Gregory was a huge fellow with hairy hands and he did not use them lightly. Wrenching Gregory's wrists behind his back he clapped a pair of handcuffs on to them, then lifting his great boot he gave him a kick on the behind that sent him flying head first into the ditch under the rock wall. His yowl of pain was cut short as the fall drove the breath out of his body and, since his hands were secured behind him, he went down flat on his face, cutting his cheek badly on a stone. For the next minute he was practically out and when he got back his wits he found that he had been lugged to his feet.

Von Ziegler had evidently fared no better, as between gasps of pain he was cursing fluently in German. The two of them were thrown into the back of the airman's car and the big fellow sprawled on the seat, planting his huge feet on top of them, while another policeman took the wheel. The car started with a jolt and began to run down the road towards Hamar.

'Here's a pretty kettle of fish!' thought Gregory. 'To be pinched while operating as a British agent against the Germans is the fortune of war, but to be caught and shot as a German spy is a bit too thick! What the devil does A. do now?'

He realised that there was nothing to stop him producing his British passport and disclosing to the Norwegians the real reason for his being with von Ziegler; but at the back of his mind persisted the nasty, worrying thought that they might not believe him. Von Ziegler was carrying a pass to which he obviously had no right, so Gregory felt sure that when they were searched the Norwegians would also regard his passport as a forgery.

In ordinary times he would at least have been allowed to get in touch with the British Consul and would have been assured of a proper trial at which steps could have been taken to prove his true identity, but from that morning of Tuesday, April the 9th, the times in Norway had become extraordinary. After a hundred years of peace the people had suddenly woken to the unbelievable—they were at war—a full-scale invasion of their country was taking place. Under cover of darkness, foreign troops had entered all their principal cities. Screaming shells, hurtling bombs and spates of machine-gun bullets were exploding and spattering amongst them. They had been taken entirely off their guard, and were now fighting for their very existence. With such an upheaval in progress all normal judicial procedure would have been thrown overboard and they were living from minute to minute while they took such steps as they could for their protection. Two enemy spies, caught red-handed, would almost certainly be shot after the barest formalities. Gregory did not at all like the look of things.

The cars pulled up in the main street of Hamar and the two captives were lugged into the police-station. For the time being they were allowed to sit on a worn pitch-pine bench while the German-speaking police sergeant who was in charge of the party that had caught them held a long telephone conversation. The other policemen stood round eyeing them malevolently, and only waiting for a chance to give them another beating-up should they show the least signs of any attempt to rush the door which led to a short passage and the street.

Gregory's bottom hurt him abominably where the big fellow's boot had landed, and he had to sit sideways on the hard bench, which was extremely uncomfortable, but the cut on his cheek was not deep and the blood had already dried. Von Ziegler, he noticed, had a lovely black eye which was beginning to colour up, and his white collar had been torn away from its stud where somebody had grabbed him at the back of the neck.

After about twenty minutes the dumb-looking, walrus-moustached inspector arrived whom they had seen outside the house occupied by King Haakon. The sergeant made his report and the inspector stared grimly at the prisoners, after which he gave some order and the other men moved towards them.

Von Ziegler stood up and, squaring his shoulders, began to talk quickly but firmly. He went on for about five minutes, while the men scowled angrily at him, but the old inspector seemed considerably troubled by what he said and, when he had finished, gave another order; upon which his men led both the prisoners away and locked them up in a fairly roomy cell with two beds and a wash-place.

'Well?' asked Gregory, who had not understood a single word of all that had been said.

'They were going to shoot us out of hand,' said von Ziegler, 'but I managed to get the old boy rattled. He's just a country policeman and I imagine he's reached the rank of inspector only by doing his job conscientiously for the best part of forty years, and avoided any responsibility unless his little book of rules has given him chapter and verse for taking it.'

'How did you manage to get him scared?' asked Gregory curiously.

'I admitted quite frankly that we were German officers in civilian clothes. I also admitted that we were communicating with the enemy—there was no sense in denying that, seeing that we were actually caught on the job—and that as we were not in uniform the penalty for our offence was death; but I told him that the police had no power to pass or to carry out such a sentence. I insisted that, however brief our trial, it must be held by the military and that sentence and execution must be carried out by them.'

Sitting down gingerly on one of the beds Gregory lit a cigarette. 'That was a damned clever line. I take it that you were gambling on the fact of there not being any troops in the town? I wonder, though, that he believed you.'

Von Ziegler grinned. 'He didn't at first—I could see that in his rheumy old eyes—but I told him that it was quite definitely a piece of international law. I pointed out that at four o'clock this afternoon Oslo had surrendered to General Count von Falkenhorst and that our troops were also in possession of Stavanger, Bergen, Trondheim and Narvik; that his people, therefore, hadn't a hope in hell of holding the rest of the country and that we should be in full possession of it inside a week. I reminded him that immediately afterwards an investigation into events in every town would be carried out with our usual German thoroughness and that we had plenty of sympathisers in Hamar as well as in other places; that if he liked, therefore, he could have us taken out into the back yard and shot, but that he would never be able to cover it up; it would be reported directly German troops arrived here and perfectly legal reprisals would be carried out against him. Our *Gauleiter* would have him shot, with the whole of his firing-squad that shot us, and all their families would be sent to a concentration-camp in Germany. After all, that's perfectly true, you know—except the part about its not being legal for police to shoot enemy spies. These Norwegians can't go shooting German officers like you and me and not expect to pay for it; so really I've done the old boy a good turn by scaring the wits out of him.'

Gregory nodded. 'Yes; our comrades would inflict pretty sweeping penalties for the loss of an Air Attaché and a Staff-Colonel. I think you handled the situation magnificently. Unfortunately, though, the bluff you put up has only saved us temporarily. Our lives are still hanging by a hair; the moment any troops turn up we shall be handed over to them and promptly executed.'

'Maybe,' said von Ziegler, by no means happily, 'maybe; but things will start to happen long before any Norwegian troops come on the scene.'

'What sort of things?' asked Gregory. 'Have you got some Fifth Column people among those ferocious-looking policemen who will come and let us out later on, when the excitement has quietened down?'

'No; unfortunately I haven't. These country folk are much more difficult to get at than the Norwegians in the towns. The thing I'm thinking of may give us an opportunity to escape, but on the other hand it may settle our problem for good and all.' The airman began to pace a little nervously up and down the narrow cell, as he added: 'Have you got that Will, Baron?'

'Eh?' Gregory almost said: 'What Will?' but he checked himself in time and replied instead: 'Why d'you ask?'

'Only that you may need it, unless it goes up in smoke with you. This place is going to be bombed to blazes in less than half an hour.'

'Hell's bells!' Swinging round, Gregory stared at him. 'So that is what you were signalling about?'

'Yes. I ordered three squadrons to come up at twelve-thirty and blow Hamar off the face of the earth.'

'Phew!' Gregory whistled. 'The devil you did! But *why*, in God's name? I thought you wanted to get the King alive?'

'I did—this morning. But we couldn't go into that château on the lake and carry the old man off now he's surrounded by a lot of friends and loyal police—we wouldn't have stood a chance—and from the policy point of view it doesn't very much matter which we do—secure his person or kill him. The essential thing is that since he's decided to fight we must render him powerless to inspire his people. It would have been fun to fly him to Germany, but once that became impossible, it was up to us to bring about his death in any way we could.'

Gregory drew heavily on his cigarette. 'I suppose the idea was that we should sit up there in safety on the mountainside while Hamar was blown to bits, then come down and inspect the ruins to make certain that he hadn't escaped?'

'That was the scheme; but, unfortunately, things have panned

76

out rather differently. I told them to begin on the château, then to go for the road-junction and the railway station in case he escaped the first salvo and tried to get away; and lastly, to plaster the whole town in case he had taken refuge anywhere after leaving the château. I suppose this police-station is as solid a building as anything hereabouts, but if our *Flieger* do their stuff properly it's not going to be a very jolly party for you and me now. Still, there's a chance that part of the building will be damaged and that we may be able to escape in the ensuing confusion.'

Gregory's brain was working overtime again. The first thing was to get a warning to the King before the German planes came over, and that should not be difficult. He had only to bang on the cell door and start creating a fuss, upon which the German-speaking sergeant would be brought along; he could then tell the man what was intended, and it was quite certain that the police would not waste time inquiring why Gregory had chosen to give the warning, but would take immediate steps to see that the King removed himself to a place of safety.

Such a course meant giving himself away to von Ziegler, but that was immaterial now that the German had done his worst and was a captive. They would both be removed to a place outside the town until after the air-raid, and von Ziegler would definitely be shot immediately troops arrived in that area, but Gregory might get off through having given the warning which had saved the King.

On the other hand, he might not. It would probably be reasoned that he had given the warning only out of sheer funk for his own life, which did not affect the fact that he had communicated with the enemy for the purpose of bringing about the King's death, and jointly with von Ziegler he would still be held responsible for the destruction of the town and for the deaths of any Norwegians who were killed in the air-raid. On further consideration he did not think that there was much chance of the Norwegians reprieving him because he had given away the fact that the raid was to take place. It was much more likely that he and von Ziegler would be torn to death by an infuriated mob in the light of the blazing ruins.

Time was passing with horrifying swiftness and he knew that he had got to think mighty quickly if he was to get both the King and himself—not to mention the wretched inhabitants of Hamar—out of this ghastly mess, and for about ten agonising

77

minutes he could think of no way out at all.

Suddenly the idea came to him that it might be possible to use the information he possessed as a bargaining counter, and he said quickly to von Ziegler: 'This isn't good enough. Our boys may get the King but they'll probably get us too; and if they don't, it's a hundred to one that we'll be lynched afterwards by a howling mob. I'm perfectly prepared to die for the *Fuehrer,* but we can be much more useful to him alive.'

The airman was a brave man, but the last ten minutes had done him no good at all. Little beads of perspiration were standing out on his forehead and he had gone quite pale about the gills. He knew, just as well as Gregory did, what an extraordinarily slender chance they stood of getting out of that police-station alive, and he said after a moment:

'Yes. It was one thing to take a sporting chance of being wounded or killed in an attempt to get the King, but it's another to have to sit here waiting for almost certain death—as we now have to. I wasn't reckoning upon being trapped like this. What d'you suggest?'

'You'd better leave this to me,' replied Gregory. 'Just get me that police sergeant who speaks German.'

Von Ziegler hammered on the door and when it was opened spoke to the warder, who shut it again and a moment later returned with the sergeant.

'Look here,' said Gregory, 'my friend and I have been thinking things over. We fully realise that we shall be shot directly some of your troops turn up, and we've been wondering if we couldn't save our lives by doing a deal with you. We are in possession of very important information; something which may change the whole fate of Norway. As a German officer and nobleman I give my word for that. My proposal is that we should give you this piece of information and that, in exchange, you should allow us to walk out of here immediately afterwards as free men. If you don't agree—all right, we're not talking; we'll go to our deaths with our mouths shut—but you'll regret it as long as you live.'

'I must send for the inspector,' said the sergeant cautiously.

Gregory shook his head. 'Sorry, there's no time for that. This matter is of the utmost urgency, so you must make the decision yourself. My friend and I have excellent reasons for wanting to be outside this station as soon as possible, and the information will be no good to you unless you act on it at once. If you haven't made up your mind in two minutes the deal is off.'

The sergeant was a much more intelligent-looking man than the old inspector and he did not waste further time beating about the bush. Instead, he said quietly: 'In that case you must give me your information and leave yourself in my hands. If I consider that the information is really worth it I'll let the two of you go.'

The man had an open, honest face and Gregory knew that the only thing that he could do was to trust him, so he said: 'All right; I'll take your word for that. We were signalling, as you saw, to one of our planes. It went back to Oslo with the information that King Haakon has taken refuge in the château here and with orders for three squadrons of bombers to come up and blow the place to hell. There is no means of cancelling the order, so you've got about twelve minutes left to warn the King and get the inhabitants out of the town.'

'Right,' said the sergeant. 'You're free. Out you go—both of you!' Then he yelled an order in Norwegian to the astonished warder and raced for the telephone. A moment later Gregory and von Ziegler stood out in the street mopping the perspiration from their brows—but free men.

'*Mein Gott!* You handled that well,' sighed von Ziegler. 'And you were right; we should have been crazy to stay there and let ourselves be blown to bits. Now we're free again we'll get the King tomorrow and still live to wear Iron Crosses of the First Class for the job.'

His car was still standing outside the station and he ran towards it. As he started it up and swung round the wheel Gregory jumped in beside him, yelling: 'Hi! Not that way—back to the hotel! I want to collect my car.'

'We haven't much time,' muttered the airman.

'Time enough for that,' replied Gregory, 'and it may prove useful.'

'*Schön!*' Von Ziegler put his foot on the accelerator and the car sped down the street. Realising that at that time of night the garage would be locked, they drove straight to the hotel entrance. When Gregory raced up the steps he heard a fire-alarm ringing loudly; a warning had just been telephoned to the hotel and the night-porter had had the sense to set the alarm going as the quickest way of rousing the guests.

The bedless crowd who had settled down in the lounge to get what sleep they could were already hurrying to the cellars and other people in their night-attire were running down into the lounge from the rooms above. After one hasty glance round, Gregory saw the night-porter and grabbing him by the arm demanded the key of the garage. The man took it off its hook and thrust it into his hand. Without losing an instant he ran out of the hotel again and jumped on to the footboard of von Ziegler's car, so that the airman could run him round to the garage gates.

The open space outside it was blocked with the cars of refugees who had selected the hotel as a temporary shelter for the night, and when Gregory got the door open he found that the garage also was jammed to capacity with cars; so he did not bother to look for his own, as it might have taken him a quarter of an hour or more to get it out. Instead, he ran his eye swiftly down the front line and selected a car of the same make, which his ignition key would fit. Thrusting it in, he turned on the engine, then glanced at his watch; there was still about five minutes to go. Getting into the car, he sat back and lit a cigarette.

He waited there, keeping an eye upon the minute-hand of his watch and listening with all his ears for the sound of aeroplane engines. Three minutes passed, then von Ziegler came dashing in.

'Come on!' he yelled. 'Come on! What the hell are you waiting for?'

'All right,' Gregory called back. 'I've been trying to find my own car but it must be somewhere at the back, and it's only just occurred to me to take this one instead.' As he spoke he drove slowly out of the garage, but directly he got the car on to the road he stopped again and, getting out, lifted the bonnet to examine the engine.

'Come *on*!' shouted von Ziegler. 'They'll be over in a minute!'

'Right,' yelled Gregory. 'Let me just fix this,' and he pretended to tinker with the carburettor. He had been at it for about a minute when he caught the faint hum of aeroplanes. 'There they come,' he thought. 'Just like the old Boche—punctual as a clock.' And slamming down the bonnet he jumped back into the car.

Von Ziegler's car was already in motion and he was cursing furiously. He had meant to drive north out of the town immediately they left the police-station, and so get ahead of the Royal party, as it was a hundred to one that the King would renew his flight in that direction. But Gregory's insistence on collecting his car had necessitated their going to the southern end of Hamar, and now it was too late to drive back through the town. Unless he was prepared to risk being caught in the open street he had to take the road south: which was just as the crafty Gregory had intended that it should be.

They were hardly outside the town when the planes roared over. Three parachute flares dropped; a second later the first stick of bombs landed with a frightful crash in the grounds of the château. The speeding cars felt the impact but they were now far enough away to be out of danger from a direct hit, though there was still a chance that they might be caught by a flying piece of metal. Realising this, both of them pulled up and, jumping out, scrambled down into a ditch.

The earth shook and quivered as flight after flight of planes came over and salvo after salvo of bombs hurtled down half a mile to north of them. A number of people who had fled imme-diately on receiving the warning were out there on the roadside near by, but others who had lingered had been caught, and from where they were they could hear the screaming of the wounded.

Very soon the flames from the burning buildings lit the sur-rounding countryside almost as brightly as daylight, and as Gregory crouched beside the author of this havoc he watched the drawn, bitter and terrified faces of the people about him. One man was muttering to himself unceasingly, and although Gregory could not understand what he said he knew that the poor fellow was solemnly and persistently, from the bottom of his heart, cursing Hitler and all his workers; while near him lay a woman who was sobbing quietly.

At first the bombing had been down on the lake-shore, then it had shifted to the railway station, which was on higher ground, and along the road to the north, over a mile away from them; but soon the German airmen, having thoroughly plas-tered their first targets, began to attack any buildings that they could see by the light of the flames, and some of the bombs fell very much nearer.

The noise was positively deafening as out of the night sky the planes shrieked down, practically on to the roof-tops, before letting go their bombs. Hamar was totally undefended and the raiders had nothing whatever to fear from diving right on to their objectives. A large bomb caught the last house to the south

81

of the village and the whole building seemed to dissolve in a sheet of flame and smoke while brickbats and pieces of metal hurtled hundreds of yards through the air in all directions. One lump of rubble caught a woman who had injudiciously raised her head above the level of the ditch and she let out a piercing scream as she slumped sideways.

At last the pandemonium subsided and, locking their cars, Gregory and von Ziegler walked back among the crowd to the entrance of the town. The havoc that had been created was absolutely frightful. Hardly a building was left standing, and those that remained were in flames. Burning beams, steel girders and masses of rubble choked the roadway, and it was some small consolation to Gregory to see that the bombers had done their work so thoroughly that it was now impossible for von Ziegler and himself to get through the town in their cars until the road was cleared. He could only hope that the King and the Crown Prince had managed to get away to the north before the air-raid started.

As everybody was speculating on what had happened to the King it was not difficult to get news of him, and von Ziegler soon learnt from people in the crowd that he had succeeded in getting clear of the château but had been caught at the railway station. It seemed that he had gone there believing that a train, for which he had given orders to take him farther north first thing in the morning, was already in the siding. The station was almost a total wreck but the building in which the Royal party took shelter had escaped the first attack, and immediately afterwards they had been bundled into a car that had managed to get away before the Germans bombed the road to the north.

Gregory hid his satisfaction while condoling with von Ziegler, who was furious; not so much at the King's having got away, for he had more or less reckoned that the warning of the raid would give him time to do so, but at the fact that with the road blocked he would be unable to follow him, perhaps for many hours.

When they had confirmed these rumours Gregory remarked: 'Don't you think it would be wise for us to get out of the town again? It's true that the sergeant gave us our freedom but we might find ourselves in a nasty mess if we were recognised by one of those ferocious policemen. Now that they know we're German officers it's quite on the cards that they might turn the mob on us, and if *that* happens we'll never see Berlin again.'

'You're right,' von Ziegler agreed. 'Come on; let's get out of this.' And they began to pick their way south again over the heaps of rubble, among which the inhabitants of Hamar were already searching for their belongings and endeavouring to cope with the innumerable fires that were destroying the remnants of their property.

'I think the best thing is for us to sleep in the cars until morning,' the German added. 'With refugees still streaming north from Oslo they'll have to clear the main street, as there is no way of getting round the town except by a long detour through the mountains, so with luck the road may be passable again soon after dawn.'

Even down there in the valley it was very cold, once they were away from the area of the burning houses, but they had thick overcoats and, fortunately, there were rugs in both cars, so when they reached them they curled themselves up on the back seats and settled down to get some sleep.

Gregory was pretty tired after his twenty-two-hour day but before he dropped off he reviewed the situation. The war had now started in deadly earnest by the German invasion of Norway that morning; and he had a fine little private war on his hands into the bargain. So far he had kept his end up. Twice in fifteen hours he had saved King Haakon from capture or death and secured him another clear start; but von Ziegler was no mean opponent, and Gregory wondered for just how long he would be able to continue to outwit him.

8

To Catch or Kill the King

Von Ziegler woke first and roused Gregory. Full day had come and the sun was shining. During the night many refugees in other vehicles had pulled up near them. Evidently the road through Hamar was not yet clear, as the long line of cars and vans was stationary and their owners were either lounging about near them or busy preparing picnic meals for themselves at the roadside.

When they went forward to have a look at the town they found that, with the exception of one big fire which was still raging near its centre, the place was now only a blackened ruin. Many of the walls were still standing but there was hardly a roof to be seen and most of the houses were just empty shells or huge piles of rubble which had collapsed in the roadway. However, quite a considerable amount of progress had already been made in clearing the main street and gangs of townsfolk reinforced by a number of refugees were hard at work shovelling away the great heaps of brick and dragging clear the fallen beams.

Keeping careful watch for the police, they set about trying to find some breakfast, but not a shop was left where they could buy anything and none of the people whom von Ziegler questioned had anything to sell, so they had to content themselves with cigarettes and a few pulls from their flasks. It looked as though the road would be clear by mid-morning and, as they had no wish at all to run into one of the policemen who had caught them the night before, they retired to the cars, where Gregory, curling up in his, managed another two hours sleep.

Shortly after eleven o'clock von Ziegler roused him again to say that the long line of vehicles was on the move and, joining the procession, they set off. The going was now even slower than it had been the day before as the cars were able to pass through the partially-cleared streets of the town only in single file; the pace of the column was that of its slowest member and there were constant halts for no apparent reason. At last, when they got on the clear road to the north they were able to go a little faster, as both cars had the police notices stuck on their windscreens and the refugees gave passage to them wherever possible.

About five miles farther on von Ziegler pulled up on a grassy stretch at the roadside and produced a map which he consulted while Gregory joined him for a cigarette. It was a large-scale map of German origin and every building was marked upon it. The airman pointed to a solitary square that stood a little apart from a cluster of rectangles, denoting the village of Jesnes.

'That's the place I'm looking for,' he said. 'It can't be far now; judging by the contours, it's just round the next bend. We'll find friends there and if these blasted refugees haven't eaten them out of house and home we'll get some breakfast.'

They crawled on for another mile and round the bend entered Jesnes, where von Ziegler turned right, up a steep, winding side-road, until he reached the gates of a chalet which stood about a hundred and fifty feet above the village. Here they got out and the airman tinkled a bell, upon which a flaxen-haired, fresh-cheeked maid with voluminous petticoats, came out of the house and along a short path of chipped stones to ask them what they wanted.

On the previous night they had had their guns taken from them but they had not been searched after the inspector's decision to hand them over to the first troops that arrived in Hamar, so von Ziegler still had his Norwegian police pass on him. He showed it to the girl and asked to see Professor Elvdalen, but it proved unnecessary for her to fetch her master as at that moment he appeared on his own doorstep.

The Professor was a plump, rosy-faced man of about forty, and on the girl's showing him von Ziegler's pass he asked them to come inside. The house was a well-kept but unpretentious place with the type of furnishings that are bought on the hire-purchase system, and Gregory judged that Elvdalen was probably a minor official of some kind—perhaps to do with the fisheries or the forests—as the only thing which made the living-room into which their host conducted them at all out of the ordinary was that on one wall there was a number of large-scale maps of the district, which had evidently not been pinned up recently for they were yellow from exposure.

When the girl had gone about her housework von Ziegler spoke to Elvdalen in Norwegian, upon which the plump man immediately straightened himself up and gave the Nazi salute. Having acknowledged it von Ziegler introduced Gregory, and it was found that the Norwegian could speak a little German but not very much, so von Ziegler did not use that language for giving him instructions.

These resulted in the Professor's going out to give some orders to his maid and then settling down to make a number of telephone calls. While he was still at it the maid came in bearing a heavily-laden tray with hot coffee, eggs, cold meat and preserves. Except for the *brodchen* in the hotel at Hamar, Gregory and von Ziegler had had nothing at all to eat for over thirty hours, so they set to with a will. They were still eating when Elvdalen finished his telephoning and came over to report. The King had reached Lillehammer, about thirty miles farther north, in the small hours of the morning and there was reason to suppose that he intended to stay there, for the time being at all events.

'Why?' asked Gregory, and the airman replied:

'Because it is at the entrance to the great Gudbrandsval Valley and there is no town of any importance farther north until one reaches Trondheim. He can't go there because we have already occupied it, and if he's going to continue any attempt to govern the country he must make his headquarters in a town where communications will be reasonably easy with the other large towns that the Norwegians are still holding.'

Gregory nodded. 'From what I remember of the map, the valley is over a hundred miles in length, so there are plenty of places where he could go into hiding in it; but, of course, if he did that he'd have great difficulty in keeping any control over the situation at all.'

'Exactly. And the thing that makes me pretty certain that he intends to establish permanent headquarters at Lillehammer is that he is staying with the Sandvigs.'

'What has that to do with it?'

'It was old Sandvig who fathered the collection of Norwegian peasant arts. He went in for the gaily-printed chests and cupboards that they have in their houses, and for silver-work and embroidered costumes, but his interest didn't stop there. He also collected the most interesting specimens of the ancient Norwegian log-houses with their oriental-looking gables and had them re-erected round the shores of a small lake on his estate at Maihaug, outside Lillehammer. Elvdalen learnt from his informant that there has been great activity going on out there all this morning and that they are fitting up these old show-houses with beds, wash-basins, etc. As the houses are fairly well scattered over the estate the people who occupy them will naturally be much safer from air-raids than they would be if they were concentrated in two or three large buildings in the town, so it looks to me as if the King intends to house his Ministers and staff in them while he stays with the family who own the place.'

'I see. And what do we do now?'

Von Ziegler yawned. 'First I must try and get through to Oslo to make fresh arrangements, but the lines must be terribly congested so that may take some time. While Elvdalen is getting me my number we'll have a bath and a shave.'

This was welcome news to Gregory as, although the good meal had appeased his hunger, he was still feeling stale from a night spent in his clothes and his bristly chin was begrimed with dirt from the ditch in which they had sheltered from the air-raid and with smuts from the burning buildings.

While they bathed, the maid cleaned up their soiled garments and when they were dressed again the fatigues and discomforts of the past night were forgotten, but they found that Elvdalen had failed to get through to Oslo. He reported that the bombing of Hamar had destroyed the telephone exchange there and had cut direct communication with the south, so calls to Oslo could be got through only via Lillehammer and a long circuit of village exchanges; the delay reported was at least five hours.

'We can't wait all that time,' said von Ziegler impatiently; 'I'll have to use other methods. As the line to the north is still functioning we ought to be able to get through to Ringsaker. It's only about ten miles north along the road and I've got a man there who could do the job for us.' Turning to Elvdalen he told him to get a Ringsaker number and in less than five minutes the call was put through. Taking the instrument von Ziegler himself spoke. When he put it down he was smiling.

'That's fixed,' he told Gregory. 'My man there has a secret wireless so my new instructions will reach our Oslo Air Head-quarters in the course of the next few minutes.'

'Fine,' laughed Gregory, but inwardly he was cursing. These damned Germans seemed to have a hundred strings to their bow. How could any ordinary army put up a prolonged resist-ance against a people who had secret agents established in almost every hamlet?

Von Ziegler led the way out to the hall and began to take a swift leave of the Professor, who expressed the honour he felt at their having made use of him. Gregory would have liked to smash in the face of the treacherous Norwegian who was sell-ing his country and stood there fawning on its enemies; but he had a better plan. He had purposely left his cigarette-case in the sitting-room and, leaving the others in the hall, he went back to fetch it.

Elvdalen had been smoking a heavy pipe and he had laid it down in an ash-tray on his desk. Taking from his waistcoat pocket a small phial of cyanide, which he always carried, Gregory inserted a little of the deadly powder into the hole of the pipe-stem. No human court was needed to convict the Pro-fessor; a higher court had decreed that when he betrayed his King it should be before a witness who was also prepared to act as judge and executioner. Gregory's act was carried out with cold deliberation and when he rejoined the others he only felt a mild gratification at the thought that Elvdalen was now most unlikely to live to enjoy the rewards of his treachery. Five minutes later the two cars were descending the winding track to the village.

On the main road there was still a long line of vehicles streaming north but this time they had no great distance to go and they arrived at Ringsaker at half-past two. The place was a fair-sized country town and it stood on a long, narrow arm of the great Mjose Lake, which ran all the way from Hamar to Lillehammer.

Von Ziegler drove straight through the town and some way beyond it until they reached a point where the foothills of the mountain range rose sharply to the right of the road but on its left was a mile-wide strip of flat, cultivated land between it and the Lake. Driving through an open gateway into a meadow, he pulled up and got out. Gregory followed suit and they sat down on a near-by bank to smoke some cigarettes that Elvdalen had pressed upon them.

There was no reason at all why von Ziegler should not have taken Gregory into his confidence as to what the next move was to be, but the adventurous airman evidently derived considerable pleasure in producing one rabbit after another out of the hat for the edification of his companion, who was technically his senior officer, and by now it had become more or less accepted between them that Gregory should ask no questions but only offer useful advice if they got into any difficulty; so he controlled his impatience to know why they should have halted outside Ringsaker instead of going straight on to Lillehammer.

As they were still many miles from King Haakon's new headquarters it seemed pointless to halt here if another air attack on the King had been ordered, and he could only assume that von Ziegler had made a rendezvous at that spot with the man who had the secret wireless-station in the town. But once again he proved wrong.

Just before three o'clock von Ziegler got to his feet and began to pace restlessly up and down. Gregory noticed that he kept glancing at the sky to the southward until, after a few moments, he suddenly gave a whoop of joy and cried: 'Here they come!'

Following the German's glance Gregory could just make out a number of tiny black specks in the sky, which were growing in size with considerable rapidity, and a second later the droning note of the aeroplanes was quite clear. 'Perhaps,' he thought, 'they're going to bomb the King again after all, but, if so, why should we have pulled up in a spot where we have no possible chance of seeing the effect of the attack and it will take us at least an hour to reach the scene of the raid to find out if it has proved successful?'

Then the shape of the planes became perceptible and he saw that they were not dive-bombers but troop-carriers of the JU 52 pattern. As he watched six of them roared over and out of each tumbled a succession of what looked like large black parcels. For an instant he thought that they must be some new type of bomb, but there seemed no point whatever in bombing these quiet fields and meadows on the lake-shore. A second later the parcels burst and a wavy object billowed out above each. They were men descending from the aeroplanes by parachute.

Gregory was intensely interested. He knew that the Russians had formed parachute battalions years ago and it had seemed to him then that the idea was an excellent one. Such troops could land far behind an enemy's lines and seize aerodromes or strong points and cut communications almost without interference. He had spoken of the idea with considerable enthusiasm to a Staff Colonel of the British War Office, but the Colonel had poured cold water on the scheme. He had said that the Russian experiment had not proved at all a success, as many of the men had injured themselves on landing, and that Britain could not afford to risk that sort of thing happening to her fellows; also that the parachutists landed so far apart from one another that they afterwards had great difficulty in forming up into a coherent unit and therefore could be picked off or rounded up and captured separately before they had time to do any serious damage.

Those arguments had not seemed to Gregory to hold water, for he considered it part of a soldier's business to risk being injured in training just as an R.A.F. pilot has to risk his neck while learning to fly, and he felt that it must be possible to reduce the number of casualties on landing to an insignificant proportion if the parachutists were given proper training. Moreover, if they floated down on to a patch of peaceful countryside, far from any troop concentrations, who was going to capture or kill them before they succeeded in joining up, however widely they were dispersed on landing?

The Colonel had not attempted to argue the matter further,

but had implied that the whole thing was rather the sort of comic-opera business that one might expect from people like the Russians, and that it did not really come into the sphere of serious soldiering.

Gregory had again heard of parachute troops being used in the Polish Campaign; this time by the Germans. But the reports about it were rather vague and, whatever British Military Intelligence may have known about the actual facts, the Press had inferred that most of the Germans who made parachute descents in Poland were spies, dressed in civilian clothes, whose business it was to spread false reports and sabotage communications. It was, therefore, with positive fascination that he now saw for himself that the Germans had adopted the new technique and actually had companies of fully-equipped troops specially trained to make parachute-landings.

The spectacle was the most charming thing to watch. The planes had circled round and were on their way back to Oslo, but the whole sky to the west of the road was dotted with the green hemispheres of the wind-filled parachutes as they floated gracefully down carrying either a man or a big, tubular drum. The drop was not a great one, as the planes had passed over at about five hundred feet, and in a few minutes the soldiers were landing all over the fields for a mile or more either side of the place where Gregory stood. Even the refugees streaming along the road, who had at first been terrified by the approach of the German aircraft, had now, in many cases, halted as though spellbound at the sight of this manœuvre which seemed more like a number in a military tattoo than an act of war.

A few of the parachutists were dragged as they landed or became caught up in trees and bushes, but after cutting themselves free from their parachutes most of them remained where they had fallen for about a minute, as though acting on a routine drill, to recover from the shock of landing. Then the officers' whistles sounded and, springing up, they began to run at full speed towards the drums which had been landed with them.

One of these had fallen into a ditch quite near Gregory and he saw some of the men fling themselves upon it. Ripping open its zip fasteners they pulled out an amazing variety of items, including automatic rifles, leather ammunition-carriers, two heavy machine-guns and a squat, fat-barrelled affair that looked like a cross between a trench mortar and a small howitzer.

Within five minutes the platoons had assembled and were numbering off so that the officers could make certain that none of their men had been stunned in his fall and was missing. The second that this check-up had been completed the officers gave an order and the men dispersed again in little groups to take up positions behind the most advantageous shelter immediately available from which they could cover the road against any possible attack.

Von Ziegler then went forward and introduced himself to the nearest platoon commander, upon which the officer gave a signal by whistle and a few moments later they were joined by two other officers; a major who commanded the parachute troops and his second-in-command. Introductions were made all round and although, technically, Gregory was the senior officer present and the paratroop commander, Major Helder, the second senior, it was clear that von Ziegler was still to be regarded as the director of the whole force. After informing Major Helder that the capture of Lillehammer and the person of King Haakon was the objective of the expedition he gave him certain orders which were rapidly carried out.

Having recovered from their astonishment at seeing German troops descend from the air most of the refugees were hurrying on again, though some of them in a panic had abandoned their vehicles and were taking to the hills on the far side of the road; but the column halted again, as the parachutists who had landed a mile farther to the north had drawn a cordon across it. The hundred-and-forty-odd troops turned the Norwegians out of the best cars available in the traffic jam, made all the other vehicles drive into ditches or fields and formed up in a long, unbroken column. For the time being Gregory decided to go with von Ziegler and the Major. They drove along to the head of the column and it set off for Lillehammer.

Among the commandeered vehicles were three motor-cycles and German soldiers mounted on these now went ahead to clear a way for the column. Soon they caught up with the last refugees who had got through before the road was closed and, waving their automatic pistols with threatening shouts, they drove all stragglers right into the roadside so that the German column was able to pass with a minimum of delay.

Gregory wondered why the parachutists had not been dropped nearer Lillehammer, but as they advanced the reason became obvious. The strip of flat meadow-land to the left of the road gradually narrowed until it gave place to a steep bank with pine trees, running down to the water, and on the right-hand side the slope rose, even more steeply, towards the mountains. Evidently von Ziegler had chosen the site as the only one suitable for a parachute-landing south of the town he meant to attack.

At first Gregory hoped that someone who saw the Germans might telephone a warning of their approach to Lillehammer but he soon saw that precautions were being taken against this. Every few hundred yards one of the motor-cyclists dismounted and, swarming up a telephone pole, cut the cables so that no one in the scattered houses which they passed could get through to the north. News of their approach could not be carried by word of mouth, either, as they were moving faster than the procession of refugees. Within an hour of landing the motor-cyclists reached a sharp curve in the road. Two of them again cut the column of refugees and the third rode back to report to Major Helder that Lillehammer was in sight a mile farther on round the bend.

After consultation with von Ziegler and Gregory the Major began to make his dispositions for the attack. Half the troops were ordered out of their cars and down the bank to the water's edge. For many miles past this long arm of the Mjose Lake had had the appearance of a river and it had gradually narrowed until here it was no more than two hundred yards wide. A number of the Germans began to blow up rubber boats that had formed part of the contents of the drums which had been dropped with them, while others cut branches with which to paddle themselves across; the intention being that one half of the force should continue along the road and that the other half should advance along the far side of the water so that Lillehammer could be attacked simultaneously from two directions.

While the troops were still busy blowing up the boats von Ziegler said to Gregory: 'The men in the cars will have to wait here until the others are ready to go forward.'

'Quite,' Gregory agreed. 'But in the meantime, since you and I are in civilian clothes, don't you think it would be as well if we drove on in one of the cars to see if the Norwegians have posted a guard at the entrance to the town?'

Von Ziegler shrugged. 'As they can't know that there are any German troops within miles of them that's most unlikely; and if we meet with any opposition our fellows on the other bank will be able to enfilade and outflank it.'

'Oh, certainly. But as the King is in the neighbourhood there's just a chance that some local reservists have been erecting a road barrier, and I really think it's up to us to spy out the land and make quite sure that our men are not exposed to any unpleasant surprises.'

'Perhaps you're right,' the airman admitted, 'and we can't be too careful. Major Helder will need a car so we'll leave him mine. The men who were in yours have gone down to the river, so we can use that.' As he spoke he walked towards it and, getting in, they drove at an easy pace towards the town.

It was just the opportunity for which Gregory had been waiting. During the whole of the last hour he had been acutely conscious that it was up to him somehow or other to get another warning through to the King of this new danger that threatened him, yet he had been completely powerless, for he was at von Ziegler's mercy so long as they were surrounded by troops; but now that he had the airman on his own again he had at least an even chance of overcoming him, since the weapons of both had been taken from them by the Norwegian police the night before.

Gregory believed in never taking any unnecessary risks, and von Ziegler was sufficiently powerful to knock him out in a scrap by a lucky blow, so he decided that the best thing to do was to drive straight in to the police-station and hand the German over to the authorities; then they could telephone to the King a warning of what was impending. But his plan was frustrated by an irritating though quite simple mishap.

Earlier that morning he had realised that his petrol was getting pretty low, but as he had not been driving the car for the past hour he had not thought about the matter since, and now, with a sudden sputtering of the engine, the petrol gave out. Fortunately they were only half a mile from the first houses of the town and two hundred yards ahead there stood a petrol station, so they got out and walked towards it.

In front of the station there was—somewhat to Gregory's surprise—a handsome Rolls-Royce which was just being filled up. As he and von Ziegler halted beside it, waiting to ask the pump attendant if he had a tin of petrol, the solitary occupant of the Rolls turned round, looked at Gregory and, flinging open the door of the driving-seat, jumped out. He was a tall, thin, prosperous-looking individual with a drooping moustache and a beautifully-cut suit of Glenurquhart tweeds. Advancing on the petrified Gregory he exclaimed in English with jovial delight:

'Well, I'll be jiggered! If it isn't my old friend, Gregory Sallust!'

As Gregory was in civilian clothes there was nothing whatever about him to indicate that he was posing as the *Colonel Baron* von Lutz, and the tall man's recognition was so convincingly confident that Gregory knew that he would never be able to persuade von Ziegler that any mistake had been made. At that second he caught the German's eye; in it amazement was struggling with sudden comprehension and the dawn of fanatical hatred.

9

When Greek Meets Greek

Gregory could almost see the thoughts racing through the German's brain. He was putting two and two together with extraordinary rapidity. He had been too wrapped up in his own plan to kidnap or kill King Haakon to wonder why a German staff-colonel should, within five hours of the invasion, have completed any work he had to do and be at liberty to set off into the blue as a casual helper in this wild chase. Here was the explanation. His companion for the last twenty-seven hours was not a German officer at all, but a British spy. The Rolls-Royce car had a diplomatic number-plate, so evidently its owner was an Englishman who had escaped from the British Legation in Oslo, and he had given away this old friend of his, Mr. Gregory Sallust, without realising what he was doing.

It must have been this spy who had somehow managed to warn King Haakon to leave his Palace at a moment's notice. It was this wolf in sheep's clothing who on the previous night had suggested that instead of remaining in the police-station to be bombed they should give warning of the air-raid; so he had managed to save the King again on the specious excuse that if they saved themselves they could always capture or kill him the following day. Now it was this snake that he had been nurturing in his bosom who had proposed that they should go ahead of the column to make quite certain that Lillehammer was undefended; but evidently his intention had been to get yet one more warning to the King so that he could leave the town before the German troops came up. Von Ziegler was an ambitious man and he had counted upon receiving signal honours from his *Fuehrer* for the capture of King Haakon; now he saw how step by step his plan had been foiled by the British agent whom he had been fool enough to take as his companion and confidant.

With a roar of rage he sprang; but Gregory side-stepped and put out a foot to trip him. For once Gregory had met his match. Von Ziegler was still much too concerned for the preservation of his own plans to be willing to risk sabotaging them further for the joy of injuring the man who had tricked him. The thing uppermost in his mind at that moment was the urgent necessity of escaping from the two Englishmen, who might try to hold him prisoner, and of getting back to his troops round the bend of the road. He had leapt at Gregory only in order to drive him out of the way. Swerving suddenly, he jumped into the driving-seat of the Rolls. Its tall owner grabbed at him but he fended him off with one hand while releasing the brake with the other. Next minute the big car slid away in a cloud of dust.

Gregory could not help admiring the tactics by which von Ziegler had made his get-away and he smiled at the Englishman. 'Well, Gussy, old friend, I'm afraid that's good-bye to your Rolls.'

The Honourable Augustus Langdon-Forbes stared after four thousand pounds' worth of the world's most excellent machinery, which was now streaking southward. Then he looked ruefully at Gregory.

'Who's your ill-mannered friend? I seem to know his face.'

'You should,' Gregory replied. 'He's the Air Attaché at the German Legation in Oslo and he rejoices in the name of Captain Kurt von Ziegler.'

'Of course. Still, damn'd unsporting of him, I think, to make off with my car like that without so much as "by your leave".'

'There *is* a war on, Gussy, old thing,' Gregory remarked quietly.

The other's eyes suddenly flickered with amusement. 'So I gather. In recent months we've even had one or two dispatches about it from London.'

'I should have thought you might also have seen something of it yourself in the last few hours. Did you by any chance pass through Hamar early this morning?'

'Yes; and I found it a most regrettable sight—most regrettable. I see no reason at all why we and the Germans shouldn't kill one another, if we feel that way, without burning up the houses of a lot of unfortunate Norwegians.'

'The Germans considered that they had an excellent reason. They were out to capture King Haakon—and they'll get him yet if we don't do something about it. Do you by any chance speak Norwegian?'

'A word or two. I've been *en poste* here for over two years you know.'

'Enough to make yourself understood over a telephone?'

Augustus Langdon-Forbes' brown eyes twinkled again. 'I might succeed in that.'

'Come on, then; you must get on to the police—or, better still, to the Sandvig's house, where the King is staying, and warn him to get out at once. There's a column of German troops lurking round the corner up there all ready to come racing into the town, and another lot are making their way up through the trees on the other side of the water.'

'God bless my soul! D'you really mean that, Gregory? I know the German motor-cyclists are pretty swift movers but I never thought that they'd get here as quickly as this.'

Gregory had turned and was striding towards a long, low building just beside the petrol station, as he replied grimly: 'They didn't come on motor-cycles; they dropped straight out of the sky like a lot of lovely fairies who had been cursed by a wicked witch and turned into sausage-eating hoodlums with two-ton boots.'

'Parachute troops, eh?' Augustus said lazily.

'How did you guess, Gussy dear?'

'Oh, we are not altogether without our sources of information,' the diplomat shrugged, 'and I had a sort of idea that they might try out their new technique if they decided to go for Scandinavia.'

'Then why the hell didn't you pass on your "sort of idea" to the War House?'

'We did, old fellah—we did; but the wallah who received this epic testimony to our foresight and care for our country's weal probably thought we were pulling his leg. After all, it's asking a bit too much to expect a British general to believe in fairies.'

As they hurried into the low building Gregory realised that it was not, as he had supposed, the rather spacious bungalow of the owner of the petrol pumps, but some sort of club. There was a man behind a desk in the hallway, which opened into a broad lounge-room where a number of Norwegians with worried faces were earnestly talking together in little groups.

Langdon-Forbes stepped forward and proceeded to air his word or two of Norwegian. This proved to be a complete and rapid command of the language, without any attempt to speak it as it was spoken by the Norwegians, and his rather high, clipped accent still branded him as Winchester and Balliol although he was speaking in a foreign tongue. What he said to the man behind the desk Gregory did not know, but the man was galvanised into instant activity and two minutes later Gussy was speaking swiftly and clearly on the telephone. As he hung up the receiver he said to Gregory:

'Well, that's that. Dr. Koht, the Foreign Minister, is with the King and I spoke to his secretary, whom I know personally, so they will be on their way in half an hour.'

'Half an hour?' exclaimed Gregory. 'That's no good; the Boche are only just round the corner; once they start they'll be in the town inside ten minutes—and they may start at any moment.'

'Sorry; but the King is in his bath. He's had rather a trying time, poor old chap, and he thought a bath and a bit of massage would restore him. They'll tell him at once, of course, but it's bound to take him a quarter of an hour or so to get dried and dressed.'

'Has he any troops out there to defend him?'

'No. I asked about that, but Lillehammer is not a garrison town and so he hasn't even an acting unpaid bombardier for escort—only a few policemen with those funny old revolvers.'

Gregory groaned. 'We must try and gain him a flying start somehow. I know! We can't stop the troops across the water but what we *can* do is to stop the motorised column by making a road barrier. We'll have to be darned snappy about it, though. Go and talk to those chaps in there; tell them as quickly as you can what's happening and get them to lend a hand dragging out the furniture.'

Langdon-Forbes advanced into the open doorway of the

lounge and raised his high-pitched voice. There was instant silence, and after he had spoken for a moment a fat man stepped forward and said something to him; upon which he turned to Gregory.

'Our luck's in. This place is the Lillehammer Rifle Club and our friend here, who is its President, suggests that all the members should get their rifles.'

'Splendid!' Gregory nodded to the fat man and added: 'But for God's sake tell them to be quick!'

The President called loudly to his friends and a stampede to the gun-room ensued. Two minutes later the first members of the club to reach it came hurrying back with rifles and boxes of ammunition. As they started to run out on to the road Gregory spoke quickly again to Gussy.

'Tell them that I'm a British officer and that they'd better let me take charge while you act as my interpreter. They won't stand an earthly if they line up out there in the open. The Germans have got tommy-guns and will simply shoot them to ribbons. The thing to do is to man the windows of the club and lie in wait until the Germans come down the road.'

Gregory's suggestion was adopted and under his directions the clubmen began to smash the long line of windows; afterwards removing the fragments of glass to prevent their flying when the Germans fired at the place. They then sorted themselves out inside the building while Gregory stood in the doorway watching the curve of the road half a mile away. Word was passed round that not a shot was to be fired until he gave the Norwegian word of command, with which Langdon-Forbes furnished him.

The preparations for the ambush were only just completed in time. A moment later he saw the Rolls suddenly shoot round the corner, and it was followed by a string of about sixteen other cars containing the parachute troops.

He stepped back a little in case he was spotted and von Ziegler took a flying shot at him when the Rolls drew level. Unconsciously holding his breath, he waited until the first four cars had passed him; then with all the strength of his lungs he roared the word for 'Fire!'

There was a deafening crash as the thirty-odd rifles of the clubmen flashed at the German column. The cars were a bare twenty yards away, the attack was totally unexpected and the fusillade created absolute havoc among them. It was as though

98

the drivers of the first eight cars had suddenly been struck with madness. From an orderly, fast-moving procession the leading half of the column was instantly thrown into the utmost confusion. Cars swerved, skidded and crashed into one another. Two of them plunged headlong down the bank on the far side of the road; one was caught sideways-on by a tree, while the other, rocketing from side to side, plunged into the water. A third came roaring towards the club-house but hit a telegraph-pole, which it tried to climb and became stuck with its front wheels eight feet in the air. A fourth charged a petrol pump and, turning over, burst into flames.

Above the din could be heard the screaming of brakes as the drivers in the latter half of the column tried to pull up. They bunched in an almost solid jam, swivelled in all directions across the roadway, and the Norwegians sent a second volley into them. Gregory took in the general scene with grim satisfaction, then his glance ran swiftly along to the leading car—the Rolls—and remained fixed there. One of the back tyres had been exploded by a bullet and the car had run up the bank about fifty yards past the club-house.

As he watched he saw von Ziegler, Major Helder and another German officer climb out of it. Helder staggered a few paces then fell, either dead or wounded. The other officer turned and sent a stream of bullets out of his automatic towards the club-house, but von Ziegler, with his head low, was running hard towards the town. Suddenly he halted and shouted an order to the officer. The officer yelled something to two other men, who had just scrambled from the third car, and all three of them abandoned the fight to pelt after von Ziegler.

Somebody in the club-house drew a bead on one of the men and he was hit in the back as he ran. Flinging up his arms he pitched forward on his face, but von Ziegler, the officer and the other man managed to reach cover before the marksman could fire again.

Gregory cursed softly to himself. It was the German Air Attaché who was the brains of the party and he had got away with two armed comrades. He was not the sort of man to have fled from the fight on account of cowardice, and the fact that he had drawn two others off with him showed that, although he might consider the ambush into which his party had fallen as an infuriating setback, he was still unshaken in his determination to capture or kill King Haakon.

99

However, von Ziegler was without a car for the moment, and even with two armed men to help him, both of whom were in uniform and so likely to prove a target for the revolvers of the Norwegian police or the brickbats of the population, he would probably have considerable difficulty in getting another; so Gregory did not feel that he was called on to risk his life by giving chase immediately.

To have left the shelter of the club-house would certainly have been to do so, for, in spite of the devastating surprise attack, the Germans were now fighting back with determination and ferocity. Those who had escaped death or serious injury had climbed out of their cars and taken refuge behind them or in the ditch at the far side of the road and were blazing away with their tommy-guns at the club-house windows.

The Germans lost over thirty men before the Norwegians sustained a single casualty, but after that it became more or less tit-for-tat. Allowing for the many casualties which the Germans had suffered in the first few minutes after the attack opened, their numbers were now about even with those of the Norwegians; and although the soldiers had enormous fire superiority, that was largely offset by the fact that every one of the clubmen was a trained marksman.

Drum after drum of machine-gun bullets spattered into the club-house, annihilating any marksman who was rash enough to expose himself for more than a quarter of a minute, but every German who showed a limb was an instant target for half a dozen well-aimed rifles. Several of the Germans attempted to throw hand-grenades, but two of them were shot down in the act so that the grenades rolled away and exploded near them, causing further casualties, after which the others desisted, as they could not lob the bombs far enough while lying down.

Gregory and Langdon-Forbes had had no time to get rifles before the attack but immediately it had been launched and Gregory had had a chance to assess its results they dashed inside and collected a couple of weapons from the armoury; then for the next ten minutes they did their share by firing alternately out of the narrow window of the wash-place.

It was Gussy who spotted three Germans behind an overturned car who were fitting together the parts of one of their miniature howitzers. Gregory popped up his head for a second to get a glimpse of them and he knew that if once the gun were allowed to come into action the club-house would very soon be rendered untenable by shell-fire. With a swift word he sent Gussy along a passage to tell the others what was happening, so that the gun's crew might be put out of action by fire from different angles.

Gussy returned to say that he had found a Norwegian ex-Army Colonel who had volunteered to take half a dozen good men out through the back of the premises; they were to make their way along behind the rifle butts, which would give them cover from the road until they reached a point where they could enfilade the men with the howitzer. For another five minutes the battle raged with undiminished fury. The air was now thick with smoke and the acrid smell of cordite, but the Germans had not gained a foot of ground and as the clubmen were now exercising greater care they were sustaining fewer casualties.

Suddenly there was a blinding flash from behind the overturned car; it was followed instantly by the roar of an explosion. The first miniature shell had fallen just behind the clubhouse and the tinkling of glass could be heard as the panes fell from the shattered windows. There was another flash and the club-house seemed to rock as a second shell pierced its low roof and exploded there, making a gaping hole in the ceiling above the lounge. A third shell followed, pitching right into the long room and causing many casualties; but at that moment the party that the Norwegian ex-Colonel had taken out came into action. Seven good men and true, all first-class shots, emptied the magazines of their rifles into the crouching group of Germans and the gun's crew was annihilated.

A second later a whistle blew and the fire of the Germans slackened. The officer who was commanding what remained of the enemy force evidently considered that they had had enough and was drawing his men off. In several cases as the Germans retreated they had to expose themselves for a few seconds while wriggling back from one piece of cover to another, and during the process the Norwegians got four more of them; so Gregory estimated that there could be only about twenty Germans now left uninjured out of the seventy-odd who had made up the original force. Soon afterwards the firing ceased altogether and the Norwegians were able to assess their own casualties. They had lost five dead and nine wounded; half that number having been accounted for by the single shell which had burst in the lounge. Gregory, Langdon-Forbes, the President of the club and the ex-Colonel then held a brief council of war.

Through Gussy, Gregory explained that a second party of Germans, over seventy strong, were approaching the town on the far side of the water and that, if possible, these also must be ambushed and held off. He added that the leader of the expedition, who was in civil clothes, and two other Germans had succeeded in getting through and were now, presumably, already in the town. It was to be hoped that by this time the Royal party had got away, but von Ziegler would certainly attempt to follow them and, as he seemed to have German agents all over the place, he would probably endeavour to bring up another force of parachutists or send an SOS for bombers to attack the King. In consequence, it was of the utmost importance that he should be caught before he could plot further mischief.

As Gregory knew von Ziegler by sight it was agreed that it would be best for him to go after the airman, with Langdon-Forbes to help him and act as interpreter, while the ex-Colonel took command of the clubmen and did his utmost to hold the town so as to give the King as long a start as possible before the Germans entered it.

On checking up they found that there were twenty-one clubmen still uninjured, three who were only slightly wounded, and six male members of the staff, all of whom were capable of handling a rifle. It was considered unlikely that the surviving Germans from the motorised columns would attack again for some little time and providing they could be prevented from advancing towards the town that was all that was required. In consequence, it was decided to evacuate the club-house and leave it to be shelled by the Germans. With the President in charge, the six members of the staff and the three slightly wounded men took up a position among the trees on the slope at the right of the road, so that they could fire down on the Germans when they proceeded to advance along it after having pounded the club-house to pieces. All the unwounded members, with the Colonel in command, were to make their way through the trees into the town and occupy houses along the shore so that they could ambush the second German force when it came across the water in its rubber boats. They were also to carry as many rifles and as much ammunition as possible, since they knew that they would find plenty of men in the town only too willing to join them, and with these reinforcements the Colonel hoped to hold the Lillehammer waterfront for some considerable time, if not indefinitely.

There was not a moment to be lost, as it would be touch and go as to whether the Colonel could get his men down to the waterfront in time to prevent the Germans landing. Immediately these decisions had been made everyone set about collecting such arms and ammunition as they could carry. The staff took charge of the seriously wounded and made preparations to take them out into the woods, while the main body of clubmen hurried off through the trees. They entered the town from its east side and as soon as they reached the main street Gregory and Gussy took leave of the Colonel and the others, wishing them the best of luck and congratulating them upon the splendid show which they had put up in defence of their King.

The two Englishmen then set about making inquiries for von Ziegler and the soldiers who were with him. They soon learnt that the three Germans had entered the town by way of its main street about half an hour before and, threatening the crowd through which they passed with their tommy-guns, had entered the only store in the place, which contained a men's outfitting department. As soon as they had gone inside a section of the crowd had rushed off to get the police; but as almost the entire police force of Lillehammer was out at the suburb of Maihaug, where they had been protecting the King, only two policemen could be found. Very gallantly they had entered the store armed only with revolvers. Rumour said that they had found the two German soldiers changing into civilian clothes, but the third man was standing by them holding a tommy-gun and with a single blast of fire he had cut the two wretched policemen practically in half.

About five minutes later, by leaving the store through its back entrance the three Germans had evaded the crowd which had collected in the main street, but they had soon been spotted and a hue and cry ensued. One sportsman had fired at them with a shot-gun from a first-floor window, slightly wounding one of them in the leg, and they had been driven back to the main square of the town. There they had fired a couple of bursts which had killed and wounded a number of people and had forced back the crowd; they had then piled into a stationary car and driven across the square towards the north.

By this time, however, as nearly every Norwegian shoots by way of recreation, and there is some sort of firearm in practically every house, a number of citizens were arriving on the scene with guns, having either heard that there were Germans in the town or been attracted by the sound of shooting. They had sent a ragged volley after the car which had punctured one of the tyres and, it was thought, killed one of the Germans, who was standing up with his tommy-gun thrust out of the back window, as he had dropped his gun and been seen to collapse in a heap; but the car had got away.

Although accounts varied a little, Gregory gathered that von Ziegler had been gone only five or ten minutes, and it was obvious that he would not be able to get far with one of his back tyres flat. The Germans would have to stop and put on the spare wheel as soon as they were clear of the town, so there appeared to be every chance of catching them if immediate action were taken. A tall, fair young farmer, who had given the most coherent account of the affair, had his car handy and offered it for the pursuit; so with the two Englishmen beside him he thrust his way through the crowd and they piled into his ancient, open Ford. The Ford looked a ramshackle affair and its back seat was occupied with crates of live chickens, but the engine had plenty of go in it and to the cheers of the assembled multitude the car bucketed out of the town.

They had hardly reached the open road when they heard fresh sounds of firing, and turning to peer back over the chicken crates Gregory saw that the new battle for Lillehammer had started. The narrow, forty-mile-long arm of the Mjose Lake merged just below the town into the Gudbrandsdal River, which ran twisting and curving up the whole length of the hundred-mile-long valley ahead, ending in a chain of lakes which almost connected with the fjords on the Atlantic coast fifty miles south-west of Trondheim. At Lillehammer the river was a good hundred and fifty yards wide, and the Germans were now endeavouring to cross it in their rubber boats. As the car sped up the steep road that ran along the cliff face of the mountains the little figures down on the river grew more distant, but before the car rounded the first bend Gregory saw several of them tumble into the water, and, knowing the folk of this rural town to be so well equipped with weapons and with men who knew how to use them, he had every confidence that the old ex-Colonel would manage to prevent the Germans crossing, at least until night came and they were able to do so under cover of darkness.

On their rounding the bend the young Norwegian farmer

gave a whoop of joy. There on the road ahead, barely a mile farther up the slope, were the Germans. Their car was halted and they were changing the ruined tyre. Gregory wondered if he should risk a shot with his rifle over the windscreen but decided that the car was bumping too badly for him to stand the least chance of scoring a hit. Next moment he regretted his decision as the Germans had completed their work and, jumping into their car, went on again.

The farmer settled down to the grim chase but it soon became apparent that his old Ford was not up to the job of catching the car that von Ziegler had stolen. From a lead of a mile the Germans drew ahead to a mile and a half and as they rounded a second bend, about three hundred feet above the river, the pursuing party saw something which greatly perturbed them. They now had a view right across a broad bend of the valley and they could see the distant line of the road on the far side of the great dip. A little cloud of dust immediately caught their attention; it came from four cars, all proceeding at the same pace and close together. None of them doubted for a minute that it was the Royal party, and the cars were only about four miles ahead of the Germans. Some members of the Royal party might be armed with automatics but it was most unlikely that they would have anything more lethal, whereas von Ziegler had a tommy-gun with him; if he managed to catch up the King and his ministers things might go very badly with them.

Resting his rifle on the top of the windscreen Gregory began to fire over it, but after wasting half a dozen rounds he gave up. It was quite impossible to get the Germans at that distance when both he and his target were in constant and erratic motion. He spoke urgently to Gussy, who held a short conversation with the farmer.

After a moment Gussy turned and shouted: 'Yes. He says there is a road—or track, rather—which serves a few sheep-farms up in the hills ahead; it joins the road at the inner bend there and comes out on the far side of the spur. It'll be a close thing, but if this old bus doesn't jib at the gradients there's just a chance that we might cut von Ziegler off.'

Right!' yelled Gregory. 'Tell him to take it.'

A mile further on they left the road and took the track which wound up into the mountains. It was only about six feet wide and its surface was absolutely appalling. Patches of loose shale alternated with stretches of bare earth intersected by deep gulleys down which water from the melting snows was now trickling. In parts it was more like a river-bed than a highway. There were periods when they had to fight down their impatience as their speed was reduced to six miles an hour, but the old Ford stuck it gamely and climbed slope after slope until they reached the pass, where the track wound for about two miles between grassy hillocks.

Up there they had difficulty in keeping to the winding way, as they had reached cloud level and the misty wisps half-obscured the lonely scene making it seem utterly unreal, so that they all felt as though they were only dreaming this nightmare chase. It was very cold and their clothes were soon half-saturated with the damp, clinging mist; but at last they reached the end of the level stretch and began to descend on the far side of the spur.

This proved even worse than the climb as they slithered and skidded from turn to turn, often in considerable peril of their lives; but the farmer had been born and bred in these lonely, inhospitable mountains and was used to driving his rickety old bus along just such tracks in all weathers. His performance absolutely staggered his two passengers, who perpetually had their hearts in their mouths, but each time the car seemed within a second of hurtling over the unguarded precipice, which was always within a few feet of them, he managed to check it and bucket down to another hairpin bend until he finally brought them safely back on to the main road.

They glanced swiftly to right and left. The King's party was out of sight but the Germans were streaking towards them less than a mile away. Gregory's heart gave a bound when he saw that they had succeeded in intercepting the enemy, but he knew that without the farmer they could never have done it as they had achieved their object only by a matter of minutes.

Without waiting to be told the young Norwegian drew his car right across the centre of the road so that there was no more than three feet between its rear and the rock wall or between its bonnet and the precipice. The Germans could not possibly pass. Gregory and Gussy jumped out with their rifles and knelt down behind it, while the farmer, who had no weapon, ran to the side of the road and grabbed up a large piece of rock.

With a screech of brakes von Ziegler's car pulled up ten yards away. Gregory had crawled under the Ford and in one swift glance from beneath it he saw that the airman was driving.

Instantly the car stopped his companion opened fire with a tommy-gun. The bullets spattered into the old Ford like lumps of hail bouncing on to the corrugated-iron roofing of a hen-house. Gussy gave a cry and, grabbing his shoulder, dropped his rifle. He had exposed himself too soon.

For a second there was silence, then Gregory fired from beneath the Ford. His bullet drilled a neat round hole in the unbreakable-glass windscreen of the German's car and the man with the tommy-gun fell backwards spitting blood.

Unnoticed by the others the farmer had crept along the gully by the cliff-face, where a mound of outcrop gave him a little cover, until he was within six feet of the other car. Suddenly he sprang up and hurled his lump of rock. It saved von Ziegler's life as he ducked back at the very second that Gregory fired again; while the rock, landing on the wheel of the car, first smashed it then fell into the airman's lap. A second later an automatic which he must have obtained from one of the soldiers spat twice and the farmer clutched at his throat. Gregory saw the blood well up between the young Norwegian's fingers before he uttered a gurgling cry and sank down on the heap of shale.

'Now,' thought Gregory, 'it's von Ziegler or myself.' But he was mistaken. The third German had not been killed as the car sped out of the town; he was only wounded, and suddenly he came into action, leaning out of the back of the car to throw a hand-grenade.

It bounced and rolled until it came to rest near the rear of the Ford. Gussy was kneeling there, holding his injured shoulder, and Gregory knew that his friend might be blown to bits in a matter of seconds. Reversing his rifle he thrust it along under the car and knocked the hand-grenade away so that it rolled towards the cliff-face. Next instant it went off.

They were protected by the car from the flying pieces but the blast caught both of them. Gussy was knocked backwards in the roadway and Gregory was rolled sideways from beneath the car. The bomb, having exploded at the back of the Ford, had had the effect of driving it forward so that of its own accord it suddenly ran across the few feet of road. Its front wheels went right over the precipice but with a loud clang of metal on stone it came to rest hanging half over the gulf.

When Gregory picked himself up he saw that the explosion had knocked Gussy unconscious. Grabbing him by the coat collar he dragged him back under cover of the rear end of the Ford, which was still on the road. But the German who had thrown the bomb had wrought better than he knew, as by blowing the Ford half over the cliff he had cleared the way for von Ziegler's car.

Gregory heard the engine start into life. His head was still rocking but he seized his rifle, and as the car roared by he poured the remaining contents of the magazine into it. But it did not stop. It charged on in a wavering, zigzag course and Gregory remembered having seen the rock hurled by the young farmer come hurtling down on the steering-wheel. Snatching up the unconscious Gussy's rifle, he fired after it, aiming for the petrol tank. His third was a lucky shot; the car limped on for another hundred yards then came to a halt. Springing to his feet he gave chase.

He knew that in doing so his life was hanging by a thread as now that he was running down the open road without any sort of cover one of the Germans might lean out of the stationary car at any second and shoot him; but his blood was up and he was determined to get von Ziegler or die in the attempt. Dodging from side to side and ducking as he ran, to make himself a more difficult target, he raced on. To his amazement no shots came at him, but when he was within fifty yards of the car von Ziegler got out of it. The airman held an automatic in his hand but he did not attempt to use it. Instead he took to his heels and ran.

Pulling up with a jerk Gregory raised his rifle and called on him to halt. Von Ziegler took no notice so he aimed at the middle of the airman's back and gently squeezed the trigger. The rifle clicked but it did not go off; he pressed the trigger again and still there was no report. Jerking back the bolt he saw that the magazine was empty.

Instantly he set off in pursuit. A glance at von Ziegler's car as he reached it showed him that both the other Germans were dead. One was slumped in the front seat, having been killed by the bullet that he had sent through the windscreen; the other lay sprawled across the back with his mouth hanging open, and Gregory knew that he must have finished him only a few minutes before when von Ziegler had driven past the wrecked Ford.

Jumping on to the running-board of the car Gregory hauled

aside the dead German in the front seat and pulled out the man's tommy-gun; but its lightness told him what to expect. A swift examination of the magazine showed him that he had been right—that, too, was empty—and evidently that was why von Ziegler had not taken it.

The airman was now half a mile away, still pelting down the road with his automatic clutched in one swinging hand. Gregory wondered how many bullets remained in the weapon. When one is unarmed it is no picnic to go after a man who has a gun, but Gregory knew that if the adventurous Air Attaché once got away he would get in touch with some more of his Fifth Column people before many hours were past, and that might cost King Haakon his life that night or on the following day; so it never even occurred to him to give up the chase.

Instead, he stripped off his overcoat so that he could run faster and, picking up the empty rifle, set out at a steady, loping trot. He was not a crack runner but he was tough as nails and he felt confident that if he husbanded his strength he would be able to wear the German down.

It was getting on for six o'clock but Gregory knew that there was little fear of his losing von Ziegler in the darkness, as up there in central Norway at this season of the year there were still many hours of daylight to go.

Had his mind been less occupied he might have admired the scenery, since it was truly magnificent. The great mountains swept away on either side of the valley, their lofty peaks shrouded in mist and snow. Many of the slopes were fringed with pine-woods and down in the bottom of the valley, where the river curved like a silver ribbon hundreds of feet below, the young green of spring was already showing in the herbage that fringed the river-banks.

As it was, he thought of nothing but the bent figure ahead of him pounding along the twisting road. Twice he lost sight of it as it shot round a corner, and his only fear was that von Ziegler might halt and ambush him from behind one of the spurs round which the snaky road curved every half-mile or so. But apparently the German's only idea for the moment was to try to out-distance his pursuer.

After turning the second corner there was a longer stretch of road ahead and Gregory saw that he was gaining on the airman. He had decreased the distance between them by several hundred yards and he thanked his stars that he had had the forethought to abandon his overcoat, as the skirts of von Ziegler's coat were flapping round his legs.

Gregory's breath was coming in gasps but he was a long way from being beaten yet and he saw that von Ziegler was now glancing anxiously over his shoulder from time to time as he ran. Deciding to try to end the business Gregory put on a spurt and in another half-mile he had come up to within fifty yards of his quarry. Von Ziegler glanced over his shoulder again, ran on for about ten yards, then suddenly halted and swung round. Gregory knew that the next second spelt life or death.

He was staring right down the barrel of von Ziegler's pistol and decreasing his distance from it every moment. He counted three as von Ziegler aimed and suddenly bounded sideways. The pistol flashed but the bullet sped harmlessly past its mark. 'One,' thought Gregory; and recovering his balance he jumped again. 'Two,' as the pistol cracked again—and again von Ziegler missed. 'I wonder how many more bullets he's got.'

But von Ziegler did not fire a third shot. As Gregory lurched back to the centre of the road he saw that the airman had turned and taken to his heels once more. Now there were only twenty yards between them.

Gregory's spurt and the great effort of springing from side to side had taken it out of him; he was sweating now and panting like a grampus. For about five minutes the German kept his lead, but Gregory had reverted to his old loping trot and gradually he drew ahead again.

Fifteen yards—twelve yards—ten yards—eight yards—five yards—three yards. Every moment Gregory thought that von Ziegler would swing round and fire at him again; this time point-blank and with little chance of missing. Yet he dared not act prematurely. When only two yards separated them he lifted his empty rifle and, gripping it by the stock and the barrel, swung it up above his head; then with all his force he hurled it at the back of von Ziegler's neck. The rifle caught the German right across the shoulders; his automatic went off in his hand as he staggered and pitched forward on his face. Next second Gregory had flung himself right on top of him with a triumphant gasp.

For two minutes they lay there struggling in the roadway. Von Ziegler was tough, but Gregory was even tougher. By twisting the airman's wrist he made him drop his automatic, then he got his hands upon his throat.

It looked as though von Ziegler was finished. But suddenly he kneed Gregory in the groin. The stab of pain forced Gregory to relax his grip, and the agile German wriggled from under him. Both of them struck out at each other's face as they lay for a second side by side, but both landed only glancing blows. Then, as though by mutual consent, they rolled apart and staggered to their feet.

Next moment they were in a wrestler's clinch, swaying violently from side to side, each striving to throw the other. Gasping and grunting they staggered first one way and then the other across the road while exerting all the power of their muscles. Both were so intent on their struggle for mastery that neither noticed when their violent shuffling brought them right to the edge of the precipice, Suddenly, over von Ziegler's shoulder, Gregory glimpsed the shimmering river far below.

His heart missed a beat as he realised that the airman's feet were planted on the very brink of the cliff. If the earth gave way, locked as they were in a deadly embrace, they would both go hurtling down into the five-hundred-foot gulf that yawned within inches of them. Relaxing his hold he made a violent effort to break the German's grip. Von Ziegler thought that his enemy was weakening and with a grin of triumph exerted all his strength to tighten his clutch. Gregory threw his whole weight into a backward jerk and at the same time struck the German a terrific blow in the face. Von Ziegler gasped and his hands came apart from behind Gregory's back. For a second Gregory was free and he stood there panting.

Next instant the earth beneath the airman's left boot gave way. In a desperate endeavour to regain his balance he clutched at Gregory's arm. For a fraction of time he swayed there, but his whole weight was now on his right foot. It proved too great for the unsupported slab of earth beneath it. As his other foot sank through the crumbling mould Gregory made a last frantic attempt to wrench himself free but the clutch on his arm was like an iron vice. As von Ziegler slid down over the edge Gregory was jerked forward and they both plunged into the abyss.

10

A Strange Armistice

Gregory's face was within a foot of the airman's, as he had been dragged forward head-foremost almost on top of him. In that last half-moment of their struggle he had seen the sudden realisation of the awful end which threatened them dawn in his enemy's face. Von Ziegler's mouth hung open, although no sound came from it, and his brilliant blue eyes seemed to start right out of his head.

At such a moment time ceases to exist and as Gregory hurtled downwards with his arm still in his enemy's vice-like grip, he was amazed to find that he could still think coherently. He found himself subconsciously registering the map-like scene which lay below them; the broad, curving river, the jutting rocks which broke it here and there, churning it into foam, and the fresh spring green of the meadows along its banks. He even found himself thinking what a pity it was that he hadn't got a salmon-rod. Then, in a split second, he was mentally rocking with laughter that such an idea should have come to him in such a situation.

He knew that he ought to be thinking of his approaching death and recommending his soul to God but, although he had a firm belief in the hereafter, he had never paid much tribute to any deities other than the old pagan gods who made life for a full-blooded man very well worth living; and he saw no reason why now, in his extremity, he should cringe before a more modern deity whose devotees denied the flesh and followed a way of gloom.

He had often said in a half-joking way that if ever he were brought before the Judgment Seat he would proclaim aloud that the Judge, having given him his body, his instincts and his opportunities, could bring no charge against him for having put them to good purpose; that if the Judge were not prepared to acknowledge the truth of that he would have no more to say, since one might just as well be ruled by Hitler, and that in that case he would set his wits to work to escape at the earliest possible opportunity from the heavenly concentration-camp.

Now that he was actually about to die he was not in the least afraid. Death held the answer to so many fascinating problems. He wondered . . . His thoughts had moved a considerable way in those few seconds after he was dragged over the edge of the precipice, but he was not destined to speculate any further.

With the suddenness of a blind being drawn across a window the strip of landscape that he could see between von Ziegler's feet and the cliff face was blotted out by a greyish-green curtain. For another second the wind whistled past Gregory's ears as the greyish-green thing that had obscured his view positively leapt up to meet them. With a frightful thump von Ziegler hit the grey-green mass. Instantly everything blacked out for Gregory as his face was flattened against the airman's chest.

His breath had been driven from his body and for a few moments he could only gasp like a fish on a bank while a queer, tingling sensation ran through all his limbs. At last, realising that he was still alive, he very cautiously raised his head a little while keeping his throbbing body absolutely lax. Peering from side to side he saw that they had landed upon a ledge no more than ten feet wide at its broadest point and about twenty-five feet in length, with both its ends tapering in until they vanished into the main sheer wall of rock. The next thing he discovered was that his nose was bleeding, then that one of his legs was still dangling over the awful void. Drawing it in he raised himself a little more and immediately an awful pain shot through his shoulder.

At first he thought that he had broken it but soon he came to the conclusion that he had only wrenched it badly and after cautiously flexing his other limbs he was extremely surprised to find that he had not injured himself in any other way. Von Ziegler had acted as a human mattress for him and had broken the force of his fall.

Kneeling up, he began to examine the airman, who was only semi-conscious and groaning softly. He had landed feet-first. One leg, which had doubled under him, was broken and Gregory thought that he had probably also injured his back; but it was a cut at the base of his skull, where his head had hit a stone, that had rendered him unconscious.

Using his sound arm Gregory drew the airman away from the edge of the ledge to a safer spot under the cliff face, and getting out his flask he forced some of its contents between the injured man's lips. Von Ziegler choked a little, blinked, opened his blue eyes and muttered:

'Where—am I?'

'Somewhere between Heaven and Hell,' Gregory replied grimly.

'What—what happened?'

'You fell over the edge of the precipice and you dragged me with you, but evidently it was your lucky day. Had you pulled anyone else over it's a thousand to one that you'd be a deader by now—a nasty little heap of pulped human matter that would just fall to pieces directly anyone tried to pick it up; but your patron devil slipped up in letting you choose me for your companion in your attempt to get to Hell before you were sent for, because my patron saint wasn't having any. As they couldn't kill one of us without the other it was agreed that the matter should be referred to the big Chief for his decision. In the meantime we are suspended between earth and sky. If my man wins somebody will come along and pull us up to safety, and if your man wins we shall sit here until we're either frozen to death or die of exhaustion.'

'*Donnerwetter!*' muttered the German, '*Donnerwetter!* How my head hurts!'

'I'm afraid you haven't been listening,' said Gregory amiably, 'but you'll gather the facts of our present situation for yourself all in good time.' He raised his voice and added: 'How is your back?'

'Aching—aching all over.'

'Any special pain anywhere?'

'No.'

'Can you move your head?'

Von Ziegler nodded it backwards and forwards twice, then groaned.

'Good,' Gregory said approvingly. 'If you can do that your spine's not broken, and the cut on your head is nothing much so you're not in bad shape, really, except for that broken leg. From what I can see of things, we must have fallen thirty to forty feet and it was lucky for you that this ledge has a little earth on it, with a layer of old pine-needles, otherwise you would have been smashed to bits.'

'Water,' groaned von Ziegler.

'He asked for bread and was given a pancake,' grinned Gregory, lifting his flask, which still had a little of the Norwegian Punch in it, to the German's lips.

The patient gulped down the rum-flavoured liquor without

114

complaint and with a sigh closed his eyes again, so Gregory thought that he had better allow him to rest for a little, while he mopped at his own nose and considered the situation. His recent escape from death had given him a temporary forced cheerfulness; hence his facetious burblings to the still dazed German; but he soon sobered down and the more he thought about the position the less he liked it.

The ledge could not be seen from the road above, so there was no chance that someone coming along it might spot them and bring help. Moreover, they were too far down the cliff to be able to hear passing motor traffic for any distance so they could not send up a great shout to attract attention just at the moment that a vehicle was approaching. By the time they heard it the car or lorry would be rattling away from them, and they could not sit there shouting all the time.

Crawling to the edge of the ledge Gregory peered over, but the distant valley far below offered no better prospect. No one down there could possibly have seen them against the dark rock, except with a pair of binoculars, and there was no village or even house anywhere in sight along the foot of the cliff, the attention of whose inhabitants might possibly have been attracted by the dropping of large stones.

If they had gone over near the wrecked cars there would have been a decent possibility that the first arrivals at the scene of the affray might have seen them while examining the Ford that was hanging out half-over the cliff; but they were now a long way from the Ford. Of course if Gussy were still alive he would cause a search to be made; but was he alive, and, if so, what would be the result of such a search?

The search-party would probably examine the road and the cliffs for a few hundred yards on either side of the two cars and, on no trace of the missing men being found, Gussy would assume that von Ziegler had got away and that Gregory was still pursuing him; perhaps in some desolate valley miles away up in the mountains. He could hardly be expected to guess that his friend had chased the German for the best part of three miles and that after a set-to they had fallen over the cliff together.

At the time of the King's escape from Lillehammer there had been no traffic at all upon the road, because for about an hour before that the Germans had cut off the stream of refugees at the southern side of the town and except on market days there was normally little traffic in the late afternoons between

Lillehammer and the villages along the valley. But Gregory reckoned that even if the Germans got possession of the place it was unlikely that they would hold up the flood of refugees indefinitely, so that long before darkness came an unending stream of traffic would be pouring along the road overhead.

For a time he sat there listening intently. Once or twice he caught the faint purr of a motor engine and the note of a distant horn; then, about half-past six he became aware of a steady vibration that gradually increased until it was a regular hum and rumble, occasionally punctuated by the sounding of Klaxons or hooters. Either the remnants of Major Helder's motorised column south of Lillehammer had been mopped up or the Germans had taken the town and released the traffic; whichever was the case the refugees were on their way north again.

Filling his lungs, Gregory began to yodel for all he was worth. He kept it up for about five minutes but nothing happened, so he had a rest. Then, after a bit, he tried again; and for the next hour he spent alternate periods yodelling and resting, but with no result. At the end of that time his voice was cracked and husky so he gave up altogether and acknowledged to himself that as nobody on the road had heard him during the past hour it was unlikely that they would do so even if he had been able to keep his vocal efforts going all night.

Another idea then occurred to him. Since he could not make himself heard he might perhaps succeed in making their presence felt. Part of the ledge was covered with a fall of loose shale and, selecting a piece, he endeavoured to pitch it up on to the road. Until he tried he had no idea how difficult it is to throw a stone almost vertically upward. Had he been able to stand further back he could have managed to land some of his missiles among the procession that was passing above, but although he risked standing almost on the edge of the ledge he could not even get one up to within ten feet of the cliff-top. They sailed up for about twenty-five feet, seemed to hover for an instant and then, infuriatingly, came whirring back at him. After a score of fruitless attempts he abandoned that game also and gloomily sat down beside the half-comatose German.

He had had nothing to eat since the late breakfast which Elvdalen had provided that morning so he was beginning to feel distinctly hungry. Fortunately he had on him a large slab of chocolate such as he always carried by way of iron rations for

116

an emergency. Taking it out he broke off a bar apiece for von Ziegler and himself and they sucked it slowly, but it did not make a very satisfying meal, and the bulk of the contents of both their flasks had already been consumed so they allowed themselves only a swallow each, saving the remainder with the rest of the chocolate as a last reserve for the following day.

It had now become distinctly cold and having no overcoat Gregory began to dread the coming night; but von Ziegler did not appear to feel the cold as he was now in a fever. Gregory had made him as comfortable as he could by scraping up the dried pine-needles to form a pillow for his head but he had no means of setting the airman's broken leg or washing the cut at the back of his skull. They spoke little but all the enmity seemed to have gone out of them owing to the common peril they were now sharing. Both realised that the other had only been doing his duty as he saw it, and although the airman had stopped at nothing in his attempts to get King Haakon, Gregory knew quite well that he would have been equally ruthless if he had had the least chance to get Hitler.

Very, very gradually the light paled but it was still a long way from sunset when Gregory started to shiver. After a bit he got to his feet to try to warm himself a little by walking up and down their barless, narrow prison. Von Ziegler, who was still feverish but had recovered a little, glanced at him and saw that his face was blue with cold so he sat up and undoing his overcoat began to struggle out of it.

'What the devil are you up to?' Gregory asked through chattering teeth.

'Getting my coat off,' replied the airman. 'Come and give me a hand, then we'll lie down side by side and share it.'

At first Gregory refused to accept the chivalrous offer, but von Ziegler was insistent. He pointed out that there was no question of there being any personal vendetta between them and that if Gregory had wished to carry the World War on to the little ledge he could easily have pushed his injured companion over hours ago. But such an act had obviously not even occurred to him; on the contrary he had done his best for his enemy and had fed him with his chocolate. Clearly then, von Ziegler argued, as long as they remained on the ledge the war had ceased to exist for them and until they were rescued or died there they ought to share the few assets they had.

This reasoning so exactly embodied Gregory's own views

that he gave way and they curled up together under the German's overcoat to get as much warmth as they could from each other's bodies.

Gradually the long twilight gave place to darkness and the stars came out in the clear, cold heavens above. Von Ziegler slept little but tossed in feverish restlessness all through the night while Gregory only dozed for stretches of a few moments between long bouts of wakefulness. Morning found them hollow-eyed and miserable. The coming of the new day did not bring them new hope and as they munched the remainder of the chocolate they were both wondering how many hours of agony they would have to endure before they died.

Soon after the sun was up they heard the flapping of wings and a big eagle soared by. The bird veered suddenly and came to rest upon a piece of rock about ten feet from where they were lying, eyeing them malevolently. The sight of it filled them with fresh dread. Eagles are carrion-eaters but they like fresh meat even better than a corpse. Both men were travelled and knew enough about the royal bird of prey to realise that if its nest was near by it might easily attack them and would almost certainly do so when they were too weak to resist. Such a feathered menace was capable of pouncing upon a full-grown sheep and with its talons buried in the poor brute's body lifting it for thousands of feet to its eyrie in the mountains. It would prove a redoubtable antagonist even to a strong, fit man armed with a thick club, as it could attack him from above, and, if it once got home, tear out its victim's eyes with two pecks of its great curved beak.

Gregory did the only thing there was to do. It was better to risk a fight with the brute there and then than to wait until they were so weak that it would have them completely at its mercy and tear strips from their living flesh. Reaching out his hand he grabbed a large stone and flung it.

The stone caught the eagle on the breast and it sailed into the air with an angry squawk. As he scrambled to his feet he grabbed up a larger stone and heaved that. It missed, but the great bird turned in its flight and drew off for the moment. Von Ziegler had struggled into a sitting position and threw another stone which brushed the eagle's tail feathers, while Gregory grabbed up two more. For a second the bird hovered, then in a beautiful curve, with its great wings at their full spread of six feet, sailed away.

The brief episode filled them both with such horrible forebodings that they did not even discuss it; but both hoped that by their immediate attack they had ensured that the bird would leave them in peace and go in search of easier prey.

The murmur of traffic was still coming from overhead so Gregory began to shout again, but after a time he gave up as it was quite obvious that nobody up there on the road could hear him. Fortunately the day was fine, and now that the sun was shining they began to feel slightly better as, even in that northern latitude, its rays warmed them a little. Von Ziegler's fever was no worse but his broken leg pained him badly, and Gregory's left shoulder hurt him every time he moved it; but they had had such a bad night that in spite of their aches and anxieties they decided to settle down again and try to get some sleep. For an hour or so they dozed, but both sat up with a start on hearing a sound that they had already come to dread—it was the flutter of great wings. The eagle's nest must be somewhere near and it resented their presence as it had come back to see how they were getting on.

Grabbing pieces from the pile of loose shale they both went into action simultaneously. The eagle rose at once, then swooped towards their heads, but by a lucky shot Gregory struck it on the beak. With a loud squawk it swerved and flapped up into the air above their heads. Both of them sent more stones whizzing at it. The stones missed but made it swerve again. For a second it hovered, black and menacing, twenty feet above their upturned faces then, suddenly folding its wings, it dropped like a plummet straight on to them.

They had no weapons with which to defend themselves and von Ziegler could not even stand up, but Gregory struck out with his fist at the bird's evil, rapacious face. Its razor-sharp beak came within a foot of his head but his fist landed on its muscular neck. One of the brute's talons ripped his coat from shoulder to elbow and he shuddered mentally as the brute's beady, red-rimmed eye stared into his own; but once more, its attack having failed, it swerved and the tip of its wing brushed his hair as it circled outwards away from the ledge to prepare for another swoop.

Next second there was a loud report. The eagle croaked, twisted in the air and dropped from sight. Instantly Gregory turned up his face and began to bellow with all the force of his lungs. A moment later a head was thrust out over the edge of the cliff above and its owner shouted back in Norwegian. A hand was waved and the head withdrawn. Gregory sank down with a sigh. They had been found and now it was only a matter of waiting until help reached them.

Twenty minutes drifted by, but they hardly noticed that in the immense relief at the thought that help was now definitely at hand; then several heads were thrust out over the edge above and a rope with a big slip-knot in it was lowered. Gregory fixed it securely under von Ziegler's armpits and, fending himself off from the wall of rock as well as he could, the airman was drawn up to safety. A few moments later the rope was lowered again and having attached it to himself Gregory was in turn hauled up to the cliff edge, where willing hands dragged him back on to the side of the road from which he had descended in such a terrifying manner some eighteen hours before.

He then learnt through von Ziegler that it was the eagle which had been the means of saving their lives. Some refugees in a passing car had been watching the bird as it dived and swerved, when suddenly they had seen stones shoot past it, apparently hurled from the naked cliff-face. They had realised at once that the stones could only have been flung by human beings trapped on a ledge down there, but before they could set about their rescue they had had to wait until a car that had a rope in it came by. He also gathered that the attack on Lillehammer the previous evening had been defeated and that the survivors of the German force had retreated along the road to Hamar, the ruins of which, it was said, had been occupied on the previous day by a second detachment of parachute troops.

Their elation at the prospect of rescue had temporarily renewed their strength and made them forget their hurts, but this burst of nervous energy soon wore off and it became obvious to their rescuers that they were chilled to the bone, injured and exhausted. A short discussion took place among the crowd of Norwegians, and a father and son who had no women with them very decently agreed to turn their car round and drive the two strangers back to Lillehammer, which boasted the only hospital within fifty miles. The back of their car was half-filled with trunks and suit-cases but some of these were shifted round so that the groaning von Ziegler could be propped up with his broken leg stretched out before him, and Gregory squeezed into the front seat between the two Norwegians.

After being hauled up von Ziegler had still had his wits about him sufficiently to realise that his rescuers might become extremely hostile if they discovered that he was a German, so when he told Gregory how the eagle had led to their discovery he had used a few sentences of halting English. The pain that he was in had prevented his saying very much but the Norwegians had taken it for granted that he was a Norwegian himself and that Gregory was an Englishman. It now transpired that the driver of the car could also speak a little English and he and his son were both curious to know how their passengers had become stranded on the ledge of rock thirty-odd feet below the level of the road.

Gregory pulled his tired brain together in an effort to provide an adequate answer to this difficult conundrum without giving too much away. If he told the truth, von Ziegler would, he felt sure, be handed over to the military authorities at the first opportunity and shot either at once or as soon as his leg was mended; yet after the experience they had been through together he had a curious feeling that this would not somehow be quite fair to the man whom he himself had been ready and anxious to shoot the previous afternoon. Von Ziegler was no danger to anyone at the moment, and it seemed to Gregory that until he was in a better state to cheat death, if he could, a sporting chance ought to be given to him and that their personal armistice should continue.

He therefore told the driver that their fall was the result of an accident. He said that they had got out of their car the previous evening but had neglected to put the brakes on before doing so. It had then suddenly run forward and as they had tried to prevent it going over the cliff his friend had been knocked down right at the edge of the precipice; the car had plunged into the abyss and his friend had rolled over the edge, where he had been left hanging by one hand. He had rushed to the rescue but had slipped and so, just as he had grasped his friend's wrist, they had both gone over, but by extraordinary good fortune they had landed on the ledge below.

He knew that with the invasion crisis in full swing neither of the Norwegians would bother to check up the story about the missing car by wasting time looking for its wreckage; and they both accepted his account of the affair in good faith.

Half an hour later they reached the Lillehammer hospital, a fair-sized building with low gabled roofs like those of a Swiss chalet. The place was already crowded with casualties from the

121

affray on the previous day, but extra beds had been put up and Gregory and von Ziegler were accommodated in a small, bright room, facing south, that was normally used as a sitting-room for the nurses. The place was spotlessly clean and the medical attention of the highest quality. A doctor and nurses took charge of them. Von Ziegler's leg was broken and reset under an anaesthetic and Gregory's wrenched shoulder adjusted; then they were put to bed between fresh, clean sheets, with a rosy-cheeked, golden-haired nurse in attendance.

The invasion had actually taken place in the small hours of Tuesday morning and it was now Thursday afternoon, yet to Gregory it seemed weeks since he had been in a comfortable bed without anxieties, so, although it was still early, after a bowl of excellent chicken-broth which satisfied his immediate hunger he dropped off to sleep in a relaxed and contented frame of mind.

They both woke early the following morning and Gregory found that von Ziegler, while still in considerable pain, was well enough to talk, so he told him about the explanation that he had given on the previous day as to how they had become marooned on the ledge of rock and that he had refrained from disclosing the German's real identity.

Von Ziegler expressed his gratitude and said that an occasion might later arise when he could repay Gregory's forbearance, in which case he would certainly do so. In the meantime, it was agreed that their armistice should continue at least until both of them were out of hospital, and to prevent complications the airman said that while he was there he intended to pose as a Swede, since he spoke Swedish fluently and the change of nationality would prevent the checking-up of any awkward questions that he might have to answer about his address and occupation.

After breakfast they asked for news, and before going to fetch them a local paper—which was the only one available— their golden-haired nurse brought them up to date. On the Wednesday many German transports had been sunk in the Kattegat and Skagerrak, but in addition to Oslo, Bergen, Trondheim and Narvik the Germans had managed to establish themselves at Kristiansand, Stavanger, Egersund and Vallo. There had been a number of air-raids and the industrial district of Porsgrund had been severely bombed. The British and German Fleets had been in action at various points along the Norwegian coast, but no details were yet available except that five British destroyers had steamed into Narvik Fjord against seven German destroyers. One British and one German had been sunk and two British and three German badly damaged, but the British had also succeeded in sinking seven German supply-ships and partially wrecking the quays.

Gregory wondered why, when we had such immense naval superiority, five of our destroyers should be sent in against seven Germans, but even with the odds against them the British seemed to have put up a remarkably good show, as they had evidently gone in to destroy the supply-ships and had had to concentrate their fire upon them before becoming free to return that of the enemy destroyers.

When it arrived the local paper gave further particulars of the events of the previous day. The headline was devoted to the reaffirmation of Norway's rejection of the German demand for a Quisling Government by M. Nygaardsvold, the Norwegian Premier, and the rest of the front page was devoted to King Haakon's escape, the attack on Lillehammer and Mr. Churchill's speech in the British Parliament. Von Ziegler gave Gregory a translation, and after hearing it he felt that although the British might declare that Hitler's attack on Scandinavia was a fatal strategic blunder the Nazis had carried out the job with amazing speed and efficiency.

Reading between the lines he could make a pretty good guess at what had happened. With brilliant and impudent daring the Germans had sent a squadron, led by the *Scharnhorst*, right up the coast of Norway. Immediately the British had learnt of this they had dispatched their battle-fleet north in pursuit with the intention of cutting off the Germans when they turned and made for home. In the meantime, the rest of the German Fleet, in three squadrons, had convoyed their main landing-forces to Oslo, Bergen and Trondheim where they had forced the defences of these three ports and covered the landing operations with their guns.

The British were probably somewhere about half-way up the coast when they received news of this and apparently they had detached a squadron led by the *Repulse* to follow the *Scharnhorst*, while their main fleet had turned south again, arriving too late to intercept the Germans there but in time to sink a number of their transports bringing up reinforcements on the following day. The *Scharnhorst* must have arrived off Narvik at about the time that the other German forces arrived off the more southerly Norwegian ports. She had sent her destroyer flotilla up the fjord to assist in the capture of the town but had herself continued with her escorting cruiser, the *Hipper,* on her northern course with a view to drawing the British away from Narvik and up into the Arctic.

When the *Repulse* had come up it had appeared out of the question to let the *Scharnhorst* get away, so apparently the British Admiral had left his destroyers to bottle-up the German forces in Narvik while he continued with the chase. He had caught the *Scharnhorst* and severely damaged her, but by sheer bad luck she and her companion had managed to get away under cover of the mist and snow. Meanwhile, although his force was inferior to that of the Germans the commander of the destroyer flotilla had decided with a gallantry typical of the British Navy to go in to Narvik and destroy the supply-ships before the enemy could land any considerable quantity of munitions from them.

That was about the size of it. The Germans had acted with such boldness that they had succeeded in pulling the wool over the Allies' eyes for the first few vital hours of this brilliantly-executed operation. Rough seas and bad visibility had probably greatly hampered the British and they had made the best out of a bad business when they had at last got to grips with such portions of the enemy as had not escaped them. But what Gregory could not understand was why the British Fleet had not been cruising off the Skagerrak all ready to intercept the Germans if they took up the challenge issued to them by the mining of Norwegian waters on the Monday. Even less could he understand what had happened to the British Army. The Germans had made their landings early on Tuesday morning and it was now Friday, but apart from rumours which had been officially denied there was no news of a single British Tommy having as yet set foot on Norwegian soil.

When the doctor came he said that Gregory had been worse shaken by his fall than he had realised and that he must stay in bed for at least three days. As there seemed nothing that he could do for the moment which might give the Nazis a head-ache, he accepted the doctor's order quite cheerfully. He loved staying in bed reading, smoking and dozing when he had nothing better to do. Moreover, he knew that while he was there he would have less occasion to move his injured shoulder and that after the strain of the past few days the rest would do him a lot of good.

During the night it had occurred to him that the Honourable Augustus Langdon-Forbes might possibly be in the hospital, so when the doctor—who spoke quite good English—had finished his examination Gregory made his inquiry. To his delight he learned that Gussy had been brought in on the Wednesday evening and he obtained permission to go along in a borrowed dressing-gown to see his friend, for ten minutes.

He found the diplomat in one of the proper wards. Gussy had a nasty wound, as he had been hit by three bullets from the tommy-gun, but it had been cleaned up at once and was going on as well as could be expected. He had also been slightly concussed by the explosion of the hand-grenade, but he was already over the worst effects of that and his forty hours in bed with excellent medical attention had restored him to his normal philosophic calm.

He was amazed to see Gregory and hear of his narrow escape from death, as when he had come-to and found both Gregory and von Ziegler gone he had naturally assumed that the German had succeeded in getting away and that Gregory had gone after him, so he had imagined that by this time they were probably miles away up the Gudbrandsdal Valley. To his delight, Gregory learnt that the young Norwegian farmer was not dead but also in the hospital, although he was still in danger as one of von Ziegler's bullets had penetrated his throat.

In a low voice Gregory told Gussy of his understanding with von Ziegler, and Gussy agreed that as the German was now rendered harmless by a broken leg it would be rather an unsporting business to take any steps which would result in his being shot. By this time Gregory's ten minutes were up, so he retired to his own room and went back to bed; but later he had a talk with von Ziegler, who at once acquiesced in the suggestion that he and Gussy should swap beds so that the diplomat could share the little room with Gregory, and the arrangement was carried out the following morning.

That day the news seemed better, as the British had occupied the Faroe Islands and were guarding Iceland, while the R.A.F. had made some large-scale attacks on the German-occupied Norwegian ports, and on the Friday the Navy had sealed the Baltic with vast minefields; but there was no news yet of any Allied troop-landings.

On Sunday they heard that there had been a second action at Narvik. The 31,000-ton battleship *Warspite* had accomplished a brilliant feat of navigation and led the way up the long narrow fjord with another destroyer flotilla. The squadron had silenced the land-batteries which the Germans had established on the shore and had destroyed every one of the six remaining German destroyers stationed there. The Admiralty also announced that the *Admiral Scheer* had been torpedoed and the *Karlsruhe* sunk; but there was still no news of any Allied Expeditionary Force, although both the British and the French Governments had announced days before that they would render Norway every possible assistance against the common enemy.

As Gregory talked it over with Gussy he was almost in despair. He simply could not understand what the military were up to. The crossing from British to Norwegian ports could be accomplished in some thirty hours and even if they had not had troops ready to sail at once, as it was reasonable to assume that they would have, twenty-four hours seemed ample to embark light elements for a first force which could seize all sorts of small places and strategic points along the coast before the Germans could get to them. Tanks and heavy guns could come later, but even a few companies pushed in here and there would have made later operations on a larger scale infinitely easier.

Neither Gregory nor Gussy could see why the Allies had not had a considerable number of small units in Norway within three days of the German invasion. Such scattered bands could have penetrated inland without waiting for transports, other than their ammunition carriers, since they were operating in a friendly country and so could live on the land. They could have made contact with the Norwegian troops, blown up bridges, seized railway junctions and done all sorts of things to hamper the Germans. Yet a whole week had been allowed to go by in which nothing had been done. Meanwhile, the Germans were not losing a moment but, according to all reports, were constantly reinforcing their Army by air, despatching flying columns upcountry in all directions and digging themselves in at their bases so that they would be ten times as difficult to dislodge when at last the Allies arrived on the scene.

By Monday the 15th Gregory was allowed to get up, but his shoulder still required daily massage. As there had been no further fighting in the Lillehammer district his bed was not required immediately so it was agreed that he should retain it for the time being in order that he could remain with Gussy, whose wound was progressing well but who it was expected would be confined to bed for another fortnight at least.

Now he was well on the road to recovery again Gregory was naturally anxious to get home. Without any definite plan to follow and no knowledge as to the Allies' intentions it did not seem that he could serve any useful purpose by remaining in Norway a day longer than he had to, and during the time that he had been laid up he had been thinking a great deal about Erika. The sooner he could get back to England the sooner he would be able to rejoin her and Kuporovitch in Holland and he was convinced that now that Hitler had really started the war in earnest he would not be content with the conquest of Norway. The next act would almost certainly be an invasion of the Low Countries; then, whether the Allies went to their assistance or not, the big scene of the war was due to open, as there would either be a terrific pitched battle in Flanders or, if the Germans were allowed to march through it, on the Franco-Belgian frontier between the end of the Maginot Line proper and the sea.

If he could get into Holland before that opened he felt certain that Erika and Kuporovitch would already have prepared the ground for him to do further useful work, and he was eager to play another hand against the Nazis as he was to have Erika in his arms again, but the devil of it was that first he had to get out of Norway.

To begin with he had assumed that that would be fairly easy, as he had counted on British landings, upon which, by contacting the British he would be able to get back to England via one of their bases; but the Allies had not as yet established any bases and as the days went by the Germans were extending their control from all the principal ports over larger and larger stretches of the Norwegian coast. Their moves were so swift that no one in Lillehammer knew from day to day which new point they would seize next; so to make for any port now meant running the risk of walking straight into them. He knew that by once more posing as a German he could evade capture, but that would not help him to get back to England, as each port that the Germans occupied would automatically be sealed to any but their own coastal sea-traffic. It seemed, therefore, that the only thing he could do was to remain where he was until the situation clarified a little.

On the Wednesday, the 17th, they heard that Allied troops

were operating in the region north of Trondheim, and on that following day it was definitely confirmed that the British at long last had landed at Namsos the previous Tuesday. The only ways to get to Namsos were by road up the Gudbrandsdal Valley or to go south again to Hamar, then east to Elverum, where the Norwegian Government had now established their headquarters, and thence up the Osterdal Valley. But both these great parallel valleys ended south of Trondheim and Trondheim was in German hands, so it looked as though there might be considerable difficulty in getting through to the British base.

On consideration it seemed to Gregory that since the Allies had at last come to the assistance of the Norwegians and committed themselves to sending an Expeditionary Force they would have to make other landings further south, otherwise they would virtually be wasting troops to little purpose; and another two days of inactivity proved him to be correct.

On Friday the 19th news came through that a second Allied force had landed at Andalsnes, some distance south-west of Trondheim, and it became clear that the first intention of the Allied General Staff was to execute a pincer movement from north and south with a view to defeating the isolated German forces at Trondheim and recapturing Norway's ancient capital. It still seemed to Gregory, however, that they would yet have to make a third landing, still further south, if they wished to establish themselves in Norway before the Germans had dominated two-thirds of the country, including all its principal industrial and agricultural centres, so he decided to sit tight for another day or two.

One good thing which seemed to have come out of Hitler's assault on Norway was that it had put new life into the French. Daladier had seemed a good man, yet there was no doubt about it, from their almost total inactivity during the whole of the winter, that the French were not really bringing a fighting spirit to the war; but the shock of Hitler's coup now appeared to have shaken them up. The Daladier Government had been replaced by a new ministry under Paul Reynaud, who had come to office, just before the invasion, with such a dubious reception that it looked as if he would not be able to stay the course for more than a few weeks; yet by a magnificent fighting speech delivered at the time of the Allied landings Reynaud had suddenly swung the whole French nation behind him.

128

The British, it now transpired, had also landed troops near Narvik earlier in the week, although they had not yet succeeded in forcing their way into the town. They were carrying out terrific aerial attacks night after night on the German-occupied Norwegian seaplane-base at Stavanger, while the Germans were apparently employing enormous numbers of their aircraft for attacks on Allied shipping. In the meantime the Norwegian Army had established several ragged fronts in Central Norway and was endeavouring to confine the Germans to the areas they had already occupied; but the Germans were reinforcing their armies by air-borne troops each day and it was now said that General Count von Falkenhorst had over 60,000 troops at his disposal. The Germans, too, had succeeded in bringing over large numbers of light tanks and armoured vehicles, against which the Norwegians had no adequate protection; so the enemy was spreading out fanwise from Oslo and constantly pushing further north.

On Tuesday the 23rd Gregory learnt that two battles had taken place on the previous day in the Trondheim area. The British had taken Stoeren, thirty miles south of the city, while their Northern Force was advancing along the shore down the inland end of the Trondheim Fjord. However, the Germans had sent warships up the Fjord, which had not only severely shelled the British columns as they pressed forward but had landed troops in their rear, thereby cutting off their advance detachments. The result had been a nasty check for the Allies and they were reported to have sustained many casualties.

On Wednesday, however, he received better tidings. British troops had actually been seen coming down the Gudbrandsdal Valley, so it looked as though sufficient forces had now been landed to take care of Trondheim and also justify an advance to the south. A few more days at most and they should reach Lillehammer, so he could remain there now with a quiet mind and, as soon as they put in an appearance, go down their line of communication to their base, and so home.

It was now a fortnight since the affray on the mountain road in which Gussy had been wounded, and as his injury had received expert medical attention within a few hours it was healing well. It would be several weeks yet before he could use his arm again but he had recovered from the loss of blood and was able to get up for an hour or two every day. Gregory played chess with him and they spent many interesting sessions discussing the war and the international situation, as although Gussy appeared at first sight to be a fool he was actually an extremely knowledgeable man. Both of them were of the opinion that as the Allies held the seas they could put more troops into Norway by water than Germany could possibly send by air; so that although the Germans had the enormous advantage that they had been given so long to consolidate their positions in the south the Allies would easily be able to establish a front in Central Norway which would contain them there and gradually wear them down.

It was on the evening of Thursday the 25th that they heard the sounds of cheering and Gregory went out at once to see what was happening. He found that the excitement was caused by a company of the Leicester Regiment which was marching into the town. They looked fit and well and were evidently the advance guard of the British Army, so they were receiving a great ovation from the Norwegian inhabitants. As he stood watching them with a pleased smile on his face he felt a touch on his elbow and turned to see that von Ziegler was standing beside him.

He had seen the German from time to time during the last fortnight, and for the past few days von Ziegler had been hobbling about on crutches, but while they had maintained their armistice, by an unspoken mutual consent, they had refrained from any form of fraternisation.

'Well, what d'you think of them?' asked the airman.

'They look pretty good to me,' said Gregory guardedly.

The German grinned. 'Yes—the men look all right. But I was thinking of their equipment. I see that your officers still carry those clumsy old-fashioned revolvers of the same pattern that they used in the Boer War; while the men are armed only with rifles and have the air of being about to take part in an act at the Aldershot Tattoo.'

'True,' Gregory agreed. 'But there are their Bren-gun carriers coming along behind them and I imagine that they're marching in column of threes like this only to make a semi-formal entrance to the town.'

'Oh, quite. But they have no motor-cyclist scouts, no armoured cars, no tanks, no flame-throwers, no anti-aircraft guns, not a tommy-gun between them and no aerial protection; so how do they propose to operate against a German armoured column when it puts in an appearance?'

130

The question was an awkward one but Gregory replied quietly: 'I don't doubt they'll make out all right. This is only the advance guard and you can be quite certain that they have plenty of tanks in support on their way down the valley.'

'You think so?' von Ziegler drew slowly on his cigarette. 'Of course, even poorly-armed flying columns like this could have done an immense amount for you if you had had them here a fortnight ago, but now that we have a fully-mechanised army established in the south, is it wise to send infantry against it? I should have thought that the tanks would have provided the advance guard.'

'They probably will when contact is established with the enemy.'

Von Ziegler grinned again. 'Now, look here, Sallust, you saved my life and I want to repay that. I'm going to tell you something and you can take my word for it that my information is correct. As you know, I have any number of reliable agents in this country and I have naturally been keeping myself well-informed as to what is going on.

'Our Air Force has been playing the very devil with your bases at Namsos and Andalsnes, so you're having very great difficulty in getting your heavy equipment ashore. Your trouble is that, for some reason best known to yourselves, you allowed us to seize every air-base in Norway; so while we can operate from close at hand your people are having to rely almost entirely upon their Fleet Air Arm, and that was not intended to support large-scale military operations.

'You may have some tanks up the valley, but there can't be very many of them, so these poor devils are in for a thin time. We have an armoured column advancing north by this road, and it's only a few miles away, so before dawn at the latest we shall take Lillehammer and any of your men that are left will be driven back up the valley. I say "any of them that are left" because our aircraft will be letting go twenty tons of bombs on this place in about half an hour, and that's really what I came out to tell you. If you want to save your necks, you and that flowing-moustached friend of yours had better get out of here while the going's good.'

11

'He Who Fights and Runs Away . . .'

'Thanks,' said Gregory quickly. 'That's very decent of you. As you made no stipulation that I should keep this to myself I take it that you don't intend trying to prevent my passing it on?'

Von Ziegler shrugged. 'I could hardly expect you to do otherwise, and I have no objection at all, since I feel sure that I can rely on you not to have me arrested as the source of your information.

'You see, the fact of your warning the officer in command of these troops will not materially affect the military situation. In addition to the armoured column which is now approaching Lillehammer, a second armoured column captured Elverum last night, so King Haakon and his Government are on the run again, and the way is now open to us up the Osterdal Valley. In consequence, this British force is already outflanked, and hour by hour its situation will become more precarious as our Eastern column moves north. Still, that needn't worry you as it will be destroyed or driven back by our Western column which is moving direct on Lillehammer. With these two armoured divisions advancing up the parallel valleys we'll have you out of Stoeren and Dombaas inside a week, so nothing you can do now will prevent us relieving Trondheim.'

Gregory gave a wry grin. 'We'll see about that, but for the moment you've certainly got the whip-hand of us and I must get busy. Anyhow, I'm very grateful and, personally, I wish you the best of luck.'

'The same to you,' called von Ziegler as Gregory hurried away into the hospital.

Gussy was sitting up in bed reading a ten-days-old copy of *The Times* which had somehow found its way into Sweden and then across the border. In a few swift words Gregory told him what was happening, asked him to warn the doctor so that the hospital could be evacuated and said that immediately he had done so he had better get the nurse to help him dress. He then dashed out again and ran down the street to the central square of the town where the British troops had now formed up.

A freckled-faced young Captain in a fur jerkin was standing

in front of the men with several other officers, a Norwegian interpreter and the Mayor of Lillehammer, with whom they were arranging the matter of temporary billets for the troops. Without wasting a second Gregory barged in amongst them and addressed the Captain.

'My name is Sallust. That won't convey anything to you, but I'm an Englishman and I've been in Norway since the latter part of March, on special duties. I've just received reliable information that a German armoured column is approaching the town and that the German Air Force is going to bomb it in about twenty minutes; so you'd better withdraw your men and tell the Norwegians to get into their air-raid shelters.'

'Thank you,' said the Captain. 'Mine is Renetter. Would you be kind enough to put your hands above your head?' He turned quickly to a sergeant. 'Search this man for arms and examine his papers.'

Gregory shrugged, but he did not put up his hands and he waved away the sergeant as he said: 'I suppose you think I'm a Fifth Columnist?'

'That's it,' the Captain nodded. 'Ever since we set foot in Norway we've been meeting gentlemen of your kidney who've been spreading false rumours and telling us to evacuate positions when there was no need to do so; we've developed special techniques for dealing with people like you.'

'Well, in this case you're wrong,' Gregory smiled, producing his passport. 'Run your eye over that, and if you think it's a fake you'd better come up with me to the hospital. Langdon-Forbes, who was attached to the British Legation in Oslo, is there and he will vouch for my identity.'

'I see.' Captain Renetter looked a little undecided. He had been trained for good honest fighting and he detested the uncertainties which were now thrust upon him by the Nazis' new methods of warfare.

'Come on!' snapped Gregory. 'I'm not going to stand here to be bombed—if you are. For God's sake order your men under cover. That's the least you can do if you won't take my word for it that they'd be much better out of the town altogether; and come up and see Langdon-Forbes.'

Puffing at a pipe that he had just lit Renetter refused to be hurried, but after a moment's thought it seemed to him that, anyhow, there could be no harm in getting his men into some of the nearby buildings, so he gave the necessary orders while the interpreter passed on to the Mayor the information about the anticipated air-raid. He then nodded to Gregory.

'Right-oh; you'd better lead the way, and I warn you I'll shoot you if you attempt to play me any monkey tricks.'

In this somewhat undignified manner Gregory proceeded at a swift pace up the hill, the Captain following with a quick but apparently leisurely stride. At the hospital they found everything in a bustle. The nurses and male-attendants were already shepherding the less serious cases down into the air-raid shelters which had been prepared during the past fortnight, while outside the building were three ambulances, to which others of the staff were carrying out the bedridden on stretchers.

They found Gussy dressed and a nurse was just completing the adjustment of a sling to carry his arm. The lean-faced Gregory was of such a type that he might well have been taken for a dark-haired Briton, a southern German or even a Frenchman, but about Gussy there was no question at all. His beautifully-cut suit of Glenurquhart tweed positively screamed Savile Row and no one but a British diplomat could possibly have sported that long, drooping moustache in the year of grace 1940 and got away with it. Captain Renetter had hardly to exchange two sentences with him before he was confident of his *bona fides*; which automatically established Gregory's as well.

'Where did you get this information?' he asked.

'Sorry, I can't tell you,' Gregory replied promptly, 'but I'll take my oath it's authentic. There's one German armoured column advancing up the Osterdal Valley and another which will be rattling through here within a few hours. You can't possibly resist tanks, flame-throwers and ground-strafing aircraft with infantry, so the sooner you pack up and get out the better.'

'I'm afraid I can't do that. My orders are to advance south until I contact the enemy and then to go into action.'

'But good *God*, man! There's no sense in doing that when you've already been told that you'll be up against immensely superior forces! Your men will only be massacred. You'd much better get back up the valley. Blow up a bridge if you can find one, to halt their tanks, then hang on there until reinforcements reach you.'

Renetter shook his head. 'I wouldn't care to retreat until I've at least put up some sort of a show.'

'All right, then,' shrugged Gregory angrily, 'hang on if you insist, and ambush the tanks from houses on either side of the main street; but if you do that, it's a hundred to one that you'll be cut off and surrounded here, which is a senseless way to try to serve your country.'

'Thanks! but I think that I'm the best judge of that,' replied the Captain a little stiffly. 'After all, I'm a soldier.'

'True.' Gregory's eye glinted. 'I'm sure that you'll put up a jolly good show and die very gallantly. But the trouble is, my young friend, that you do not yet understand what you're up against. I, on the other hand have spent several months in Germany since the war, so I know very much more about the German Army than you do. Incidentally, I also happen to have won my Military Cross when you were still in your perambulator. However, probably you're a braver man than I am. I mean to get out before this place gets too hot to hold me.'

'I'm sorry,' Renetter apologised, handsomely if a little awkwardly. 'I didn't mean to be rude or anything but it seemed as if you were suggesting that I should run away from the Germans.'

'That's quite all right,' Gregory assured him with a smile; 'it's your show and you must use your own judgment, but knowing the facts I'd see to it anyhow that you leave yourself a good line of retreat open, because I'm afraid you'll need it. Best of luck to you. Come on, Gussy.'

Together they walked out into the pale, spring sunshine. The Captain flicked his battle bowler with a smile and went off down the hill to his men while Gregory and Gussy joined the small crowd that was gathered about the three ambulances. They were now loaded up with four stretcher-cases and a nurse apiece, but the driver of the rear car was missing, as he had run off a few minutes before to collect some valuables from his house. The doctor was anxious to get the convoy started and said that they would not wait for the man if they could find another driver. Gregory at once volunteered and got into the driving-seat with Gussy on the box beside him. The doctor jumped on the leading car and the little cavalcade set off.

The leading ambulances, moving at an easy pace on account of the injured people who formed their cargo, ran down the hill towards the main square, but Gregory did not follow. Jamming his foot down on the accelerator he tore along the side-road in which the hospital was situated and, clanging his bell to clear the way ahead, turned down a number of other side-streets towards the northern entrance to the town.

'Hi!' exclaimed Gussy. 'Steady on! Think of your poor passengers.'

'I am,' said Gregory grimly, swerving to avoid a farm-cart. 'If we had stayed in a column we'd have made a tempting target for a Nazi bomb once we got out on to the open road, and we need every ounce of speed this bus will give us if we're to get well clear of the others before the trouble starts. It's better for the people behind us to have a bit of a shaking-up than to be blown to bits.'

They left the town a quarter of a mile ahead of the other two ambulances and streaked up the gradient of the valley road along which they had chased von Ziegler a fortnight earlier. When they had covered a bare three miles they heard the crash of bombs behind them but gradually the noise faded in the distance, and for the sake of the invalids inside it Gregory eased down the pace at which he was driving the ambulance.

'Poor devils!' he muttered, suddenly.

'You were thinking of the troops and that Captain feller,' said Gussy slowly.

'Yes. I'd hate to have been in his shoes. I should have felt just the same about things myself. The very idea of retreating from the enemy without even firing a shot seems cowardice—particularly when one's young and it's against orders. I felt an awful cad trying to scare him into getting out, but I was right, you know.'

'Um; I'm afraid you were. Infantry can't possibly hold up an armoured column unless they are equipped for the job.'

'That's what makes me so livid,' Gregory went on. 'They're going to be slaughtered because the people whose job it was to equip them were still thinking in terms of war as it was twenty-five years ago; they stand no more chance against Nazi shock-troops than the archers of mediaeval times would have stood if they had been sent against the grenadiers and batteries of artillery which took the field at Waterloo. I wish to God the whole damned Army Council was in Lillehammer at this moment instead of that poor Captain and his boys!'

'It's no good getting excited about it,' Gussy replied quietly, 'and it isn't really fair to blame the Generals.'

'Oh, I know what you're going to say,' retorted Gregory, with swift sarcasm; 'it's not really the Generals' fault; it's the fault of the Treasury, with their eternal cheese-paring and obstruction. Every time the soldiers ask for a new weapon the Treasury argues that it isn't necessary and vetoes it on account of the expense. There's a lot in that, but all the same . . .'

'No,' Gussy cut in. 'The Treasury only does its job of protecting the taxpayer. Every Government department blames the Treasury for its own shortcomings, but all the Treasury actually does is to prevent waste and try to ensure that whatever money is available is spent to the best advantage. If you really want to know at whose door you ought to place the deaths of those young men who are going to die in Lillehammer tonight when they try to halt the advance of the German armoured column, I'll tell you. It is the fault of the British public.'

'The old get-out of collective responsibility, eh? No, that won't do.

'But it's the truth, Gregory. The fact that we're a Democracy gives us the right to elect our own Government. We've done so numerous times since the last war—and who did we elect? For years we kept that vain, visionary wind-bag, Ramsay MacDonald, in power.'

'You mean Stanley Baldwin kept him in power,' Gregory interjected.

'I was coming to Baldwin. MacDonald was only a small-time Pacifist, who sold his Party for the shadow of Power; and Baldwin was clever enough to use him as a stalking horse. He didn't mind the Loon from Lossiemouth posturing as P.M. for a spell now and then providing that he retained the real power himself, and either through Ramsay or as the acknowledged Chief he ruled Britain for fifteen solid years. He knew what was happening on the Continent—he admitted it in the House of Commons again and again—and made specious promises that the nation should be properly rearmed so that any threat of future aggression could be checked; but the only thing that those two cared about was remaining in power. They feared that if they went to the country with a rearmament programme they might lose their jobs, so they kept on promising but they did nothing whatever about it, and from having had the finest Air Force in the world Britain's air strength was allowed to shrink to sixth place. They reckoned that they could count on peace continuing for as long as they were likely to hold office and that someone else would have the job of tackling Hitler when they'd gone.'

'And they were right,' said Gregory bitterly. 'The conscientious objector died full of years and honours on a luxury liner, and the other patriot made a graceful exit after the Coronation, to the cheers of the assembled multitude, with an Earldom and a K.G. Just think of it—all that the Most Noble and Puissant Order of the Garter used to stand for. Doesn't it make you utterly sick?'

'No. If you employ ambitious and unscrupulous men as the managers of your business you must not grumble when you find out one day that they have robbed the till. But you put your finger on it just now when you said "the cheers of the assembled multitude". I remember those cheers for Baldwin at the time of the Coronation very well. Honest Stanley had just sacked his King and the public felt that he had handled a tricky situation remarkably well. Handling tricky situations was his long suit. Read your *Hansard* and see how for year after year he effectively spiked the guns of men like Churchill and Beaverbrook, causing them to appear to be ambitious trouble-makers when they were really only trying to bring home to the nation the frightful peril into which it was drifting. But honest Stan got away with it every time—and the public cheered him for it.

'And that, Gregory, is the point I want to make. It was the Nation that by the exercise of a free vote put him in power and kept him there. People like you and I who knew a thing or two may have been alarmed at the manner in which he completely ignored the growing power of Hitler, but we didn't want another shilling on the income tax, and we hadn't the guts to vote Socialist; while the people who don't pay income tax were just as much to blame; they took what he said for Gospel because they preferred to watch a football match or go dog-racing rather than take an intelligent interest in the international situation for themselves. You and I and all the other millions of men and women who voted for the Baldwin-MacDonald combine, from 1923 to 1937, are the criminals responsible for the situation of those boys of ours in Lillehammer today. That, Gregory, is the terrible, inescapable truth.'

Gregory sighed. 'God! What a comment on Democracy!'

There was little traffic on the long, winding, mountain road except when every few miles it curved down to a place where the valley broadened out and they passed through a village. Occasionally a German aircraft hummed high overhead. They were used to that, since during the whole of their stay in Lille-hammer German planes had passed up the valley several times a day on reconnaissance flights; but now Gregory kept a wary eye upon them as he knew that von Ziegler would have reported the presence of British troops in Lillehammer and so at any time the Nazis might start aerial attacks on the British lines of communications.

By four o'clock in the afternoon they had covered about twenty miles and entered the village of Holmen, to which the doctor had said he meant to evacuate the patients as there was a cottage hospital there, so in the market-place Gregory pulled up. They had passed several detachments of British infantry outside the village and a temporary halt had been made by a battery of artillery in its square, from which Gregory concluded that this was the head of the main column for which the company at Lillehammer was acting as advance guard. While they waited for the other two ambulances to come up Gregory and Gussy got off the driver's seat and, waylaying a lieutenant who was crossing the square, told him what was happening further south.

The lieutenant said that he was already aware of the situation as a field wireless had just come in to say that the British in Lillehammer were now in actual contact with the enemy, but that they had no need to worry as the main force that had been dispatched down the valley, of which his unit formed part, would soon be moving up in support; then he left them as the order 'prepare to march' was given.

They watched the column pass and found that it consisted only of a battalion of infantry, a battery of artillery and half a company of R.E.s with a mixed collection of vehicles bringing up the rear; which greatly perturbed Gregory as he had expected that it would be a much larger force—at least a Brigade, or possibly a Division. Its tail end had hardly disappeared when the doctor arrived with the other two ambulances, so Gregory and Gussy went over to him. He was just about to give them directions how to reach the cottage hospital when Gregory said:

'I don't want to butt in, but there must be another cottage hospital further up the valley, and if I were you I should take your patients on there.'

'But why?' protested the doctor. 'Your troops were already at Lillehammer when we left and many more of them have just gone by, so the valley will now be held. We may have to put up with air-raids, but apart from that we shall be safe enough with twenty miles between ourselves and the Germans.'

'Twenty miles is nothing to fast tanks,' said Gregory bluntly; 'they could cover that in an hour; and without wishing to appear disloyal to my own people I doubt very much if these lightly-equipped troops will be able to hold up a German armoured column for long. We must get behind something much heavier before we can consider ourselves really safe.'

'I see,' replied the doctor thoughtfully. 'In that case, then, perhaps we'd better drive on to Ringebu.'

Accordingly they proceeded north once more. They had covered about five miles when they heard a faint but distinct thudding behind them and Gregory looked at Gussy.

'It sounds as though the Boche have spotted that British column and are giving it the works.'

Gussy nodded. 'That's about it. I wonder, though, that we haven't seen some of our own aircraft by this time.'

'There's not much hope of that, I'm afraid. Von Ziegler told me that they've secured all the landing-grounds in Norway, so the only support that our troops will get is from the Fleet Air Arm in the neighbourhood of the coast.'

For half an hour they drove on in silence, another German plane droned overhead, then a sudden rat-tat-tat struck their ears. Gregory needed no telling what that meant. It was the sound of machine-guns, and next second a sharp ping-ping-ping of bullets striking on metal came from their immediate rear.

Gregory was still leading the small convoy and they were running along a low stretch of the road which here was only a few feet above the level of the broad river. The mountains rose steeply to his right but to his left there was a shallow ditch and then a belt of pine-trees between the road and the water. Without an instant's hesitation he swung the ambulance round, charged the ditch and bumped violently over the bank into the fringe of the wooded strip, pulling up with a jerk just before his bonnet came into collision with a tree.

'Oh, my arm!' gasped Gussy as the ambulance jolted to a halt.

'You're lucky still to be able to feel it,' muttered Gregory somewhat unsympathetically. 'If I'd stayed on the road another minute we would probably both have been shot through the head.' Scrambling down, he dashed round to the back of the ambulance to see if any of his passengers had been hit.

There was a line of ten neat, round bullet-holes in the roof and seven or eight of the bullets had gone through the body of an old lady who had been admitted to hospital with a broken thigh during the previous week. Blood was still pouring from her on to the occupant of the lower berth but she had died almost instantaneously and neither the nurse, who was riding inside, nor any of the other three passengers were hurt.

Leaving the nurse to cope with one of her charges who had given way to a fit of hysteria, Gregory ran out on to the road. The second ambulance had charged a telegraph-pole. The driver was lying over his wheel with blood pouring from his head, and the doctor, who had staggered out on to the road, fell dead at Gregory's feet; but the third ambulance seemed to have escaped, as it was streaking along the road half a mile away.

The solitary murder-plane had turned and just as Gregory put his hand on the quivering driver's arm it came streaking down again for a second attack on the now dispersed convoy. Dropping to his knees he wriggled underneath the ambulance. With a hellish clatter the machine-gun opened fire and bullets streaked into the roof above his head. There was a loud wailing cry, an awful gurgling shout, then silence as the plane ceased fire and zoomed up again. Gregory felt a warm splash on the back of his neck and knew that it was human blood dripping through the floor-boards.

Crawling out, he got open the door and in one glance took in the shambles that Hitler's disciple had made during his evening's sport. Two of the patients were dead, riddled with bullets, and the young nurse was writhing in agony with half her face shot away.

There was little that he could do for her except to find the doctor's bag and give her an overdose of morphia. She was losing so much blood that he knew she would be dead long before he could get her to any place where her life might have been saved by proper attention, so he had no hesitation in sparing her what pain he could. Having thrust the morphia pellets into her mouth he sat there in a pool of blood on the floor of the ambulance, holding the poor girl's hands until her moans ceased and her remaining eye glazed over.

Gussy and the other nurse had joined him. The driver was now dead. The other ambulance had not come back as the man who drove it was doubtless scared out of his wits and now intent only on getting his own passengers and himself to a place of safety; but Gregory and the nurse, with Gussy's one-handed aid, managed to get the two unwounded patients out on to the roadside. Gregory then went back to his own car. To his fury, he found that it was stuck. Owing to the trees on either side he could not turn it, and the bank over which he had charged was too steep for him to back it up. Having told Gussy how he had ditched himself, he set off at his long loping stride along the road for help.

Three-quarters of a mile further on he found a farmhouse among the trees. The farmer was quietly working in his yard and had probably heard the machine-gunning but known nothing of its object or results. When he saw that Gregory's clothes were soaked with blood he dropped his pitchfork and came out at once on being beckoned from his gate.

The next hour was spent by Gregory and the farmer carrying the remaining five patients along to the farm, where the farmer's wife and daughter busily employed themselves making ready for the reception of the invalids. Fortunately, each stretcher in itself constituted a bed, and the surviving nurse, who had been in Gregory's ambulance, was able to take charge of the patients.

During the whole business they hardly spoke as all of them were filled with a bitter, furious rage, which was utterly beyond expression, at the scene of murder they had witnessed. The farmer's wife provided them with a meal and although Gregory would have liked to push on he felt that now that dusk was falling he and Gussy had better stay where they were for the night; so after they had eaten he went out and fetched two more stretchers as beds for them, leaving the dead bodies of their occupants on the floor of the second ambulance.

During the night there were sounds of distant firing, but how distant was impossible to judge, as the noise of the explosions echoed for miles up the deep valley. There was also the almost constant drone of aeroplanes overhead, but no bombs were dropped in their vicinity.

In the morning Gregory held a consultation with Gussy and they both decided that they could do no good by remaining where they were. The patients had warmth, shelter and food in the farmhouse and the nurse was quite competent to look after them until they could be moved; but the problem which faced the two Englishmen was that of transport.

142

After breakfast Gregory went out to have a look round the place and he found that in addition to several horses the farmer had a pony and trap, so he suggested that Gussy, who had ample funds, should buy it. The farmer was loath to sell, and on being pressed, demanded a price that was nearly three times the proper value, but Gussy had no intention of being caught by the Germans if he could possibly help it and during the early hours of the morning the firing had sounded considerably nearer. In consequence, although he was sulky at being rooked, he paid up without further argument, and with Gregory driving they set off towards Ringebu.

On their way they passed further detachments of British troops, but the sight did not cheer them particularly, as there were no heavy tanks in evidence and their numbers were not sufficient to justify any hope that they would be able to hold up the German column. At Ringebu they tried to get a train, but during the hour they waited on the station platform the only two-coach local which passed through, going north, was crammed with British wounded; so after buying enough food to keep them going for twenty-four hours they continued their journey in the pony-cart.

Soon they had more trouble with the Germans' planes, as now that the battle was joined these were in constant evidence attacking British troop-concentrations wherever they could see them. For the German airmen it was a Roman holiday; except for occasional bursts from Bren guns they met with no opposition at all, so they were able to sail up and down in a leisurely fashion machine-gunning anything that took their fancy. Half a dozen times during the morning Gregory halted the trap in the best cover that he could find and lay doggo while fresh flights of Germans went over, and whenever he caught sight of a few khaki figures he was extra cautious. The Germans seemed determined not to give their enemies a moment's rest and, in consequence, the British had been compelled to split up into little groups, which made their way in single file through the trees at the roadside or along the gullies where they could throw themselves flat immediately they were menaced by the Nazis.

By midday they reached the village of Graaho, where they halted to give the pony an hour's rest and eat their lunch; and here they ran into a Staff-Colonel who was known to Gussy. Without saying very much it was clear the Colonel knew enough of the truth not to take too optimistic a view of the situation.

He said that the landings had been absolute hell as the weather had been lousy and nine out of ten of the men had been violently seasick; which had not helped matters, as the Germans had seized all the best ports and the British had been left only a few rickety piers at which to land. He added that they had met with a much stronger resistance outside Trondheim than they had anticipated and that the men were getting a bit fed up by being perpetually harassed from the air; but that, all things considered, they were in pretty good spirits and eager enough to have a cut at the enemy. On this optimistic note he drove off to get first-hand news of the progress of the battle that was raging further south.

By mid-afternoon Gregory felt that more could not be asked of the pony, so they halted at the village of Otta, having accomplished over thirty miles in the course of the day. Every inn in the valley was crowded out with refugees who had streamed north during the past fortnight, but the innkeeper found a cottager who was willing to let them a room with a double bed for the night and a stable for their pony.

Next morning they went to the railway station in a second attempt to get a train, but all the previous day the Germans had been bombing up and down the valley and they had obtained direct hits on the track on both sides of Otta, so until the line was repaired trains could not now get through from either direction. Returning to the cottage at which they had spent the night, they harnessed the pony and set off once more up the seemingly interminable valley.

They had to follow the same watchful procedure as on the day before, since the German aircraft were again active, strafing and bombing almost without intermission. Fortunately, the road was almost empty, as the farming community of the rich Gudbrandsdal Valley were staying 'put'. The Germans were to the north and to the south of them, so there was nowhere for them to go, except up into the snow-topped, inhospitable mountains to the east or west. The refugees who had flooded the valley earlier in the month apparently felt the same, since they seemed to have abandoned any attempt at further flight and stood about in groups at the roadside and in the villages, waiting anxiously for the latest rumours and speculating as to whether the Germans would be arriving in a few hours or if the British would succeed in holding them back.

At Broendhaugen Gussy bought some more food while

144

Gregory talked to some British Tommies who were connecting field-telephone lines with the installation in the tiny village post-office. The men knew little of what was going on but Gregory was not surprised at that; as a subaltern in France in the old war he had often had to wait until the newspapers arrived from home to learn if an attack of two or three days before in a neighbouring sector had proved a success or failure.

The men grumbled because the German planes constantly interfered with their work, because their own Air Force was apparently at home, in bed asleep, because their sheepskin jerkins hampered their movements, because of the cold and because their rations were late in arriving; but Gregory was not at all perturbed by their attitude. He knew that the British Tommy is a born grouser and that the only time when his officers need worry about him is when he sits still and says nothing. Naturally, they did not like being bombed and machine-gunned, but in all other respects they were rather enjoying themselves. With their extraordinary facility for overcoming suspicion among foreigners by a cheerful grin and graphic gestures they had already made friends with the local inhabitants, and one of them was nursing a baby while the woman who owned the little general shop in which the post-office was situated was cooking them a meal in her kitchen.

When Gregory told them that he was going to Dombaas they said that he had much better stay where he was, as they had come up from there on a truck that morning and the place was in ruins. As it was the railway junction at the head of the Valley the Germans had been bombing it almost without cessation for the last forty-eight hours. However, Gregory knew that if he meant to get to Andalsnes he had no option, as it was only by going through the junction that he could get on to the road to the port; so, having eaten a scratch meal, he and Gussy wished the soldiers luck and set off once more.

They could see where Dombaas lay long before they got there as the situation of the little town was indicated by a mile-high column of smoke. When they drew nearer they saw that fires were burning there which it was far beyond the capacity of any small-town fire-brigade to put out, even with the assistance of the military; and while they were still half a mile from the nearest houses a flight of German planes came over to unload yet another cargo of bombs, which added to the havoc and confusion.

British military police were directing traffic along a side-road that skirted the town, since it was quite impossible to go through it, but the side-road was already a quagmire, as it had been churned into a sea of mud by British tanks, and cars were now having to bump their way over the fields that lay at the sides of the worst stretches.

They had accomplished another thirty miles, and it was now well on in the afternoon, so they pulled up at a farmhouse about a mile to the west of Dombaas. Every room and barn was crowded with refugees from the nearby town, but they managed to find a corner in one of the outbuildings in which to shelter for the night. It was very much colder up there than it had been down in Lillehammer and they would have suffered severely had it not been for the human warmth of the unfortunate Norwegians who were packed like sardines into the wooden building. There was nowhere at all in which they could stable the pony, so while Gussy kept their places Gregory secured a feed of hay for the animal and rugged it up on the lee side of the barn.

There was little sleep for them that night; it seemed as if Goering had turned the whole of the German Air Force on to Dombaas. Explosion after explosion shook the earth as the bombs rained down with rarely more than ten minutes' interval between salvoes.

Haggard, weary, unshaven, they went out the following morning to find that their pony and trap had been stolen. Gussy was furious. As a rich man he had an extremely well-developed sense of the rights of a property-owner and the fact that he had paid through the nose for the outfit made him feel even more bitter about it; but Gregory accepted the incident philosophically. He pointed out that Gussy could hardly have expected to get the pony and trap back to England with him and he would probably have had to give it away in any case when they reached Andalsnes. He suggested that the best thing they could do was to go out on to the road and try to get a lift on one of the British Army lorries.

For the best part of three hours they stood shivering at the roadside trying to induce the drivers of the occasional vehicles that passed going westwards to stop and give them a lift; but the men all shrugged their shoulders with a helpless gesture and drove on. At last one of them pulled up half a mile down the road to examine his engine so Gregory raced after it and

146

tackled him. He then learnt why the others had refused to stop. The orders were that the troops were to treat the civil inhabitants with every consideration and render them every possible assistance which did not interfere with their own duties; but they were forbidden to give any refugee a lift on an army vehicle.

Gregory pleaded that as he and Gussy were Englishmen they were in an entirely different category, but the driver refused to risk it. He said that if Gregory could get an order from an officer he would take them willingly, but not otherwise, and on the lonely stretch of road no officer was available.

As Andalsnes was over seventy miles away it was not a jolly prospect to set out on foot, but Gregory decided that it was the only thing to do, so they started to trudge down the long, bleak road which followed the line of the railway upon which no trains were now running.

While they plodded on round curve after curve that disclosed seemingly endless vistas of misty mountains they discussed the military situation, although they knew little about it. As far as they could judge there was probably only about a Brigade operating in the Gudbrandsdal Valley, and from what they had heard it seemed that the British had not as yet penetrated to the Osterdal Valley at all; so if the Germans were coming up that as well, and had no opposition to face, it seemed quite on the cards that they might come round behind the British somewhere south of Trondheim; in which case the British would be caught between two fires.

Gussy remarked how lucky it was that a great mountain-range separated the two valleys, as otherwise the German Eastern column might have crossed the watershed and made a descent direct on Dombaas, thereby cutting the British off days earlier and much more effectively. But owing to the snow on the heights, and the almost impassable roads, that, fortunately, seemed out of the question.

Gregory devoutly hoped that Gussy was right, but it seemed to him that the whole German drive was being conducted with such brilliant initiative that he would not have put anything past the German General Staff, and about three o'clock in the afternoon his pessimistic forebodings were confirmed through a totally unexpected happening which proved an extraordinary stroke of personal good luck for them both.

At the wail of a Klaxon behind them they moved to the side

of the road to get out of the way of an oncoming car, automatically turning their heads as they did so. As the car raced by Gussy caught a glimpse of its solitary passenger; it was his friend, the Staff Colonel, and the Colonel was looking straight at him. A hundred yards further down the road the car slowed up and, as the Colonel had no hesitation in breaking a regulation for two Englishmen, one of whom was a member of His Britannic Majesty's Diplomatic Service, they were taken aboard.

As soon as they were settled they gave the Colonel an outline of their adventures during the forty-eight hours since they had last seen him, and asked how things were going.

He looked tired and despondent and said quite frankly that he did not at all like the look of things. The fact that the Germans were able to come and go in the air without the least opposition was proving little short of disastrous. Our men were game enough, but no sooner had they established themselves in a position than the Germans bombed them out of it and machine-gunned them from the air. The company of Leicesters in Lillehammer had been almost annihilated and their supporting troops had fared little better. For the past two days the Germans had been driving ahead, up the Gudbrandsdal Valley, smashing all resistance with their tanks and aircraft, while they had raced up the Osterdal Valley to Tolgen without meeting any opposition at all, so that they were now only about seventy miles south of Trondheim. Worse; with almost unbelievable daring they had launched a four-pronged attack over the mountain-range and were already reported to be nearing Dombaas and Stoeren. Orders had been issued for an immediate withdrawal from the Gudbrandsdal, but with the railway cut in a dozen places and the Dombaas road-junction rendered impassable by constant bombing it was going to be touch-and-go as to whether the British would succeed in getting out of the trap.

The Colonel had not been out of his clothes for a week and they could see from his drawn, lined face how the strain of his responsibilities was telling on him. Soon after he had told them the bare facts he dropped off to sleep, in spite of the bumping they sustained from the ruts of the road which had been badly cut up by the heavy military traffic.

Twice during the afternoon German planes came over and machine-gunned them from the air, but even that did not wake the Colonel, and the chauffeur seemed already to have had sufficient experience of this form of attack to evade it by clever alterations of his pace from a crawl to sudden spurts, which put out the Germans' aim until they flew off to find easier targets. Gregory and Gussy, too, dozed between these strafings as they were both feeling the effects of the restless night they had spent, and neither the general situation nor the grey, wintry-looking afternoon was an encouragement to cheerful conversation.

At seven o'clock they drove into a small town and the car pulled up in front of a good-sized brick building which had the appearance of a school; but there were no children about. One of its wings had been shattered by bombs, and a British sentry was posted on the gate, beyond which were parked a number of camouflaged cars, so Gregory rightly assumed that the place had been taken over as a British military headquarters. As the car stopped the Colonel roused himself and, glancing round, told them that they had arrived at Andalsnes.

'Thank God for that nap,' he muttered as he got out. 'I'm feeling lousy now, but after a cup of tea I'll be myself again, and I don't suppose I'll have a chance to shut my eyes for another forty-eight hours if I'm to get through the work that our new movements will entail. Come inside and I'll arrange for somebody to fix you up with permits to get out of this damned country; I'm sure you'll understand if I have to leave you in someone else's hands from now on.'

As they thanked him Gregory thought what a lot of utter nonsense was talked about the cushy jobs of the gilded staff. However desperate a battle the troops could generally doze for a few hours during the nights and had to be taken out of the line to rest after ten days' fighting as the absolute maximum, but in an operation of this kind the staff had to work on indefinitely, day and night, with the responsibility for every move on their over-burdened shoulders.

The Colonel passed them on to a hollow-eyed captain, who attached a special chit to each of their passports, then took them into a Mess where he told an orderly to look after them and said that they had better wait there until they were sent for.

No regular meals were being served in the Mess but there were plates of sandwiches and biscuits laid out on the table and the orderlies fetched them a fresh pot of tea. Staff-Officers came in from time to time, munched a few sandwiches, gulped down cups of steaming tea, exchanged laconic remarks and hurried back to their work again. The evening had closed in grey, wet and cold, a misty rain streaked the windows and it seemed to

Gregory and Gussy that they sat there for an interminable time.

At last, about one o'clock in the morning, the Captain returned and put them in charge of a Corporal, who, he said, would take them down to the harbour. Gregory asked if he thought that they would have to wait long on the ship before it sailed, to which he replied with a grim smile:

'I don't think so; quite a number of ships will be leaving Andalsnes for England tonight.'

In the darkness they could see little of the town or the fifth-rate harbour with its one rickety jetty, where the Army had performed the remarkable feat of landing an Expeditionary Force when at last the powers that be had completed their long-drawn-out arrangements and decided that the force should sail. German planes were overhead again and others were dropping bombs somewhere further to the south while searchlights swept the sky and anti-aircraft guns manned by the British in the town replied to the raiders. By the flash of the bombs they could make out the silhouette of destroyers and cargo-boats standing out in the deeper waters of the fjord, while by the light of the parachute-flares that were being dropped they could discern many smaller craft and rafts nearer inshore.

Down on the wharf there were several hundred soldiers and they soon discovered that many of the troops were French, so at first they assumed that the British were being reinforced by a new landing of Allied troops; but they soon discovered that, on the contrary, the French were loading their gear on to the small boats preparatory to going back to the ships that had brought them, and that the English troops were also man-handling guns and carriers on to the rafts that lay at the water's edge.

Gregory and Gussy looked at each other as another parachute-flare dropped from a German aircraft and lit the scene. 'Got it?' said Gregory.

'Yes,' said Gussy. 'We're chucking our hand in.'

'That's it. Hitler's made Norway too hot to hold us. I expect the decision was taken only a few hours ago as a result of the German outflanking movement from the Osterdal towards Dombaas. I only hope to God that the Boche don't hear that we're evacuating before we get clear of the harbour.'

'They will if *La Baronne Noire* learns of it through French sources,' Gussy remarked pessimistically.

Next second there was a blinding flash as a bomb fell on some sheds fifty yards from the wharf's edge. There were shouts and yells as the men ran for cover and flung themselves flat. Another bomb—another—and another came down, all within a radius of a hundred yards, and when the din of the explosions ceased they could hear the screams and moaning of the wounded.

When Gregory cautiously got to his knees he found Gussy beside him but they had lost the Corporal in the confusion.

'Come on,' said Gregory; 'any damned boat'll do; it's no good staying here to be murdered.' As he spoke he swung himself down into a motor-launch that was bobbing at the wharf's edge, already half-full of soldiers, and stretched up a hand to help the still partially-disabled Gussy in after him.

More men scrambled down until the boat was packed, then the naval petty-officer who was at the tiller gave the order to cast off and the launch cautiously nosed its way out among the other craft.

Even during those few minutes three more sticks of bombs had dropped, this time on the town, and lurid flames leapt up from the shattered buildings. Overhead there was a horrid, irregular droning as the Boche planes circled above their targets, and before the launch was thirty feet from the jetty it suddenly seemed almost to leap out of the water. Another salvo had been dropped plumb on the embarking troops.

The fires that had been started now lit an incredible scene of horror and confusion. Some of the boats, with their human cargoes, had been blown to fragments; others had capsized, having been thrown right over on their keels by the huge water-spouts that the exploding bombs had sent up, and others, again, partially damaged, were now sinking. Scores of men were struggling in the water, yelling for help, and as they were hauled aboard the undamaged craft their clothes dripped red from the blood of their dismembered comrades.

The overloaded launch shot forward again; the naval petty-officer steering it with what seemed miraculous skill, between other boats and wreckage, to get away from the wharf which was now a roaring furnace. Out in the fjord the ships had switched on their searchlights and were replying with their anti-aircraft guns. The whole sky was like a firework display of bursting shells and sweeping arcs of light; but wave after wave of German planes still came over, launching their bombs upon the town, the ships and the wharf with equal persistence.

Just before they reached the destroyer for which they were heading there was a slight lull and Gregory said to Gussy: 'This

151

is no ordinary raid; it's Fifth Column stuff; the Germans have been tipped off about the evacuation and they've sent up every plane they've got that's capable of getting off the Norwegian airports.'

'That's it,' Gussy agreed, pulling his long moustache. 'I only hope it'll be a lesson to our people to take a stronger line with the Fifth Columnists we've got at home.'

The destroyer on to which they were taken was soon crowded with troops, but it did not put to sea, as its boats were needed to carry more British and French troops off from the wharf to the transports which were further down the fjord. The sailors who were not manning the anti-aircraft guns or the boats had turned themselves into nurses and were tending the wounded to whom all the available below-deck accommodation upon the destroyer was turned over; so the unwounded had to remain on deck in spite of the bitter cold.

By the light of the burning houses, the bursting shells, the parachute-flares and the searchlights the scene was now lit nearly as brightly as if it were day, so even distant groups of figures could often be made out quite clearly. From their position on the deck near the stern of the ship Gregory and Gussy could see that all attempt to embark guns, vehicles and material had now ceased. The men were just jumping off the burning wharf into the first boats that could take them, but there was no pushing and no panic, in spite of the frightful gruelling that they were receiving, so evidently they were abandoning their equipment under orders.

For an hour or more Gregory assisted by passing ammunition for an anti-aircraft gun. The work kept him warm and gave him the satisfaction of feeling that he was helping in the uneven fight against the enemy. But they were firing at such a rate that the ammunition gave out, after which he could only crouch, shivering, behind a ventilator.

At last the short, terrible night was over and the grey light of dawn began to dim the searchlights and the flash of the explosions. Some of the transports were already moving down the fjord and at about half-past four the destroyer hoisted in her boats and followed; but the evacuation was by no means over. Gregory knew that the troops which had been coming off in the past few hours were only recently-arrived reinforcements; few of them had even been outside Andalsnes, let alone seen any of the fighting. It would be days before all the troops

152

that could be saved from the Gudbrandsdal Valley *débâcle* could be got back and embarked; and now that the Germans knew what was happening they could be trusted to see to it that not a shipload escaped without its quota of casualties.

The seamen cooks had been working without cessation, boiling great cauldrons of tea lashed with rum for the cold and exhausted soldiers, and as the destroyer steamed out of Andalsnes Gregory managed to procure two mugs of the piping-hot brew for Gussy and himself. When he got back from the queue he saw that they had rounded the bend of the fjord but the position of the town was still marked by a dense pall of black smoke that hung over it. With chattering teeth they gulped down the welcome tea but they had not yet seen the last of the enemy. As the convoy formed up in the broader waters a flight of bombers roared over and one small steamer nearby received a direct hit on its stern, which caused it suddenly to list to port, then turn right over.

The convoy hove-to and boats were lowered to rescue the survivors who were floundering about in the ice-cold water. Before the boats were well away the German bombers turned and came hurtling down again. The ships had long since run out of anti-aircraft ammunition, so they were virtually defenceless except for the Bren and Lewis guns with which some of the soldiers opened fire. As Gregory watched, one plane burst into flames and, turning over, pitched headlong into the fjord. A sudden cheer went up, but it wavered out into a groan as the other planes drowned it in a hellish tattoo, deliberately machine-gunning the survivors from the capsized troopship and the boats that were setting off to their rescue.

With muttered curses and half-choked by the intensity of their bitter fury the spectators stood there impotent to help their comrades but vowing vengeance in their hearts. More dripping, wounded and exhausted men were dragged on to the already crowded decks of the destroyer and she proceeded on her way.

By the time they reached the open sea the men had sorted themselves out a little. A number of those who had fallen in the water were now in borrowed clothes lent to them by the sailors; others had stripped and stood shivering in their greatcoats while their uniforms were being dried in the boiler-rooms. Every one of the sailors had given up his bedding, under which, and a number of tarpaulins, the troops sheltered as best they could from the bitter wind and the salt spray that was now flying over the bow of the ship. Many of them were seasick and the long day and night that followed seemed like a timeless span of unending misery.

At midday on the Tuesday they put in to a Northern port and the heterogeneous collection of French and British troops, some with uniforms, some without, hollow-eyed, stubble-chinned and incredibly weary, crawled ashore to the reception stations on the docks that had been made ready for them.

As civilians with special passes Gregory and Gussy were allowed out of the dock at once, and an hour later they were on a train for London. Gregory had secured a paper, and before settling down in his corner to sleep he glanced at the front page; a short news item caught his eye and he began to laugh uproariously.

Three neatly-dressed business men and a spick-and-span officer, who shared the carriage with them, and had eyed the two bedraggled strangers with considerable misgiving, glanced up disapprovingly.

'What is it?' Gussy asked, as his friend continued to laugh almost hysterically.

Gregory controlled his shouts of mirth and spoke with sudden intense bitterness. 'Two days ago a German was caught with a camera in a forbidden area on the South Coast. The magistrate fined him twenty shillings and let him go. Is Sir John Anderson a traitor or a lunatic; or is it just that nobody has yet told him that for eight months Britain has been at war with the most formidable, unscrupulous and merciless horde of fanatic-ridden brutes that have ever blackened the pages of history?'

12

'Seek Out and Destroy the Enemy'

For the next three days Gregory kicked his heels in London. Sir Pellinore Gwaine-Cust was away on some special business and not returning until the Saturday.

After his long absence he found London surprisingly unchanged. The sandbags were still there but there was no other evidence of war and it was considerably fuller than it had been when he had left it at the end of the previous October. The people were as well clad as ever; nine out of ten of the West End shops were still open and doing good business, so that the gaps among them were hardly noticeable. In the clubs where he lunched everybody was quite cheerful, although some of the officers to whom he talked were a little perturbed about the situation in Norway. An American journalist had apparently blown the gaff during the previous week in a sensational article which had been given a prominent place in the United States Press. He stated that the British had been cut off at Lillehammer and that while the Germans were complete masters of the air and showed splendid initiative, the British, as usual, were quite inadequately equipped for the most modern type of warfare.

As yet nobody knew that the Allies had actually been thrown out on their ear and were now evacuating as fast as they could go, but Gregory kept that to himself, since he was every bit as good at keeping his mouth shut when it might do harm to open it as he was at stating his opinion with fearless disregard to consequences when he thought that a good purpose could be served by so doing.

Apart from the feeling that Britain had had a bit of a setback in her Norwegian campaign, everybody was still full of complacent optimism. They took it for granted that Hitler would either have to attack the Maginot Line and lose a million men to no purpose, or quietly submit to being strangled by the Blockade.

Gregory was not prepared to make any predictions upon Hitler's next move, but of one thing he was quite convinced—Hitler had no intention of fading from the scene through sheer inanition, although it seemed highly probable that the British Government might do so.

On the afternoon of Saturday, May the 4th, his faithful henchman, Rudd, whom his safe return had made as happy as a sand-boy, took a telephone message that Sir Pellinore was back and would be happy if Gregory could dine with him that night. When he got in Gregory rang up to say that he would be there; and 8.15 found him, lean, bronzed and very fit-looking after his few days' rest, at 99, Carlton House Terrace.

When he was not actively at war himself he believed in ignoring to the best of his ability any war that might be in progress, so, according to his peace-time custom, he had donned an admirably-cut, double-breasted dinner-jacket, and no one who saw him could possibly have associated him with the filthy, bloodstained vagabond who had crossed the North Sea in a destroyer five days before.

As Gregory was ushered into the great library on the first floor, which in daytime had such a lovely view over St. James's Park, the elderly baronet came striding forward from the fireplace and placed both his huge hands on his visitor's shoulders. Sir Pellinore measured six feet three in his socks and from his great height he stood for a moment looking down on Gregory; then he boomed:

'Well, you young rascal, so you've got sick of gallivanting about the Continent at last, eh? Dining and wining and womanising in Berlin and Helsinki and Oslo, and five months overdue from that mission I sent you on. But, damme, I'm pleased to see you.'

'It seems to have escaped your memory that I've done a few other little jobs on my own account since then,' said Gregory mildly.

'I know, I know.' Sir Pellinore brushed up his great white cavalry moustache as he strode over to a side-table, where he proceeded to pour out two handsome rations of old, bone-dry Manzanilla sherry. 'The way you bluffed Hermann Goering into sending you to Finland was an epic, and that German programme for world conquest that you got us was worth its weight in hundred-pound bank-notes. But after that I suppose you felt that you had earned a holiday and went to Norway for some fishing.'

'That's it,' Gregory grinned. 'I had good sport, too; only, instead of salmon, I was after water-rats.'

'So I gathered. And if only the Government had acted on your information we wouldn't be in our present ghastly mess. But what have you been up to since the invasion?'

'Oh, I saved King Haakon's life several times and pottered round a bit, generally.'

'Ha, that sounds interesting. Tell me about it.'

'I will later on, but first of all what about Erika? I've been worrying myself silly as to whether she succeeded in reaching Holland and managed to get in touch with you.'

Sir Pellinore's bright-blue eyes twinkled. 'She's safe enough. I think I ought to break it to you gently, though. You've got a rival, Gregory, my boy.'

'Eh? Say that again,' said Gregory.

'Yes. After all, you can't expect to leave a lovely woman like that trailing about Europe all on her own without anyone to hold her hand or tuck her up at nights. I will say you're a good picker, though, and she's worth six of that Hungarian witch that you produced some years ago; although Sabine was admittedly an eyeful.'

A slow smile broke over Gregory's face. 'You old rogue! You've seen her, then?'

'Yes. Where d'you think I've been these last three days while you've been sleeping your head off in London? That young woman of yours has a pretty taste in food, too. We dined last night at the *Fillet de Sole* in Brussels.'

'How was she?'

'As pink as a peach and as plump as a partridge. And we were getting on famously. Great pity I had to fly home this morning—great pity. Another few days and we'd have got to the tucking-up stage.'

Gregory helped himself to another glass of the bone-dry sherry as he laughed: 'At your age? You ought to be ashamed of yourself!'

'What's age got to do with it?' Sir Pellinore ran a large hand over his fine head of white hair. 'A woman's as old as she looks and a man's as old as he feels. Don't be deceived by that rot in *Debrett* that says I'll never see seventy again. I'm somewhere in the early thirties.'

'My arithmetic must be at fault, then. I had an idea that way back in the 'eighties you had already acquired a reputation for having an eye for a horse or a pretty woman and an infinite capacity for vintage port.'

'Ha, you're jealous, eh? That's what makes you dig up that old story. Not a word of truth in it, either. Everyone knows that I've lived a life of simple rectitude within my modest means.'

'I might be able to manage a life of simple rectitude myself if I had your income,' murmured Gregory. 'What is it now— eighty-thousand a year?—or have you touched the hundred-thousand mark?'

'There you are! Jealous again of my little successes in the city. But jealousy won't get you anywhere. You know you won't be able to keep that young woman of yours for a week if only we can manage to get her over here.'

'I wish to God you could,' said Gregory seriously.

'So do I.' Sir Pellinore stopped his chaffing. 'She's being very useful to us, but I've always held that it's wrong to flog a willing mare. After the many services she has rendered she ought to be brought out of danger for a few months at least, but she's got a bee in her bonnet about its not being right to accept the hospitality of Britain while we're at war with her country. I did my damnedest to persuade her to take a rest but I couldn't budge her an inch.'

At that moment the elderly butler announced dinner, so they went downstairs, where Gregory found that the war did not, so far, appear to have in the least affected the magnificent kitchen maintained by his plutocratic host. Over the rich, well-chosen meal he told Sir Pellinore of his adventures in Norway and gave him a much more detailed account of the time that he had spent in Germany, Finland and Russia than he had been able to send from Leningrad in the long letter that he had despatched via the Consul there and the Moscow Embassy Bag. The magnum of Louis Roederer 1920 that they drank had lost the exuberance of its youth, but mellowed to the flavour that only age can give, and was perfection from never having been moved out of Sir Pellinore's cellar since the day it had been laid down. They had finished it and were already on the old brandy by the time Gregory came to the end of his recital and, after a short pause, remarked: 'Well, how goes the war?'

'It doesn't go,' replied Sir Pellinore glumly. 'The Government is dying on its feet and for months past it's been dead from the neck up.'

Gregory swivelled the old brandy thoughtfully round the very thin, medium-sized, balloon-shaped glass and smelt its rich ethers appreciatively. 'So I rather gathered from the people I've met in the last few days. It seems that the Socialists and the more energetic Conservative back-benchers are getting a bit fed up with Chamberlain.'

'Chamberlain,' boomed the baronet, 'was right about Munich—right every time. We wouldn't have stood a dog's chance against Hitler if we'd gone to war with him then. Chamberlain was clever enough to trick him into giving us a year to rearm, and in spite of the innumerable things that should have been done and yet were not done, at least the groundwork was laid which saved Britain from immediate and probably irremediable defeat. Whatever may happen to Chamberlain now, when history comes to be written he will assume his rightful place as a great and far-seeing Prime Minister who had the courage to accept the odium for having made Britain eat humble pie over the surrender of Czechoslovakia so that she might have a chance to save herself.'

'What's the trouble now, then? Is he a tired man, or is it that his heart isn't really in the war?'

'He's getting on in life and he hasn't been too well, so probably he's feeling the strain; but it's not that, entirely, and I'm convinced that, although he did his absolute utmost to avert this terrible calamity which has overtaken the world, once the war was on he became as determined as any man in this country to do his damnedest to defeat Hitler. He is very shrewd and extraordinarily far-sighted. He only came into politics comparatively late in life and his long experience of business is an enormous asset to him in many ways, but he was raised in the tradition of Birmingham, where for a century past it has been the habit of the great manufacturers to deal honestly with their customers all over the world, but slowly and methodically, on the theory that there's always plenty of time and that it is better to reject an order from a doubtful source than to risk a bad debt by snatching it from under the nose of a competitor.

'Such methods are of little use when you're up against a gangster. In dealing with Hitler honesty is *not* the best policy and there is *not* plenty of time thoroughly to investigate possibilities before every fresh liability is entered into. Risks *must* be taken, and not a moment of a single day should be lost in reaching definite decisions which may help to bring the war to a speedy conclusion. That is why, although Chamberlain served us well in peace, he is not a good war leader.'

'But surely,' Gregory interjected, 'there must be many energetic men who are pressing him all the time and stressing the necessity of his developing a more vigorous policy?'

'There are; but Chamberlain does not trust them. He has a deep-rooted suspicion as to the motives of anyone who even faintly smacks of the "go-getter" mentality and he refuses to recognise that it is the "go-getters" who win wars. The trouble is that he's a very unapproachable man; he doesn't make friends easily, but when he does he's very loyal to them and relies upon their opinions which are definitely not the opinions of the nation. He listens only to this little group of life-long friends, and the tragedy of it is that nearly all these people who hold high office under him are the proved incompetents who served under Baldwin; the men who lowered the prestige of the British Empire to such a parlous state that we dared not even face up to the Italians over the Abyssinian business—let alone tackle the reborn German nation at the time of Munich.'

'What d'you think'll happen?' Gregory asked.

'Chamberlain's days as Prime Minister are numbered. Not a doubt of that. This Norwegian affair will be the finish of him. I hope that for his own sake he will retire and leave it to history to vindicate him as a great English gentleman and a fine states-man; but I doubt if he'll do that.'

'D'you think Churchill will succeed him?'

'One can only pray that he will.' Sir Pellinore suddenly became enthusiastic. 'Churchill is the most inveterate enemy the Germans have ever had, and it's the Germans that we're fighting. For years he has stood, a defiant and almost solitary figure in the House, warning the nation of the peril into which Baldwin was allowing it to drift. I'm very proud today to be able to say that I have always believed in Churchill—even in his darkest hours, when nearly everyone had turned against him. He has the attributes of real genius in that he would have made a great name for himself in any profession that he had chosen. His writings alone would have made him famous, because they have a quality that is unique and outstanding. The Admirals who worked under him when he was First Lord will all tell you that he would have made a great sailor, and had he continued in the Army there is little doubt that he would have gone down to history as a great military commander. He possesses qualities of imagination far beyond those of any of our other leaders and apparently perennial youth, which makes him ready and willing to consider new ideas; a lion's courage and a wonderful human touch which goes straight to the hearts of all who come in con-tact with him. He has served in practically every high office of the State and his policy with regard to Germany has been con-sistent, so it is only fair, now that he has been proved right after all these years, that the Premiership should go to him; and what's more, it is the wish of the people.'

'It seems a foregone conclusion that he'll get it, then.'

'Unfortunately, that's very far from being the case. The people have no say at all in who is to be Prime Minister. The House of Commons have no say. Even the Cabinet has no say. It rests almost entirely with the outgoing holder of the office.

Chamberlain will go to the Monarch and when he hands in his resignation he will suggest his successor. The unwritten constitution is that the Monarch should either accept that nomination or send for the leader of the Opposition; and although we want the Socialists in, because they have some really first-class men like Bevin and Greenwood, they are not strong enough to carry the whole war on their shoulders with the other half of the country distrusting and criticising their every action.'

'Couldn't the King turn down the outgoing Prime Minister's nomination and send for somebody else who was in the same Party?'

'He could, but it would be contrary to all precedent and liable to prejudice the detached position of the Throne, the very strength of which lies in its aloofness from the dirt and chicanery of Party politics. Therefore it is most unlikely that the Monarch would take such a step even in a major crisis.'

'In that case Chamberlain may nominate Sir John Simon or Sam Hoare, and from what you say the King's only alternative would be to send for Attlee.'

Sir Pellinore nodded his white head. 'That's the situation, and it's a very worrying one indeed; because, short of a public upheaval that would split all three parties from top to bottom and force a General Election—which is the very last thing we want just now—there would be nothing at all that anybody could do about it. This will be the last and most momentous decision that Neville Chamberlain is called upon to take; but even hedged in as he is, I don't think he can be in much doubt as to the nation's wish. It now remains to be seen if he really has the greatness with which I credit him and nominates Churchill, who criticised the Government so long and so bitterly before he was taken into the Cabinet, rather than one of his old friends with whom he has seen eye to eye for so many years. Let's go upstairs now, shall we?'

'Hurrah! The fatted calf!' cried Gregory, as on entering the library his eye was caught by a long-necked, cobwebby bottle which had been set ready on a salver with a corkscrew, duster and glasses beside it.

'What's that?' Sir Pellinore cocked a bushy white eyebrow. 'Oh, you mean the pre-1914 Mentzendorff's Kümmel. Well, we said we'd knock a bottle off when you got home again—and by Jove you've earned it!' Picking up the duster he carefully cleaned the top of the bottle, inserted the wide, spiral corkscrew and with a skilful twist extracted the cork. He had a theory that even the best of modern servants did not understand the handling of fine liquor so he always insisted on uncorking the greatest rarities from his cellar himself. Having carefully wiped the lip of the bottle he poured out two portions and handed one to Gregory.

For a full minute they savoured its wonderful bouquet, then lifting his glass Sir Pellinore said: 'To Hell with Hitler!'

Following his example Gregory added: 'And here's Long Life to Churchill as Britain's Victory Premier and later first Duke of Chartwell.'

They drank and were silent for another minute; then Sir Pellinore exclaimed: 'Gad! What glorious tipple! They don't make stuff like this in Russia these days; but there it is—the whole darned world's gone to pot in this last half-century.'

'By the by,' said Gregory, 'talking of Russians, did you meet my tame Bolshevik General when you were in Brussels?'

'What, Kuporopoff? Yes. He's a grand feller—man after my own heart.'

'Kuporovitch,' Gregory corrected him.

'That's it. Of course, he's a child compared with me but he's old enough to remember Paris as it was in its heyday. After we'd seen Erika home last night he and I had a rattling good yarn over some '96 Yquem that he had discovered in some pub or other, comparing notes about the high spots. Yes; I liked your friend, Kupothebitch—he's definitely one of us, although he is a foreigner.'

As he was speaking Sir Pellinore strode across to his desk. Pulling open one of the drawers he produced an envelope which he handed to Gregory. 'Little something for you, my boy; it'll buy you a bottle or two of good liquor while there's still something fit to drink left in this decadent world.'

Gregory glanced at the contents of the envelope and gave a gasp. It was a cheque for £10,000.

The elderly baronet was grinning with delight, obviously as pleased as a peacock with himself. 'Surprised you, eh? That extra nought was one more than you bargained for—but you've earned it.'

'It's—it's positively princely,' Gregory stammered. 'Even if I'd been working for money I shouldn't have expected a tenth of this.'

'Why not? You've killed more Germans so far in this war

than the entire Brigade of Guards, and I'll bet that their keep has cost the nation more than 10,000 Jimmy-o'-goblins.'

'I can't see the Government setting such a high value on my services, though,' Gregory smiled.

'Oh—the Government; no, they never have understood that if you want real brains and ability you must be prepared to pay for them. That's why there are so many duds among the Civil Servants. But this is my affair. You carried all that was left of my poor boy back out of the Hell of the Somme, Gregory, and I had only the one—that is, as far as I know—so I've always meant to see to it that you were decently provided for. You've been down in my Will for years for quite a tidy sum, but by the time we've finished with this damned house-painter feller none of us may have any money left to leave anyone. That's why I added the extra nought—thought you might just as well have a bit on account for pocket-money, while the going's good.'

'I just don't know how to thank you, sir; but I'm sure you know how I feel.'

'That's all right, my boy; that's all right.' Sir Pellinore gave Gregory's shoulder a little jerky shake and turned away to refill the Kümmel glasses. 'Now, what are your plans? It's no good my asking you to take a holiday while there's a war on; I know you too well for that, and naturally you're anxious to get back to that pretty wench of yours on the other side.'

Gregory nodded. 'You must give me her address and I shall want you to get me a new passport visaed for France, Belgium, Holland, Switzerland and Italy; one that Goering had faked for me is good only for the British Empire and Finland.'

'Right. That shall be done through special channels so that you have it in time to leave on Monday morning's plane. Have you any particular line that you mean to follow up?'

'No. I was hoping that Erika would have started a hare in Holland or Belgium by the time I was able to join her. But I take it that if she'd got on to anything she would have let you know about it.'

'She's been doing good work—damn' good work. That, of course, was really why I went on to Brussels after I'd finished in Paris. Her written reports made such interesting reading that I thought it worth the extra time to get further particulars from her by word of mouth. She and your friend—what's-his-name? —Kuporopoff—have been putting the tabs on Hitler's secret weapon right, left and centre during these past three weeks.

He's got scores of attractive young women in Holland and Belgium, and these little pink rats are playing exactly the same game as they played in Norway.

'I've been able to put such a dossier in front of the more energetic members of the Cabinet that I believe they'd force an issue on it if it weren't for the fact that a Cabinet crisis on other grounds is blowing up already. Unfortunately Chamberlain can't be persuaded that these neutrals are, all against their own will, neutrals no longer and that for their sakes as well as ours we should go into the Low Countries at once instead of leaving it to Hitler to choose his own date and forestall us.'

Gregory frowned. 'Isn't there a risk that if we went into them uninvited they might appeal to the Nazis for assistance? If they did, we'd be in a fine mess, you know; because not only would the quite useful Belgian and Dutch armies be added to our enemies but by such an act of unprovoked aggression we might do ourselves almost irreparable damage with the United States, and that would be playing Hitler's game with a vengeance.'

'Nonsense, boy, nonsense! These little countries are not frightened of *us*; they know perfectly well that even if we had to occupy them temporarily we should give them back their full independence the moment the war ended. What's more, even during our occupation we should treat their populations with every consideration, see to it that they received adequate supplies of food and pay them handsomely for anything like rolling stock and so on that we had to commandeer for our military operations. But if Hitler once goes into these places he'll never march out again of his own free will. They'd be given *Gauleiters* and made permanent vassal states of Germany. He would commandeer everything he wanted, and if he paid for it at all he'd only do so in useless marks. To feed his own people he'll strip their larders as bare as Mother Hubbard's cupboard and, naturally, in the event of a German occupation of the Low Countries we should extend our blockade to them; which means that if the war is not over by next winter five million Dutch and Belgians are going to starve to death. They know that, Gregory, as well as I know that you've got that old scar above your eyebrow.'

'Then why the hell don't they make a secret pact with us to go in on a certain date?' Gregory asked in a puzzled voice. 'They could afford to risk a spot of bother if French and British troops were already landing in their ports.'

'They daren't,' Sir Pellinore boomed. 'They're scared stiff that while the negotiations were going on their intentions would leak out. With our present Government in power six weeks at least would elapse before all our little cooks and bottle-washers had been consulted and completed their preparations. Long before that Hitler would have got wind of it that the Dutch and Belgians were plotting to come in against him. Then he'd have a perfect excuse for invading them first; and you can just imagine the manner in which he would take it out of the poor devils. That's why they positively dare not *ask* us to lift a finger.

'On the other hand there's nothing to prevent us making our preparations in secret, then arriving at their ports one morning and simultaneously wheeling the left end of the main Allied Army over the Franco-Belgian frontier. There would be a formal protest and within six hours they would accept the situation. We should be able to establish ourselves on a line from Amsterdam to Antwerp and along the Albert Canal before Hitler could get there. That would secure to us the ports and the coast-line, which is all that really matters, and within another six hours it's three to one that the Dutch and Belgian armies would be fighting with us.'

Sir Pellinore began to pace up and down as he went on angrily: 'As it is, if we sit tight and wait until Hitler decides to march in on a date of his own choosing, we shall find ourselves in an even worse mess than we are over the Norwegian business. Holland and Belgium will almost certainly resist the aggression and call for our assistance. If we don't go to their help the effect on world opinion will be deplorable and the whole of the coast-line from the Zuider Zee to Dunkirk will fall into Germany's hands within a fortnight. Alternatively, if we *do* go to their assistance you may bet your bottom dollar that there will be no troopships ready to be flung into the Dutch ports to support the Netherlanders and our Army will have to leave the protection of the fortified line that it has been digging all through the winter, to wheel into Belgium at a moment's notice; and I suppose you realise what *that* means?'

'That they'll have to fight in the open,' said Gregory.

'Exactly. Having lost the value of surprise they will no longer be able to pick the most advantageous position for giving battle; they'll have to take the Germans on wherever they find them, which means tank for tank, gun for gun, man for man; and as the Germans have at least four tanks, four guns and four men for every one of ours we shall stand a first-class chance of being scuppered. As long as we remain behind the extension of the Maginot Line the advantage lies with us, but once we move out of it we shall be risking a major defeat and the destruction of our first-line Army, which might set any prospect of victory back for years. In fact, I'll go further. If the Germans annihilated the British in the open fields of Belgium through sheer weight of numbers, the way would be open for them to invade northern France and outflank the Maginot Line proper. Then the organ-grinder might get his courage up sufficiently to launch an invasion of France's south-western provinces. If he did, the French would be caught between two fires and it might put them out of the war altogether.'

'My hat!' exclaimed Gregory. 'That's a pretty picture! But d'you think that Mussolini really means business? He's been banging his little drum a lot again lately.'

Sir Pellinore shook his head. 'No; he's a cautious feller, and clever as a cartload of monkeys. He's exploiting our reverses in Norway now to try to blackmail us into lifting our blockade so that he can get some more old iron through for Hitler; but the one good thing which has come out of this Norwegian show is that it has enabled the Navy to inflict enormous damage on the German fleet. It's been so crippled that while maintaining the same ratio of safety-margin in the North Sea we've been able to despatch many units to strengthen our Mediterranean squadrons. As you'll see in tomorrow morning's papers, we have now massed a positive armada at Alexandria. That's our reply to the ice-cream hawker.

'Another thing; all the odds are in favour of the French down on their Italian frontier; not only are they better fighters than the Italians but the ground is to their advantage. The French have only one ridge of mountains to cross to get down into Italy, and in that ridge are situated the great hydro-electrical power stations which supply the whole industrial area of Turin and Milan. If the French captured or destroyed those generating plants Italy would be out of the war in a week. The Italians have a much harder row to hoe. They have three ridges of mountains to cross before they can get down into France proper, and even when they got there there's nothing vital that they could destroy which might seriously cripple the French war effort. No. I'm still convinced that Mussolini is only bluffing and hasn't the least intention of risking his own neck to help his gangster friend. The only possible case in which he might be tempted to send his waiters over the top would be if the Allies had suffered a major defeat and France was practically down and out. *Then* he might screw his courage up to play the part of the jackal, but not before.'

'I see. Well, let's hope that if Hitler *does* go into the Low Countries the politicians will not overrule the Generals and insist on our going into Belgium. In any case, it's obvious that we're not strong enough to defeat the German Army yet. Our game is to wait and let the Blockade do its work this winter, while we triple the size of our Army and Air Force so that we can launch a decisive offensive in the spring.'

'That's it. But Hitler is not the man to wait for our convenience and he may decide to go into Belgium and Holland any day, so the more information you can get the better. Erika and Kuporovsky will have a dozen interesting lines for you to follow, but to what sort of devilry they'll lead you, God in heaven only knows.'

'There's nothing special that you want me to keep my eyes open for while I'm out there, then?'

'No. Unless . . . By Jove! That's an idea! Have you ever heard of the Black Baroness?'

'Yes,' said Gregory slowly. 'Kuporovitch mentioned her once in Oslo. Paula von Steinmetz received her instructions to move to Holland from someone who was referred to as "the Black Baroness", but he couldn't learn anything about her; and Gussy Langdon-Forbes mentioned the Black Baroness to me on one occasion when he was talking about German Fifth Column activities; but a bomb burst just at that moment and I forgot afterwards to ask him who she was.'

Sir Pellinore filled up the Kümmel glasses. 'Her real name is *La Baronne* de Porte, and don't imagine that she's a coloured woman. She's French, as white as we are, and she used to be very beautiful; but as she is over fifty now she's a bit part-worn. She is a great friend of that traitor Bonnet, and she wields enormous influence with quite a number of people whose decisions may affect the lives of untold millions.'

'Queer,' muttered Gregory. 'I've never even heard of her.'

'That's hardly surprising, as she is one of those *really* clever women who prefer wielding great power in secret to receiving the public acclaim of the mob, and later, perhaps, hearing the

167

same mob howling for their blood. I met her once and she has a dead-white face with jet-black eyes and hair. It may be from her eyes and hair that she gets her nickname; but I've an idea that it was given to her because she always works under cover in the same way as the old "Black Hand" which invariably struck in secret.

'Her husband, the Baron, was a millionaire financier, and you know how greatly the ruling caste in France has felt itself to be threatened by Communism in recent years. When *Madame la Baronne* became interested in politics her very able brain naturally sought some antidote and, not unnaturally, it turned to Fascism. She made many friends in high places in Italy, and later she was received at Berchtesgaden by the *Fuehrer*. Exactly what those two plotted together nobody knows, but it's a very curious thing that during the last few years whenever a woman has brought about the downfall of a European statesman with pro-Ally leanings the name of the Black Baroness has cropped up vaguely somewhere in the background of the story.'

'You think, then, that she may be the brains behind Hitler's secret weapon?'

'I don't know. I'm only certain of one thing—that they entered into some devil's pact. We have ample evidence that the *Baronne* would prefer to see a Hitler-dominated France in which she and her friends survived than a Communist France in which they would automatically go under. I suggest, therefore, that she may be Hitler's great whore mistress. She knows so many important figures on the European scene, and it would be easy for a woman of her brain to find out what their weaknesses are and the type of girl that they would be likely to fall for. If I'm right, she would then send very detailed instructions to Berlin, and the Gestapo would go through their whole list of beautiful harpies. When they had selected the one they considered most suitable the *Baronne* would take the girl under her wing for a time and so arrange matters that ample opportunity was given to her to ensnare the intended victim.'

'It sounds feasible,' Gregory agreed. 'Anyhow, I'll certainly keep a look-out for her.'

Far into the early morning hours these two cronies, so far apart in age yet so near in outlook and in spirit, discussed many matters of interest with unflagging enthusiasm. The bottle of old Kümmel was empty and two beakers of champagne had followed it, when at last Gregory stood up to go. As he thanked his host he said: 'If I can manage to get on the track of the Black Baroness, what d'you wish me to do about it?'

Sir Pellinore shrugged. 'Need I go into details? Even if she does not control Hitler's secret weapon that woman is poison, Gregory. I know for a positive fact that she has been responsible for at least two suicides, and that while she is high in the councils of our Allies she is in reality hand in glove with the enemy. If she could be put out of action permanently it would be as great a victory as the destruction of a German Army Corps.'

Gregory did not speak for a minute; then he said: 'Are you suggesting that I should murder her?'

The elderly baronet's merry blue eyes suddenly went very cold and hard, as he replied quietly: 'We are at war. The age of chivalry, alas, is past. Since our leaders still fail to realise what Britain is up against it lies with people like you and me to save our country, however repulsive to our personal feelings the methods may be which we are forced to employ. The only instructions that I can give you are those which have made England great—whatever the age, whatever the weapons—"seek out and destroy the enemy".'

13

The Enemy is Found

Erika had never looked more lovely. Her cheeks were flushed, her eyes were shining. For some reason best known to herself she had put on full evening-dress although she was dining alone in the charming apartment that she had taken in Brussels. As she came into the dining-room her new butler drew back her chair with the quiet assurance of a perfectly-trained servant and with a deft movement brought the little handwritten menu-slate a few inches nearer to her, as he said in French:

'I was not aware that *Madame* had given her cook permission to go out this evening and that she would have to dine off cold dishes in consequence. If *Madame* would prefer something hot, I have the good fortune to be a passable cook so I could manage some *Oeufs poché Béndictine* or an *Omelette pointes d'asperges* with the eggs that are in the kitchen.'

'No, thank you, Pierre; *Consomm éen gelée saumon froid*

and *fraises des bois* will do very well,' Erika replied quietly, but her hand trembled as he placed the iced soup in front of her with a little bow and left the room. Even the cold soup—easiest of all dishes to master for anyone whose intense excitement has robbed them of their appetite—proved difficult for her to swallow, and she was hardly half-way through it when the perfect man-servant appeared again noiselessly beside her.

'Jacqueline is about to leave now, and she wishes to know if *Madame* has any further orders for her before she goes,' he said deferentially.

'N-no. There's nothing—thank you.' Erika could hardly get the words out; she leaned back and closed her eyes as the man smoothly removed her soup plate and disappeared again.

A moment later as she heard the click of the front door she sprang up from her chair. At the same second the butler returned, and next instant she had flung herself into his arms.

'Gregory—darling!' She was half laughing, half crying. 'It was absolute *torture* to have you here all the afternoon yet not be able to say a single word to you because of these silly servants.'

'My angel!' Gregory smiled, when he had kissed her until they were both breathless. 'Today I've learnt what poor St. Anthony must have felt when he was tempted in the desert. To be in the same room with you and denied the joy of even touching your hand!'

'Must we keep up this farce?'

He nodded. 'I'm afraid so, for the time being at all events. If I were seen with you in public by any one of a hundred people who are in Brussels now the whole game would be up; but I simply couldn't bear to be in the same city and have to remain content with talking to you on the telephone. That's why I sent you a note round at midday to hire me as your man-servant. Anyhow, we'll be under the same roof—and that's a lot.'

'But, darling, we shall simply never be alone together. It was sheer luck that it happened to be my cook's evening off tonight, and I had a frightful job trying to think up a plausible excuse to get my maid out of the flat for a few hours. They're certain to think there's something fishy going on if I often send them out together in the evening.'

'There are the nights, angel,' Gregory whispered with a mischievous grin.

'Yes, my sweet—yes. I shall positively live for them. What

fun it will be to lie in bed waiting for you to tiptoe down the corridor after a long, long day of make-believe that you are only my servant.'

'I am your servant—for all eternity,' he murmured, and caught her to him again in another swift embrace.

'There!' gasped Erika, when at last she drew away from him. 'That really is enough for—for about five minutes. Our salmon will be getting cold.'

'It's cold already, sweetheart,' he laughed.

'Why, so it is; but I've been in such a state all day that I haven't been able to take in a single thing except that you're safe and with me once more. Come on; let's sit down and eat it.'

He did not bother to fetch another plate; they shared the dish with the gaiety of two naughty children who had broken into a larger; which brought back memories of the meals that they had had together when she had hidden him for a day and a night in her bedroom in Munich.

As they ate they talked, volubly, nineteen to the dozen; firing questions at each other, gabbling replies, incredibly eager to know how every moment of each other's time had been spent since they had parted.

Gregory learnt to his great satisfaction that, as far as she knew, through the assumption of the name Yonnie Rostedal, which was on the Norwegian passport that Paula had secured for her, she had so far succeeded in preventing any members of the German Embassy learning that she was in Brussels. Paula and two or three other German girls who had known her in Norway and travelled to the Low Countries at the same time as herself all believed that she had assumed her Norwegian *nom de guerre* to avoid the unwelcome attentions of a wealthy young Dutchman; about whom she had put out the story that he was so madly in love with her that when she had been in Holland the year before he had threatened to kill her and himself if she would not take pity on him. This also provided an excellent excuse for her to refuse invitations to parties and to go out very little in public, as they naturally assumed that she was afraid that she might run into this most undesirable lover. Such a life of semi-concealment naturally greatly restricted her personal opportunities for gathering information, but that was where Kuporovitch came in, and they formed an excellent partnership.

The ex-General, having been cooped up in Russia for twenty-six years, knew nobody in European society. Even the names of high officers, diplomats, leaders of fashion and all except the leading statesmen were totally unknown to him, so he had no background of knowledge from which to draw inferences when he heard them mentioned; but as Paula's lover he had become *persona grata* with the most important section of the German Fifth Column which was working in Holland and Belgium, and so constantly heard references made to key personalities in a dozen countries.

Fortunately he possessed an excellent memory, so he was able to repeat parrot-wise to Erika most of the conversations he had heard: and as she had moved for so long in international society she was able, in the great majority of cases, to get the full import of what had been said; upon which she wrote out her reports for Sir Pellinore.

For a few days after their arrival in Holland they had stayed at the Brack's Doelen Hotel in Amsterdam, but then Paula had received instructions to move to Brussels, and the other two had accompanied her. Paula had taken a furnished apartment on the *Boulevard du Regent,* the 'Park Lane' of Brussels, and Erika had taken another near by in the *Rue Montoyer,* which lies between the *Parc Leopold* and the Royal Palace; while Kuporovitch had gone to the Hotel Astoria.

The Belgian Fascist leader, Degrelle, had called on Paula immediately she was settled in and arranged for her to meet the Comte de Werbomont, a member of King Leopold's household who had very soon fallen for her youthful, opulent charms. The Count, being a married man, was able to visit her only in secret, and as most of his time was occupied in attendance upon the King he knew nothing about Kuporovitch, who, since he had to share Paula with somebody, found the arrangement highly satisfactory. Erika, meanwhile, was supposed to be engaged on some extremely tricky piece of work for the Gestapo which was so secret that she could not tell even Paula about it; all of which worked in admirably with the fact that she very rarely went out.

As Erika had reported personally to Sir Pellinore three nights previously there was no necessity for her to go into great detail with Gregory about the German Fifth Column activities, but she gave him a general layout of the situation and said that she was convinced that Brussels was the centre of the whole network of the German espionage system in the two threatened countries. Gregory waited patiently until she had finished, then he asked her if she had ever heard of the Black Baroness.

'*Die Schwartze Baronin,*' Erika said thoughtfully. 'Yes. Mention of her has occurred now and again but never in connection with anything of sufficient importance to be worth putting in any of my reports.'

'What sort of things?' Gregory asked.

'Oh, just social gossip. She was staying with Degrelle, I think, about the time we got here and I believe poor Susie von Ertz dined with her one night.'

'Why d'you say "*poor* Susie"? I thought her rather an attractive, jolly girl when we met her in Oslo. Has anything gone wrong with her?'

'Why, yes. I told Sir Pellinore; but of course you wouldn't know. Susie was given a Dutch aeroplane designer to look after, but they slipped up somewhere, and his wife found out. The poor man was so upset that he poisoned himself. Unfortunately for Susie, he chose her bedroom to take his life in; so, of course, the police were called in, and they've been trying to pin a charge of murder on her.'

Gregory made a grimace. 'Poor little devil. The police are probably right, though.'

'What makes you think that, darling?'

'Well, presumably she's been under arrest since the tragedy occurred, so she must have dined with the Black Baroness beforehand. From what old Pellinore tells me, the Baroness has been hovering vaguely in the background of so many tragic "accidents" that I should think it's quite on the cards that she blackmailed Susie into giving her aeroplane designer the poison with the promise that they would help her to fake things to look like suicide afterwards.'

'Who is this Black Baroness woman, Gregory? Now I come to think of it I asked Susie, after she told me that she'd dined with her, how anyone had come by such a curious nickname. Susie just said that it was because she's such a striking-looking woman with hair and eyes that are as black as pitch; but the word seems to have a much more sinister implication than that.'

'She's a Frenchwoman and her real name is the Baronne de Porte.'

The Baronne de Porte!' Erika exclaimed. 'But, *of course*, I know quite a lot about her.'

'Then you're better informed than I was up to three nights ago, my sweet.'

'Darling, when I was selling armaments with Hugo Falken-stein it was my business to find out about such people. Her husband, the Baron, was a great industrialist and she married when she was quite young, but left him before she was twenty-four. She then went in for high finance, on her own account, and she has the Midas touch, so that in a few years she had amassed a great fortune; but that's years and years ago. When making big money began to pall on her she started to take an interest in politics; perhaps because she was already an intimate friend of Paul Reynaud's.'

'Reynaud's!' Gregory repeated. 'But, good God, he's the new Premier of France.'

Erika shrugged. 'Oh, her affair with him started when he was only a promising lawyer, way back in 1916. It must have burnt itself out long ago.'

'Thank God for that.'

'Later she travelled a lot,' Erika went on, 'and she often used to stay in Rome and Berlin. In both she made many friends and there is no doubt that she acquired pro-Fascist leanings. Just after Munich she became very intimate with Baudoin, the President of the *Banque d'Indo-Chine,* and he is a person who wields enormous influence behind the scenes. Both of them, quite naturally, are rabid anti-Communists, but I've always believed that the Baronne was a patriotic Frenchwoman. It's a grim thought that anyone like that should actually have gone to the length of tying up with the Nazis and be working for them now that her country is at war with Germany.'

'Well, she is; and what you've just told me about Susie, together with the fact that the Baronne was staying with Degrelle, and that it was Degrelle who arranged for Paula to meet the Comte de Werbomont, seems to confirm Pellinore's belief that it's she who picks the most suitable girls for the chaps the Nazis want to get into their toils, and makes the neces-sary social arrangements so that each selected lovely can be thrown in the chappie's path quite naturally. I've got to get on to this Baroness woman. D'you know if she's still in Brussels?'

Erika shook her golden head. 'No; I haven't the least idea, but we'll talk to Stefan about it tomorrow and see if he can find out anything.'

'That's it,' Gregory agreed. 'You had better arrange for him to meet me somewhere for a quiet chat in the afternoon. One of the parks would probably be the best place. Then go out yourself so as to leave me free to slip away from my duties for an hour.'

'I'll telephone Stefan in the morning and tell him to meet me by the Tritton Fountain in the *Parc Leopold* at three o'clock; then you can turn up in my place.'

'Good. I heard that he got on splendidly with old Sir Pellinore.'

'Who could fail to do so?' Erika laughed. 'What an amazing person he is! Nowhere else in the world but England could have produced such a character. His education is appalling. He shouts at foreigners in English and takes it for granted that they will understand him. To hear him talk one would think that he knew nothing about anything at all except the idiosyncrasies of women, sport, food and drink; yet he has a flair for going straight to the root of any question and underneath it all such a shrewd brain that if he were pitted against Ribbentrop, Litvinov and Laval together I believe he'd have all three of them tied in knots. I thought him charming and I fell for him completely.'

Gregory grinned and stood up. 'I can see that it was quite time for me to reappear on your horizon. And now, d'you know what I'm going to do to you? I'll give you three guesses.'

With a mocking smile she put her arms round his neck. "How could I *possibly* guess, my sweet? But something tells me that I was a very rash woman to remain alone in my flat for the evening with such an attractive, forward butler.'

'You've guessed it in one, angel,' he laughed, and swinging her off her feet he carried her from the room.

At three o'clock the following afternoon Gregory was seated on the rim of the fountain in the *Parc Leopold,* reading an early edition of the evening paper. He noted that the British withdrawals in Norway were having a deplorable effect on the world press and that the little countries were, in consequence, getting into a worse state of jitters than ever through the fear that Germany would next attack one or other of them.

The Swedes had been in a state of unofficial mobilisation ever since the Germans had gone into Norway, nearly a month before, but they were still keeping up as bold a front as possible and shooting down any German planes that flew over their territory. Carol of Rumania was singing a very small song again and promising Hitler further commercial advantages to the detriment of the Allies. Hungary, sandwiched between Italy and Germany, had now given up all attempt at playing one off against the other and was pretty obviously doing exactly as she was told by Berlin; while the Dutch and Belgians were calling up more and more classes of conscripts and now frantically building road barriers as a precaution against a sudden invasion. Yet a strong feeling still seemed to run through the people of both countries that if only they kept their heads and refrained from giving offence to Hitler he might yet spare them, as being more useful to him while going concerns from which he could draw considerable quantities of foodstuffs and other supplies than as conquered areas of devastated territory.

By the time Gregory had scanned the most important news items Kuporovitch put in an appearance. The Russian looked very well and prosperous, having, apparently, equipped himself with a new wardrobe since his arrival in Brussels.

'Hullo!' exclaimed Gregory. 'You *are* looking a swell!'

Kuporovitch beamed. 'You also. We might be different people from the two men who met in Kandalaksha. I like Brussels; it is much more pleasant for me than Oslo, because everybody here speaks French; it might almost be Paris—but not quite. But it is very expensive.'

'Naturally,' smiled Gregory, 'if you get your clothes at the best tailors and stay at the Astoria.'

The Russian shrugged eloquently. 'What would you? I had meant to live quietly on my savings, but everything here is a temptation to me. How can I resist having of the best and spending the money necessary to mix with elegant people when for a quarter of a century I have lived in the so-called workers' paradise, where there is not even anyone interesting to talk to? I must not go on in this way, though, otherwise in a year or so I shall have spent all my money and have to take some filthy job. Being a General does not fit one for becoming a commercial traveller or a pen-pusher in an office.'

'You needn't worry, Stefan; you have a job already. I told you that when I got back to England I would somehow manage to refund any expenses to which you had been put on Erika's account, but I intend to make good your own expenses as well and give you a fat cheque for the excellent work you've put in; so you can consider your savings as still intact and that you'll have money in hand into the bargain.'

176

'*Sacré Nom!* That is good news indeed; because this job is very different from the degrading occupations that I have been visualising for myself—and, let me tell you, the little Paula improves immensely upon acquaintance. She was born with a great aptitude for loving, but she is a far more accomplished *amoureuse* now that I have had a little time to train her. But tell me about yourself.'

For some twenty minutes Gregory gave a graphic outline of his doings, after which he asked what Kuporovitch knew of Madame de Porte, alias the Black Baroness.

The Russian had never heard of Madame de Porte, but he said that mentions of the Black Baroness had been made by Paula's friends from time to time. He recalled that when Paula had broken the news to him that she was leaving Norway she had said: 'I understand that the Black Baroness has a new job for me in Holland,' and a Belgian politician, who had recently returned from a visit to France, had stated quite casually that after a dinner-party given by a French Cabinet Minister he had had a most interesting conversation on the political situation with the Black Baroness; but Kuporovitch could not recall definitely any other occasion upon which her name had cropped up. Without any grounds to justify the idea he had assumed that the woman referred to had acquired her nickname because she was a half-caste or Creole from one of the French African colonies or Martinique.

Gregory disabused him about that and asked him to tackle Paula on the subject as he wished to find out the Baroness's present whereabouts with the minimum possible delay.

Afterwards they talked for a little about Paula's set and it transpired that Kuporovitch was having the time of his life. In spite of war conditions which had to some extent affected the capital of neutral Belgium it was far gayer than Oslo had been, and the vortex of this strange, unnatural gaiety while the outer world stood grimly to its arms was Hitler's 'Secret Weapon'. There were an even greater number of German, Austrian and Hungarian women, all picked for their looks and with ample funds at their disposal, who had big apartments in which night after night they gave extravagant private parties for their co-workers and the Belgians of their acquaintance. In addition to looking after her own special lover of the moment it was part of each girl's job to get to know as many Belgians of good standing as possible and, since all the girls were of good birth and living outwardly respectable lives, they were permeating all the higher stratas of Brussels society, which enabled them to collect an immense amount of information for the Gestapo.

After an hour with Kuporovitch, Gregory went back to Erika's flat to take up his duties as butler, and when the two maids were sound asleep that night he discussed with her plans for the following day.

They considered it would be unwise for them to risk being seen together about the city, so Gregory suggested that they should take a picnic lunch and eat it in the Park of Laeken, which is outside the capital and is to Brussels what Kew Gardens is to London; so on the following morning she told her maids that she would be out for the day and left the flat about eleven o'clock.

Gregory was in the pantry cleaning silver. Having given her a quarter of an hour's start to buy their lunch at a delicatessen store he removed his baize apron and took down his black coat from its hook on the door.

The maid, Jacqueline, looked at him in surprise and remarked: 'Where are you going at this time of day, *Monsieur* Pierre?'

'Somewhere where unfortunately I cannot take a pretty girl like you, *Mademoiselle* Jacqueline,' he replied mysteriously, 'and I shall not be back until about six o'clock this evening.'

She preened herself at the compliment, but persisted: '*Madame* would not be pleased if she knew that you were neglecting your work during her absence to go out on your own affairs—and for the whole day too!'

'But she will *not* know,' he smiled mischievously, 'because you, my pretty one, are not going to tell her and you are going to see to it for me that Cook does not tell her either.'

'You take a great deal for granted, *Monsieur* Pierre.'

'No. I am a psychologist and I can tell from your features that you are as kind-hearted as you are good-looking.'

She bridled again. '*Monsieur* Pierre, you are a flatterer! But what about your work? There'll be a fine row if the dining-room's not put ship-shape and the silver's still uncleaned when *Madame* gets back.'

'Yes. I might get the sack; and that would be most unfortunate, because I like it here. I am an artist, you see, and it makes a world of difference to me if I work in a place with a girl like yourself who has good taste in hats.'

'What do *you* know about *that*, *Monsieur* Pierre?'

'I saw you come in the night before last, *Mademoiselle* Jacqueline, and I thought that little black affair you were wearing quite ravishing. It occurred to me this morning that you might like to buy yourself another.'

'And why? Hats cannot be bought every day on a lady's-maid's wage, *Monsieur* Pierre, and, as a matter of fact, it was *Madame* who gave me the black one that I was wearing on Monday.'

'How wise of *Madame*; I am sure that it suits you infinitely better than it suited her,' lied Gregory.

'Now you are being foolish,' replied Jacqueline loyally. 'As well as being a very kind lady, *Madame* is most beautiful—in fact, I do not think that there is anyone so beautiful in all Brussels.'

'There!' exclaimed Gregory. 'What a tribute for one woman to pay another! I knew from the shape of your little nose, which turns up so attractively, that you were a girl with the most generous instincts. But this hat we were speaking of—a new one of your own choice. I had a little legacy not long ago from my poor old uncle, who was valet to a French marquis, so I am in funds.' He produced a hundred-franc note and toyed with it a moment. 'I was wondering if I could persuade you to do my silver for me and tidy the dining-room and, as a very small return, buy yourself that little hat out of this?'

Jacqueline was in fact a generous girl, and as he had got on the right side of her she would quite willingly have done his work for him on this occasion, but Gregory knew that there might be others and that unless he was prepared to make love to her—which he was not—she certainly would not be willing to make a habit of doing his jobs while he went out, presumably to amuse himself elsewhere. That was why he had invented the legacy, as ordinarily she would probably not have liked to take money from another servant; but believing that he had just come in for a nice little sum she would feel that if he chose to spend it on getting his work done for him by somebody else, that was his affair.

With a shrug and a smile she took the proffered note. 'All right; run along, then, and I'll put things right with Cook for you. Are you sure, though, that you can spare this money? It seems a lot for so small a service.'

Gregory nodded. 'Yes; I could really have afforded a good holiday, but I prefer to keep in work providing that I can arrange matters so that I have a little time to attend to my own affairs.'

She laughed. 'I do not mind work, and it is always nice to have the opportunity of earning a little extra money.'

'*Bien. Au revoir, Mademoiselle Jacqueline.*' Bunching the finger-tips of his right hand he kissed them to her while winking his left eye. It was a curiously un-English gesture but absolutely in keeping with the part that he was playing and, fully satisfied that he had got the maid just where he wanted her, he went out to keep his appointment with his mistress.

On Sunday, May 5th, his last day in London, the sun had suddenly appeared in all its glory to revivify a Europe which had suffered from the severest winter within living memory and now, three days later, it was still shining; so it really seemed that summer had come. For the last two days it had been as warm as June and the women of the Belgian capital were already bringing out their light summer frocks, which lent an air of gaiety to the city that was extraordinarily refreshing to Gregory after his many months in Finland and Norway. Erika had dressed very simply for the occasion in order that her clothes should not contrast too strongly with the neat but ready-made black jacket and pin-striped trousers which Gregory had bought for himself on the morning that he had come to her as her manservant.

Out at Laeken they admired the gorgeous Chinese pavilion and the Japanese pagoda made of carved woodwork specially brought from Japan. They were not allowed inside the Royal Palace but entry was permitted to the great conservatories with their fine array of tropical plants and flowers. The azaleas were in blossom and smelt quite heavenly. Afterwards, on a grassy bank in the great park, they ate the things that Erika had provided for their picnic lunch, while the children played happily in the near distance. Then all through the long hours of the sunny afternoon they lay there side by side, quite oblivious of anything except each other, as is the habit of lovers the world over.

It was a new experience for the *Frau Gräfin von Osterberg,* spoilt darling of the German aristocracy, to be kissed and lie with her head pillowed on the chest of a man in a public park; but after her first shocked protests 'that people were looking

180

and that that sort of thing positively was not done' she had to admit that it *was* done by the great majority of young women even in the most civilised countries and—as Gregory laughingly told her—if she chose to come out with her butler she must accept the canons as to what was and was not done in a butler's normal sphere of life. After that she threw her hat on the grass and settled down to enjoy herself, thinking what a marvellous man Gregory was at finding good reasons for everything he wanted to do, and how clever it had been of him to provide a totally new setting for their love-making instead of allowing them to waste this precious afternoon in sitting decorously looking at each other.

By seven o'clock they were back in Brussels, separating before they reached the flat so that Gregory could go in first and resume his duties before she arrived; and although they were unable to speak together privately during the evening it passed for both of them with the happy feeling of two children who had played truant from school for the day and managed to get away with it.

On the following morning, May the 9th, a note arrived by hand from Kuporovitch to Erika. In it he said that Paula had made various tactful inquiries the previous day and informed him, when he had seen her at night, that the Black Baroness was staying under the name of Madame de Swarle, at the Hotel Weimar in Rotterdam.

When Erika had passed the note to Gregory he whispered to her to go out and ring him up, then to come back to the flat about an hour later as though she had been doing some local shopping. When she rang up he answered the telephone and for Jacqueline's benefit put on an act as though he had just heard the most disconcerting news. He told her that his old aunt was dying and that he must get leave from *Madame* at once to go to her as there might be another nice little legacy involved in the matter, which, could he have but known it, gave added impetus to an idea that had entered *Mademoiselle* Jacqueline's pretty little head the day before.

It was obvious that he liked her and not only was he a very attractive man but he had money of his own with which he was very generous; therefore it might not be at all a bad thing if she tactfully inspired him with the idea of proposing marriage. She knew that if she once started an affair she would be treading on dangerous ground, because it was quite certain that such a good-looking fellow had had plenty of affairs with other women, so he would almost certainly try to seduce her. She was well aware that men who seduce girls don't usually marry them afterwards; but she felt that if only she could manage to keep her head everything would be all right; which was unfortunate because in point of fact she had no reason at all to worry herself one way or the other.

Quite unaware of the agitation he had aroused in the breast of his pretty co-worker, Gregory met Erika in the doorway when she returned and, with voluble protestations as to his desolation at inconveniencing *Madame,* begged to leave to rush off to the bedside of his dying aunt.

The leave was duly granted and a quarter of an hour later, carrying a small suit-case which contained all his possessions in the character of butler, he left the flat. By a curious coincidence Erika went out again a few minutes later and, as she expected, found him waiting for her a few hundred yards down the street. Together they drove to the Hotel Métropole where Gregory had parked his own baggage on his arrival in Brussels, under his German pseudonym of Colonel-Baron von Lutz. Taking a room under the same name he went upstairs so that he could change into one of his own tailored suits, while she spent five minutes sitting in the lounge, then took the lift up to join him.

'What d'you intend to do, darling?' Erika asked, trying to keep out of her voice the new anxiety she had felt.

He looked unusually thoughtful as he replied: 'To tell you the truth, my sweet, I haven't the faintest idea. It's up to me to put the Black Baroness out of action, somehow.'

'Do you mean *murder*?' Erika said softly.

'An ugly word to apply to the execution of a traitor.'

'I shouldn't have used it. Killing is not murder, in any case, when two countries are at war; and that is not altered in the least by the fact that you and I don't wear uniforms and that our war lies behind the battle-front. Of course you must kill her, Gregory, if there is no other way; and you must have no more scruple about it than you would have had about shooting down that Nazi airman who machine-gunned your ambulance in Norway.'

'You're right, angel—absolutely right. All the same, I must confess that the idea of killing anyone in cold blood makes me feel horribly squeamish and my allotted enemy on this occasion

182

being a woman makes it ten times more repulsive to me.'

Erika stood there, her face very white and her blue eyes wide. 'Why? You're not an ordinary man, Gregory; you're far too good a psychologist still to believe the childish myth that women are really God's little angels and on an altogether higher spiritual level than men. You know as well as I do that the two sexes don't really differ except in outward form. Women have the same appetites as men, the same instinct of self-preservation; they can be as courageous and generous or as cowardly and mean; and since the female of the species has been theoretically the under-dog until very recent times, she has had to get what she wants by cunning and trickery, so her instincts for lying and every form of deception are much more highly developed than those of the male. What is more, All she lacks in strength she makes up for in cruelty, so when one comes down to stark reality there are no grounds whatsoever for refraining from killing an evil woman with as little scruple as one would kill an evil man, when either is one's enemy in war-time. Grauber and his friends made up their minds about that long ago; and I don't blame them. I don't think that I'm a really evil woman, but you know quite well that they would kill me without the slightest hesitation if they could catch me.'

Gregory sighed. 'Your reasoning is unanswerable, but we have no proof of any kind that she has actually instigated murder, and I'm hoping that I may not have to go to extreme measures. Perhaps, if my luck is in, I'll be able to trap her some-how and get her locked up in a fortress for the duration of the war.'

It was agreed that Erika should remain in Brussels unless she heard from Gregory that he wished her to leave and that in any case he would rejoin her as soon as possible. After a lingering farewell they tore themselves away from each other and Gregory took a taxi to the station. He was in Rotterdam by four o'clock.

Before leaving the station he went to a telephone kiosk and rang up the desk at the Weimar Hotel. Speaking in a rather high-pitched voice he said that he was an official of the French Embassy and that a parcel had arrived which should be posted to Madame de Swarle, and would they please give him her room number so that he could address the package fully.

The desk clerk replied that Madame was occupying Number

141, a suite on the first floor; upon which Gregory thanked him and hung up.

He then drove to the hotel and, going up to the desk, said that he wished to book either a suite or a comfortable room; but the desk clerk found him a rather pernickety customer. He didn't want a room facing on to the street, because of the noise from the traffic; he didn't want a room that was too high up because Hitler might let loose his *Blitzkrieg* at any time and the higher up one was the more danger from bombs. On the other hand, he didn't want a room down on the first floor because that consisted almost entirely of luxury suites, which were too expensive. Having rejected half a dozen suggestions with the plan of the hotel before him he finally settled on Number 242, which was the nearest he could get to being immediately above the Baroness.

When a page had shown him to his room he took a quick look out of the window, then went to bed, on his old theory that there was nothing like getting all the sleep that one could during the daytime if there was any likelihood at all that one might not get any the following night.

At a quarter to eleven he awoke, bathed, shaved and dressed; then, going down to the restaurant, where dancing was in progress, he ordered himself a substantial supper and a bottle of champagne.

By two o'clock in the morning he was back upstairs in his bedroom leaning out of the window, further to investigate the possibilities of the fire-escapes, of which he had already made a cursory examination on his arrival. There was no fire-ladder that could be reached from the window out of which he was looking, but one ran down the wall alongside the window of his private bathroom next door; and as in hotels bathrooms are nearly always built in tiers, to facilitate hot water and drainage systems, it seemed reasonable to suppose that the bathroom of the Baroness's suite lay below his bathroom.

Having examined his gun to make certain that the mechanism was working smoothly he put a small black whalebone truncheon into his breast-pocket, tied a silk handkerchief over the lower part of his face and pulled a soft hat well down over his eyes. He then put out the lights, went into the bathroom, swung himself out on to the fire-ladder and, treading softly but firmly, descended to the level of the window below.

It was in darkness but a chink of light came from between

184

the curtains of the window to his right, which he assumed to be the Baroness's bedroom. She was still up, apparently. He had hoped that by waiting until nearly half-past two in the morning he would catch her in bed and asleep; but he had the facility of moving with almost cat-like stealth when he wished, and it did not matter materially whether he caught her awake or asleep, providing that she was alone and that he was able to take her by surprise; so he decided to go forward.

The bathroom window was about a quarter open so he eased it down to its full extent and, wriggling in over its top, lowered himself gently to the floor. The room was not in total darkness as, although there was no moon, Rotterdam was not yet blacked out and some light was given by uncurtained windows on the other side of the big square well upon which the rooms faced. He could just make out the line of the bath, the wash-basin and the shelves; but as he turned towards the door he moved with great caution, since a bathroom with its bottles and glasses is a tricky place for an uninvited visitor at night-time when with his elbow he might so easily brush something which would crash to the floor and give away his presence.

Reaching the door he turned the handle right back and pressing the door open a fraction stood there with his ear to the crack, listening intently. He could hear faint sounds of movement but no voices, so it seemed that the Baroness was alone. Opening the door further he slipped out into the passage and softly drew it to behind him. There was a light in the corridor and what he presumed to be the bedroom door was open about a foot. He could hear the movements more plainly now. After another pause of a full minute he tiptoed forward. As he came level with the partially-open door he drew his gun; then giving the door a sudden shove he flung it wide open.

The movement was so swift that the woman who was in the room had not a second to grab any weapon she might have had, or even open her mouth to shout, before she found herself covered from the wide-open doorway.

The room was a bedroom with three entrances; the doorway in which he stood and two other doors, one on his right which led to the bathroom and was shut and a second, just ajar, which evidently led to the sitting-room. A big wardrobe and most of the drawers in the room were open, and they were all empty. Two suitcases stood near the bed and the woman was bending over a white rawhide dressing-case; he had caught her just as she was completing her packing. The fact that she had packed for herself indicated that she had no maid with her, so evidently her visit to Rotterdam under the *nom-de-plume* of Madame de Swarle was highly secret.

One glance was enough to satisfy Gregory that Madame de Swarle was unquestionably the Baroness. Her dead-black hair was quite straight and cut short, with a fringe making a line across her forehead so that her pale face stood out startlingly from it; and from beneath a pair of level eyebrows her jet-black eyes stared at him with an inscrutable expression. She was small and slim, and to the casual glance she certainly did not appear to be the fifty years that Sir Pellinore had given her. Her figure was perfectly preserved and apart from a faint network of wrinkles at the outer corners of her eyes her face looked like that of a woman of thirty. The only splash of colour was her mouth, which was heavily lipsticked a vivid scarlet. Gregory understood at once why she had such power over men. She had a subtle and peculiar sexual attraction which seemed to exude from the poise of her whole figure and her red mouth. He could not have defined it, but there was something about her—warm, soft, pulsating.

She stared at him across her open dressing-case but she was perfectly self-possessed. There was no trace of fear in her dark eyes at the sight of this masked unknown man who threatened her with a gun. She remained absolutely still and did not even open her red-lipped mouth to ask him what he wanted, but waited quietly for him to speak first.

He wondered for a second where she could be off to at this time of night, but that did not concern him for the moment. Stepping into the room and closing the door behind him he said in a gruff, low voice:

'*Madame* is said to have some very nice jewels. I want them. Take off your rings and those pearls, put them in that dressing-case and bring it over here to me.' He knew that any papers that she might have would be in the dressing-case, and it was these that he was after; but he wanted her to believe him to be an ordinary hotel thief.

'And if I refuse?' she said in a low, musical voice.

'Then, *Madame,* you must take the consequences. I want those jewels and I mean to have them. Also, I do not intend to risk a long term of imprisonment by chancing your giving an alarm while I tie you up and gag you. There is a silencer on this automatic. If you refuse to do as I tell you I shall have to shoot you.'

She raised her voice and cried with sudden defiance: 'I *do* refuse!'

Gregory gave her full marks for courage although he felt certain she could not realise how very near death she was at that second. She was gambling upon the fact that few jewel thieves will deliberately commit murder. They may shoot if they are surprised during a theft, in order to escape capture, but not once in a thousand times will they kill purely to secure their loot when they are the masters of a situation.

But he was not a jewel thief and it was his duty to put this dangerous woman out of business just as much as it is a sentry's duty to fire upon an enemy whom he may see creeping towards him across no-man's-land. It was a perfect opportunity to settle the matter once and for all. The silencer on his gun would prevent the shot being heard. Within two minutes he could be back in his bedroom. In ten, abandoning his suitcase and its contents which had no marks by which he could be identified, he could be out of the hotel; and he could take her jewels to provide a motive for the murder. Travel presented no difficulties in these countries which were still at peace and long before her body was discovered he would be over the Belgian frontier. Certain interested parties might guess that the Baroness had not been killed purely for the sake of her jewellery, but they had good reasons for keeping their mouths shut. When he reappeared in Brussels as Erika's butler there would be nothing whatever to connect him with the crime. He was very tempted to squeeze the trigger of his automatic.

Yet somehow he could not do it. If she had attempted to reach the bell or to grab any weapon that she might have had in her open dressing-case she would have been a dead woman; but she did nothing of the kind; she just stood there staring at him, and the only expression which he could fathom in her eyes was a look of interested curiosity as to whether he meant to shoot or not.

'All right,' he said. 'I'm not shooting for the moment; but I will if you move your lips by as much as a millimetre. Stand back from that case and put your hands up!'

She did as he had ordered and, stepping forward, he slammed down the lid of the case, pressed home the locks and picked it up.

Her lips twitched into a sudden smile. 'It is not, then, my rings and my pearls that you are after?'

For a second he debated whether he should continue his bluff and forcibly strip the rings from her fingers or if he should content himself with the suitcase, thereby giving away the fact that he had really come for her papers, and get out as quickly as he could. But in either case she would raise the alarm the moment he had left her suite, so he had somehow to render her incapable of doing that until he was at least clear of the hotel. It occurred to him that the easiest way to do so was to get her into the bathroom, where there was a good supply of large towels. By gripping her throat with one hand he could prevent her screaming until he had pouched his gun; then he could wrap one large towel round her head and tie her up with the others. So he said:

'All in good time. I'll have the rings and the pearls in a minute, but I expect you've got some other trinkets in this case so I'm taking that as well.'

He brandished the gun again. 'Now, you've got it coming to you this time unless you obey me. Quick march! Out of here and along the passage to the bathroom!'

Somewhat to his surprise, she did not again refuse to be intimidated, but walked unhurriedly past the foot of the bed and across the room to the door leading into the passage.

As she opened it Gregory followed her with his gun in one hand and her dressing-case in the other. He was just about to cross the threshold when he heard a faint noise behind him. Swinging round he saw that the door of the sitting-room had opened. In it, covering *him* with a gun, stood his old enemy, *Herr Gruppenführer* Grauber.

14

The Hurricane Breaks

For once Gregory cursed the acuteness of his hearing. If he had not heard that faint creak as Grauber had opened the sitting-room door he would not have swung round. In consequence, he would still have had the Baroness covered had Grauber called on him to put up his hands; which would at least have created a stalemate wherein he could have held her life in pawn for his own. But, in turning, he had had to take his eye off the small, dark figure in front of him. At that moment she had produced a little mother-of-pearl gun from somewhere on her person; so on swinging back to her he found that he was now covered from two directions while his own gun was not pointing at either of his opponents.

'Step back into the room and throw that gun on the bed!' commanded Grauber in his high, piping voice.

Gregory hesitated. Had it not been for the Baroness he would have risked a shot from Grauber's pistol while he took one flying leap down the passage; but she was barring his path. Realising that he was cornered he stepped back into the bedroom, but he did not relinquish his pistol.

'Drop that gun!' ordered Grauber again, but Gregory took no notice. He had swiftly decided to play the same game with Grauber as the Baroness had payed with him.

If the Gestapo Chief had known whom he was addressing it is highly probable that he would have shot Gregory out of hand. He could have got away from the hotel with as little likelihood of having to answer for the crime as there would have been of Gregory's being arrested for the murder of the Baroness had he shot her five minutes earlier : but the silk handkerchief hid the whole of the lower part of Gregory's face and his hat was pulled well down over his eyes, so Grauber had not yet realised that, by a stroke of sheer luck, the Englishman with whom he had such a long score to settle had fallen into his hands and was entirely at his mercy. He thought, as Gregory had assumed he would, that he was dealing with an hotel thief, and even Gestapo chiefs do not shoot down ordinary burglars without provocation.

Grauber shrugged and came mincing forward into the room. Gregory noted that he had lost none of his bulk since their last encounter and his pale, solitary eye had the same dead look which hid his extraordinarily shrewd intelligence.

'Since you will not relinquish your gun,' he purred, 'I advise you to keep it down; because if you raise it by a hair's breadth I will put three bullets into your stomach.'

Gregory nodded and, stepping back another pace, lowered his head a little so that his hat brim hid his eyes and would make any chance of recognition less likely.

The Baroness re-entered the room, quietly closing the

passage door behind her, as she said: 'Thank you, *Herr Gruppenführer,* for disembarrassing me of this creature. It was fortunate that you so kindly agreed to wait until I had done my packing so that you could see me to the air-port.'

Up to that point they had all been speaking in French but the Baroness had addressed Grauber in German and he replied in the same language, assuming either that Gregory did not understand German or that, if he did, a common thief would not be in a position to gather the import of anything that was said. Still covering Gregory with his gun Grauber clicked his heels and bowed.

'It is a pleasure to have been of service, *Gnädigefrau Baronin,* but I fear that this annoying incident will interfere slightly with our arrangements. As you are due to leave the air-port at 2.45 you have no time to lose; you had better carry your bags into the sitting-room while I keep this man covered, then ring for the porter to take them down and leave at once.'

This little speech cheered Gregory considerably, as it implied that neither of his captors wished to be involved in a scene. Evidently Grauber's intention was to remain with him in the bedroom while the Baroness sent for the night-porter and made her departure. It seemed, therefore, that if he were prepared to surrender the dressing-case, which he was still holding, Grauber might let him go once she was clear of the hotel and could not be delayed as a police witness on account of the attempted burglary. That suited him all right, as his principal anxiety at the moment was to get away before Grauber recognised him and put half a dozen bullets into his body; so when the Baroness stepped up to him and gripped the dressing-case he relinquished it without attempting to grab her and swing her in front of him as cover for his body, as he otherwise might have done.

As she carried the case through the open doorway she said over her shoulder to Grauber: 'There is no immediate hurry. I am travelling by my own plane so my pilot will await my convenience. I think, therefore, it would be better if I telephone down at once to tell the management about this hotel rat so that I can be here to make the necessary statement when he is handed over to the police.'

'Damn the woman!' thought Gregory. 'Why in Hades couldn't she let well alone?' He had no pull with the Dutch Government and no possible explanation for being in the

Baroness's suite. Moreover, he was standing there masked with a pistol in his hand. There was a perfectly clear case of attempted burglary and menacing with arms against him, which was a very serious matter. If he were once handed over to the police the law would take its course and he would find himself sentenced to a long term in a Dutch prison. But, to his relief, Grauber said:

'No. That would not be wise, *Gnädigefrau Baronin*; you might be held as a material witness in the case, and that would derange all our plans. Also, it is vital that you should leave at the time arranged. As it is, we allowed only a quarter of an hour for you to get clear of Schiepol and well out over the coast, where you will be in no danger of running into an air battle. You are much too valuable to us for us to risk anything of that kind, and our bombers will be over Rotterdam at three o'clock. You are late already; you must not lose another moment.'

'Hell's bells!' thought Gregory. 'Air battles—bombers over Rotterdam in the next twenty minutes—we've been caught napping again, blast it! Hitler is launching his *Blitzkrieg* tonight.' But in spite of his suppressed excitement there was nothing whatever he could do about it.

The Baroness had carried her other two cases out of the room, and she turned in the doorway to reply swiftly: 'I had no idea that zero hour was so near, but don't worry; I shall be off the airport well before three o'clock.'

'*Gute reiser, Gnädigefrau Baronin*.' Grauber clicked his heels and bowed once more as she closed the door with a muttered, '*Danke Schön, Herr Gruppenführer*.'

'Now,' Grauber addressed Gregory, speaking once again in French as he walked over and perched himself on the end of the bed, 'one word from you or one movement of that gun during the next ten minutes and I shall shoot you where you stand. I can easily press the trigger of your gun afterwards and say that I suddenly came upon you in the room here and it was you who fired on me first. As you are a masked man who obviously came here with felonious intentions everybody will believe me. So, rat, keep a still tongue if you wish ever to be able to wag it again with your thieves fraternity.'

Gregory nodded, indicating that he understood, but he did not trust himself to speak in case Grauber recognised his voice, and for several minutes they remained eyeing each other but practically unmoving, while various sounds coming through the sitting-room door told of the porter's arrival and then, by a loud slam of the outer door of the suite, that both the porter and the Baroness had departed.

For another five minutes Grauber remained sitting there and during them Gregory, who still had his own gun in his hand, was sorely tempted suddenly to bring it up and shoot him; but the Gestapo Chief had the drop on him, as his automatic was already levelled and he had only to press its trigger. Gregory might have killed his enemy or perhaps, as his aim would necessarily be wild, have only wounded him, but at that point-blank range it was quite certain that he would have paid for his fun with his life and it did not seem to him that the game was worth the candle.

A gilded sun-pattern electric clock set in the wall above the sitting-room door stood at seven minutes to three when Grauber, evidently considering that the Baroness had had ample time to get clear of the hotel, stood up again and piped in his effeminate falsetto: 'Now that there is no longer any danger of my friend being involved in this business I propose to hand you over to the police.'

Gregory bit his lip with annoyance. During those moments of waiting he had become confident that Grauber intended to let him go so as to save himself trouble. With a German invasion due to break at any moment it had seemed that a Gestapo Chief would have a score of urgent matters to occupy him, and the last thing he would want at such an hour of crisis was to spend his time dictating statements to Dutch policemen about a common burglar who, after all, had not even succeeded in getting away with anything. But Gregory remembered with dismay that Grauber and his colleagues had a habit of perfecting all their arrangements down to the last detail beforehand, so the real probability was that now that the balloon was actually due to go up he had nothing whatever to do but sit back and watch the well-oiled wheels of the Nazi machine begin to turn as it roared forward on the lines that had been so carefully laid down for it.

For a second he thought of trying to argue Grauber out of his decision. He knew well enough that no plea for mercy would have any effect, but if he said that he spoke German, had understood Grauber's remarks that the *Blitzkrieg* was being launched at that moment and that he was a German Fifth

Columnist who had work to do for Germany, there was just a possibility that Grauber might have let him go; particularly as Fifth Columnists in countries outside Germany were largely recruited from the criminal classes, which would lend a certain plausibility to such a story. But the trouble was that if he once opened his mouth Grauber still might recognise him and, as they were alone, kill him without further argument; so he decided that he dare not risk it.

Having spoken on the bedside telephone to the man on duty downstairs, while never taking his solitary eye off Gregory for a single second, Grauber replaced the receiver. With his free hand he took out his handkerchief and dabbed at a small boil on his chin, and Gregory caught a whiff of the rather sickly perfume that he always affected. Then the German perched himself on the end of the bed once more as they waited for the night-porter and the police to arrive.

Gregory, meanwhile, was wondering frantically how he could get out of this wretched mess in which he had landed himself; but the evidence against him as he stood there was so obvious that any plea of innocence would only be laughable. The Dutch police were efficient and it was most unlikely that they would allow a burglar who had been caught with a weapon in his hand the least loophole for escape on the way to the police-station; in fact, he would almost certainly be handcuffed to one of them. In the course of the next few days he would come up for trial, as even an invasion was unlikely to interfere with the normal criminal procedure in a coast city like Rotterdam that was many miles from the German frontier. Then he would be sent down for two or three years' hard labour, and he did not see how even Sir Pellinore would be able to help him.

He had got thus far in his gloomy speculations when there was the sound of a pass-key turning the lock of the outer door and a moment later the night-porter entered the room with a plain-clothes man, who had 'hotel detective' written all over him, and two uniformed policemen.

Grauber immediately addressed the plain-clothes man in French. 'As you probably know, my friend, Madame de Swarle, has just left the hotel. I had to see her on urgent business but I could not get here before two o'clock. I have had no opportunity to secure accommodation for myself, so she said before leaving that I had better take over her suite and sleep in this room for what is left of the night. She had hardly been gone five minutes when I went into the bathroom and caught this fellow in the act of wriggling through the window. Fortunately, I had a gun on me so I was able to hold him up, but you will notice that he is armed; and if I had not drawn my own weapon very quickly would have shot me. Kindly remove him. I will visit the police-station in the morning to charge him with felonious entry.'

The detective looked at Gregory. 'Have you anything to say?'

Gregory silently shook his head, but from under the brim of his hat he snatched a glance at the clock; its long hand now had only half a minute to go before it reached the hour.

'Right, then,' the detective nodded to the policemen. 'You'd better take him along, boys.'

Grauber had lowered his gun at the entry of the police. Gregory suddenly stepped back and raised his, pointing it not at the police but at Grauber. 'One moment!' he cried, using the husky voice in which he had spoken to the Baroness. 'Remain quite still all of you, or I will kill this man.'

The night-porter had started forward, but he checked himself. For half a moment all six men remained rigid, like a set tableau. Gregory was listening with all his ears for the hum of aeroplane engines, praying that the Germans would be on time. The others were staring at him, wondering what he meant to do. A full minute passed, but no sound broke the stillness.

'Well?' exclaimed Grauber at last, turning with a sneer towards the two policemen. 'Are you going to remain standing there all night while this man threatens me?'

In vain Gregory strained his ears. For once the Germans were late in launching their programme. Knowing that he could hold the situation no longer he played another card. Lifting his free hand, he jerked down the handkerchief that covered the lower part of his face.

'*Gott in Himmel!* Sallust!' With a shout Grauber sprang up from the bed. But Gregory had him covered, so he could only stand there snarling with anger at the thought of the opportunity to revenge himself that he had now lost.

'So you recognise me at last,' Gregory said smoothly. 'I am glad of that, because I wanted these gentlemen to be given clear proof that I'm somebody who is known to you.' He swung round to the others. 'Now let me make it clear what has been happening here. I am not a burglar; I've stolen nothing; and the only thing with which this man can charge me is with breaking into Madame de Swarle's suite. If he does that I shall counter-charge him, because I challenge him to prove that he has any right here either. Again, if he charges me with threatening his life I shall charge him with threatening mine; and on that count I have the advantage because when you entered this room he was actually holding me up with his pistol.'

The four Dutchmen looked extremely puzzled. The whole matter had now taken such a totally different turn from anything they had anticipated, and while they followed Gregory's reasoning they did not see what they ought to do. At last the detective said:

'That's all very well; but it was the other gentleman who called us in and he wouldn't have done that unless you had been threatening him.'

'Oh yes, he would,' said Gregory: 'because he had the draw on me and it's in his interests to get me locked up for the night —or longer if he can manage it—so that I'm out of his way; but I'll bet you a hundred *gulden* to twenty-five *cents* that if you take me to the police-station he'll never turn up to charge me with anything in the morning.'

'Can you explain what you were doing here?' asked the detective.

'Yes. You Dutchmen have got yourselves mixed up in an international quarrel; I am an Englishman, at present employed upon a special mission for my country; while that fat, repulsive thug at the end of the bed there . . .' Suddenly he broke off, and exclaimed: 'Listen!'

It was now three minutes past three; no aeroplanes were droning overhead but in the silence that followed his exclamation they could all hear the sound that he had been the first to catch: it was a low, irregular thudding in the distance.

'D'you know what that is?' he said quickly.

The detective shook his head.

Gregory smiled grimly. 'At three o'clock Hitler loosed his *Blitzkrieg* and those are German bombs falling on your airport out at Schipol. What is more, as I was just about to tell you, the repulsive individual who so rashly brought you up here is *Herr Gruppenführer* Grauber, Chief of the Gestapo Foreign Department, U.A.—I, and for the last few minutes he has been just as much your enemy as mine. I shall hold you responsible to your Government if you fail to arrest him instantly.'

The four Dutchmen gasped. So the thing that they had been

195

dreading for months had happened after all, in spite of their efforts to placate both Hitler and the Allies. Their peaceful, prosperous country was to be made a battle-ground and devastated in the Titanic struggle of the two mighty antagonists. The distant thudding of the bombs continued; almost as one man they swung angrily upon Grauber.

With pardonable satisfaction Gregory watched them close in upon his enemy. He had got himself out of a very awkward mess and, triumph of triumphs, succeeded in snaring the German in his own net. He now had little doubt that the Dutch would take very good care of Grauber until an extradition warrant could be obtained for his transfer to England and trial for the murder of Tom Archer in Hampstead during the previous October; but Gregory had underrated his opponent.

Grauber stood up and smiled blandly at the angry Dutchmen. 'Gentlemen,' he said, 'you have only this crook's word for it that those are German bombs you can hear falling, even if they are bombs at all. The English have been planning to invade your country for a long time and it would not surprise me in the least if it is they who have attacked you without warning. In any case, I'm quite willing to accompany you to the police-station provided that you take this unscrupulous desperado, who is wanted for several murders in Germany, with you as well.'

His calmness and the thought that, after all, they as yet had no proof that Gregory was speaking the truth swiftly modified the anger of the Dutchmen towards Grauber; they looked from the German to the Englishman with doubtful expressions, until Gregory said:

'That suits me. Let's all go to the station.'

The detective nodded, one policeman took Grauber's arm and the other Gregory's arm. They filed out, went down in the lift and, leaving the night-porter, into the street. As they reached it the roar of aeroplanes sounded in the dark sky overhead and a fresh series of explosions came from a new direction. These had quite a different note from the first and Gregory felt certain that they were gunfire down at the docks. He could only pray that if the Germans were playing the same game there as they had played in Oslo the Dutch were resisting.

The Police Headquarters lay in the centre of the city, only a short distance from the hotel, and when they reached it they found that the normal quiet of its early morning hours had been rudely disturbed. Instead of only the small night-staff being in evidence policemen were still pulling on their uniform jackets as they hurried out from the dormitories to the street, while a little knot of senior officers had already gathered in the charge-room, where one of them was shouting down a telephone. Before the detective or either of the policemen had a chance to say anything Grauber boldly addressed an Inspector:

'I wish,' he said loudly in German, 'to see Chief Inspector Van der Woerden; I have been taken into custody on a false charge, but the Chief Inspector knows me and will see to it that justice is done.'

The Inspector frowned and shook his head. 'We can't disturb the Chief at a time like this, and if you're a German citizen it's just as well that you've been taken into custody. You'll be safe enough here, but when the news that Hitler is attacking Holland gets round—as it will in the course of the next few minutes—you'd stand a good chance of being lynched if you remained out in the street.'

'It *was* the Germans bombing the air-port out at Schipol, then?' Gregory cut in triumphantly.

'Yes; it must have been, because we've just had it over the telephone that German troops have made a surprise landing on the wharfs down in the harbour, though how they managed to get there without our Navy intercepting them is a complete mystery.'

'I can tell you,' Gregory said grimly; 'and it's your own fault for not learning the lesson of Norway. They've probably been coming into the port for several days in cargo ships and barges, but they've remained concealed under the hatches until their zero hour.'

Grauber shrugged his massive shoulders and taking out a visiting-card thrust it at the Inspector. 'If the *Fuehrer* has decided to take the Netherlands under his protection you should be grateful. He will save you from the English. In the meantime I insist that you send for Chief Inspector Van der Woerden.'

The Inspector stared at him angrily. 'That's quite enough from you. Hitler is not the master of Holland yet, and I tell you that the Chief Inspector is too busy for us to disturb him at a time like this.' Swinging round to one of the policemen he asked: 'What was your reason for bringing these two men in?'

The man piped up in a sing-song voice: 'At two hours fifty-five we were called into the Weimar Hotel by the house detective. We ascended with him and the night-porter to Suite 141 on the first floor; there we found these two men, both with automatic pistols in their hands. The one states that he is a German, the other that he is an Englishman. It was the German who rang the night-porter for police assistance and when we arrived on the scene he was covering the Englishman with his weapon. Both charge the other with breaking into the suite and with threatening violence.'

Grauber made a swift gesture, brushing the statement aside, as he said to the Inspector: 'That is an accurate account of what occurred, but it has no bearing upon the present situation. It is now clear that the *Fuehrer* has decided to give his protection to your country. If you are wise you will accept that protection peaceably; if you are foolish you will resist. But nothing you can do will prevent the German Army being in full control of your country within a week. Then, my friend, there will be a reckoning. For those who have conducted themselves creditably there will be no trouble, but for anyone who has arrested a German citizen and not given him a reasonable opportunity to state his case there will be very big trouble indeed.'

'So you're up to your blackmailing tricks even before you've conquered the country,' Gregory cut in furiously. 'Don't you listen to him, Inspector.'

The Inspector had gone red in the face and looked as if he was about to strike Grauber, but the German went on imperturbably: 'I am a high official of the Nazi Party and when Holland is conquered my word will be law here. For your own sake you should think well before incurring my displeasure—particularly if you have a wife and children. Either you fetch Chief Inspector Van der Woerden immediately so that I can make proper representations to him, or you will have to answer to the German authorities within the next few days for having refused my request—and by that time we shall have concentration-camps in Holland as well as in Germany.'

'Don't allow him to intimidate you, Inspector,' Gregory cried. 'This man is a Gestapo agent and it is people such as he who are at this moment signalling with lights to the aircraft that are killing honest Dutch citizens with their bombs. If you deal with him according to his deserts he won't be alive to tell any lies about you by the time the Nazis get here.'

But the Inspector was badly shaken. It was not even certain

yet that his Government would decide to fight, and even if they did, how could thirteen million Dutch stand up to eighty million Germans; particularly when those Germans had the mastery of the air? Privately he doubted if the Dutch Army could hold out for very long even with Allied aid, and after that Government, officials and people would have to submit to the Nazi bosses whom the Germans sent them. He *had* got a wife and children to think of and, after all, the German was not asking to be released, only that a higher official should be sent for to hear what he had to say. What the Chief Inspector might decide was not the Inspector's business, and by sending for him he could relieve himself of the whole unpleasant business.

'All right,' he muttered sullenly. 'Chief Inspector Van der Woerden is in the building somewhere, I think.'

'How nice,' sneered Grauber, in his thin falsetto, 'and how fortunate for all concerned.'

While the Inspector left them they stood there in the charge-room, to and from which policemen and civilians were now constantly hurrying. In the next few moments the news came through that German troops had crossed the Dutch frontier and that Amsterdam was now being bombed. The sound of the cannonade down by the harbour increased in violence, and the irregular rat-tat-tat of machine-guns was added to it. Just as they heard that the aerodromes at Brussels and Antwerp were also being bombed the Inspector returned with his superior, a short, stocky man with a grey moustache.

Grauber clicked his heels and bowed. 'I regret to have taken you from your duties at such a time, Chief Inspector,' he said formally, 'but your police are holding me upon a very minor charge which cannot easily be substantiated. If I give you my word to hold myself at your disposal, will you permit that I am released at once?'

'He's a German agent!' cut in Gregory; 'I insist that you should hold him here, otherwise he'll engineer further death and destruction among your people.'

The Chief Inspector glanced coldly at Gregory and said in a toneless voice: 'I know this gentleman. I am perfectly aware that he must now be considered as one of Holland's enemies, but it so happens that he is a member of the staff of the German Embassy; therefore he has a right to expect certain diplomatic courtesies.'

'He's no more a member of the Embassy staff than I am,'

199

Gregory cried, 'and even if he were you'd be insane to let him loose in Rotterdam tonight. If you do he'll go straight down to the docks and give all the help he can to the enemy troops there who're trying to capture your city.'

With barely veiled hostility the Chief Inspector replied smoothly: 'Kindly mind your own business and refrain from attempting to interfere in mine. The affair at the docks will soon be settled and Holland is not yet at war with Germany.' Then he turned to Grauber. 'I accept your word, *Herr Gruppenführer,* that you will report to the Dutch authorities within twenty-four hours if you are called upon to do so. You may go.'

'I thank you, Chief Inspector.' Grauber clicked his heels again, bowed from the waist and without a glance at Gregory walked quickly out of the station.

It was about the clearest instance of a Gestapo tie-up with a foreign police official who was on their books as a reliable Fifth Columnist that it could have been possible to witness. Gregory was absolutely wild with rage and the old scar on his forehead stood out a livid white. He turned furiously upon the Chief Inspector. 'How *dare* you let that man go! He's a murdering Gestapo thug, and you know it, you damned Fifth Column traitor!'

Suddenly, in his white-hot anger, before anyone could stop him he snatched up a heavy round ebony ruler from a nearby desk and struck the Chief Inspector with it a terrific blow across the head.

For a second Van der Woerden's eyes started from their sockets, round, goggling, horrible. His mouth fell open, blood began to ooze from a jagged line across his temple and he slumped to the floor without a sound.

With shouts of surprise and dismay the group of policemen flung themselves upon Gregory. There was a short, violent struggle, and as they wrenched him erect, with his arms pinioned behind him, the Inspector who had fetched Van der Woerden knelt down to examine him.

After a moment he looked up and said: 'That blow will cost you your life. He's dead.'

15

Prison for the Killer

Within a second of having struck the man Gregory had sobered up and the struggle with the police was not due to resistance on his part but owing to the fact that so many of them had all attempted to seize him at the same time.

Normally he despised people who lost their temper, as he maintained that those who were stupid enough to give way to anger placed themselves at a disadvantage, and if ever he had to fight he always fought with a cold, calculating ferocity, which was infinitely more dangerous than any whirlwind attack delivered without plan through loss of control. But, in this instance, his feeling of indignation and disgust had been so overpowering that he had virtually been affected by a brain-storm.

Such a thing had never happened to him before and it frightened him a little. He felt that perhaps the strain he had been through in the last eight and a half months was beginning to tell and that he was losing his grip. But as he stared down at the dead police chief he did not feel the least remorse at what he had done.

To have struck the official in such circumstances would have been bad enough, but to have killed him was infinitely worse. He knew that his act might cost him his life; and not as the price of something for which he might have been willing to give it, such as settling accounts once and for all with Grauber or dealing some major blow at the Nazis, but without anything to show for it, as a convicted murderer in a prison yard. Nevertheless, apart from the personal peril into which the act had brought him, he would not have undone the deed even had he had the chance.

Van der Woerden had known that his country was being invaded by the Germans. Even as he had stood there he was aware that the Nazi forces which had entered the port in secret were killing the very men who looked to him as their own officer for leadership and the citizens whom it was his duty to protect; yet he had deliberately allowed a German secret agent to go free so that he could continue his nefarious activities and inevitably bring about the loss of more Dutch lives. The man had been that lowest of all human beings—a proved traitor to his own country—and he deserved to die.

The Inspector stood up and gave an order in Dutch. Gregory was hurried down a corridor and thrown into a cell. The steel door clanged-to behind him.

He was quite calm again now and already thinking about what measures he should take. Producing pencil and paper from his pocket he wrote out two telegrams; the first was to Sir Pellinore:

'HAVE EXECUTED DUTCH POLICE INSPECTOR ACTING AS GESTAPO AGENT STOP UNDER ARREST ROTTERDAM STOP PLEASE INFORM FOREIGN OFFICE AND GET LEGATION TO DO THEIR BEST TO POSTPONE TRIAL TILL SITUATION CLARIFIES.'

The second, which he addressed to the British Minister at The Hague, ran:

'HAVE KILLED DUTCH POLICE INSPECTOR BELIEVING HIM TO BE GERMAN AGENT STOP UNDER ARREST ROTTERDAM STOP KILLING JUSTIFIED ON GROUNDS THAT IT TOOK PLACE AFTER INVASION AND VICTIM WAS ACTIVELY RENDERING ASSISTANCE TO ENEMY STOP SEND LEGATION OFFICIAL TO RECEIVE DETAILED PARTICULARS STOP PELLINORE GWAINE-CUST LONDON WILL GUARANTEE MY BONA FIDES.'

On reading these through he thought that they were pretty good. There was nothing like carrying the war into the enemy's camp and surely the first line of defence against murder was to state categorically that it was not murder at all but justified killing in the execution of one's duties. Officially, of course, the British Legation could not give any assistance to a secret agent but, for once, he felt that his entirely unofficial position should stand him in good stead. His situation was that of an ordinary British citizen travelling in Holland who had got himself into trouble, and it was incumbent on his Legation to investigate the matter and see that he received fair play.

Sir Pellinore would probably storm and rage when he got his telegram. Anxious as Gregory was, he smiled as he imagined the sort of thing that the elderly baronet would say: 'There's that damned feller—can't move ten yards without killing somebody or getting them killed on his account, and now he's had the impudence to drag me into it.' But Gregory felt quite certain that however annoyed Sir Pellinore might be he would get on to the Foreign Office immediately and pull every available wire which might ring a bell in that most intelligent and powerful of British institutions.

So far, so good, but there were two thoughts which made Gregory extremely uneasy. He had seen quite enough of the new German methods of warfare in Norway to be under no illusions as to how a *Blitzkrieg* worked. The Germans were already attacking Rotterdam from the sea and bombing the Dutch airports; within a matter of hours landings by parachute-troops could be expected and these together with the innumerable Fifth Columnists that the enemy had established in Holland, would be destroying all communications; so it was highly probable that neither of his telegrams would reach its destination. Further, while he was sitting in his cell, Queen Wilhelmina was probably signing a proclamation placing the country under martial law. In that case any civilian who killed a member of the armed forces or of the police would be liable to be tried by court-martial and summarily shot. By morning, therefore, he might find himself in the last and stickiest corner of a career which had already had far more than its fair quota of sticky corners.

Having given the police time to cool down he banged upon his cell door and, on the warder's appearing, asked him to fetch the Inspector, whose name, he learnt, was Fockink. Some quarter of an hour later the Inspector arrived and inquired what he wanted. He produced the two telegrams that he had written out, together with a 50-*gulden* note, and asked for them to be sent off at once.

The Inspector, like most educated Dutchmen, could understand English. He read the messages through and was visibly impressed on seeing that one asked the assistance of the British Foreign Office, and that the other was addressed to the British Minister at The Hague. He had not forgotten the manner in which Grauber had threatened him if he refused to send for his superior and the fact that bombs were still falling did not make him feel any love at all for the Germans, so he said quite civilly:

'I'll send these off if I can, but there's so much trouble in the city now that I'm afraid it's very doubtful if they'll get through.'

'Have the Germans succeeded in penetrating from the harbour to the centre of the town, then?' Gregory asked.

'No; but they must have had scores of agents living here, as fighting seems to have broken out in half a dozen places. One party has seized the broadcasting station and another attempted to storm the telephone exchange. Troops and police are trying to round them up now but they must have had secret stores of arms as they're all carrying tommy-guns and hand-grenades. Each group, too, appears to be trained in street-fighting and properly led so it's a very different matter to putting down an ordinary riot, and we're not organised to contend with this sort of thing.'

Gregory shrugged. 'Even if you were, you wouldn't stand much chance if many of your senior officers are like that fellow Van der Woerden—just waiting for the opportunity to sell you to the enemy.'

'Are you quite sure that German was not on the Staff of their Embassy?'

'Certain of it; I know him well; he's the Gestapo Chief, *Gruppenführer* Grauber. And even if he had been an accredited diplomat, that's no possible excuse for letting him go at a time like this when his country has just invaded yours without the slightest provocation.'

The Inspector nodded. 'You're right there. I wish now that I'd refused to send for the Chief Inspector. Still, as I did, the fact that he died from your blow means you'll have to stand your trial for murder.'

'I know,' Gregory smiled suddenly, 'but in the meantime I'd like to know how you propose to treat me. Am I to be regarded as a sailor who has killed a man in a drunken brawl or as a political prisoner who may have acted rashly but was working in the interests of your country as well as his own?'

Inspector Fockink hesitated a second, then he said: 'Quite unofficially, of course, I don't mind confessing that I understand your motive and that you have my sympathy. In any case, I'm prepared to give instructions that you shall receive such amenities as the station affords. If you've got money, so that you can pay for them, you can send out for any food you want, cigarettes, drink, etc. You may smoke as much as you like and have paper and pencils to write letters or prepare your defence —in fact any reasonable request you care to make will be granted.'

'That's decent of you,' Gregory replied. 'How about news? I'm naturally pretty anxious to know what's going on.'

'You can have any papers that you like to send for.'

'I'm afraid that's not much good; I can't read Dutch, and at a time like this I imagine it's extremely doubtful as to whether the English and French papers will come in as usual.'

'All right, then. Most of the warders can speak quite good German. I'll lift the regulation which forbids warders to carry on conversations with prisoners and each time they come into your cell they can give you the latest news.'

"Thanks,' said Gregory. 'I'm very grateful.'

When the Inspector had left him, Gregory glanced at his watch and saw that it was five to four. Guns were still firing, machine-guns were still beating their horrid tattoo; occasionally there drifted through the barred window of the cell a distant shout or the sound of hurrying feet; but there was nothing more that he could do to aid himself and, locked up as he was, there was nothing that he could do to help the Dutch defend their city, either, so he decided to go to bed and try to get some sleep.

In spite of the distant thudding and the rattling of the windows he managed to drop off about four-thirty but the warder woke him two hours later. He gave the man money to send out and buy him meals, drink, cigarettes, a war map to pin up on the wall of his cell and some English novels; and asked that his bag should be collected from the hotel; then he dozed again until the things arrived and, shortly afterwards, lunch was brought to him.

The warder gloomily gave him the news. It seemed that most of the German commercial travellers who had descended on Rotterdam in recent weeks were really soldiers in disguise. Each of them had known exactly what to do and where to go when the moment came, so they had rapidly consolidated into definite units several hundred strong, and as they had seized certain buildings which readily lent themselves to defence it was proving a very difficult matter to turn them out.

Since dawn the sky had been black with planes, and parachutists having captured the Schipol airport troop-carriers were now landing much greater numbers of Germans on it. An hour after the Germans had invaded Holland and Belgium they had gone into Luxemburg and launched a great offensive in the Moselle sector, where the Franco-German frontier and the Maginot Line proper ended. Both Holland and Belgium had appealed to the Allies for aid and at eleven o'clock it had been announced that the British and French would give them every possible assistance. It was reported that a Franco-British Army had already crossed the frontier and was wheeling through southern Belgium to meet the Germans.

Gregory received these tidings with very mixed feelings. It was good that the two countries had decided to fight. Their Air Forces were, unfortunately, negligible but Holland could put 600,000 men in the field and Belgium the best part of 1,000,000. True, the Dutch equipment was not very up to date but they were a stout-hearted race who had proved their courage many times and took a place second to none in the annals of those nations which had fought and endured to secure their independence. As a nation the Belgians were a much younger people and they were a mixed race of Flemings and Walloons, so Gregory doubted if they had the solidarity of the Dutch; on the other hand, their Army was not only larger but was said to have been greatly improved in recent years. Taking even the most cynical view, he felt that this 1,600,000 new enemies which Hitler had acquired overnight would at least inflict considerable damage on him before they could be put out of action—which was something definitely to the good.

As against that, he well remembered the manner in which Sir Pellinore had laid down the law to him less than a week ago on the subject of strategy in the Low Countries. He had made it very clear that as long as the British stood upon the Franco-Belgian frontier it would be extremely difficult for the Germans to inflict a major defeat upon them; but that once they moved out of their fortified zone they would have to meet the Germans tank for tank, gun for gun and man for man.

In the evening he learnt that in addition to innumerable Dutch and Belgian cities the Germans had also bombed Nancy, Lille, Colmar, Lyons, Pontoise, Béthune, Lens, Hazebrouck, Abbeville and Calais, but that the Dutch had blown up the bridges on the Yssel and Maas so that the first onslaught of the northernmost German Army had definitely been checked.

The Germans were reinforcing their troops in Rotterdam harbour by landing men from seaplanes and they had captured the great bridge over the river, but the situation in the centre of the city remained obscure. Gregory did not think the fighting was very near, but salvoes of bombs were being launched from time to time near enough for him to hear them whistling through the air. At ten-past ten a big fellow falling about a hundred yards away shattered the window of his cell. It was not pleasant to remain locked up during almost continuous air-raids, but the Police Headquarters was a massive building and Gregory felt that he was infinitely safer there than he had been at Andalsnes and managed to get some sleep between raids.

On the Saturday morning news came which put him into a more cheerful frame of mind. At nine o'clock the previous evening Chamberlain had announced his resignation and Churchill was the new Premier. It was good to think that Chamberlain had proved equal to the emergency and that Britain at last had a war leader worthy of her.

The local news was also good. The Germans had not succeeded in making any deep penetration into Holland and were being held at Delfzyl, the key position at the extreme northern end of the new greatly extended Allied line. In the previous day's fighting the small Dutch Air Force had behaved with great gallantry and more than a hundred German planes had been brought down over Holland, while a further forty-four had crashed on French territory. Hitler was certainly not getting it all his own way.

After Gregory had lunched, Inspector Fockink, now begrimed and unshaven but still resolute, entered the cell. He told Gregory that in the normal course of events he would have been taken before a magistrate the previous morning, but that with enemy troops holding various key positions in the city all normal judicial procedure had had to be temporarily suspended.

Gregory asked, jokingly, if there was such a thing as a writ for *habeas corpus* in Holland, and, on the Inspector's inquiring what he meant, he explained that it was an ancient law, considered by Englishmen to be the keystone of their liberties, by which a man could not be held in prison for more than twenty-four hours unless he was brought into court on a definite charge laid against him.

The Inspector said that in Holland the liberty of the subject was protected by somewhat similar measures, but in the present instance he was quite certain that they would not be operative.

No replies had yet been received to either of the telegrams and the telephone lines to The Hague had been cut by saboteurs so it was impossible to ring up the British Legation; but Fockink seemed quite friendly and having accepted a drink from Gregory's small private bar gave him the latest details of the fighting. The Fortress of Maastricht, in the extreme south of Holland, had fallen with the loss of 3,000 men and the Germans had overrun Belgian Limburg; they had also captured Mal-médy and Vitry and reached the Albert Canal. This seemed amazingly good going after a bare day-and-a-half and Gregory could only pray that the Belgians would be able to hold the line of the Canal, which was their main defence, until the British came up.

The Dutch had been forced back towards Arnhem and it had now become apparent that the maximum German pressure was being exerted in this area with the objective of driving a wedge right through to the coast, and thereby cutting the whole of north Holland off from south Holland and Belgium. In the meantime, desperate fighting was taking place out at the Schipol air-port as the Dutch had now brought up strong reinforcements of their Regular troops in an attempt to recapture it.

In the evening Gregory heard that the Dutch had succeeded in retaking the aerodrome after a most bloody action in which they had lost a thousand killed and three times that number wounded. His warder was very cock-a-hoop about this victory and also about the fine exploit of the Dutch warship, *Jan van Galen,* which had made its way through a minefield laid by the Germans and shelled several of their troop-carriers which were landing reinforcements on the shore, causing them great loss. At nine o'clock Gregory went to bed to spend another uneasy night constantly broken by violent explosions.

On the Sunday his routine did not differ from the preceding days. The police were much too occupied even to give him an hour's exercise in the courtyard so he spent the day trying to shut out the now monotonous din while he attempted to read or follow on his war map the progress of the great battle that was raging.

The Germans had pierced the Albert Canal in two places and were making a rapid advance through the Ardennes. They had also launched another attack on the French front, between the Forest of Warndt and the Saar, while in Holland they had driven their central wedge past Arnhem and south of that town were reported to be within fifty miles of the coast.

During the day all sorts of stories came through about the Germans' Fifth Column activities. Apparently the Gestapo had established secret arms-depots in practically every town in Holland and organised the Dutch Fascists and other political groups to sabotage their country's own war effort when the day came. Many of these groups had also had secret stores of Dutch military and police uniforms, the use of which enabled them to issue false orders and spread defeatist rumours from what appeared to be authoritative sources.

The Fifth Columnists were being strongly supported by German parachutists dressed in civilian clothes and even as clergymen or women. These enemies within had cut communications, seized bridges to prevent their being blown up and held off the local police while German troop-carriers had landed regular troops on golf courses, arterial roads, long stretches of sandy beach and other makeshift air-grounds.

In consequence an incredible state of confusion had resulted throughout the length and breadth of the country. Nobody now knew if a policeman or an officer was a genuine executive of the State or if he was a German sympathiser employed in diverting traffic or turning back troops in order to facilitate the advance of the enemy. There were several hundred small wars going on all over the place and large bodies of troops which should have been holding the main defence system had had to be recalled into the interior of the country to try to mop up these innumerable groups of Fifth Columnists and German airborne troops.

In the evening the new British Inner Cabinet was announced. Churchill—Premier; Chamberlain—Lord President of the Council; Attlee—Lord Privy Seal; Halifax—Foreign Affairs; Alexander—Admiralty; Eden—War Office; Sinclair—Air Minister; and Greenwood—Minister without Portfolio. Later another batch of appointments came through. Simon—Lord Chancellor; Kingsley Wood—Exchequer; Lord Lloyd—Colonies; Herbert Morrison—Supply; Anderson—Home Office; and Duff Cooper—Information.

Many of the newcomers were excellent men, but it was clear that even Churchill had been unable to break down the old business of Party claims which has to be considered in any Coalition Government; whereby professional politicians who have achieved leadership by years of uninspired hack work must be given key positions, however much they may lack the necessary qualifications to fill them, instead of the Premier having a free hand to choose younger men of outstanding ability. By and large the new Government was a great improvement on the old one, but the thing which utterly dumbfounded Gregory was that Sir John Anderson had been allowed to remain at the Home Office, when for eight solid months he had flatly refused to curb the activities of the Fascists or to take even the most rudimentary precautions to prevent the same sort of thing happening in Britain as was going on at that moment in Holland.

Whit Monday, the fourth day of the battle for the Low Countries, showed no sign of a break in the weather. Ever since May the 5th the skies had been almost cloudless and it was nearly as hot as midsummer. The German thrust into mid-Holland had deepened while further south the enemy had broken right through the eastern end of the Albert Line, hurled 2,000 tanks at Tongres and now threatened the main Belgian bastion of Liège on three sides.

Over the week-end Gregory's fears for the outcome of his killing had considerably lessened, as with every hour that passed there was less likelihood of his being taken before a military court and summarily condemned to death. The Dutch authorities were learning to their cost of the incredible havoc which was being wrought upon their war effort by Nazi sympathisers among their own countrymen and there was abundant evidence from the police who had been present as to *why* Gregory had struck down Chief Inspector Van der Woerden. He therefore no longer thought that there was any danger of his being charged with murder. It was even possible that the British authorities might be able to secure his release on a Royal pardon from the Queen of Holland; but other anxieties were now beginning to agitate him.

Three full days had elapsed since his telegrams had been sent off but he had had no reply to either, and no one had come to interview him from the British Legation at The Hague, so he thought it very doubtful if the telegrams had ever reached their destination. In consequence it looked as though he would be unable to obtain any assistance from his own people until the Dutch had succeeded in restoring some sort of order in the territory behind their actual line of battle; but the devil of it was that they might fail to do so before the advancing German armies had smashed their way forward and completely overrun the whole country. If he were detained in his cell until the Germans reached Rotterdam, Grauber might appear with a squad of Black Guards to collect him; and that was a very worrying thought indeed.

On the Monday morning he had been consoling himself with the belief that he probably had at least three or four more days to go before such a calamity was liable to overtake him, but in the evening he received an extremely rude shock. With a glum face the warder told him that a German armoured column had penetrated to within five miles of the city. True, a company of tanks might be far ahead of their supporting troops but Gregory had good reason to know that wherever a German spear-head appeared its main forces very soon succeeded in following it.

He sent an urgent request for Inspector Fockink to come and see him, then turned to the map on the wall of his cell; but he did not even need to glance at it to realise that the Dutch northern armies were now in the gravest peril. For the past three days they had been putting up a stout defence along their water-line, in spite of the fact that after the first day the Germans had achieved complete air superiority and of the sabotage which was occurring right, left and centre in their rear. But now that the point of the German wedge had practically reached the coast they were cut off from their Allies, and Gregory knew sufficient of German strategy to forecast with conviction that the enemy's spear-head would now curve north towards Utrecht, thereby encircling the Dutch and rendering their position absolutely untenable.

The warder returned to say that Inspector Fockink was out superintending the defence of one of the street barricades and that no one had any idea if or when he would return. The bombing had temporarily stopped but the banging of hand-grenades and crackle of rifle-fire sounded considerably nearer, so in a decidedly cheerless frame of mind Gregory sat down to his supper.

For the last forty-eight hours he had had to make do on cold tinned-foods, as most of the restaurants near by had closed down either on account of war damage to their properties or owing to scarcity of food, which was already becoming very short in Rotterdam, all supply services having been interrupted. While he ate his Dutch ham and sausage the warder gave him the gist of a British news bulletin which had just come in.

The Queen of Holland had arrived safely in London; Churchill had put a motion to the House of Commons that Britain should fight on to a victorious finish, which had been carried by 381 votes to 0; and several new appointments had been announced. Amery—Secretary for India; Macdonald—Health; Lord Woolton—Food; and Bevan—Labour; while from Italy anti-British demonstrations by crowds of warmongering young Fascists were reported in Rome.

The news about the Queen of Holland was extremely perturbing, as it indicated pretty clearly that the Dutch goose was as good as cooked. Gregory knew that Queen Wilhelmina was a woman of great character and absolutely devoted to her people. He felt that she would never have abandoned them at such a time unless the situation was quite hopeless and she considered that she could serve them better by escaping to England and retaining her freedom than by remaining to be taken prisoner by the Germans.

He waited up till past one in the morning hoping that Fockink would return; but the Inspector failed to do so and Gregory paced the narrow limits of his cell unable to settle to anything from the grim forebodings that now crowded in upon him.

When he went to bed the cannonade which had been raging for four days and four nights without cessation was more furious than ever. It seemed as though Hell had been let loose in a dozen quarters of the city, and when he put out his light the room remained almost as bright as day, with a red glow from the many fires that were raging. During the previous nights it had been by no means easy to get any sleep, and now it was almost impossible, as he was haunted by the persistent thought that within another twenty-four hours he might be delivered, bound hand and foot, into the clutches of the Nazis.

16

The 'Fury' of Rotterdam

When Gregory roused from his fitful dozing on the Tuesday morning, in between the crashing of explosions he could hear the dull, continuous roaring of the great fires which were now consuming several portions of the city. The sky was dark and flakes of blackened ash were drifting through the bars of his broken window.

There was no coffee for breakfast, only biscuits, red cheese and bottled beer. When the warder brought this unusual meal he said that the Germans had sabotaged the reservoirs so there was no longer any water pressure, which rendered it impossible for the fire-brigades to check the advance of the flames, but that the Police Headquarters was in no immediate danger.

Gregory also learned that just as von Ziegler had attempted to capture or kill King Haakon the Nazis had also done their best to eliminate Queen Wilhelmina. Every place to which she had moved since the invasion had been indicated to the enemy by Fifth Columnists and it was only by the greatest good fortune that she had escaped unscarred from the innumerable air-raids directed at her personally. They had not even given up their attempts on her life when she had decided to leave for England and special squadrons had been sent to bomb the British destroyer upon which she had sailed, the previous afternoon.

The news from Belgium was no better. The enemy had reached the Meuse from Liège to Namur and from Namur to Sedan, and were hurling in division after division in an attempt to cross the river at Dinant. Even more sinister, in Gregory's opinion, was the news that after hammering for four days and nights at the Franco-Luxemburg frontier the Germans had broken through from Longwy to the Moselle, thereby forming a dangerous salient right in the middle of the old Allied line.

Further appointments to the British Cabinet had been announced, by far the most important being that of Lord Beaverbrook to a new Ministry of Aircraft Production. The War Office was calling for volunteers for a new Home Defence Force to deal with enemy parachute-landings and was preparing to resist a full-scale invasion—a certain sign that matters on the Continent must be in a positively desperate state, but, whatever the cause, it was a consolation to think that people in Britain had at last awakened to the fact that there was a war on.

Shortly after eleven o'clock the warder made a special visit to tell Gregory that General Winkelman, the Dutch Commander-in-Chief, had surrendered, so on the face of it it seemed that Holland was out of the war; yet the perpetual din of bombs, guns and machine-gun fire, which constantly made it necessary to shout to be heard, continued unabated.

Gregory asked again for the Inspector and learned that he had been in during the night, but only to snatch two hours' sleep in his clothes, and had then gone out again. He asked to be taken before any available authority but the warder said that everything was at sixes and sevens and that none of the police chiefs could possibly spare time to interview prisoners.

As the hours drifted by each fresh bulletin added to

Gregory's sense of frustration and depression. Just as he had anticipated, the armoured column which had reached the suburbs of Rotterdam the previous evening had long since turned north, after demolishing the makeshift road-barriers, but the main German thrust had now penetrated the eastern outskirts of the city and its fall appeared imminent.

To Gregory's surprise and relief, just after eight in the evening, Inspector Fockink appeared. His uniform was smeared with blood and dirt, his face begrimed with smoke, and he looked a positive shadow of his former self. Without any ceremony he sat down in a semi-exhausted state on the bed, and Gregory mixed him a stiff brandy-and-soda from the little stock that had been brought in while such things were still obtainable.

After gulping down half his drink the Inspector said: 'I've been trying to get here for hours but the whole city is in such a state that it's a miracle I got back at all. Half the streets are blocked by fires; the others are choked with débris from the bomb explosions or in the hands of the Germans, and wherever one turns there seem to be poor people who need help or protection from these murderers.'

Gregory nodded sympathetically. 'Yes; you must have been through one hell of a time in these past five days. Still, I suppose the actual killing will soon be over, since General Winkelman threw in his hand this morning?'

'It's that I wanted to see you about,' the Inspector muttered. 'Apparently you've been following the course of the battle, as you have a map on the wall there. You'll have seen for yourself that our northern Armies were cut off and almost surrounded. I think Winkelman was right to save his men from further slaughter and to save the towns of the north from further devastation; but that doesn't mean that we're going to make peace with those blasted Nazis. News has just come through that our Prime Minister, Jonkheer de Geer, and his Cabinet have arrived safely in England and they have already issued a statement that Holland will fight on.'

'Good for them!' exclaimed Gregory. 'Your country's taken such terrific punishment since last Friday that we couldn't have blamed you if you'd gone out of the war altogether.'

The Dutchman shook his head almost angrily. 'Certainly not. To surrender while there is a single German left on the soil of the Netherlands is unthinkable. We have our empire overseas,

214

our Navy, which although not that of a first-class Power is capable of inflicting considerable damage on the enemy, and our southern Army which will continue to support the Belgians. That is why the fight is still raging here, in Rotterdam, in spite of General Winkelman's "Cease fire" order. Two-thirds of the city is now in flames or ruins but it has become the western pivot of the new Allied line, so we mean to continue our resistance until it is rendered absolutely untenable.'

'Well done, well done!' Gregory murmured. 'But how long d'you think you'll be able to hang on to the bits of it that are still in Dutch hands?'

'Another twelve hours, perhaps, but that's about the best we can hope for. Our supplies of ammunition are running low and more and more German troops are pouring into the suburbs. The odds are that they'll have gained complete control of this vast heap of wreckage, which was only a few days ago our splendid city of Rotterdam, by the small hours of the morning.'

Gregory made a grimace. 'Well, I don't suppose we shall ever know now what a Dutch court would have done to me for killing Chief Inspector Van der Woerden, but one thing is quite certain—if I'm still here when the Nazis walk in they'll shoot me.'

'That's just what I thought, and I've made up my mind that I'm not justified in holding you any longer.'

'Thank God for that!'

'Well, after the way these Fifth Column people have stabbed Holland in the back it certainly wouldn't be the act of an Ally to hand you over as a prisoner to the Germans. God knows if you'll be able to get out of the city alive but I'm not standing on any formalities at a time like this, so if you like you're free to try it.'

'Right!' smiled Gregory. 'Even a dog's chance is better than nothing,' and grabbing up his suitcase, he swiftly ran through its contents. He had no intention of burdening himself with it but just selected the most useful items and stuffed them in his pockets. When he had done he poured a drink for himself and another for the Inspector. They solemnly drank damnation to the Nazis, then went outside together. On the doorstep they shook hands and Gregory stepped into the street a free man once more.

Erika had never been far from his thoughts during these trying days and he knew that she would have been worrying herself sick about him, so his natural impulse was to get back to her at the earliest possible moment. As the Allies were now holding a line from Antwerp to St. Trond he reckoned that apart from the danger of air-raids she was still quite safe in Brussels and would almost certainly remain there as long as there was any hope of his rejoining her; but the difficulty was how to get there.

The city lay on the north bank of the Rhine, or Lek as it is called in western Holland, and the normal route to Brussels ran south-east, across the one bridge that spans the broad river, over the Noorder Eiland and through the great dock area of the Feijenoord peninsula. The bridge, island and docks were now in the hands of the Germans, who had also occupied the whole of the Karlingen area of the eastern side of the city; so the only free exits remaining were by way of the northern or western suburbs. But to head north or west would take him further from his goal and mean that in a few hours he would find himself pinned by the Germans up against the coast. On the other hand, if he could reach the river and get across by boat to a place either east or west of the docks the rest of his journey should not prove difficult as he would be in friendly country still held by the Dutch. In consequence he decided to turn south and see if he could get through to the waterfront.

All hell was now loose in Rotterdam. The cannonade had increased to a steady drum-fire and the evening sky was one great pall of reddish smoke from the fires that were eating out the heart of the city. At Hamar he had seen how a small place can be practically blasted off the map by concentrated bombing, but this was a huge industrial area many square miles in extent and it did not take him long to realise that it had suffered in a degree that he would have thought unbelievable. The first air-raids on Helsinki were large-scale affairs but the damage they had done was simply nothing compared with the havoc which had been wrought by five days and nights of shelling, bombing and incendiarism in the great Dutch port.

Not a pane of glass remained in any of the windows; great gaps appeared every hundred yards or so in the rows of buildings; streets and pavements were torn up as though from an earthquake; water mains had burst and flooded the lower levels; thousands of slates had been blown off the roofs and littered the gutters; lamp-standards had been uprooted and thrown across the roadways; tangles of fallen telephone wire snaked across great heaps of débris; the ways were partially blocked with overturned cars, wrecked omnibuses, twisted bicycles and dead horses; here and there barricades of vehicles, torn-up paving-stones and furniture dragged from houses had been erected, among which the killed were still lying; the air was stifling from the fires that were raging and in places ashes were falling like black snow; aeroplanes droned ceaselessly overhead, bombs crashed, guns thundered, fires roared, rifles cracked and machine-guns chattered. Sheltered in his cell even the babel of sound had given Gregory no conception that the city had been reduced to such an incredible scene of chaos and disruption.

Stumbling over bricks and skirting piles of wreckage he headed south, but he had not got far before he was checked by flames and smoke issuing from a block of burning office buildings. Turning back he tried another street but found it blocked by a barricade upon which police and troops were fighting. Twenty-four hours earlier the Germans had gained a foothold on the northern bank of the river and they were now in possession of all that was left of the railway station and the Central Post Office. By street after street he tried to work his way down to the waterfront but in every case he was held up by fires or turned back by squads of armed police, while shells screamed over, bullets whined and brickbats hurtled through the smoke-laden air.

After two hours spent crouching and dodging in this inferno he gave it up as impossible and turned west. Night had come once more and the red glow from the sky lit the scene of devastation. For what seemed an interminable time he picked his way through streets half-blocked by falls of rubble and twisted girders. Here and there a leg, an arm or a human head stuck out grotesquely marking the place where a human body lay crushed and buried. Rescue parties were at work among the ruins but they could not keep pace with the casualties and while there were so many maimed and bleeding humans to be helped and cared for there was no time to collect the dead. Owing to the heat some of the corpses were already beginning to stink and their odour mingled with the stench of cordite and the all-pervading smell of burning. 'This,' thought Gregory, as he stumbled on, 'is total war—Hitler's war. Pray God that we can keep it out of England.'

Even towards the west his progress was constantly checked by other fires or police patrols and for a time he lost all sense of

217

direction, to find himself eventually right up in the north by the Law Courts. Here he came upon a new series of barricades which were being attacked by another force of Germans who had worked their way round the city, and on both sides of the barriers snipers were firing from the roof-tops at anyone rash enough to show himself in the streets. Having tried to go west again by half a dozen different turnings, without success, he entered a house, the door of which was standing open. No one was about so he made his way through into the back garden, then he began the laborious process of climbing over wall after wall down the block until at last he emerged in a side-street that was on the German side of the line of barricades.

He had not gone far when a squad of German infantry came running down the road. Without even challenging him two of them raised their tommy-guns and let fly. With that swiftness of thought which had saved his life many times before he flung up his arms at their first gesture and, letting his body relax, slumped backwards on to the pavement. The little bursts of bullets hissed over his head and spattered on the brickwork of a wall behind him. For a moment he lay there holding his breath, waiting for another burst to be poured slap into his body; but the Germans thought that they had already eliminated this solitary Dutchman who might be up to no good in the area where they were operating; without another glance at him they hurried on.

Stumbling to his feet he went forward more cautiously until at the end of the street he saw a German sentry. He had barely started to consider whether he dared risk a bullet by going on or had better turn back when the matter was settled for him. Above the dull rumble of the bombardment there came a solitary whip-like crack and for a second a stab of fire lit a second-floor window just ahead of him. The German sentry, shot from above through the back, reeled suddenly and pitched face-forward into the gutter.

A few streets further on he had to crouch in a dark archway for some moments while a German tank column rattled and bumped its way over the débris in the direction of the barricades, and ten minutes later he had to hide again from a company of infantry; but at last he reached the Zoological Gardens, right on the outskirts of the city, and it seemed that he had got clear of the Germans. Turning south-west he started to make his way through the residential district of Beukelsdijk. It was nearly one o'clock in the morning when he got on to a main road down which scattered groups of people were moving, and he realised that as they were all making in one direction they must be refugees who were heading for the coast.

The last five hours had been both nerve-racking and tiring work but as he had just spent the best part of five days either in bed or lying down he had plenty of reserves of energy, so he put his best foot forward and, taking a short rest every half-hour, passed group after group of wearily-plodding people. At about half-past three he came to a main crossroads right out in the open country and the signpost showed him that the road he had been on led to The Hook while that which cut into it from the north went to Delft. Down this was trickling another stream of refugees and as the two streams mingled at the crossroads some groups took the road south while others went west towards The Hook. Under the signpost Gregory sat down to rest again and smoke a cigarette while he considered the situation.

He had long since given up any hope of getting through or round Rotterdam with a view to trying to cross the Dutch frontier into Belgium, and it was now quite clear that his only means of getting out of Holland was by sea. The question was which road offered him the best prospect? That to the south led to the broad mouth of the river, which was less than three miles away, and he might succeed in getting a small boat there at a village on the coast; but it was said that the Germans had mined the estuary, and there was no proper port along the shore where ships would be embarking refugees. On the other hand he was pretty tired now, The Hook was still seven miles distant and he had only his legs to carry him; but, unless the Germans had got there already, in the big harbour he was much more likely to find a ship that would take him to England. Grimly he decided to face the longer journey and stubbing out his cigarette stood up to tramp on again.

He spoke to nobody, for he felt that the Dutch must now have very good reason to suspect all foreigners of being Fifth Columnists, and he had no intention of risking being lynched, or arrested again and confined in another police-station while inquiries were being made about him. If he had not considered that discretion was so very necessary he might possibly have bought a lift for part of the way, as a number of cars and carts were constantly passing, but he preferred to make quite certain

219

of retaining his liberty, so he did the whole distance on foot, arriving at The Hook at seven in the morning. Since leaving the Rotterdam Police Headquarters, some eleven hours earlier, he reckoned that he must have covered well over twenty miles and he was seriously feeling the effects of his exertions; but on entering the town he was immensely cheered by the sight of British sailors and marines.

They appeared to have taken charge of the traffic and the whole harbour area. Some were directing the stream of refugees towards the docks while others were carting ashore large cases, which Gregory guessed contained explosives. As he had been approaching the port he had heard several heavy detonations, but such sounds had become a normal background to his life during these past few days so, tired as he was, he had not taken any special notice of them, assuming that as German planes were once again circling overhead they were bombing the harbour; but he had hardly reached the docks when there was a terrific crash and a whole wharf about half a mile distant seemed to disintegrate in a sheet of blinding flame. The Navy knew their business and were seeing to it that there would not be much left in the way of harbour works by the time the Germans got there.

Good-humouredly, but firmly, the British sailors and marines herded the never-ceasing flow of refugees into the long customs sheds while Dutch interpreters who were working with them told the crowds of grimy, despondent people that they must abandon their cars, vans, wagons and all their contents as, in order that the ships which were leaving could take the maximum number of passengers, they could not be allowed to retain anything but hand luggage.

For over an hour Gregory waited in the customs shed, resting his weary limbs by lying at full length along one of the benches with his head pillowed on his arms. While he lay there further shocks more like earthquake tremors rocked the building and a number of lesser bumps together with anti-aircraft fire showed that the Nazi planes were strafing the refugees and their rescuers. From time to time batches of the patient, sad-eyed crowd were shepherded out on to the quayside, and at last came Gregory's turn to be taken on board a cargo vessel.

Now that he had a proper chance to look round he saw that one side of the fairway had already been blocked by the sinking of a dredger and two trawlers and that other vessels lying near

220

by were evidently in readiness to be used for closing the gap, when the last evacuee ship had cleared the harbour mouth. The great steel gates of an inner lock were half-submerged and twisted almost beyond recognition, and in many places fires were burning where the British had dynamited port-authority buildings and warehouses. Every now and again waves of German bombers came over to add their quota to the racket but most of their bombs fell harmlessly in the sea. Once on board Gregory found himself a corner among the crowd where he could sit on the deck with his back to the engine-room hatch, and, like many others of the exhausted refugees who were past caring about the bombs, dropped off to sleep.

When he awoke he had the curious sensation that something strange was going on, but after a moment he realised that it was only the silence which seemed unnatural. The ship was out of sight of land and for the first time in six days the crash of bombs and the rumble of guns were no longer audible. He found that it was half-past two in the afternoon but it was not until eleven o'clock that night that they put into Harwich, and even then, in spite of his British passport and reiterated statements that he was not a refugee, he had to submit to a rigorous examination by the Security Police who were exercising every possible precaution to prevent German Fifth Columnists entering Britain with the genuine victims of Nazi persecution. It was past one before he was able to get away from his unfortunate fellow-travellers, who were being specially catered for, and nearly two when he flopped into bed at the Station Hotel.

He did not wake till ten o'clock on the Thursday morning but he had hardly opened his eyes before he recalled the urgent necessity of getting back to Brussels, and to Erika, now that the *Blitzkrieg* was on, without losing a moment. He knew, without inquiring, that all passenger sailings would have been cancelled, so he at once got on to London and was fortunate enough to catch Sir Pellinore at home.

Having told his elderly friend the gist of his news he asked if permission could be obtained for him to be taken on board any naval vessel which might be leaving Harwich for Belgian waters. Sir Pellinore said that he thought matters could be arranged and that he would get in touch with the Admiralty at once.

On reaching the hotel Gregory had been too utterly weary for more than a rough clean-up, so, having telephoned down for breakfast to be brought in half an hour, he lay for a bit in a hot bath, soaking off the rest of the smoke and grime of Rotterdam. His breakfast, which consisted of China tea, smoked haddock with a poached egg, and mushrooms on toast, was a special order given on his old principle that the best meal obtainable was never too good if there was no knowing when one was going to get another. When he had finished it he felt distinctly better and turned his attention to the morning papers.

On the previous day the whole of Holland had been sub-merged beneath the Nazi flood and the Dutch were now holding out only in the island of Zeeland. The Allies were maintaining their line from Antwerp to Namur but further south enormous pressure was being exerted on the French. German armoured columns had broken through at three points between Namur and Sedan and were still attacking in spite of the fact that 150 Allied planes had spent the entire day going backwards and forwards to their bases for relays of bombs which they had hurled on the advancing Germans and the road junctions.

At midday he dressed and went out into the town where, although the weather showed no signs of breaking, he bought himself a rubber raincoat as a precaution against a choppy crossing, then he returned to await events in the hotel lounge. At two o'clock a message arrived for him from the port authorities to say that instructions had been received from the Admiralty that he was to be given passage in one of His Majesty's ships which would be proceeding to Belgium, and that he was to report to the Admiralty Building, Harwich, at eight-fifteen that night. He cursed the delay but knew that he was lucky to have enough pull through Sir Pellinore to get taken across at all.

In the evening the news was no better. From Namur to Sedan there were a million men fast locked in battle and at the southern end of this vital sector the Germans were obviously getting the best of it. They were exploiting the breaches made in the French line on the previous day. It seemed that some-body had failed to blow up the bridges across the Meuse in the face of the advancing enemy so that they were now well over the river and had captured Rocroi, Mézières, Sedan and Mont-medy; while their advance units were now several miles south and west of these places, thereby creating a most dangerous bulge in the Allied line. However, the fact that the Germans had reached Louvain, in Belgium, gave Gregory considerably more concern. Louvain was less than twenty miles from Brussels, and Erika was in Brussels.

He arrived at the Admiralty Building punctually but his temper was not improved by the fact that he was left to kick his heels in a bare waiting-room for two and a quarter hours. At last a naval Petty Officer took him down to the dock and on board a destroyer where a genial Lieutenant-Commander received him and installed him in the wardroom with the casual invitation to order anything that he wanted from the steward. At 11.10 the destroyer put to sea.

After a little he dozed to the hiss of the water rushing past her portholes and to the monotonous whirr of the turbines. At one o'clock two officers came in so he roused up, drank pink gins with them and discussed the *Blitzkrieg*. They did not stay long and when they had gone he took another cat-nap. At a quarter to four the steward brought him bacon and eggs, toast, marmalade, and coffee. Soon after he had completed his meal the ship swung round in a wide curve and on looking out of one of the portholes he saw harbour lights paling in the dawn. Ten minutes later, having thanked his hosts, he was on the quayside at Ostend.

A passport officer gave him the latest news. The Belgian Army was fighting splendidly in the north and the British were holding the German attacks in the centre. The situation further south, however, gave cause for anxiety as the French Armies in the neighbourhood of Sedan were giving up more and more ground and seemed quite incapable of holding the terrific German attacks which were being launched against them.

Even at that hour the quayside was a bustle of activity. Hundreds of Belgian refugees were waiting to get away in the ships that were sailing for England or France. Among them moved many khaki figures, French and British officers and details who during these past few days had been making all the innumerable arrangements necessary for converting Ostend into a new forward base for the Allied Armies. Just as Gregory was passing out he heard his name called and turned to find that he was being hailed by a Guards Captain of his acquaintance, one 'Peachie' Fostoun.

'What the hell are you doing here?' grinned Peachie.

'Same as you, presumably,' Gregory grunted amiably; 'only I have somewhat more subtle methods of waging war. Have

223

you just come down from the line, or have they made you a permanent base wallah?'

'They wouldn't dare.' Peachie flicked open his cigarette-case. 'I graciously consented to come down to arrange the Brigades' supply of caviare, but I'm going up again in about an hour's time.'

As it was still technically before dawn Gregory managed to raise a laugh. 'Don't tell me that the Army has at last gone in for code words, otherwise for "caviare" I shall write in re-inforcements.'

'Have it which way you like,' Peachie shrugged.

'How are things going?' asked Gregory.

'They're lousy. This Fifth Column stuff would take the grin off the face of a clown in a pantomime. When we went into Belgium on Friday morning everything was grand; in every village the populace was waiting to give us the big hand. They chucked cigarettes and chocolate at us by the bucketful and at every halt the women kissed the troops until you couldn't see their mouths for lipstick, but by nightfall things weren't quite so rosy. There was still a hundred miles between us and the Germans but all sorts of nasty low-down tikes began to snipe us from the house-tops. Some of them even chucked hand-grenades in the path of our Bren gun-carriers, from the woods through which we were passing, and we began to think that it wasn't quite the sort of war that we had bargained for.

'The following day things became really unpleasant. German parachute-troops started to float down out of the sky by the hundred; the nearest ones provided good sport for some of our better marksmen with their Brens but the devils came over in such numbers that we couldn't account for one-tenth of them. Then, apparently, the Boche started landing troop-carriers with horrid little howitzers and while the troops were proceeding along the road soulfully singing "Little Sir Echo, Hullo! Hullo!" you could never tell from one moment to the next when one of these things would start blazing off from a farm-yard or behind a haystack.'

Gregory nodded sympathetically and the garrulous Peachie went on:

'I don't mind telling you, it got on our nerves a bit as, after all, it wasn't like real war at all, but just a sort of dirty assassination party. The further we went, the worse it got, until every time a young woman threw us a bunch of flowers we ducked as though there was a Mills bomb concealed in it; but at least it had one good effect—it made the men so angry that they were screaming mad to get at the Jerries.

'By Monday we'd contacted the enemy, and you can take my word for it that once the party started it was war with the lid off. We hardly saw a German but they came over in their tanks by the train-load. We held the tanks all right, but the thing that is a bit shattering is their Air Force. Heaven knows what's happened to ours—we've hardly seen a British plane—but Goering's chaps are as numerous as grouse in August. The moment one has held a tank attack they come hurtling down out of the sky to play merry hell with their bombs; and they're not content with that, either; if they see a trace of movement they let fly with their machine-guns. It seems to me as though they are using dive-bombers for artillery. Anyhow, it makes it devilish difficult to hold on to any one position for any length of time; and if one gets a lot of casualties which necessitate a retirement their tanks immediately come on again; added to which, with all this trouble going on behind the lines one never knows when one's going to be shot in the back. It's not at all like any war that we've been taught to anticipate.'

'Naturally,' said Gregory; 'since you're a quarter of a century behind the times. Never mind, my young fellow-me-lad, we can be quite certain that the good old British spirit will stand up to the strain. After all, surely you don't expect modern equipment and modern training. That would be letting the old school down and asking much too much of your tutors.'

'We shall manage somehow,' said Peachie, a trifle huffily.

'Of course you will,' Gregory beamed. 'Anyhow, the best of luck! I've got to get along to the station.'

'Where are you off to?' Peachie inquired.

'Brussels.'

'Have you a special permit?'

'No. I didn't know that one was required.'

'It is; and it would take you days to get one. We're doing our best to make the battlefronts a closed area. You can come out, and welcome, but you can't get in unless you prove that you're Winston Churchill or Anthony Eden.'

'That's awkward; I've got very urgent reasons for wanting to get back to Brussels.'

'Well, you won't—I'll bet you a pony. Unless . . .' Peachie hesitated. 'I suppose you really are doing a job of work?'

'Sure thing,' Gregory nodded. 'I'm not wearing my beard or my rubber-soled shoes at the moment but I've got the hell of a sting in my tail for all that.'

'In that case I could get you through by giving you a lift in my car. I shall have done all I can here in another couple of hours, then I'm going straight back. Meet me in the lounge of the Splendide at seven o'clock.'

'Thanks, Peachie, that's darned good of you; and, joking apart, I am helping a bit to push the old boat along.'

As Peachie Fostoun hurried off Gregory made his way to the great luxury hotel on the sea-front. For him it called up pleasant memories of a week he had spent there long ago with a lady who had loved him very dearly and whom at that time he had considered to be the most desirable among all women; a happy state of affairs for two young people who with one war then only a memory, and another not even visualised as a remote possibility, had been able to devote themselves without let or hindrance to the entirely engrossing subject of each other.

In spite of the early hour the hotel was as busy as if it were mid-morning on a day in race week. There had been three air-raids on Ostend that night so many people had come down from their rooms to sit in the lounge and their number was constantly being added to by refugees arriving from Brussels, which somewhat perturbed Gregory.

When Peachie turned up they went into the bar to have one for the road and Gregory asked: 'What is the latest authentic information? Is there any likelihood of Brussels falling within the next twelve hours?'

Peachie shrugged. 'We're not actually trampling our way over the German dead to victory, but it's quite fair to say that we're holding our own. The Boche gave Louvain hell yesterday, but it didn't get them anywhere. Now the fight is on our men are behaving magnificently and you can sneer at the equipment as much as you like, but such as it is, we've got no complaints about it. Maybe we haven't gangster weapons like the Jerries but our stuff's better quality and we've already found that when our lads get face to face with the enemy they're worth three to one of them every time. I don't think there's the least likelihood of a withdrawal to Brussels unless it's suddenly made necessary by either of our flanks caving in, and the Belgians are putting up a splendid show in the north.'

No papers were available but a British Naval Officer who was in the bar told them that things were reported to have taken a turn for the better. Apparently a telegram from the Generals Giraud and Huntziger to Monsieur Reynaud had been published and in it the two commanders who were responsible for the Sedan area, where the Germans had broken through, stated categorically that they were getting the situation in their sectors under control. With this distinctly cheering item of information Gregory and Peachie went out to the car, which Peachie was driving himself, and set off.

Bruges was no great distance, and normally they should have reached it in less than three-quarters of an hour, but an unending stream of traffic moving towards the coast made a normal speed impossible, so it took them double that time. From Bruges they went on along the straight, poplar-fringed road towards Ghent, but their pace came down to a crawl as in addition to the refugee column, which occupied more than half the road, they now encountered a great number of breakdowns which, with the west-bound traffic moving round them, blocked the road entirely. They had expected to be in Brussels by lunchtime but it was one o'clock when they entered Ghent. As they had already been on the road for over five hours' most exasperating driving they pulled up at a restaurant on the Place d'Armes to snatch a quick meal. Just after they had given their order a Major, who was a friend of Peachie's, came in and they asked him to join them.

The Major took a by no means cheerful view of things and, as he was a G.S.O.2, attached to the Second Corps, his information could be considered as authentic as any that could be secured in the sea of rumours that were flying round. He said that the Germans had surprised both the French and the British by the direction of their thrust, the weight of their tanks and the numbers of their aircraft. Apparently the Meuse sector had now become a deep bulge and a number of German armoured columns were right through, having penetrated the whole depth of the fortified zone at the western end of the Maginot Line. Most alarming of all, this threat to the southern flank of the Allied Armies operating in Belgium had become so serious that an order for their withdrawal had been issued early that morning and the British were now retiring to fresh positions west of Brussels.

Greatly perturbed by this new and disconcerting possibility

227

that the Germans might be in Brussels before him Gregory urged haste on Peachie and having bolted their meal they hurried back to the car; but the time saved proved of little value as outside Ghent their pace came down to a positive crawl. Evidently the news that the capital was to be abandoned had sent half a million Belgians scurrying out of it along the roads to the west and south, so that the procession of refugees had now swollen to a triple line of crawling vehicles and patiently-plodding people. In vain Peachie pounded at his Klaxon while Gregory cursed and swore. The sullen-looking, sad-eyed crowds either would not or could not get out of the way and the long, hot afternoon developed into a kind of tread-mill which sometimes afflicts one in a dream, where one is striving very hard to get somewhere but finds that one's legs will not obey one's will. Nevertheless, mile by mile they made gradual headway, reaching Alost at six o'clock. They snatched a drink at the crowded hostelry there then pressed on again by the evening light.

Now they were well within the sound of the guns and occasionally a German plane came over to unload its bombs on railway sidings or the villages through which they passed. By eight o'clock they were within six miles of Brussels and met the first of the retiring troops. All day, here and there in the endless procession, they had seen cars, ambulances and supply-wagons which belonged to the French and British Armies, but this group of weary, dust-covered men had a totally different appearance; they had obviously been in the thick of it, and Peachie pulled up to ask an officer if he could give him any particulars of his own unit.

The officer said that he had not run across the Guards Brigade for several days. He knew nothing of the general situation as he and his men had been ordered out of the line only that morning, after three days' very hard fighting, as they thought to rest; but they had no sooner reached the billets allotted to them at Nosseghem than they had been ordered out again with new instructions to retire through Brussels to Assche. 'Hence,' he added with a smile, 'our rather part-worn appearance; it's four days since we've had a chance to clean up.'

From that point on they passed many units of the B.E.F. Some, which had borne the brunt of the early fighting, looked pretty war-worn, while others were spick and span, being units of reserve divisions that had not yet been thrown into the battle.

As the twilight deepened the numbers of refugees gradually lessened, until the road became almost entirely occupied by the military. Peachie was now pulling up at every hundred yards or so to ask passing officers if they knew the whereabouts of his unit and at last on a crossroad, among a group of officers who were standing there studying their maps, he saw his own Colonel.

The Colonel told him that the Guards were at Uccle, just south-west of the capital, and that if he took the road to the right he would find the village about three miles along it. Peachie then introduced his passenger and said that Gregory was anxious to get through to Brussels as he had work of importance to do there.

'I'm afraid it's too late to do that,' said the Colonel promptly; 'the Germans have already occupied the city.'

'That won't stop me,' Gregory replied. 'I speak German fluently and I have a German passport, so I could easily pass myself off as a German agent.'

The Colonel brushed up his moustache and eyed Gregory with considerably more interest. 'In that case it's up to you, but I'd strongly advise you to wait until morning.'

'Why, sir?'

'Because, although the whole front is in a state of flux, we have established some sort of line just behind Brussels, so there's a mile or two of territory outside the suburbs which is more or less no-man's-land at the moment. It will be dark by the time you get there and during the night the sentries on both sides will be potting at any moving object they may see, so the fact that you're in civilian clothes won't be the least protection to you. But if you wait until daylight you should be able to walk straight through the battle-zone and you only have to risk being killed by a stray shot or shell, as neither side is likely deliberately to shoot down a civilian.'

Gregory immediately saw the sense of this argument. Ever since he had been released from the Police Headquarters in Rotterdam he had been cursing the succession of delays which had prevented his getting back to Erika, but now that the Germans had got to Brussels before him there was no longer quite as much point in his pressing forward without the loss of a moment. He felt confident that she would have had the sense to evacuate before the Germans arrived, and was probably now somewhere among one of the columns of refugees that had left

229

Brussels that morning; so his only reason now for wishing to get into the city was because he felt sure that she would have left some message for him in her flat to say where she intended to go.

Once he knew that, even with the country in its present state of confusion, he would probably be able to reach her in another twenty-four hours; but as long as he had no idea at all where she had gone, with every form of communication broken down, it might take him days—or even weeks—to find her. It seemed, therefore, that for the sake of securing any message she might have left him it was not worth risking being shot in a night-crossing of no-man's-land, when by waiting for a further eight or ten hours he would be able to cross it with comparatively little danger.

Peachie suggested that Gregory had better come with him to Uccle and take pot-luck for the night about any accommodation that might be going there; so on Gregory's agreeing they took leave of the Colonel and turned down the side-road.

At the village they found Peachie's battalion temporarily resting, as there was now a lull in the fighting, the Germans being fully occupied with the take-over of the Belgian capital. A Mess had been established in a large farmhouse and while Gregory and Peachie ate a meal there they listened to the accounts given by several officers of the last two days' fighting. All of them were extremely bitter about the Fifth Column activities in Belgium. One of their brother-officers had been shot through the back of the neck and killed when walking down a road miles behind the line, and another had halted his car in a quiet area to offer two Belgian peasant women a lift, upon which one of the women had pulled out a pistol and shot him through the head.

They said that we had no weapon at all to compete with the Germans' small, quick-firing howitzer and that at short range our old-fashioned rifles were almost useless against the tommy-guns which were carried by every German infantry-man. On the other hand, everyone present agreed that the Germans were a poor lot when it came to hand-to-hand fighting; thy would not face the bayonet at any price and, in spite of constant bombardment and machine-gunning from the air, every time our men got a chance to get at the enemy they were putting up a magnificent performance.

In the Mess Gregory saw a copy of the order that General

230

Gamelin had issued that day. It said: 'Any soldier who cannot advance should allow himself to be killed rather than abandon that part of our national soil which has been entrusted to him.' So, clearly, for the Supreme Commander of the Allied Armies to have played his last card by such a backs-to-the-wall command, the situation was really critical.

The farmhouse was filled to capacity but Peachie managed to secure a double bed for Gregory and himself in a cottage near by, and they slept on it in their clothes, ready to be up and doing at a moment's notice in any emergency.

At five o'clock they were wakened by shells screaming into the village and knew that the battle was on again. The Germans had taken Brussels in their stride and now that daylight was approaching they were launching new attacks upon the hard-pressed British. In the farmhouse the Mess orderlies were going about their business quite unperturbed and to Gregory's surprise and pleasure he was given bacon and eggs for breakfast as well as lashings of hot tea. Reports had come in from the advance company that German tanks were approaching so the remainder of the battalion was already mustering in the village street. Gregory saw no cause to delay any further and knew that he would only be in the way of the others if he did, so he thanked his hosts and, wishing them luck, set out along the road to Brussels.

There were a number of other civilians about, mostly villagers or refugees from the city. With what appeared to Gregory the height of foolhardiness, they ignored the German planes which were once more buzzing overhead and the shells which were bursting only a few hundred yards away, to stand about on the higher ground so that they could get a good view of the battle that was opening, but their presence suited him very well as it meant that he was in no way conspicuous.

He had scarcely covered half a mile when the planes dive-bombed the village; but fortunately, by that time, the troops had moved out of it, scattering to north and south to take up their positions. A few hundred yards further on a crossroad was being crumped every few moments by the shells of a German heavy battery, so he took to the fields and gave it a wide berth. Five minutes later a British Tommy popped up from behind a hedge and called on him to halt, threatening him with a rifle; but Gregory spoke to him in English, giving him the names of half a dozen officers of his battalion, and told him that it was his job to go forward to get information.

'Crikey!' exclaimed the Tommy. 'You don't mean to say we've got a Fifth Column too?'

'Yes; I'm it,' Gregory laughed.

'Right-oh; pass, chum; but you've got your work cut out against half the German Army dressed as Belgians.' The man put up the rifle and waved him on.

Twice more he was challenged by solitary Guardsmen but each time they let him through and although a few bullets were now whistling about he continued to walk forward, considering that to display himself openly in his civilian clothes was his best protection. Yet on crossing a field towards a group of houses he had a narrow squeak; a machine-gun opened fire, tearing up the grass about ten yards to his left. He could not tell if the gun was badly aimed or if it was fired by a Jerry who thought it would be fun to scare the wits out of a solitary Belgian, but he leapt for the ditch and lay there until the gunner ceased fire; then he cautiously crawled forward on his hands and knees until he came to the nearest house. Standing up, he walked round it, and on turning the corner to get on to the road again he ran straight into a patrol of German infantry.

A *Feldwebel* immediately pointed an automatic at him so he shot up his hands and spoke in German. 'It's all right, Sergeant; I am a German officer on special service. Hold your fire for a minute while I show you my passport,' and slipping his hand into his breast-pocket he produced the now much-worn document which had so often established his identity as *Oberst-Baron* von Lutz.

The Corporal glanced at it, called his men sharply to attention and saluted. Gregory pocketed the passport again and with a little nod to the group walked on. British shells were now screaming overhead and the staccato rattle of machine-guns interspersed by the occasional crack of rifles showed that the battle had been joined in earnest behind him; but now that he had crossed no-man's-land the most perilous part of his dangerous morning walk was over.

As he advanced the houses became more frequent and many of their occupants were standing at their windows or in the street, so the further group of Germans that he met took no notice of him. A long column of tanks clattered by and from the dents and scars upon them he saw that they had already done considerable service. By eight o'clock he had left the suburbs and penetrated to the centre of Brussels. It had taken him just seventy-two hours to do the journey from Rotterdam which he should normally have accomplished in an hour and a half.

It was a very different city to that which he had left fourteen days earlier. The streets were almost deserted except for the columns of German troops. Shops and houses were closed and shuttered, but he noticed with relief that the city did not seem to have suffered much from aerial attack. Here and there a bomb had wrecked a building or blown a hole in the road but the damage was not one-thousandth part of that which had been done in Rotterdam.

In the neighbourhood of the Royal Palace the damage was more severe, so it seemed that the Germans had been up to their old game of endeavouring to eliminate the Head of the State, but as he turned into the Rue Montoyer he saw that it was practically untouched. There was only one great gap among the houses, where a bomb had cut like a knife clean through the block.

Suddenly he looked again and halted, utterly aghast. The empty air above that great pile of débris was where Erika's flat had been; the whole building had been blown to fragments.

17

Dark Days in Brussels

For a long time Gregory was too stunned to do anything but stand there, staring at the empty gap between the houses where Erika's apartment had been. He was very far from a pessimist by nature yet, perhaps because they had escaped so many dangers, it had never occurred to him that Erika might be the casual victim of an air-raid. As he stared he began to suffer untold agonies, one symptom of which was a real physical pain right down in the pit of his stomach, at the thought that she was irretrievably lost to him.

Unnoticed by him an elderly man had shuffled up behind him, and he started as a thin, quavering voice at his elbow said in French: 'That was a big one—that was. I live three streets away, but we heard it above all the rest, and I said to my wife,

I said: "That's a big one—that is"—and sure enough I was right. Twenty bodies they took out of that pile of ruins, and I wouldn't be surprised if there's more of them buried there yet.'

'Go away!' snapped Gregory, turning on the old ghoul furiously.

'All right, all right.' The elderly man looked slightly offended. 'I'm only telling you what I saw. Six men, nine women and five children they brought out, though most of them were in bits, and I don't doubt there's more bodies under that heap yet.'

'Go away!' repeated Gregory. 'Go away.' Then, as his un-solicited informant turned to dodder off, it suddenly occurred to him to ask: 'What time did the bomb fall?'

The old man piped up with an angry squeak. 'Find out for yourself; I'm not giving any more details to a rude fellow like you.'

In one stride Gregory had caught him up and, seizing him by his skinny neck, shook him like a rat. He dropped his stick, his hat fell off and his pale-blue eyes showed wild panic.

'Now,' said Gregory; 'answer me! When did that bomb fall?'

'Two nights ago—near on one o'clock,' choked the little man, and taking to his heels the second that Gregory released him he began to run down the street.

Gregory groaned. At one in the morning Erika would almost certainly have been at home; but his faculties were beginning to return to him and without another glance at the retreating figure he had assaulted he started to run down the street in the opposite direction. There were no taxis to be had or he would have secured one an hour earlier, directly he had reached the centre of the town; so he ran and walked alternately all the way to the Hotel Astoria.

When he arrived there twenty minutes later he found that the hotel was still open but had been taken over as a German Staff Headquarters. There were a number of cars outside, a sentry was posted on the doorway and officers were constantly going in and out.

Having thrust his German passport under the sentry's nose, which resulted in the soldier's springing to attention and pre-senting arms, he hurried inside. To his relief he found that the Belgian head porter had been retained to continue his duties. He inquired at once if the man knew what had become of Kuporovitch.

The porter told him that the Russian had left Brussels early the previous Tuesday morning in a car, with a lady.

Gregory's heart bounded with hope, only to sink again a moment later as the porter went on to add that the car belonged to the lady, who was a great friend of the Russian gentleman, as during the past five weeks she had often called at the hotel and taken meals with him in the restaurant. That could only refer to Paula, as was confirmed when Gregory asked the porter to describe the lady and he said that she was very good-looking with dark hair and with a rather high colour. He was quite certain that no other lady had been with them and that Kuporovitch had departed without giving any hint as to his destination, or leaving any message for anyone.

He thanked the man and staggered out into the strong sunshine of the street. It seemed a little odd that Paula should have fled from Brussels, as there was no earthly reason for her to be afraid of the advancing Germans; but on second thoughts Gregory realised that if she remained in captured territory she would become useless to them. Evidently her instructions had been to get out before they arrived so that she could continue her work in western Belgium or France in the rôle of a refugee from Nazi persecution. But he could not understand at all why Kuporovitch had failed to leave some message for him. The Russian must have known that Erika's death now left him as the sole link between the Allies and the activities of Hitler's secret weapon in the Low Countries, and although it seemed that, for Gregory, the end of the world had come, he realised in a dull fashion underneath his pain that the war must go on.

It was that thought which stirred him into fresh activity. While the old man had been talking to him his imagination had conjured up a ghastly picture of his beautiful Erika, her golden hair in wild disorder, her blue eyes open but dull and blood trickling from the corner of her mouth, as she lay crushed and broken among those ruins. In the last half-hour that nightmare vision had kept returning to him and he knew that he must exorcise it from his brain if he was to retain his sanity. The only way to do that was to work and to kill Germans—that was it— work and kill—work and kill—so that his mind should be occupied for every moment of his waking hours. Then when he dared to think of her again he must think of her only as he had seen her in Munich, or on that first evening that he had played butler to her in Brussels—as gay, laughing and unbelievably beautiful.

He had walked some distance without even thinking where he was going; but now he checked himself and turned down the hill towards the centre of the town. When he reached the broad Boulevard Anspach he halted opposite the Metropole Hotel. There were three cars outside and at that moment a porter came out carrying some luggage; so the hotel was evidently still open and had not yet been taken over by the Germans.

As he stepped forward to enter it a fresh wave of pain engulfed his whole mentality. It was here, barely a fortnight ago, that he had said good-bye to Erika. For a second his footsteps faltered; he thought of turning round and making for the Grand, but he knew that now, if ever, he must be firm with himself. Bracing his muscles he went in, reclaimed the suitcase which he had left there under the name of Colonel-Baron von Lutz and asked for a room. There were plenty of rooms available, as four-fifths of the guests had fled bag and baggage the previous day, but the desk clerk told him that most of the staff had also left, so he would have to put up with certain inconveniences. He said that he did not mind that and the clerk gave him the key of a room with directions how to find it, as there was no page available to take him up.

Once upstairs he turned on a hot bath, stripped and got into it. For over an hour he lay soaking there, keeping up the temperature by adding more hot water from time to time. He had not done too badly for sleep since his escape from Holland— a good night at Harwich and about six hours in the cottage outside Brussels where he had wakened that morning—and his exertions since leaving England had not been great; so he was not particularly tired after the seven or eight miles that he had walked since dawn; but the hot water helped to relax his mind as well as his limbs and while he lay there he tried to plan what his next move should be.

During his days of imprisonment and of subsequent travel the Black Baroness had never been far from his thoughts. The fact that when he had run her to earth Grauber, of all people, had been in her suite, and that the Gestapo Chief had treated her with great deference, fully confirmed his belief that she was not only hand-in-glove with the Nazis but regarded by them as an ally of considerable importance. That she had got the best

236

of him in their first encounter only made him the more determined to find some way of putting a stop to her activities; but the question was how to set about it.

Her meeting with Grauber in Rotterdam, only an hour before the *Blitzkrieg* was due to open, indicated that her work in Holland had been completed and that she had met him to receive fresh instructions for future operations in some other field; so the probability was that when she had flown out of Holland she had gone to France or Britain. For Gregory to reach either, now that he was behind the German line, presented certain difficulties, but these, he felt, were by no means insurmountable. He had crossed the battle-line in safety only that morning and as long as the contending forces remained in a state of fluidity he saw no reason why he should not cross it again without any greater risk than that which is run by a soldier who is engaged in open warfare; but it would mean another long and tiring journey on foot and when he got through to friendly territory he did not quite see what he was going to do there.

Now that he had lost touch with Paula and Kuporovitch he had no means of getting fresh information about the Baroness's movements, and by this time she might be anywhere from Edinburgh to Monte Carlo; so it seemed that he might spend weeks snooping about in city after city without coming upon any trace of her and, meanwhile, close at hand the greatest battle in history was raging. The more he thought it over the more certain he became that he could serve his country to much more useful purpose at this hour of crisis by remaining where he was and learning anything he could of the Germans' intentions, before endeavouring to recross the firing-line, than by setting off now, empty-handed.

Having shaved and dressed he went down to the restaurant, and found that it presented a very different scene from when he had last entered it. There were now few civilians at the tables but many groups of German officers and, not for the first time, he thought with some bitterness of the enormous advantages reaped by the enemy from being the aggressor. Just as in the last war the Germans could, and did, render any town or village within range of their guns either untenable or dangerous, while in a retreat they deliberately razed every house to the ground so that our men should not even have the benefit of roofs under which to shelter; whereas, since we always fought in friendly

237

territory we had to respect property, even to some extent in the actual battle area, and when the enemy made a victorious advance he could use captured towns as safety zones for troop-concentrations or to give his men rest and enjoyment with complete immunity, as there could never be any question of our shelling such cities as Brussels, Oslo or Amsterdam.

In spite of the shortage of staff an excellent meal was still obtainable, as no food stocks had yet been commandeered and the supply in Brussels was abundant; but for once in his life he took no interest in ordering his meal and accepted the waiter's suggestion without comment, asking the man at the same time to bring him any papers that were available.

The waiter returned with the single sheet of an emergency edition which had been run off the press about ten o'clock and was the only paper that had been published in Brussels that morning. From a small sketch map he saw that the bulge south of Sedan had considerably enlarged and was spreading towards the west, while in the south the Germans had nearly reached Rethel. Liège and Namur were now both surrounded but were fighting on. The most alarming news, however, was a report that the Belgians had abandoned Antwerp. That seemed to Gregory an extremely serious matter as the great fortifications of the city formed the bulwark of the northern end of the Allied line, and if the Germans once broke through there they would have outflanked the Northern Armies.

When his food came he realised that he was still feeling too sick to eat more than a few mouthfuls, so he abandoned the uneven contest, paid the bill and went out to see if any of the shops were now open. He found that quite a number of the smaller places had taken down their shutters in preparation to doing business with such of their old customers as remained in the city or with the troops of the all-conquering Army, since shopkeepers must do their best to earn a living even when their city has been occupied by an enemy.

Having bought himself a few necessities he took them back to the hotel, then went out again, taking the road which led east towards Louvain. Nearly all civilian traffic had ceased, so he had made up his mind to a long, dreary tramp; but in the suburbs he was fortunate enough to see an empty farm-cart proceeding in the direction that he wanted to go, so he hailed the driver and secured a lift.

The man told him that the Germans had commandeered the

238

hay in his barn that morning and had made him take it in for them to a depot which they had established on the outskirts of the city, and that he was now returning home. Gregory said that he was a commercial traveller who had been caught in Brussels and wished to get back to his family in Hasselt, as he was acutely anxious to learn if his wife and children had escaped harm. The two of them then exchanged gloomy forebodings about the fate that had overtaken their country, as the farm wagon trundled on through the afternoon sunshine with the sound of the guns behind it growing gradually more distant.

As they proceeded down the long, straight road they soon came upon many signs of the previous day's battle; shattered tanks, guns and Bren-gun carriers lay wrecked or overturned on the road and in the fields to either side of them. They had lost all their martial glory and looked now rather pathetic; as though they were just old toys that some gargantuan child had thrown down and kicked about in a fit of temper. The German mortuary units were evidently still occupied in burying the fallen from the holocausts that had taken place earlier, further east, as they had not yet come up. Here and there sprawled khaki or field-grey figures; some twisted or lacking limbs, others lying quite peacefully as though they had taken the afternoon off to sleep in the fields under the warm rays of the May sunshine. German and English dead and vehicles were inextricably mixed so that there was no pattern discernible in this aftermath of battle, except occasionally round an abandoned gun where a whole crew had been knocked out by a shell or machine-gunned from the air.

Gregory was not interested in the tanks, but he *was* interested in the bodies and, without allowing his companion to notice what he was doing, he carefully took mental notes about the position of several of the dead Germans who lay near enough to the road for him to see them clearly.

About six miles outside Brussels the farmer pulled up and said that his farm lay down a side-track to the left of the road. Gregory got down and, thanking him, continued on foot in the direction of Louvain; but when the wagon was out of sight he turned round and started to walk back again.

He kept a sharp look-out, as German staff cars and bodies of troops were passing every few moments in the direction of Brussels, and he knew that if he were caught at his ghoulish purpose he would be shot without argument. Leaving the road he walked along behind the hedge until he was within ten yards of the nearest body that he had marked down. He was now able to get a much closer view of it and having taken in all the details he gradually worked his way back through field after field to look carefully at the others; then, having made his choice, as it was only six o'clock he lay down under a hedge to take a nap until darkness should cover his further operations.

When he awoke the moon had risen, but it was low in the sky so its light was just enough to be excellent for his purpose without being sufficient to make it likely that he would be seen by the troops that he could still hear every now and again rattling along the road. Going to the body he had selected he unbuttoned the dead German's uniform and exerting all his strength forced back the arms, which were already set in *rigor mortis,* until he could wriggle the tunic off the body. He next dealt in similar fashioned with the man's breeches, gaiters, boots and under-garments until the body was stark naked. He then stripped off his own clothes, stuffed them in the dead man's haversack and put on his outfit so that if he were searched at any time he would not be wearing a single article of clothing which would have given away the fact that he was not a German.

The boots were a trifle large but otherwise the uniform fitted passably well, as Gregory had taken great care to select a man as near his own height and build as possible. Before he had set out he had realised that it would be like looking for a needle in a haystack to try to find a dead Staff-Colonel, as such minor war lords are not killed in every battle and, even if he had been able to do so, it was a hundred to one that the Colonel's uniform would have proved hopelessly ill-fitting on himself; so fit being more important than rank he had despoiled an *Uber-Lieutenant* with the reservation that he would adjust the matter of his rank later.

As the officer had been shot through the eye his uniform was undamaged and passably clean, but his steel helmet proved too small so Gregory had to find another which fitted him better. He then collected the dead German's automatic, spare magazines, gas-mask, Ziess glasses, and other gear. By the time he had finished hanging things on himself his appearance in every detail was that of an *Uber-Lieutenant* of the 153rd Bavarian Infantry Regiment, fully equipped in battle kit. He then set out on the trek back to Brussels.

Ahead of him now, on the far side of the city, the night sky was constantly lit with the flicker of guns and shell-bursts, while along the road down which he was walking the never-ending columns of German troops went forward to reinforce their comrades. It was half-past four in the morning when he at last reached the Metropole, and the night-porter, not having seen him go out dressed as a civilian, had no reason to express surprise because he came in dressed as a German officer. With a gruff *'Gute nacht'* he crossed the hall and went up to his room, where he doffed his borrowed plumage and got into bed.

Not having left any orders to be called he awoke late on the following morning, and his first sensation was one of uneasiness. It seemed as though some dire calamity threatened him; yet for a few seconds he could not think what it was that he feared. Then, like a light being clicked on in a darkened room, the awful truth seared with a blinding glare through his brain. Erika was dead.

For some moments he lay almost stunned again, but after a little he recalled his resolution of the previous day and, getting up, dressed in his stolen uniform. It was nearly twelve o'clock by the time he came downstairs and he saw that a number of German officers were already congregated in the lounge, chatting and laughing over their *apéritifs*. He made a quick survey of them but to his disappointment there was no one of Colonel's rank present so, seating himself at a small table where he could keep an eye upon the door, he ordered a drink and sent for the morning paper.

It was now two double-sheets again, but a glance at the head-lines showed that it was already under German 'protection'. Dr. Goebbels' men had lost no time in getting their claws on the Brussels Press. As Gregory's eye roved over the heavy black print he saw with a little shock that it was Sunday, the 19th, as his periods of sleep in recent days and nights had been so erratic that he had been under the impression up to that moment that it was only Saturday.

The German drive continued with unabated vigour. Their spear-head had now veered almost due west, towards St. Quentin and the Channel ports, so evidently their intention was to endeavour to sever the Belgians, the B.E.F. and certain French divisions just south of it from the main French Army; but Gregory did not view this new development altogether pessimistically.

In 1915 the Germans had followed much the same procedure. Although the way had been almost clear for a direct march on Paris, instead of wheeling down on to the French capital General von Kluck, who had commanded the right wing of the German Army, had suddenly turned west in an endeavour to seize the Channel ports before they could be reinforced from England.

In doing so he made the cardinal error of defying the first rule of strategy, which is that a commander should never march his troops *across* the front of an unbroken enemy. Von Kluck's mistake had been due to the fact that he believed that he *had* broken the British at Mons and Le Cateau, and shattered them so severely that it would be quite impossible for them to take the offensive for many weeks to come; but, as it turned out, the British were by no means beaten. Together with the French Army which General Gallieni had rushed by omnibus and taxi-cab from Paris, they had faced about and, flinging their whole weight against Von Kluck's exposed flank, achieved the victory of the Marne. That battle had robbed the Kaiser of both Paris and the Channel ports and, in the estimation of the most far-sighted strategists, deprived Germany once and for all of any hope of ever achieving complete victory, by giving *time* for the British Empire to mobilise its vast resources before France could be put out of the war.

It seemed to Gregory that a very similar situation was now developing, and that if Gamelin threw his reserves in at the right moment he ought to be able to take this new German thrust in the flank and perhaps roll the German Armies up in confusion right back out of Belgium, as swiftly as they had poured into it.

A small news item stated that Marshal Pétain, the eighty-four-year-old hero of Verdun, had joined the French Government as its Vice-President the previous night, and that, too, seemed a good omen, as the leadership of this great veteran of the last World War was well calculated to strengthen the resistance of the French troops.

Gregory sat there drinking for the best part of an hour and a half before he saw a Colonel come in; immediately the Colonel sat down with some other officers he got up and strolled out of the lounge.

Crossing the hall to the cloakroom he produced a fifty-franc note from his pocket, handed it to the elderly woman who was checking-in the coats and said casually: 'All the pages seem to have run away, so I must trouble you to slip out and buy me a rubber sponge and a shaving-stick.'

The woman looked at him in surprise and murmured: 'It is not my business to run errands, *Monsieur*.'

'Do as you're told!' snapped Gregory, suddenly changing his mild manner for that of the brutal invader.

'But, *Monsieur*,' she protested, 'I am in charge of the coats and the things that people have left here.'

'Do as you're told!' he repeated harshly. 'You Belgians must learn to take orders from your betters without argument.'

'*Oui, Monsieur, oui*,' the poor woman exclaimed nervously, and as she hurried away Gregory called after her: 'When you get back you'll find me in the lounge.'

Immediately she had disappeared he left the counter over which the coats were thrust and, walking a few paces down a side-passage, entered the door of the cloakroom. Most of the coats there were the field-grey great-coats of German officers; each had been neatly folded and placed in a large pigeon-hole. Gregory ran his eye swiftly over what appeared to be the most recent additions to the collection, as they were low down in the rack, and after pulling out two he discovered the Colonel's. Producing his pocket-knife he swiftly cut the rank badges from the shoulders.

Next he pulled out several other officers' coats one after the other, jabbed his penknife into them, making ugly slits, tore off buttons or badges and thrust them back into their pigeon-holes. The whole job was accomplished in less than five minutes, then he strolled back to his table in the lounge, where the old woman found him when she returned with the sponge and shaving-soap.

Thanking her with a haughty nod he tossed her five francs and sat on there for another few minutes; then he went upstairs and proceeded to affix the Colonel's rank-badges to the shoulders of his own tunic in place of those of the *Uber-Lieutenant*. There was no reason whatever why anyone should suspect him of the theft as he had camouflaged it so skilfully by mutilating a number of other coats as well as the Colonel's. The cloakroom woman would excuse herself to their infuriated owners by saying that she had been compelled to leave her post to run an errand for another officer and the damage would undoubtedly be attributed to some unknown Belgian who had chosen to express his hatred of the Germans by this petty malice. The great thing was that now that he had secured both a passably fitting uniform and the right rank-badges he was all set to resume his activities as *Oberst-Baron* von Lutz once more.

After eating his lunch in a nearby restaurant, to avoid any chance of being involved in the scene which was certain to ensue when his victims reclaimed their coats, he spent the afternoon in the main streets of Brussels and at the railway station, carefully noting the regimental, divisional and corps badges of the officers and men whom he saw so that he could get a good idea as to which units were apparently being quartered in Brussels and which were passing through to the front. The battle, he noted, seemed to have drifted further west since the previous night, although the British heavies were still spasmodically shelling the station and certain road junctions outside the town. By evening he felt that he was sufficiently well-informed to enter into conversation with some of the German officers, and for that purpose he made a round of such bars as had reopened.

During the six days that followed, Gregory slipped into an uninspired routine. The husk of the man was still there, as he stuck grimly to his determination to absorb himself in work, and every moment of his waking hours was conscientiously spent in restaurants, cafés and bars, wherever large numbers of German officers were gathered together; but it seemed that the shock of Erika's death had numbed his brain and temporarily robbed him of all initiative.

After a comparatively brief stupor Brussels had gradually come to life again. Owing to the petrol restrictions imposed by the Germans and the dislocation of Belgian industry the traffic in the capital was still far below normal, in spite of the many German Army vehicles that were constantly passing through the streets, and the bulk of the civil population had the subdued, anxious air of people who had suffered a great bereavement—as indeed many of them had; but nearly all the shops were open again and the whole centre of the town was thronged with the thousands of Germans who were passing through or now quartered in Brussels.

Gregory found no difficulty whatever in entering into casual conversation with scores of officers each day and despite standing orders that they should not mention troop movements or casualties, even among themselves, the great majority of them ignored these regulations to discuss all phases of the war with the pseudo Staff-Colonel without the least restraint.

In those six days he learnt enough about individual units, and how they had fared in Hitler's victory drive, to fill half a dozen dossiers; but the trouble was that none of the people he contacted were high enough up to be in a position to give away anything of major importance. He wanted to unearth something really useful before leaving Brussels in an attempt to get it through to British G.H.Q. or Sir Pellinore, and such items about contemplated operations as he did succeed in picking up were on each occasion ante-dated and rendered useless by the extraordinary swiftness of the German advance.

On the Monday they were at Cambrai and Peronne, and the French front in the whole of the threatened area had given way in a general mix-up.

On Tuesday, Amiens and Arras fell, while through a corridor between these two towns motorised detachments were rushed to seize Abbeville. By evening it was reported that they were threatening Le Touquet and had reached the coast, cutting the Allied Armies in two so that there was now a gap between them thirty miles wide.

On the Wednesday the French were said to have recaptured Arras, while the British were counter-attacking in force at Douai, so that the gap had been reduced to twelve miles; but the Germans had already poured great quantities of tanks through it and were disrupting the Allies' communications right, left and centre, while enemy advance units had turned north and were dashing up the coast towards Boulogne and Calais.

On Thursday the Germans entered Boulogne and captured the town in spite of heavy shelling from the British Navy. On the north of the gap the British were now thrusting south towards Cambrai, between the Rivers Scarpe and Scheldt, while in the south the French were endeavouring to retake Amiens; the obvious intention of both armies being an attempt to reunite somewhere in the neighbourhood of Albert, thereby cutting off all the German motorised units which had broken through towards the coast.

On the Friday the Germans launched another hammerblow further east, in the Sedan sector, but it seemed that the French had got their second wind and were holding on there; and, although the German-controlled Press made no mention of any reverse, it was whispered among the officers in Brussels that the French had recaptured Amiens. The B.E.F. was reported to be fighting hard on the Cambrai-Valenciennes road, but the gap was nearly thirty miles wide again and German divisions were still pouring through it. The situation in Boulogne and Calais was obscure but the papers proclaimed confidently that they were in German hands and it seemed that for every sector in which they were temporarily checked they scored fresh successes in two others. So great, too, was the strength of the German Army that, in spite of all these offensive operations which they were conducting simultaneously, that day they launched yet another furious onslaught against the Belgians in the extreme north.

On the Saturday the situation became even more obscure. The Germans claimed the capture of Courtrai and Vimy while it was officially stated that the Belgian Army with the 1st, 7th and 9th French Armies and the B.E.F. were completely cut off; but it was difficult to see from which direction Courtrai and Vimy had been attacked, as these French Armies and the B.E.F. now seemed to be fighting on several fronts at the same time, and, in fact, it became generally recognised that in the north all trace of any coherent line had now disappeared. Over an area exceeding 20,000 square miles of territory, some 3,000,000 armed men were in one colossal mix-up, with unit fighting unit, wherever it came upon the enemy, and out of this incredible confusion only one coherent plan now emerged—that the Germans were straining every nerve completely to surround and destroy the whole of the Allied Northern Army.

With every day that passed Gregory had believed that the German effort must slacken, and when he had learnt on the Monday that General Weygand had superseded Gamelin as the Allied Commander-in-Chief he had felt confident that the great strategist would find some way in which to avert the peril in which the Northern Armies stood. He had realised that Weygand would need several days at least to alter the disposition of his main forces, but that made Gregory all the more hopeful that when the blow fell the Germans would be too exhausted to counter it effectively, so that it might be carried through to a sweeping victory; but the end of the week came without any news of a great French counter-offensive. Even their efforts to break through from the south appeared to have lessened, while instead of the German effort petering out it seemed ever to increase in violence.

It was the huge hundred-ton tanks, which Hitler had had made at the Skoda Works during the winter while the Allies were sitting still so complacently, that had been responsible for the initial break-through across the Meuse at Sedan, and there was no doubt about it that the German weapons were in every way superior to those of the British and French, but it was not these factors alone which were giving Keitel and von Brauchitsch their victories.

Battles had to be planned, great feats of organisation undertaken to supply the fighting troops at the end of the ever-lengthening lines of communications and, above all, the men who drove the flame-throwing tanks, cast the pontoon bridges over the rivers and ran forwards over mile after mile of enemy territory spraying bullets from their tommy-guns, had to possess enormous powers of endurance. There was no getting away from it that the German Generals were supreme above all others at their business, that the regimental officers were staggeringly efficient and that the German rank and file were proving in every way worthy of their brilliant leadership. They might be inhuman brutes who allowed no considerations of mercy or humanity to stand in their way, and even add to the horror of this most horrifying of all wars by machine-gunning helpless civilians to create further panic and confusion, but Gregory, whom no one could ever have accused of defeatism yet who never shirked facing facts, frankly admitted to himself that out of a broken people Hitler had welded a nation of iron men who were achieving a stupendous victory.

It was a little after six o'clock in the evening on Saturday, May the 25th, when walking along the Avenue du Midi that Gregory's eye was caught by a trim figure just in front of him. There was something vaguely familiar about the jaunty step of the dark-haired young woman in her neat black coat and skirt; then, a second later, he recognised the absurd little black hat. It was *Mademoiselle* Jacqueline. In two strides he was beside her and had grabbed her arm. For a second she stared up at him in angry surprise, then he saw recognition, amazement and hate follow each other swiftly in her dark eyes.

'*Mon dieu!*' she cried as she strove to jerk herself away. 'You —Pierre—a German officer!'

In his excitement he had completely forgotten how he was dressed and her exclamation gave him the reason for the anti-pathy with which she was staring at him; but he was too anxious to hear anything she could tell him to care about that for the moment, and could only gasp out: *'Madame*—what happened? —Tell me—tell me!'

'So!' she almost hissed. 'I thought you were a queer sort of servant paying me to do your job and always going out instead of doing it yourself; then suddenly clearing off four days after you arrived. But you weren't a servant at all; you were a spy— a beastly German spy. It was you, I suppose, who had us bombed. I'll tell you nothing—nothing—*nothing!'*

With a scream of rage she suddenly jerked free her arm and dashed off down the street as swiftly as her strong little legs would carry her.

18

The Cryptogram

For a second Gregory was about to start forward in pursuit but he checked himself in time. No German officer would so far forget his dignity as to chase a young woman through the streets of Brussels and there was a better way of dealing with the situation. Raising his hand he waved to a Belgian policeman who was standing on the crossroads and shouted at the top of his voice:

'Officer! Stop that woman and bring her to me!'

The man hesitated, but two German privates who were walking past turned their heads and seeing that the order came from one of their officers instantly leapt into action, so the Belgian followed suit; the three of them cornered the unfortunate Jacqueline and while Gregory stood placidly smoking on the pavement the policeman brought her back to him.

'Thank you, officer,' said Gregory. 'I don't think she will try to run away again.'

'Do you wish to prefer any charge against this young woman?' asked the policeman.

'Not for the moment,' Gregory replied. 'You may leave us now while I talk to her, but if she gives any trouble I shall have to ask you to take her to the police-station.'

When the Belgian had retired Gregory looked at the white-faced, frightened girl who was now standing meekly in front of him. '*Enfin, ma petite Jacqueline,*' he said quietly, 'I hope you appreciate that by trying to run away you nearly got yourself into very serious trouble. I take it that you do not wish to see the inside of a prison, but it would be easy for me to have you put into one. I could charge you with soliciting, or say that you had stolen my money, and as we Germans are now masters of Brussels my word would be taken in preference to yours. I could also, if I wished, have you sent to a concentration-camp in Germany—which you would find even more unpleasant. But I do not wish to do any of these horrid things. Instead, I am prepared to give you a handsome present which will buy you at least half a dozen little hats, if only you will be a sensible girl and tell me what happened after I left Brussels.'

Jacqueline *was* a sensible girl. Although she loathed the Germans, this one seemed quite prepared to treat her very generously and it did not appear that any question of betraying her country was involved in giving him particulars of past events; so, after a moment, she said:

'Let me see, now, you left Brussels on the Thursday, didn't you, to go to the bedside of your dying aunt? But that was just a story to enable you to get back into Germany and join your regiment; because it was in the early hours of the following morning that the *Blitzkrieg* broke.'

'Yes, yes,' said Gregory. 'Never mind about me.'

'Be patient,' she admonished him with a sudden show of spirit. 'If I am to tell you things properly I must get the dates right. Naturally, we were all terribly worried and the first air-raid was very frightening, although none of the bombs fell anywhere near us. Now, would it have been on the Monday or the Tuesday that the wicked-looking Russian gentleman came to the flat very late at night? It must have been between one and two o'clock in the morning, and he got us all out of bed.'

'Never mind about him, said Gregory impatiently; 'it is about *Madame* that I wish to hear.'

Jacqueline stamped her neat little foot. 'But I'm telling you—as quickly as I can, and I'm trying to remember if it was on the Tuesday or the Wednesday that *Madame* packed and went away.'

'Went away?' cried Gregory, and the street seemed to reel around him. 'Do you mean—do you mean that she wasn't killed by the bomb that destroyed the whole building?'

'*Mais non!*' She stared at him with wildly open eyes. '*Madame*

249

had left Brussels days before. Yes, I'm certain now, it was on the Monday night that the Russian gentleman knocked us up, then first thing on Tuesday morning *Madame* gave us a month's wages and went off, bag and baggage, saying that Cook and I could remain on in the apartment if we liked.'

'Thank God!' murmured Gregory. 'Oh, thank God!'

'It seems, then, that you were much more interested in *Madame* than you were in me, *Monsieur* Pierre?' remarked Jacqueline pertly.

He smiled and nodded. 'Yes. *Madame* is my wife—or at least she will be the moment that she can get her divorce!'

Jacqueline frowned. 'She, too, then, was a German spy and not a Norwegian lady at all. I would never have believed it of her.'

'That, my young friend, is none of your business,' Gregory said somewhat sharply, as he produced his pocket-book and took out a five-hundred-franc note. 'And now, please, you will give me the letter that *Madame* left for me.'

Jacqueline had not meant to say anything about the letter, but with considerable astuteness he had spiked her guns by implying that there had been a definite understanding that *Madame* should leave a letter for him, and she had it with her in her bag. If she denied all knowledge of it and he took her to the police-station to have her searched she might find herself in a pretty mess when it was discovered; so she swiftly decided that she had better not play any tricks with this particular German and opening her bag she handed it to him.

He ripped it open and read:

Queen Wilhelmina's flight and the news that General Winkelman proposes to surrender in a few hours have affected the situation here, so I am moving to Ghent. You will find me at the Hotel de la Poste or if there are no rooms to be had I will leave my address with the manager there. God keep you and protect you, my darling. All my love, Erika.

'Thank you,' said Gregory, passing over the five-hundred-franc note. 'You were right about the day *Madame* left, as this letter is dated Tuesday the 14th. How long after that was it that you were bombed?'

'That was on the Thursday night. The Germans had been bombing the neighbourhood of the Palace for some days. Poor

Cook was killed but I had a very lucky escape. I spent the evening at home with my father and mother and they would not let me go back through the streets while the air-raid was going on, so I didn't know anything about it until the following morning.'

'Good,' said Gregory. 'I'm sorry about Cook; she was a decent old soul; but let's hope that your luck continues through this wretched war; then you'll be able to tell your grandchildren how once upon a time you shared your pantry with a German Staff-Colonel and cleaned his silver for him while he went out to make love to your mistress. *Au revoir, ma petite Jacqueline,* and take good care of yourself.' With a smart salute he turned away and set off down the street, beaming with happiness at the surprised passers-by.

By seven o'clock he was back at the Metropole singing as he packed his bag; by a quarter-past he was downstairs paying his bill, and by half-past he was at the *Gare du Nord*. To travel he should have had a military railway voucher, but to secure one he would have had to have given an account of himself to the railway transport officer, which would have been a very tricky business and, in any case, caused him considerable delay, so he decided to travel without one.

Having found out that the next train for the west was leaving from Platform Number Five he took cover behind a tobacco kiosk where he could not be seen from the barrier but could keep his eye upon the train. The second that it started to move he came dashing out, frantically waving aside the Belgian railway official and German military police, who were standing at the barrier. Seeing his high rank at a glance the military police did not attempt to stop him but flung the barrier wide and he was just in time to leap on to the step of the guard's van.

Panting a little, but decidedly pleased with himself, he remained there until the train had cleared the station, then he went along the corridor to see if he could find himself a seat. The whole train was packed with troops going up to the front, but a junior officer promptly surrendered his place and thanking him politely Gregory sat down.

He could still hardly believe the marvellous news he had received about Erika, yet now, in a way, he wondered that he had so readily taken her death for granted. On considering the matter he came to the conclusion that it was the combination of circumstances which had caused him to do so. As far as he could then judge there had been no reason at all for her to leave

Brussels until the Friday, and the bomb had fallen on the Thursday night at a time when she would normally have been in bed, or at least in the block, and the bomb had demolished the whole building, killing, as the old ghoul had told him, twenty people. Oblivious of his surroundings he now sat there in the crowded railway carriage positively glowing with happiness.

The train chugged on into the dusk, stopping for no apparent reason every ten minutes, as is the habit of military trains behind all battle-fronts. In normal times the journey from Brussels to Ghent would not have taken more than an hour, but it was past ten when they reached Alost, which was only about half-way, and everybody was ordered out as the train was going no further, having reached rail-head.

Gregory was now within sound of the guns again and the principal activity seemed to be to the south, although he had only a vague idea as to the position of the constantly-changing front. As far as he had been able to gather, the British had put up a magnificent show during the last eight days and had been forced back only to about thirty miles south and west of Brussels, but, although they were heavily outnumbered, the greatest hammer-blows of the Germans were not being directed against them. The enemy's maximum effort, after they had reached the coast, had been directed against the French in the Rethel area, south of the Maginot Line, and in the extreme north against the Belgians. The Belgians were said to have been standing well, but on the previous night the Germans had forced them back and captured Ghent, so it seemed that the B.E.F. who were holding the line of the Scheldt were now in some danger of being outflanked both from the north and from the south; but that was as far as he could assess the position.

Outside the station there were a number of military cars and going up to one of them which had only two officers in it he asked its occupants if they could give him a lift in the direction of Ghent. They said that they were going there and would be happy to oblige the *Herr Oberst,* so he got in and they moved off into the long line of German mechanised vehicles which for many days now had been streaming without cessation towards the west.

The officer who was driving took every advantage that he could in slipping past slower vehicles and long columns of marching infantry, but even so, their pace was appallingly slow. Gregory swopped cigarettes and stories with his two companions but he was burning with impatience to get to Ghent. Erika would not be there any longer as the Germans had entered the town the previous night, but once he reached Ghent he felt confident that he would be able to secure fresh tidings of her.

Twice on their way they had to pull up and take shelter in the nearest ditch, as the R.A.F. were strafing the German lines of communication; and for minutes at a time bombs whined, crashed and thudded a few hundred yards away on or near the road. In each case the raids caused further delay as wrecked tanks, lorries and guns had to be hauled from the road afterwards and the casualties collected before the column could move on again; but shortly after midnight they reached their destination.

The sound of the guns was much louder now as a night bombardment was taking place only a few miles away. Gregory thanked the two officers who had given him a lift and left them in the Butter Market to hurry to the Hotel de la Poste. Ghent had suffered severely from German air-raids and in several parts of the city fires were still burning, but to his relief he found the hotel undamaged. There were no civilian guests in it, but it was crowded with German officers snatching a hasty meal and a drink before going forward to join their regiments or turning in for a few hours' sleep, and it looked as though the over-worked staff would be kept up all night.

After some little delay Gregory succeeded in getting hold of the manager. He recalled Erika perfectly and said that he had not been able to accommodate her in the hotel, but had secured a room for her near the University, at Number 17 *Rue des Foulons*; he had, however, seen nothing of her since. Carrying his suitcase, Gregory then picked his way through streets littered with broken glass, tiles and rubble round to the *Rue des Foulons* and finding Number 17, after some difficulty, hammered on the door.

It was opened to him almost immediately by an elderly, bespectacled man who looked like a University professor. Although it was getting on for one o'clock in the morning he and his wife were still up, as a few days before their only daughter had been seriously wounded in an air-raid and they were watching by the poor girl's bedside while she hovered between life and death.

Having described Erika, Gregory asked for news of her, and

the owner of the house said at once that the beautiful Norwegian lady had occupied their spare room by arrangement with the hotel from the afternoon of Tuesday the 14th until midday on the previous Thursday, when she had left in a great hurry. He and his wife had been out at the time and although it was possible that the lady had left a message with his daughter, there was no means of knowing if that was so, as she had been wounded little more than an hour afterwards and had been unconscious ever since.

Gregory had naturally expected that Erika would have left another note for him to say for what town she was making, but if she had had to get out in a great hurry it was possible that she had not known herself where she would next be able to take up her quarters with a reasonable chance of keeping out of the clutches of the enemy for some days. It then occurred to him that she might have considered it unwise to leave any written message for him with these people but had left some indication of her general intentions which would be plain to him; so he asked politely if he might see the room that she had occupied.

The professorial-looking Belgian nodded and, his shoulders bowed from weariness, led Gregory upstairs to a pleasantly-furnished bedroom at the back of the house. It was just as Erika had left it since, with a dying daughter on their hands, the people of the house had been much too occupied to make the bed or tidy things up.

Gregory would have liked to have buried his face in the pillow where Erika's lovely head had rested, but he was too self-conscious to do so in the presence of the Belgian. Perhaps it was his imagination, but he thought that he could just catch the faintest lingering breath of the perfume that she used in the room, which seemed to bring her very close to him and, recalling his recent despair, he felt that Fate had dealt a little harshly with him in allowing him to pass through Ghent with Peachie Fostoun on Friday the 17th when, had he only known that Erika had already taken up her quarters there, he would have been spared those nine days in Brussels and an infinity of misery.

The householder recalled him to the present by asking if, having seen the room, he was satisfied. Gregory shook his head and, stepping forward, began to open all the drawers in the handsome old chests one after another; but there was nothing in any of them.

For the next ten minutes he poked around, looking behind pictures and in cupboards, still hoping that he would find some indication as to where Erika had made for; but he could see nothing at all in the room which might hold a clue until his eye fell upon a pack of patience cards lying on a small side-table.

They were Erika's and he knew that during his absences from her she often played patience far into the night to keep her mind off her anxieties; so it seemed strange that she should have forgotten to pack them. At the second glance he noticed that although the cards were in a neat stack the top one was torn clean in half. That could hardly have been an accident, with a sudden rising sense of excitement he felt that Erika must have left the little pack of cards there with the top one deliberately torn across to attract his attention to some message that they held.

He picked them up and looked through them. There was no slip of paper concealed between them, but when he counted the pack he found that it was three cards short. Rapidly checking them through he found that it was the Queen of Hearts, the Queen of Spades and the King of Diamonds which were missing.

Turning this over in his mind he could not make head or tail of it, so he began a new search of the room to see if he could find anything which might tie up with the missing cards. He had no luck until it occurred to him to pull the bed away from the wall, and there, concealed till then by the headboard of the bed, were the three cards. They were stuck up in a row with drawing-pins over a long pencilled arrow pointing to the right. The King of Diamonds was above the point of the arrow, the Queen of Spades came next and the Queen of Hearts last.

Sitting down on the end of the bed Gregory lit a cigarette and stared at this queer cryptogram, which he was quite convinced held some hidden message intended specially for him. According to card lore only very fair-haired people are Diamonds and Erika's hair was a rich, ripe golden colour. Her eyes, too, were not China-blue but deep sapphire, so she was undoubtedly the Queen of Hearts. Paula was probably the Queen of Spades and Kuporovitch the King of Diamonds; but that did not seem to infer anything. Why should the two girls be running after Kuporovitch? Moreover, although Kuporovitch's hair was grey his eyebrows were startlingly black and he had brown eyes, so he was not a Diamond person. Again, although Paula

255

was a brunette her hair was not jet-black so she really came into the category of Clubs. The thought 'jet-black' released a spring in Gregory's brain. Paula was not a true Spade type but he knew somebody who was. The Queen of Spades was the Black Baroness.

So far, so good. Erika was on the trail of *La Baronne Noire*; but in that case who was the Diamond gentleman? A fair-haired, blue-eyed man, evidently. Could it be Paula's friend, the Comte de Werbomont? Never having seen the Count, Gregory did not know if he was fair or dark, but the thought released another spring in his brain. The Count was attached to the Royal household. With a sudden laugh Gregory snapped his fingers. The King of Diamonds was *The King*—Leopold of Belgium. The Black Baroness was after him and Erika was after the Black Baroness. Here was the explanation why Erika had not left any more definite message. She did not know where the King would next set up his headquarters, but if he could find the King both Erika and the Baroness would not be far away.

Thanking the owner of the house, he expressed his earnest hope that the daughter would recover and walked downstairs. Just as he picked up his bag it occurred to him that his next move must be to work his way back across the battle-zone, and that he would once again stand much more chance of getting through without injury in daylight than while darkness lasted; so turning to the Belgian he asked him if he would be good enough to let him for the remainder of the night the room that Erika had occupied.

As the elderly man hesitated he added quickly: 'I shan't be the least trouble to you as I don't want any meals cooked or clean sheets or anything of that kind. It's just that I must get a few hours' sleep somewhere and if you don't mind my hiring the room that will save me stumbling round in the dark for an hour or so looking for one in the town.'

Although the Belgian had no cause whatever to love the Germans he could hardly refuse; so Gregory carried his suitcase straight upstairs. Taking off his uniform he slipped into the bed, where the impression of Erika's body could still be seen, to bury his face in her pillow where he was now quite certain that he could smell the perfume that recalled for him such glorious memories.

When he awoke at seven o'clock the sun was already streaming through the window. It was Sunday again, May the 26th, and although it had been consistently fine for three solid weeks there was not a trace of any break in the weather, which seemed to have been ordered specially for Hitler.

Having washed and shaved in the fixed basin he dressed himself in the old lounge-suit that had now seen so many vicissitudes, and packed the Colonel's uniform into his suitcase; then, after leaving some money on the dressing-table for his night's lodging, he cautiously opened the door and peered out. He thought it probable that the anxious father would be sleeping now after his night's vigil by his daughter's bedside and that the mother would be sitting with the girl; but in a well-furnished house of that size it seemed almost certain that there would be at least one maid, and he was anxious that anyone who knew that a German officer had occupied the spare room for the night should not see him leave the house in civilian clothes.

Stealthily he crept down the stairs, which fortunately were old and solid. In the small hallway he caught the sound of pots and pans from a back room, but in a couple of swift strides he had crossed the hall and, lifting the old-fashioned latch of the front door, he let himself out.

Striking away from the centre of the town he headed west and having no further use for the Colonel's uniform, his first concern was to rid himself of his bag as an unnecessary encumbrance. After ten minutes' fast walking he came to an empty, boarded-up plot between two houses so, having given a hasty glance round to see that he was not observed, he pushed the suitcase through a gap in the fence and hurried on.

Outside the town he got on to the Bruges road as, in view of the fact that Antwerp in the north had fallen days before and that the situation to the south was so obscure, Bruges-Ostend seemed the most likely line of retreat for the Belgian Royal Party. The German columns were still trundling westward but nobody took any notice of him as here and there other civilians were walking along the road or standing in front of their cottages watching the seemingly inexhaustible forces of the invader.

After he had covered about three miles, shells from the Allies' batteries began to pitch on to the road and into the fields on either side of it. The German column was then broken by its transport officers into sections with a two-hundred-yard gap between each so that the sections could be rushed one at a time through the zones in which the shells were bursting. As he advanced still further the column seemed to dissolve altogether; infantry and artillery units deployed into the fields or turned up side-tracks while only tanks continued down the highway. At the entrance to a shattered village he was halted by a patrol so he produced his German passport and said that he was an Intelligence Officer going forward in civilian clothes with the intention of penetrating the British lines and securing such information as he could about their strength and battery positions.

This statement proved to be a bad break as it transpired that the Germans were not up against the British in this sector, but the Belgians, and a suspicious sergeant insisted on holding him until an officer could question him further.

On being taken before a young Captain, Gregory endeavoured to lie his way out of the difficulty by saying that he had come direct from Corps Headquarters where they had definite information that certain British units had been moved up into that area during the night.

The Captain denied this and looked as if he were going to become extremely troublesome but Gregory was on the top of his form again. He put on his most authoritative Colonel-Baron manner and declared that for the present purposes it did not in the least matter whether British or Belgians were holding that sector of the line. What *did* matter was that he should get through as quickly as possible so that he could assess their strength himself, and that if he were delayed in his mission the Corps Commander would hold the Captain responsible. At this threat, delivered with icy Prussian arrogance, the young officer caved in and allowed him to proceed on his way.

He could, he knew, have avoided such potentially dangerous encounters by having retained his Colonel's uniform, but he had felt that he might have great difficulty in finding any suitable place in which to change into civilian clothes in broad daylight when he reached no-man's-land and, although he might have succeeded in getting himself quietly taken prisoner by the British or the Belgians, to advance into the Allies' lines dressed as a German officer was positively asking to be shot on sight; so he had preferred to face the trouble of satisfying any German patrol who chose to hold him up. In the next mile he was challenged four more times, but his passport as Colonel-

Baron von Lutz and his impeccable German got him through on each occasion.

The sunny landscape now presented a most misleading appearance. The road stretched away empty towards the horizon. Not a soul nor any sign of human acitivity was to be seen on either side of it except for the occasional flash of a camouflaged gun or the puff of smoke from a shell-burst; yet Gregory knew that the countryside was alive with men lying in ditches and concealed trenches. For the last hour he had been following the roadside ditch and a dozen times had had to fling himself down into it in order to escape shell fragments; but now he followed the tactics he had employed when crossing the battle-zone between Uccle and Brussels, going boldly forward in the centre of the road, except when it was positively dangerous to do so, and making himself as conspicuous as possible. After fifteen minutes' swift, and distinctly nerve-racking, walk he crossed a low ridge and drew level with some bushes. Suddenly a voice with a strong Lancashire accent cried:

'Hi, lad, coom 'ere an' giv' an account o' thyself!'

Switching round he saw that a British Tommy was covering him with a rifle. The man had not expected that his words would be understood, as he naturally imagined Gregory to be a Belgian, but his tone and attitude conveyed his meaning clearly enough. To the soldier's intense surprise Gregory replied: 'Ay, lad, I'll coom quietly if thou'llst take me to Colonel.'

'Ba goom!' The astounded Tommy grinned at three companions who had risen beside him to peer over the bushes. ''E coomes from Lancashire.'

'Sorry to disappoint you, but I'm a Londoner,' Gregory smiled. 'I'm an Intelligence Officer and I want to see your Colonel as quickly as possible.'

The manner of the lad from Lancashire immediately changed to friendly respect and joining Gregory on the road he accompanied him another quarter of a mile along it until they reached a small wood. Concealed in the wood lay a company headquarters and the Captain, having had a few words with Gregory, attached a runner to him to take him back to battalion headquarters.

Having covered half a mile with his new guide, during which they availed themselves of all the cover they possibly could to avoid being machine-gunned by German aircraft which had suddenly arrived overhead, they reached a barn inside which a

259

Colonel and his adjutant were seated at a rickety table studying a map. Gregory said that he had just come through the enemy lines after having spent over a week in Brussels so he wished to make a report upon what he had seen of the enemy's activities there.

The Colonel replied that such information would be much more useful to Divisional Intelligence than to himself. Gregory agreed, but he spent ten minutes telling the Colonel all he could of the disposition of the German forces immediately opposite to him; then with yet another guide he set off once more.

Some way further on they had to cross a slightly higher ridge and, on looking back, Gregory could see the whole of the local battle-front spread out before him. Shells were bursting much more frequently now on both sides of no-man's-land and away to the right a German attack was developing. He could make out about thirty tanks, like huge fast-moving slugs, bumping their way over hedges and ditches. As he watched several of them were suddenly obscured by splashes of flame and clouds of smoke. A British battery had got their range and was giving it to them hot and strong. In spite of his anxiety to be on his way he felt that he must stay to witness the end of the action and five minutes later, when the smoke had cleared, he saw that a dozen of the German tanks had stopped and were burning fiercely while the others had turned tail and were hurrying back to the shelter of a nearby wood; yet another German attack had been broken.

On the far side of the hill they came to the remnants of a village which had been almost blasted to pieces and was still being shelled by the German heavies. Making a circle round it through the fields they regained the road on its far side and found there, under cover in an orchard, a number of small cars and motor-cycle combinations. The runner who was acting as Gregory's guide handed him over to one of the motor-cyclists, and when Gregory was comfortably installed in a side-car they set off at a good pace down the road. Soon they were passing other vehicles but their progress was delayed from time to time by having to dismount and take shelter from the machine-gunners of the German planes that were harassing the road; but a little over an hour later, having bumped along several curving side-roads, they pulled up at a small, white château.

After a short wait an orderly took Gregory in to a Staff-Captain and he spent the next hour dictating a long report, giving all the particulars he could about the German forces that were operating in the neighbourhood of Brussels. When he had done the Staff-Captain asked him to wait for a moment and left the room. Ten minutes later he returned to say that the Divisional Commander would like to see him.

'That's good,' Gregory smiled, standing up, 'as I was going to ask you if he could spare a moment to see me.'

The General looked a little tired but was as unhurried in his speech and as carefully groomed as though he were sitting in an office in Whitehall. For about a quarter of an hour he asked many penetrating questions, which Gregory answered clearly and briefly to the best of his ability. He then said:

'You know, sir, it was a surprise to find that the British were holding this sector. The Germans are under the impression that they're fighting the Belgians up here.'

The General nodded. 'That's quite understandable. Until early yesterday we were holding the line of the Scheldt, but the Belgians received such a terrific hammering that they were driven pell-mell out of Ghent; which exposed our flank. We had to retire to positions on the Lys and my division was sent north to support the Belgian left only last night.'

'What sort of view do you take of things, sir?' Gregory asked.

'They might be worse.' The General smiled a little thinly. 'Our men are proving magnificent. Nine out of ten of them have never seen active service before; but they're behaving like veterans. The trouble is the French having let us down so badly in the south and the enormous superiority which the Germans have in numbers. At Oudenarde, yesterday, where there was the hardest fighting that we've so far seen in the war, we estimated that the Germans had a superiority of at least four to one in men and more than that in tanks and guns. But I'm afraid I must ask you to excuse me now because I have a lot to do.'

Gregory stood up at once. 'As you've gathered, sir, my job is Intelligence, and it's of the utmost importance that I should reach King Leopold's headquarters at the earliest possible moment. Can you tell me where they are situated now?'

The General frowned. 'It's being kept highly secret, because the poor fellow is being bombed so badly. The same applies to Lord Gort's headquarters. These damned Fifth Columnists seem to smell us out wherever we go; almost before we've got our papers unpacked the bombers come over on information received from their spies. No, I'm afraid I can't tell you that.'

'Just as you like, sir, but the King's life may depend on it,' Gregory lied quietly. 'There's a plot against him, and if I don't get there in time we may all have reason to regret it.'

By the General's expression he saw that the trick was working, so he added: 'Naturally, it's up to you to take every precaution, and I can't offer you any real proof that I am not a German spy myself but . . .'

'That's just the trouble,' the General cut in frankly. 'The information you've brought in checks with what we know already or suspect, so naturally one's inclined to accept you at your own valuation. But you have no credentials and admit yourself that you're not operating in any of the M.I. services; so you can hardly expect me to trust you with an important military secret.'

Gregory smiled. 'I was about to say, sir, that there must be some things few German agents could possibly know; for instance, how the rooms are arranged in some of our West-End clubs, the best years for vintage port, the etiquette of the hunting field, and what takes place during a levée at St. James's Palace. If you care to test me out with a few questions of that kind I think you'll find you can satisfy yourself that I'm all right.'

The General accepted the suggestion and for a few minutes he fired questions at Gregory until they found that they had several mutual acquaintances, details about whose idiosyncrasies and relatives brushed away the General's lingering hesitation, so he said: 'Well, as far as I know, King Leopold is now at Ostend, but more than that I can't tell you.'

'Thanks. Now, how d'you suggest that I should get there?'

'If the matter is as urgent as you say, I'd better lend you a car and a driver.'

'I'd be very grateful if you could, sir.'

'Come with me and I'll fix it up.' The General led Gregory outside and handed him over to the divisional transport officer, who waved him away ten minutes later.

It was now three o'clock in the afternoon and as Ostend was only some thirty miles away they should have got there under the hour, but the journey took three times that time, as the German planes barely left the traffic on the road alone for more than ten consecutive minutes, and after they had passed through Bruges they had to come down to walking pace because refugees from the city, which was now being bombed almost hourly, blocked the roads once more.

In Ostend the driver was going to set Gregory down on the promenade in front of the big hotels, many of which had now been turned by the Belgians into temporary Government offices; but he told the man that he would require the car until he located King Leopold's headquarters. A long and tiring inquiry then ensued.

The King was not at his Palace on the *Plage* and, whether they knew the situation of the King's headquarters or not, officers and officials denied all knowledge of it; so Gregory was reduced to driving round the town looking for groups of military motor-cars, on the theory that wherever a number of military cars are gathered together *there* is a headquarters. His main worry was that even if he succeeded in finding the right place, unless he actually happened to see the King through a window—which was most unlikely—everybody would deny that the King was there, so he might go on all night searching in vain; but he hoped that by the cars outside the place he might be able to establish whether the King was within.

After they had combed the town for an hour and a half unsuccessfully he ordered the driver to try the roads first to the north and then to the south, as far as the nearest villages upon each; and his first choice proved lucky. Some distance to the left of the road, about three miles to the north of Ostend and just at the entrance to the little inland village of Breedene, he noticed several cars lined up outside the gate of a big private house standing in its own grounds, so he told the chauffeur to drive down the side-road towards them. One of the cars was a complete give-away; on its bonnet it carried the Belgian Royal Standard. That was quite enough to inform him that he had located the King. The next thing was to find Erika.

Ordering the car back to the main road he stopped it there, got out, thanked the driver and sent him off; then he turned towards the houses. The light was now failing so he put his best foot forward and kept a sharp look-out to right and left as he hurried into the centre of the village to see if it contained a small hotel or *pension*. He had just drawn level with an *épicerie* when a familiar figure came out of the door carrying four bottles of wine—it was Kuporovitch. And with a shout of relief Gregory bounded forward to greet the amiable Russian.

Kuporovitch turned and, recognising him, in spite of his grubby appearance from having spent much of the day crouching in ditches, hailed him with delight. Five minutes later they entered a small house a hundred yards down the street and Gregory had Erika in his arms.

For half an hour they sat in a garishly-furnished little ground-floor sitting-room, holding hands, as they told each other of their experiences and narrow escapes during the past sixteen unforgettable days, while Kuporovitch remained discreetly withdrawn in an upper chamber; but they had only given each other an outline of their doings when the woman of the house came in to lay the table for supper.

Over the meal, which Kuporovitch shared with them, Gregory went into further details of his adventures but it was not until they had finished and their buxom landlady had cleared away that Gregory asked if he had been right in assuming that Erika was on the track of the Black Baroness.

She nodded. 'Yes. She is here in Breedene, and she's staying at the Château with the King.'

'That's bad,' said Gregory quickly.

'It is even worse than you think,' Kuporovitch cut in, and Erika added:

'Yes, Gregory; we're really up against it this time. Leopold has been driven half-crazy by sixteen days and nights of perpetual bombing. If we can't do something about it, I believe that in another twenty-four hours he will surrender, and Belgium will be out of the war.'

19

A Night of Terror

'God!' exclaimed Gregory. 'But if the Belgian Army lays down its arms the northern flank of the B.E.F. will be left naked in the air.'

Kuporovitch nodded. 'They are already outflanked in the south, where the Germans have reached Lille and St. Omer. If the Belgian Army cease fire the British will find themselves fighting on three fronts and will have no alternative but to abandon the coast they are defending and cut their way through, back to the main French Army.'

Gregory looked at Erika. 'Tell me what's been going on. I

suppose the Baroness has been working on Leopold to make him chuck his hand in?'

'That's it; and I've been working on Leopold to make him stay the course.'

'*You?*'

Erika smiled. 'Yes. I'm Leopold's new girl-friend.'

Gregory made a grimace. 'I'm not at all certain that I like that. It's trying my patriotism a bit high.'

'You stupid darling!' Erika laughed. 'The poor man is much too occupied with events and overwrought by what has happened to his country to make love to anyone; but it seems that he likes blondes. It was the Baroness's idea that his mind could be taken off the war for a little each evening if he was removed from his advisers for an hour or two into the more restful atmosphere of female society, and I put in for the job of the female. But, of course, the black lady's real intention was that while he was out of the clutch of his patriotic General Staff I should instil sweet poison into his ears and persuade him that he would serve his country better by throwing in the sponge.'

'You're a wonder,' Gregory grinned. 'But how on earth did you manage to persuade the Baroness that you were the right person for such a job?'

'It wasn't very difficult, my sweet. Paula is completely under Stefan's thumb, and when we heard that her boy-friend the Comte de Werbomont was evacuating to Ghent it stood out a mile long that Leopold was going there too. Then Stefan learnt that the Baroness was also to be of the party. It seemed to me then that you must have slipped up somewhere in Rotterdam, so I decided that I had better take a hand in the game, and when we reached Ghent I arranged for Paula to introduce me to the Baroness.'

'Wasn't that mighty dangerous?' Gregory hazarded. 'Paula knows that you're not a Norwegian at all but Erika von Epp; and if the Baroness learnt that she would put the Gestapo thugs on your tail in no time.'

'Paula knows; but she will not mention it,' Kuporovitch cut in. 'I have told her that if she lets out Erika's real identity I will wring her pretty neck.'

'I see. You've got Paula into the state of mind where she's prepared to double-cross her paymasters.'

The Russian's smile was cherubic as he replied: 'She does not know any longer if she is standing on her heels or her head;

and believe me, she looks just as lovely in one position as in the other when she has no clothes on; the only thing she knows is that while I do not interfere with her ordinary duties she must do just as I tell her in all other ways.'

'Good,' muttered Gregory, turning back to Erika. 'So you were introduced to the Baroness. What then?'

'She took a fancy to me and when Paula vouched for me as pro-Nazi I could almost see the Baroness's brain turning over as to what way she could best make use of me. On the next day she sounded my feelings and having found that I was willing to give myself body and soul in the service of that scum, Adolf Hitler, she proceeded to tell me how the air-raids were making such havoc of poor Leopold's nerves and hinted that what he needed was a little relaxation from his tiresome Generals in the company of someone just like myself.'

'Yes; I get the layout now,' Gregory agreed swiftly; 'but what I don't quite see is why she should have chosen you—a comparative stranger to her—for such a vitally important job.'

'There are several reasons,' Erika told him. 'Firstly, you must remember that Paula vouched for my pro-Nazi sentiments. Secondly, while Belgium was still neutral, no special comment would have been aroused if Leopold had taken to himself a German or Austrian girl-friend, but now Belgium is at war his entourage would make the position of such a lady difficult if not impossible; whereas, they could raise no objection to a Norwegian. Thirdly, the *Baronne's* choice is probably very limited now that the country is in a state of upheaval from end to end. Lastly, although you may not have observed it yourself, quite a number of people have remarked that I am passably good-looking.'

'Pax—pax!' laughed Gregory. 'You win hands down. Of course, the second the Baroness set eyes upon your loveliness she must have realised that if you were willing to take on the job you were God's gift from Heaven; no man, half-crazy from bombing or not, could possibly fail to fall for you. But what sort of state did you find him in?'

Erika shook her head. 'Very difficult. The trouble is that the Nazis have been at him for years. After his wife died they planted a German mistress on him; then there's Professor Teirlinck of Heidelberg University, who is one of his closest friends, and that old tutor of his, de Man; both are rabid pro-Nazis and Elizabeth, the Queen Mother, is as bad as either of them. All

266

these people have preached the greatness of Hitler to him, and told him for so long that National Socialism is the cure for all ills, that his will to fight had already been seriously undermined before Belgium was invaded. He admires the Germans, their efficiency and particularly their Army, while he despises the French because their politicians are so crooked and their aristocracy is so decadent. He is very religious and he entered the war in all honesty, utterly shocked and disillusioned at the thought that the Nazis, whom he's been taught to regard as heroes, should have wantonly attacked him; but his Fifth Column friends have been dinning it into him that Hitler only invaded Belgium as a matter of strategic necessity and is perfectly willing to give him a decent deal any time he likes to ask for terms. As he is half convinced that Hitler will win anyhow, mine hasn't been an easy row to hoe; but fortunately his Cabinet and most of his Generals are pro-Ally so we've been managing to keep our end up, though how long we'll be able to do so now his Ministers have gone to Paris, God alone knows.'

'And what is the present situation?' Gregory asked.

'The situation is that in two minutes I must leave you for my evening's spell of duty. I shall be away for about an hour and a half. These sessions really last longer but I sit with him each evening now for about that length of time somewhere between ten o'clock and midnight. He is still keeping a brave face in front of his Generals and I think only the Baroness and myself, with one or two members of his personal entourage, realise the mental stresses that he's bottling up inside himself. He lets it all out to me, though, and for several days past he's been veering nearer and nearer to facing his staff and telling them that he means to quit. I'll let you know the latest directly I get back.'

As Erika stood up Kuporovitch and Gregory stood up with her and, having helped her on with her outdoor things, saw her off down the street.

When she had gone the two men settled down to drink some more of the Burgundy that Kuporovitch had bought earlier in the evening and Gregory asked the Russian to bring him up to date with the uncensored news which he had no opportunity of obtaining during his stay in Brussels.

Kuporovitch said that according to the British broadcasts the R.A.F. had been doing terrific work on the German troop concentrations and that at last they were going out practically every night to bomb the German cities. Hamburg and Bremen had already received several visits and during the previous week the power-station at Leipzig had been blown up. The British fighter aircraft were also very active and although they were greatly outnumbered by the enemy it was stated that Germany had lost 1,500 planes since the *Blitzkrieg* on the Low Countries had opened. In one case eleven Hurricanes had attacked ninety Junkers and Messerschmitts and had the best of the encounter. The British aircraft factories were now said to be working twenty-four hours a day and Lord Beaverbrook was performing prodigies of organisation which had called forth a magnificent response from the workers.

The Russian was a little vague about a new Act which the British Parliament had passed but said that the headlines had given it great prominence. Apparently, it virtually converted Britain into a totalitarian state, as the House had given the Government control over all persons and all property. They had also passed a Treachery Bill which made him laugh a lot, as it seemed quite inconceivable to him, having come from the land of the Ogpu, that Britain had been at war for nearly nine months without her judges having the power to pass the death sentence upon a German spy—even if he wounded Mr. Churchill so seriously that he was no longer in a fit state to carry on the nation's business but did not kill him, or elected to blow up Buckingham Palace provided that he did not cause actual loss of life by so doing. As a result of certain clauses in this bill Sir Oswald Mosley had been arrested with a number of other British Union of Fascist Leaders and also a Member of Parliament named Captain Maule Ramsay.

The invasion of the Low Countries had done in the United States the work that our own propaganda should have done many months earlier; it had brought home to the Americans the true facts about the world menace which the Allies were fighting, and the bombing of the hospitals, the machine-gunning of refugees and other acts of Nazi terrorism had swung American opinion to the point where the great Democracy in all but declaring war had now openly sided with Hitler's enemies. As had been expected by those who understood Russian policy, Hitler's successes in the Low Countries had caused Stalin to adjust the balance to the best of his ability by showing a cold shoulder to the Nazis and encouraging the Balkan States to resist further attempts by Berlin to dominate them.

On the previous evening fifteen French Generals had been

dismissed from their commands and the French were now taking a new line with their war communiqués. Instead of censoring all news except for official statements that everything was going splendidly, and that every withdrawal was according to plan, they admitted frankly that they had been taken by surprise in the Sedan sector by Hitler's heavy tanks and suffered grave reverses; but they declared that there was no cause for undue alarm as the position was well in hand and everything could be left with absolute confidence in the capable hands of their master strategist, General Weygand.

The British meanwhile appeared to have woken up to the fact that now that the Germans were in possession of the Channel ports it was quite possible that Britain might be invaded. In an extraordinarily short time they had formed a Home Defence army of men who had either not been called up or were over military age, and it had been announced that morning that a new evacuation was to take place in which all children were to be removed from the east and south-east coasts. In the same bulletin the news had gone forth that bluff General Ironside had been superseded by the younger, and reputedly more brilliant, Sir John Dill as Chief of the Imperial General Staff.

Kuporovitch had hardly finished giving Gregory these details when Paula came in. Up till that moment Gregory had not realised that she was staying in the same house, but accommodation in the village was extremely limited and the camp-followers of the Royal party were far too numerous to be accommodated in the Châtea. Paula's Count had managed to get off for a couple of hours that evening to give her dinner at the local *estaminet* but after a walk on the dunes, which lay between the village and the sea coast, he had had to drag himself away from his charmer to be in attendance in case the King required him. Gregory did not wonder that the poor Count was badly smitten, for in spite of the nerve-racking experiences through which she was living Paula was glowing with youth and beauty.

She still believed that Gregory was Colonel-Baron von Lutz of the German Secret Service, so he regaled her with an interesting but entirely fictitious account of his doings since they had last met in Norway. He had, he said, got back to Germany in time for the invasion of the Low Countries, and with his splendid inventive powers he described the scenes of battle as the wedge of the German Army—which he had never seen—drove its way through central Holland to Rotterdam. He had just got to a description of the city as he had actually seen it in flaming ruins when a nearby church bell began to peal.

'*Sacré nom!*' exclaimed Kuporovitch. 'Another air-raid! Someone has given away the position of that wretched King yet again!'

'What do we do?' asked Gregory. 'Is there a cellar in this house where we can take cover?'

The Russian shook his head. 'No. I inquired of the landlady directly we arrived, but there is no cellar here, and not even a trench in the garden. We must just remain where we are and fortify ourselves with some more of this passably good Burgundy.'

As the planes moaned overhead they fell a little silent. It is one thing to be on a broad battle-field, or in some great city, when enemy planes come over and the chances are several thousand to one against their dropping their bombs within a mile of you, but it is a very different matter to be sitting in a small village within a few hundred yards of a building which you *know* to be the bull's-eye of a deliberately chosen enemy target.

Crump—crump—crump. Three bombs came down in rapid succession somewhere to the south, on the sand dunes. The windows rattled and the floor quivered a little, but no damage was done.

Crash! Another fell—much nearer. The floor-boards seemed to jump, the window shattered and the broken glass tinkled down behind the drawn curtains. Paula leant forward across the table and bit her thumb hard; she had gone very white. Gregory made no bones about it himself—he did not like it a little bit. Old soldiers never do. And as he caught Kuporovitch's eye they both knew that they were feeling the same about things; although the only way in which they showed their feelings was that they puffed a little more quickly at their cigarettes.

Suddenly a low whine overhead increased to a positive scream, there was an ear-splitting detonation followed by a reverberating roar. The whole house rocked, and for a second the table left the floor to fall back again with a thud as the glasses and bottles on it fell, rolled and smashed. Gregory was thrown sideways to the floor and Kuporovitch, in his seat opposite the window, was blown backwards so that his head hit the polished boards with a heavy thud. Paula gave one scream and collapsed across the table. A bomb had fallen in the street not a dozen yards from the window.

Half-stunned, Gregory and Kuporovitch picked themselves up, while fresh whines and crashes sounded further afield as the bomber passed over, but Paula did not stir. Her head was buried on her arms, which were splayed out among the spilt wine, and blood was gushing from her side. A bomb fragment had whizzed through the window and caught her under the left arm as she was leaning on the table. It had smashed her ribs and penetrated her heart, killing her almost instantly.

Kuporovitch stood over her, gently stroking her dark hair while he murmured, 'So young—so beautiful,' and Gregory saw that large tears were streaming down his weather-beaten cheeks. In spite of the callous, casual way in which he had treated her, according to his own strange lights upon human relationships, the Russian had grown very fond of the beautiful German girl and it was obvious that he was suffering acutely at the thought that she was never to laugh again.

'Poor little devil,' Gregory said softly. 'None of us can blame her for what she was doing. It was those rotten Nazi swine who forced her to become a whore; it's pretty lousy, though, to think that in spite of all she did for them they got her in the end. Let's take her upstairs.'

Gently they carried her up to her bedroom and drew the coverlet over her warm-hued face which was now drained of blood but looked even more lovely in the peace of death. She could have felt little pain and she was gone now to a place where there were no Gestapo bullies to compel her to sell her body in exchange for her brother's life.

When they got downstairs again Kuporovitch took a bottle of brandy out of a cupboard and said: 'This is not my war, Gregory, but these Nazi swine shall pay for that. Not yet, though. You must not count upon me for help tonight in anything that you may decide to do; because I'm going to get drunk —I am going to get very drunk indeed—as drunk as only a Russian knows how.'

'O.K.,' said Gregory quietly. 'I'd keep you company and show you what an Englishman can do in that direction if it weren't that I may have to go out on the job when Erika gets back.'

Kuporovitch half-filled a tumbler with neat brandy and swigged the whole lot down, then he said: 'You'll notice, by the

271

way, that they didn't bomb the Château.'

'No. Apparently not,' Gregory agreed. 'But what d'you infer from that?'

'Simply that they didn't mean to. Ever since we reached Ghent I've been living within a few hundred yards of King Leopold. I can't remember how many air-raids we've been through; I've lost count of them; but it's shown me one thing— they don't want to get the King—their game is to scare him. They drop the bombs any damned place where it's near enough for him to hear them crashing and they don't mind whom they kill in the meantime, but they haven't dropped a bomb yet that's even been remotely dangerous to *him*.'

'I get you,' Gregory nodded. 'If they blew him to bits the little Duke of Brabant would succeed, and he would simply be a puppet in the hands of his Ministers. Belgium would fight on, and that is not according to the Germans' programme. They want the Belgians out of the war so that they can encircle the British Army. Their game is not to bomb Leopold but to drop so many bombs all round him that he gets the jitters and lets his Allies down.'

'That's the game,' Kuporovitch agreed, tipping another quadruple brandy into his tumbler. 'Well, here's luck to you people who don't like Hitler! But now little Paula's dead and you're back with Erika there's not much point in my staying here. I can probably do just as good work for the Allies in France now the battle has become general. I think I'll set out for Paris tomorrow morning. D'you realise, Gregory, that it's May again—just think of it, Paris in May.'

'Just as you like, Stefan. You've been a good friend to us. I'll be truly sorry to lose touch with you, but maybe we'll come across each other later on.'

The door behind them opened suddenly and Erika stood there. 'Thank God you're both safe!' she whispered, and sat down with a little sigh.

'We're all right, but we had one casualty, and a fatal one, here just now,' Gregory told her, breaking the news as gently as possible.

'What?' Erika's eyebrows went up. 'The old landlady—or— or—Paula?'

'Yes, Paula. One of those damned bombs fell in the street and a splinter sailed through the window; it got her through the ribs, went right into her heart. Don't take it too badly,

272

sweetheart; she could hardly have known what hit her. It was all over in ten seconds and she was dead before we could touch her.'

Great tears came into Erika's eyes as she murmured: 'Poor Paula—she was very young—and those Gestapo devils threatened they'd kill her brother if she didn't do just what they told her to do.'

'I know,' Gregory nodded. 'But in some way she's well out of it. We're going to beat the Nazis yet—you know that—and what sort of future was there in store for her? Tell me about Leopold. I wouldn't ask you at the moment, but the lives of a quarter of a million British soldiers may hang upon it.'

Erika choked back her tears. 'He's worse—nearly at the end of his tether. He's one of those artistic, highly-strung people; he adored his wife, Astrid, you know, and he's never really got over her loss, although it's said that before the war he had an English mistress of whom he saw a lot on his visits to London. He knows perfectly well that he ought to fight on, and the memory of his father seems to haunt him; but so many people round him have always told him that Hitler is great and wise and good. He feels that every Belgian is being as badly bombed as he is and that he only has to ask the magnanimous *Fuehrer* for honourable terms and he'll get them and save his people from this nightly horror. That's why he sent his Cabinet to Paris. He's clever enough to realise that if they were with him they would bully him into holding out, and intimate pretty plainly that he was a coward if he even suggested caving in. But they're out of the way now, and the final decision lies entirely with him. He's only got to sign an order and the Belgian Army will pack up. It was all I could do tonight to make him promise me that he wouldn't do anything until he had seen a friend of mine.'

Kuporovitch emptied another quarter bottle of brandy into his tumbler as Gregory looked up inquiringly.

'Yes,' Erika said, 'it's you I mean. You've got to talk to him. He's not even mentioned what he's feeling to his Generals or to the high Allied officers who are attached to his person; he's terrified of what they might say to him, but he'll take it from an outside person who is introduced by myself. You're a wonderful psychologist, darling, and you understand the tortuous ways of the human heart better than anybody that I've ever met— even Hugo, who was so marvellous. He's a pathetic figure,

273

Gregory, showing a brave face each day and breaking down each night. You've got to hold his hands and put your immense strength into him to save him from himself and from the shame that will attach to him for all time if he surrenders.'

'All right,' Gregory said gently. 'If you feel that it's up to me, I'll do everything I possibly can. When am I to see him?'

'Not until tomorrow morning. He hasn't slept for nights, but when I left him he was going to turn in and his doctor had promised to give him a really strong dose of Medinol. Orders are being given that he's not to be woken, however grave any fresh news that may come in, so it's to be hoped that in spite of the bombs he may sleep right through and be more his own man tomorrow.'

'In that case,' said Gregory, 'we'd better try to get some sleep ourselves.'

Erika sighed as she stood up. 'Yes, darling. If only those devils Goering is sending over will let us.'

Kuporovitch emptied the remaining contents of the brandy bottle into his glass and grinned at them. 'Sleep well, my children; I'm staying where I am. By the grace of God there are another three bottles of brandy in that cupboard and either I'll finish them or they'll finish me.'

He raised his glass on high, and added: 'Blessings on you; we'll meet in Paris yet—Paris in the sunshine, eh?'

'Pray God we may,' Gregory muttered.

Erika said: 'Goodnight, Stefan dear,' and Gregory followed her out into the passage and up to her bedroom on the first floor.

In the last days they had become so used to the scores of tragedies that were occurring every minute within a few miles of them that normally, having found each other again, they would have shut the tortured world around them out of their minds for a few hours to rejoice in being together once more; but Paula's death had brought things so near to them that it had robbed them both of any desire for love-making. As at any moment they might find themselves in the midst of another air-raid, they took off only their shoes and outer garments, then lay down together on the bed. The night was so sultry that they did not even draw the coverlet over them.

The raiders came again, again and again; casting their bombs sometimes into the fields north of the Château, sometimes on the sand dunes and sometimes right into the village itself. In intervals between their clinging together as the louder crashes reverberated and the whole house shook they dozed, until at last the grey daylight began to filter through the drawn blind. The air-raids eased a little after that and for a couple of hours they slept, but awoke again with a start to the sound of more exploding bombs quite close to them. As full daylight had now come, they washed and tidied themselves as well as they could in the poky little bedroom that in a normal year would have been occupied by some holiday-maker whose resources were extremely limited.

On going downstairs they found Kuporovitch lying sprawled across the sitting-room table in a drunken slumber; but he had beaten the brandy. All four bottles stood in a neat row before him—empty.

They tried to wake him to get him up to bed, but he was absolutely and completely out. Had a bomb fallen in the room he would have known nothing about it, but been blown to pieces in his sleep. Gregory got him over his shoulders, carried him upstairs, undressed him and put him in Erika's bed, since the only other lodger's room was that which he had shared with Paula and now sacred to its lone, still occupant.

Meanwhile Erika went in search of breakfast and as she was investigating the contents of a cupboard in the small kitchen the woman who owned the house came in. She had spent the night in a neighbour's cellar and on Erika's telling her of Paula's death she promised to go and fetch the village under-taker when she had heated up some coffee and cooked some eggs for them. While the meal was being prepared Erika and Gregory tidied the garishly-furnished sitting-room. The hot coffee revived them a little and they forced themselves to eat the eggs although they did not feel in the least hungry. After-wards Erika said she would go round to the Château and find out when the King would receive Gregory, while he saw the undertaker and made arrangements about Paula's funeral.

Breedene was only a little place and the undertaker proved to be the village carpenter. He said that he already had seven orders for coffins on his hands and so could not possibly promise to furnish one for Paula until the next day. But Gregory felt that all of them would like to see Paula properly buried, and Heaven alone knew where the following day would find them, so he produced a thousand-franc note, at the sight of which the carpenter promised to give his order priority and have everything ready for the funeral to take place at midday.

Shortly afterwards Erika returned. She had not been able to see the King but had sent in a message by the Comte de Werbomont, after breaking the news of Paula's death to him. The Count had been terribly cut up but he had pulled himself together and seen King Leopold, returning with a written message for Erika, which read:

'I had a good night's sleep and am feeling better. There will be conferences going on all day so I cannot see you before this evening, but as you are so insistent that I should talk to your friend bring him to the Château at ten o'clock. I give you my word that in the meantime I will not take any final decision.'

It was a perturbing thought that they must wait twelve long hours before anything further could be done to strengthen the King's will to resistance when so much hung in the balance; but they could only endeavour to possess themselves in patience.

'Do you happen to know Paula's religion?' Gregory asked.

'She came from a south German family and I'm certain that she was a Catholic,' Erika replied at once.

Gregory nodded. 'That's fortunate, as I don't expect we'd be able to find a Protestant pastor without going to Ostend. As it is, the local man can bury her; I'll go and fix matters up with him.'

While he was away Erika performed the last rites for her friend. The carpenter arrived at midday with the coffin and four villagers to act as bearers, with a farm wagon for hearse. One of them was sent off to tell the Comte de Werbomont that the funeral was about to take place and he joined them at the churchyard. Gregory kept himself well in the background, among the little group of villagers who had gathered round the open grave, in order to avoid any necessity arising for Erika to introduce him to the Count, a tall, thin man who with her took the place of chief mourner. Kuporovitch was still lying in a drunken stupor.

Erika and the Count walked back along the village street together, with Gregory following at a distance. The Count left her at the door of the house in which she was staying and Gregory joined her inside two minutes later. When he asked if she had any news as to how things were going she said:

'The Count told me just now that the French are still holding the line of the Somme in the south and that further north the Germans seem to have been halted at Calais, but their corridor from Luxemburg to the coast is now about fifty miles wide. The Northern Armies have been forced into a compact triangle with only a short base along the strip of coast between Zee-brugge and Gravelines, and such a succession of hammer-blows are being delivered against the left side of the triangle it is feared that the Belgian Armies there may be battered to pieces.'

There had been only two air-raids during the morning, but during the afternoon they came almost hourly. The landlady had disappeared again and Gregory did not like to leave Kuporovitch, who was still sleeping off his debauch, but he tried to persuade Erika to take refuge in the crypt of the church. She flatly refused, saying that if Fate ordained that he was to be killed she would rather die with him than live on without him, so they curled up on the sofa and got what rest they could, not knwing what activities the night might hold in store for them.

At seven o'clock they went downstairs and cooked them-selves a meal; then they sat smoking in the sitting-room until a little before ten, when it was time for them to go to the Château. As darkness had fallen the raids had become still more inten-sive. Many buildings were down and the northern end of the village was on fire. Fortunately the wind was blowing from the south and Gregory did not think that there was any likelihood of the fire's spreading in the direction of their house so that Kuporovitch might be burnt in bed while he still slept, but he was considerably worried as to the effect that this almost con-tinuous aerial bombardment might be having upon the mind of the King.

At the Château the servants, who knew Erika, let her pass but they would not allow Gregory through, so she sent in for de Werbomont and taking him aside told him that Gregory must remain nameless but the King had expressed a desire to see him. The Count then gave instructions that Gregory was to be allowed to enter, but the Captain of the Guard asked him to hand over any weapon that he might be carrying, so he had to surrender his pistol; de Werbomont then took them both into a small writing-room and left them.

A few minutes later he returned to fetch them and they followed him through the main hall. The Château was being used as the headquarters of the Belgian Army and Staff Officers were constantly coming and going through the passages; but they passed from the bustle and ringing of telephone bells down a short staircase to a basement corridor where everything was divided into two by a pair of heavy curtains. In normal times it had evidently been used as a recreation room, as a billiards table had been pushed up against one wall and an archery target still stood against another; but the place was now half filled with the King's luggage and personal belongings. Signing to Erika and Gregory to wait, de Werbomont tiptoed forward, parted the curtains, and said something in a low voice; then he held one of the curtains aside and beckoned the others to go through.

Although the day had once more been as warm as mid-summer the King was almost crouching in an armchair near a tiled stove. Erika made her curtsy and Gregory bowed as the curtains closed behind them. The King smiled feebly and motioned them to come forward. He looked incredibly tired and very ill. Gregory had always thought of him as a young man—almost a boy—but in spite of his slim figure and fair, curling hair he now looked well on into middle age.

Erika placed her finger on her lips and they all remained silent for a moment; then she stepped back and looked through the curtains. 'That's all right,' she said, without any ceremony, 'de Werbomont has gone. I thought he might be listening. Have I your permission, sir, to tell the sentry on the door that we are not to be disturbed?'

'Yes, Yonnie; yes, tell him that if you wish.'

Gregory suppressed a start at hearing the King call Erika Yonnie; he had forgotten for the moment that Leopold knew her only as the Norwegian, Yonnie Rostedal.

While Erika was absent Gregory remained silent, waiting to be addressed; but the King seemed hardly to be aware of his presence and sat staring at the floor. When Erika came back she said at once: 'May I present to Your Majesty Mr. Gregory Sallust? If you will talk to him as you have talked to me, I feel certain that you will find him a wise counsellor.'

Leopold roused himself and spoke with some dignity: 'I am sorry not to have been able to receive you, Mr. Sallust, at a happier time. I understand that Madame Rostedal has told you how I feel, but perhaps it would be better if I put my position to you myself. Please sit down, both of you, and help yourselves to cigarettes. There are drinks on the side-table, too, if you want them.'

Gregory and Erika both took cigarettes but they declined

278

the drinks, and as they seated themselves Leopold went on:
'Four-fifths of my country, including its capital and all its
principal cities, with the exception of Bruges and Ostend, are
now in the hands of the enemy. For seventeen days and nights
the people have been bombed, shelled and machine-gunned
unmercifully. Apart from Brussels, which we saved from any
serious damage by declaring it an open town, two-thirds of my
cities are in ruins and a million of my people lie dead or
wounded. Only a little over thirty miles to the north of us my
Armies are still holding out, but the casualties they have
suffered are utterly appalling and fresh German divisions are
constantly being hurled against them. No one can say that
Belgium has failed in her obligation to her Allies when she
called them to her assistance. She has been martyred from end
to end, and the resistance of her people has been an epic of
heroism. They have endured beyond anything that was believed
possible. How can I ask them to endure yet further? I feel now
that this murder of a whole nation cannot be allowed to go on
one moment longer.'

'Sire,' said Gregory, 'the world knows what Belgium has done
and honours her for it, but what will be the use of this great
sacrifice your people have already made if for want of enduring
to the end they are to be cast into slavery? You say that four-
fifths of your country is already in the hands of the enemy but
last time, when nineteen-twentieths was in the hands of the
enemy, your great father still fought on.'

Leopold made an impatient gesture. 'My father—my father
—everybody throws my father at my head. We all know that he
was a lionhearted saint, but I'm sick to death of being told so.'

Seeing that he had got on to the wrong tack Gregory tried
another. 'Tell me, sir; which side do you think really has the
best chance of emerging victorious from the present war?'

'How can one possibly say?' the King shrugged. 'At the time
of Munich I would have put every cent I had on Hitler, but
Chamberlain got you a year to prepare. Even last September I
considered the odds to be two to one in favour of Germany.
Hitler has welded the German nation into such a magnificent
weapon and his Air Force was at least three times the size of
those of Britain and France combined. It seemed that when he
struck his blow must prove irresistible; but for some reason best
known to himself he did not strike, and you gained a further
eight months. Every day gained by Britain lessened the chance

of a *Blitzkrieg* succeeding, and Hitler can't stand a long war, so by April I felt that the odds had become quite a bit in favour of the Allies. But look what the Germans have done in the last three weeks; it's fantastic, almost unbelievable, yet not really so very different from what de Man always told me they would do. The eight-months' respite Hitler gave you doesn't seem to have made the least difference. At the rate you've been going it will be years before you can put as many planes in the air as Goering, and if Hitler goes on as he has been going it looks as if he'll put the whole lot of us out of the war in another month.'

Gregory shook his head. 'I'm afraid, sir, that you're taking only the short view. When you look at the map of Europe Britain is only a very small place compared with the territory that Hitler now dominates; but if you look at the map of the world, you see a very different picture. Even the whole Continent of Europe *then* becomes a small place; whereas the might of Britain stretches out over six continents and the seven seas. As long as the British Navy rules the waves Hitler will never conquer Britain. It may, as you say, take us years to build up a great Air Force and a great Army, but in the meantime the blockade will be doing our work for us, and while Britain is growing in strength things will be getting worse and worse in Germany, so that when at last we *are* able to take the offensive Hitler's defeat will be absolutely inevitable.'

'I know, I know.' With his hands clasped round his knees Leopold rocked from side to side. 'But what is to happen in the meantime? Men, women and children are being killed by the thousand, and I *can't* allow it to go on.'

'You admit, though, sir, that sooner or later the Allies are bound to triumph?'

'Perhaps. Yes, I suppose so. In all but an open declaration they've got America behind them now, so if they can stick it they'll probably wear Hitler down in the end.'

'Then, it comes to a question as to *when* that end is to be. Britain will certainly not make peace until the Nazis are finished, so the only way of stopping the slaughter is for all of us to concentrate our efforts on defeating them at the earliest possible moment.'

'Of course—of course. But Belgium has already done everything of which she is capable.'

'No,' said Gregory. 'There, sir, I can't agree. It still lies in your hands as to whether the war is to be brought to a victorious conclusion in one or two years or not for three or four; and think of the hundreds of thousands of deaths that will lie at your door if it is allowed to drag on for that extra year or two.'

'I don't understand you. How can what *I* decide make such an enormous difference? I doubt if my Armies can hold out for another two or three days.'

'But it is just those two or three days which may mean the difference of two or three years later on. You see, sir, if you order your troops to cease fire now, the British and the three northern French Armies will be outflanked from the north as well as from the south, and they may sustain a major defeat in consequence. If Britain lost, say, fifty per cent of the B.E.F. in one great military disaster the damage to our future war effort would be almost incalculable. It is upon those regular troops that we rely to stiffen and lead our militiamen, when their training at home has been sufficiently advanced for them to be sent overseas. If thousands of our most experienced officers and N.C.O.s are killed fighting a desperate rearguard action it is going to take us three times as long to make our new Armies effective in the field. That is why it is absolutely imperative to the Allied cause that you should fight on and by further sacrifices enable us to shorten the length of the war.'

The King took out a handkerchief and wearily mopped his face. 'Yes; I see plainly enough that if the British first-line Army is destroyed it will take you years to build up another of anything like its quality, but it wasn't my fault that the French gave way in the south; and that's the real trouble. Now that the Northern Armies are cut off it is impossible to reinforce them, so you can consider the B.E.F. as good as lost. The fact of my Army's fighting on for another few days won't save it.'

'But it will,' Gregory insisted, 'if immediate action is taken. The B.E.F., the three French Armies and the Belgian Army together, must number at least a million fighting men. Hitler is said to have four million men under arms but more than half of them must be fighting on the southern front or doing garrison duty at home, in Czechoslovakia, Poland, Norway and Holland. The odds against the Northern Armies can't really be more than two to one, so nothing like sufficient to overwhelm the huge force we have at our disposal, in a few days' fighting.

'Listen, sir.' Gregory sat forward and went on. 'What I suggest is that you should get on to Lord Gort, the French Com-

281

mander and your own C.-in-C. and make them settle a new plan between them to throw the whole weight of this million-strong Army in the direction of Menin and Lille, with a break-through to the Somme as their objective. I fully appreciate that owing to its present position your own Army will have to form the rearguard and that in such a movement many thousands of men are bound to be killed and captured, but the Germans are now fighting on such a long front that they couldn't possibly resist the weight of a million men hurled at one thirty-mile sector between Bailleul and Tournai. The Northern Armies might lose a hundred thousand—two hundred thousand—men, and you'd have to give up all that is left to you of Belgium, but in such a case even such frightful sacrifices are of comparatively little moment. The thing is that at least three-quarters of a million men would get through, they would win a great victory by cutting off all the German divisions between Albert and the coast and within a week they would have stabilised a new, solid Allied front in the fortified zone which was being held by the British and French before you called them in to help you.'

'It might be done—it might be done,' muttered the King; 'but think of the slaughter.'

Under his breath Gregory cursed. He had caught the sound of planes again, and a moment later the bombs roared down. Leopold sat there, his hands clasped tightly together, his knuckles showing white. Suddenly he sprang up, crying:

'No, no! What's the use? My own Army would be absolutely cut to ribbons. I'll not do it! I'm going to save what's left of it.'

Gregory too had risen. 'Listen, Sire,' he pleaded. 'I'm abso-lutely convinced that if you ordered the bulk of your Army to retire secretly tonight while a number of units were sacrificed to keep the Germans occupied, and if the British and French commanders gave orders for every man they've got to be flung at the enemy at dawn tomorrow, we'd take the Germans by surprise and make a break-through. But if you won't do that, at least hang on for a few more days to give the French a chance to come to our assistance.'

Leopold shook his head. 'They won't do that.'

'Why not? Two-thirds of the French Army have not yet been in action, and it's eight days since Weygand was appointed Generalissimo. He's had time by now to make new dispositions for a counter-offensive. The Germans have been going all out for seventeen days. By this time their lines of communication must be stretched practically to breaking point and their effort almost exhausted. Weygand is perhaps the finest strategist in the world. It's virtually certain that he will have been massing a Reserve army somewhere west of Paris and the moment the Germans show signs of weakening he'll launch it north, on Lille. You simply *must* hang on to give him his chance to restore the whole situation, by breaking through to us since you're not willing to try and break through to him.'

'So you trust Weygand?' the King asked suddenly.

'Good God, why not?' Gregory exclaimed in astonishment.

'I don't. I've never liked the French. That's why I didn't want my Ministers to go to Paris; but they overruled me. You British are too trusting. You think that the French are heart and soul in this with you because Reynaud and Daladier have made some fine speeches; but half the French politicians are rotten, or in Hitler's pay, and if they had the chance they'd stab you in the back tomorrow. If you have any influence with your own Government, tell them to watch the French—and Weygand in particular. There, now I've warned you.'

'Really, sir,' Gregory protested with a smile, 'I think you're taking rather an exaggerated view of things. We all know that there are pro-Nazis like Bonnet among the French, but I find it very difficult to believe that their greatest living General is a traitor.'

Leopold shrugged. 'All right; I don't blame you—I don't know myself what to believe—that's just the trouble. Half my friends say one thing and half another. There's the Baroness. She's far better informed than most people, and she's been at me for days to chuck my hand in. She says that Hitler has no quarrel with me, or the French, but that it's the British he's determined to smash once and for all. She says that if I ask for an Armistice Hitler will give me decent terms, re-establish my pre-war frontiers and leave me in peace to rule my people. She even adds that he will help me to rebuild my shattered country. On the other hand, there's Yonnie here, who's fooled the Baroness into believing that she's a Nazi. She says that having called the Allies to my assistance, and exposed them to the full onslaught of the superior German forces in open country, I am in honour bound to carry on the war as long as there is a Belgian soldier left capable of standing upright with a rifle in his hand. She tells me that it is better that I should lose every square mile of my country—perhaps for years—perhaps for ever—

than that I should lose my soul. What am I to do? Who *am* I to believe? I don't know—*I don't know!*'

'Sir,' said Gregory. 'Why not leave the country? Your co-ruler, the Queen of Holland, has provided you with an admirable precedent; why shouldn't you take the same course? Come with us now in one of your cars to Ostend. There are British ships in the harbour. Within four hours we'll have you in London, where you'll be free of these damnable air-raids. Then you'll be able to think clearly. Let your Commander-in-Chief carry on for the moment, then tomorrow you can take the final decision in an atmosphere of calm; which is so absolutely essential to weighing such a weighty question.'

The King stood up. For a moment Gregory thought that he had won. If only he could get Leopold to London, Churchill would imbue him with his lion's spirit and there would be no more talk of Belgium's going out of the war. But once more the accursed droning of aeroplanes came overhead and the bombs crashed and thundered in the fields a few hundred yards away.

'I can't—*I can't!*' cried the distraught King. 'They're killing my people throughout the length and breadth of Belgium as we sit here. No—no—*no!* The German emissaries are waiting upstairs to hear my decision. I've kept my word to you, Yonnie. I promised that I wouldn't sign anything until I had seen your friend, but now I'm through—I'm going to make an end before they kill us all.'

Suddenly starting from his chair Leopold dashed through the curtains and above the roar of the bombs that were still falling they heard him at the door shouting an order.

Erika and Gregory looked at each other. 'What can we do? What *can* we do?' she murmured.

Gregory made a little helpless gesture with his hands. 'If Hitler's representatives are here already, God knows; but we must make a last effort to stop him somehow.'

20

Between Life and Death

For a few moments they stood there racking their brains in anxious silence; then the King returned, followed by two strangers. Both were obviously German. The one had the thin, shrewd face of a diplomat; the other looked curiously out of his element in the dark lounge-suit that he was wearing, and Gregory felt certain that he was a General. They both bowed formally to Erika and marched stiffly behind the King to a desk in one corner of the low room, at which he plumped himself down, exclaiming:

'Well, give it to me.'

The German who looked like a diplomat unlocked a flat black satchel that he was carrying and took from it two sheets of paper. One was a handwritten letter; probably, Gregory thought, a personal assurance from Hitler that if Leopold asked for an Armistice Belgium would receive generous treatment. The other had only a few lines of typescript on it and looked like a formal and unconditional request for a cessation of hostilities.

The King read the letter through, unlocked a drawer in his desk, slipped the letter inside and relocked it. He then picked up the other paper and reached out his hand for his pen. Suddenly Erika started towards him:

'Not yet,' she gasped. 'I beg you not to sign that paper yet.'

The German in the dark lounge-suit took a step forward as though about to lay a hand upon her, but Gregory placed himself between them and stood there scowling at him.

'Sire,' Erika hurried on, 'if you once put your signature to that paper you will go down in history as a traitor and a coward. You mustn't do it—you mustn't! If you cannot face the obligations into which you have entered you must let others do so for you.'

Leopold turned to stare at her. His face looked old and haggard, but his mouth was now set in a hard, wilful line that his entourage knew well as marking the pig-headed moods to which he was often subject. For a moment he remained silent, then he spoke:

'I know perfectly well what I'm doing. This is my business—my responsibility. You and your friend . . .' The rest of his sentence was drowned in the roar of a bomb.

Erika had gone round behind the desk and was close beside the King. As the bomb crashed she had been fumbling in her handbag. Suddenly, her blue eyes blazing, she pulled out a small automatic and thrust it at him.

'Here,' she cried. 'Rather than betray your Allies, it is better that you should blow out your brains; and if you haven't the courage to do that I'll do it for you.'

Gregory heard her words but he was still facing the Germans and had his back towards her. He never knew if she was actually threatening the King with the pistol. At that instant, out of the corner of his eye he saw the curtains move. The Black Baroness stepped through them and in her hand she, too, held a pistol.

Even as Gregory sprang forward it flashed twice. Erika screamed, stood swaying beside the King for a moment, then fell right across him.

Gregory swung round in an agony of fear. He was just in time to see her fall before the two Germans flung themselves upon him. He stalled one of them off with a glancing blow across the face; but the other closed with him and for a moment they struggled wildly. There was a trampling of heavy feet; the sound of the shots had alarmed the armed sentry on the door. Thrusting the Baroness aside he dashed into the room and, covering both Gregory and the German with his rifle, yelled at them to put up their hands. Flushed and cursing they relaxed their holds. Erika had lost consciousness and the King now stood with her limp form in his arms.

'You've killed her! You've killed her!' he screamed hysterically at the Baroness. 'I'll have you shot for this.'

She had slipped the automatic back into the pocket of a little silk coat that she was wearing and she curtsied as calmly as though Leopold had offered to take her in to dinner.

'As it please Your Majesty,' she said in her soft, musical voice, 'but when I came into the room I saw Madame Rostedal threatening you with a pistol and I was under the impression that I had saved your life.'

'That's a lie—a lie!' roared Gregory. 'You shot her deliberately, because you knew that she was trying to persuade the King not to sign that accursed paper. But I'll deal with you later. For God's sake, somebody get a doctor!'

Ignoring the threat of the sentry's rifle he strode across to Leopold. Almost snatching Erika from the King's arms, he carried her over to a sofa, where he knelt down beside her to see if she was dead or only badly wounded. There were two little round holes in her breast that were oozing blood, and as he knelt there staring at them there came the drone of a fresh flight of German bombers. The King, now overwrought beyond endurance, yelled at the sentry:

'Get out! Get out—and fetch a doctor!' Then swinging on the Baroness. 'You, too, get out, I say. Perhaps you meant to save my life—perhaps you didn't—how do I know? But get out of this room—get out, *all* of you!'

The Baroness bobbed again and withdrew without any sign of hurry, while the sentry ran to get the King's doctor; but the two Germans did not move. The one who looked like a diplomat pointed at the paper on the desk, and said: 'If you will sign that now, sir, we can take it with us.'

The building shook as a new stick of bombs rained down, this time on the village. Seizing a pen, the King scrawled his signature, flung the pen down and shouted above the din: 'There! Take it! And for God's sake stop this ghastly bombing!'

'At once, sir.' The German bowed stiffly as he picked up the paper. 'We can get a message through to our headquarters in about ten minutes.' His companion also clicked his heels and bowed, then they both marched from the room.

The King took out his handkerchief, mopped his perspiring face and walked over to Gregory.

'How is she?' he muttered.

'Not dead—thank God!' Gregory murmured. 'But I'm afraid for her—terribly afraid. Both bullets got her through the left lung and it's on the knees of the gods as to whether she'll live or die.'

A moment later the doctor came hurrying in. He made a swift examination and said: 'We must get her to bed at once.'

'That's it,' nodded Leopold. 'That's it; do everything you possibly can for her. I shall be leaving in half an hour; this place has too many awful memories for me to stay here a moment longer than I have to, but I wish you to remain. Don't leave Madame Rostedal until she is out of danger or—or . . .' he trailed off miserably.

'Thank you, sir,' Gregory said quickly. 'But by your recent act you have altered the whole situation; the Germans are now the masters in this part of Belgium. The Baronne de Porte heard what Madame Rostedal said to you. That will be reported; if she lives the Germans will take her into custody and directly she is well enough they'll execute her. If she can possibly be moved I must get her away before they arrive here; so if you're

287

leaving yourself I should be grateful if you would have a car and chauffeur left at my disposal.'

The doctor shook his head. 'Even if she survives she won't be fit to be moved for several weeks.'

'Never mind!' snapped Gregory. 'That is the least that His Majesty can do for her.'

Leopold nodded. 'Certainly. Doctor Hobenthal, please to give orders that my ambulance is to remain behind with you.'

Two servants were summoned. They fetched a tall, three-fold screen, which they placed on the floor near the couch, then they laid Erika gently on it and using it as a makeshift stretcher carried her from the room. The doctor had gone ahead and Gregory brought up the rear of the little procession; just as he reached the curtain he turned. The King was now alone and they faced each other across the room as Gregory said:

'I understand why you did what you have done, and I am not without sympathy for you. It was quite plain to all of us that in your hour of trial you were not great enough as a man to bear the strain that fell upon the King—but the world will not understand; and for all the years that are left to you your name will be held in contempt by all decent people.' Then with bowed shoulders he stumbled after the stretcher-bearers who carried the dear, still, white-faced figure that was more to him than his own life.

All through the night he sat by Erika's bedside while a hospital nurse, who was now in attendance, waited at its foot and the doctor tiptoed in every hour or so to make a new estimate of the patient's chances. She was out of her physical body and attached to it only by the slender, silver cord, the breaking of which means the difference between sleep and death. It was impossible to say if it would snap and she would never be able to reanimate her physical form or if that tenuous, spiritual thread would hold and she would once again open her lips to smile or sigh.

When morning came there was no change, but the doctor and nurse could not persuade Gregory to go to bed, or even to lie down. As he sat there he was not thinking of anything—his brain seemed numb—but he felt no need of sleep and sat on, unmoving, as the hours drifted by. The air-raids had ceased by the time they had got Erika to bed and the King had departed with his entourage a quarter of an hour later, so it was now very silent in the Château.

288

Shortly after midday Erika opened her eyes and moaned. The nurse sent a housemaid running for the doctor. For ten awful minutes Gregory waited for the verdict. Then the doctor said:

'There is nothing to tell you, my friend, except that now she has come round she stands a fifty-fifty chance. We shan't know which way matters will go for at least another twenty-four hours, unless she has a sudden collapse, so I insist that you must now go to bed.'

Gregory agreed quite meekly, but with Erika's temporary return to semi-consciousness his own mental powers came back to him and he wondered if Kuporovitch had survived the air-raids of the previous night, so he asked the doctor to send somebody to find out; then he undressed and got into a bed which had been made up for him in the next room.

He awoke at ten o'clock that night and found that somebody had put a dressing-gown on a nearby chair for him, so he got up, put it on and went in to see if there was any news of Erika. He found a different nurse, and Kuporovitch looking extremely woebegone, in the room, but the nurse had nothing fresh to report about Erika's state, so he beckoned to Kuporovitch and they went outside to converse in whispers.

The Russian was suffering from such an appalling hangover that he could hardly think coherently, but he said that directly he had heard what had happened he made up his mind not to go to Paris yet; he could not desert his friends at such a time.

Gregory was glad to have his company and very grateful, but he pointed out that now that the Belgian Army had surrendered the Germans might be entering Ostend at any hour. Kuporovitch shrugged his broad shoulders and said that, after all, the Germans had nothing against him, so he had nothing to fear from them. On the contrary, it was Gregory whose life would be forfeit if he were captured. Gregory knew that well enough, but wild horses would not have dragged him from Erika's side. All the same, he was extremely anxious to know how long they had, so he sent Kuporovitch off to pick up what news he could.

The Russian was away for about half an hour. When he returned he said that there were still a few officers of the Staff downstairs, who had told him that they did not think that the Germans would be in Ostend until the following afternoon. He had also arranged about a bed for himself in the now almost empty Château, and after partaking of a scratch meal with the doctor they went to bed about midnight.

Having slept his fill that afternoon and evening, Gregory got up several times during the night to inquire about Erika, but the nurse had nothing new to tell him. Early on the Wednesday morning, however, Erika became conscious for longer spells and was in great pain.

At eleven o'clock Gregory saw the doctor, who said that he thought that the patient now had a 3 to 1 chance of recovery.

'And what will it be if we move her?' Gregory asked almost in a whisper.

The doctor gave a little shrug. 'If you were to do that the odds would be the other way; a 3 to 1 chance of death. I know the difficulty you are in but I cannot possibly take any responsibility for her life if you move her so soon.'

Gregory then had to make the most difficult decision he had ever been called upon to take. If she were once caught behind the German lines he knew that with all his ingenuity he would never be able to get her through, semi-conscious and at death's door as she was; and he had not the least doubt that the Black Baroness had already reported her to the Gestapo for endeavouring to prevent King Leopold from signing the request for an armistice. Within an hour of German troops arriving on the scene Grauber's men would have her in their clutches, her real identity would soon be discovered, and when that came out there would not be one chance in a thousand of her escaping execution when she was well enough to walk to the headman's block.

It was that mental assessment 'once chance in a thousand' which decided Gregory. Twenty-five chances in a hundred were infinitely better, so he must take this horrible risk even though by his own decision he might bring about her death. Turning to the doctor, he said:

'If she remains here the Germans will execute her for certain. Therefore she must be moved. Will you ask one of the servants to pack up some cold food for us from anything that remains in the larder and make arrangements for us to start at twelve o'clock.'

The Royal ambulance was a spacious and thoroughly up-to-date affair so there was ample room for the two nurses to travel inside with the doctor while Gregory and Kuporovitch sat beside the driver. With deliberate slowness they crawled along the coast-road back to Ostend and through it towards Nieuport and Furnes, making no more than ten miles an hour, and even less where they struck a bumpy piece of road. At Nieuport they pulled up and the doctor spent some time in a telephone booth. He came back to say that every hospital and nursing-home in Furnes was crowded with British wounded but that some friends of his had agreed to take Erika into their private house.

They proceeded on their journey, arriving at Furnes shortly after three o'clock. The doctor's friends were a Monsieur and Madame Blanchard, a plump, prosperous, middle-aged couple, who received them with great kindness and did everything in their power to make the party comfortable. Erika was carried up to a bright bedroom hung with gay chintz, and the doctor and nurses were accommodated in the house. But there was not enough room for the others so it was decided that Gregory, Kuporovitch and the driver should sleep on three of the stretchers in the ambulance, which was housed in Monsieur Blanchard's garage.

All things considered, the doctor thought that Erika had sported the journey well, but one of her wounds had begun to bleed again, and he told Gregory that moving her had set her back to a fifty-fifty chance. That night she grew worse; from a slight internal haemorrhage, and Gregory was once more driven almost crazy with anxiety as he sat at her bedside all through the long hours of darkness.

It was not until midday the following day that the crisis had passed and during that afternoon and evening she took a decided turn for the better. On the Thursday night, for the first time since reaching Furnes, Gregory was able to crawl into his stretcher-bed and sleep.

On Friday morning Erika was definitely better, so Gregory was at last able to switch his thoughts to what was going on outside his immediate surroundings. Erika had been shot on Monday, the 27th, and the following morning Leopold had been denounced for his treachery by the French Premier, Paul Reynaud. World-wide indignation at the King's act had been magnified by the fact that he had not even warned the British or French Armies of his intention, so that when his own Army had laid down its arms at midnight on the Monday the unfortunate British immediately to the south of them had had no opportunity to alter their dispositions to cover their suddenly-exposed flank. However, although the Belgian Army had surrendered the Belgian people had repudiated their King and the Belgian Government had declared its intention of fighting on with the new slogan, *'Le Roi est mort—vive la Belgique!'*

With the defection of the Belgians the Northern Allied Army had been left in a position of grave peril. It was now fighting on three fronts and in considerable danger of being totally surrounded; so it seemed more obvious than ever to Gregory that Lord Gort and his French colleague would fling their armies forward in a determined attempt to break through and reach the Somme. They were reported to have some 400,000 men between them and with such a mass it was impossible to believe that under determined leadership a break-through could not be accomplished.

But by Thursday morning it had become clear that Lord Gort had no such intention. British units were already streaming back through Furnes towards the coast, and, in the afternoon Kuporovitch came back from a short walk to say that he had seen British troops occupied in destroying several supply-depots which had been established in the town.

He added that he had just heard that Narvik had been captured by a combined force of Norwegians and British, which made Gregory laugh for the first time in days. A small German force had hung out there for seven weeks in hostile country with the Norwegians shelling them from the surrounding mountains, and the mighty British Navy shelling them from the sea, while Allied troops perpetually harassed them from both shores of the fjord. Whatever German had commanded that show deserved a whole row of Iron Crosses and it was just one more feather in Hitler's helmet.

When, on the Friday, it seemed that Erika's youth and health would save her, Gregory went out to learn what he could about the situation. More and more British troops were pouring into the town down the road from Dixmude and Ypres and at the latter place a fierce battle was said to be raging. Having talked to several of the almost exhausted officers and men he learnt that Dunkirk was now the only port remaining in British hands, and, to his amazement, that an attempt was to be made to evacuate the whole of the B.E.F. from it.

This news gave him furiously to think. It now appeared that by moving Erika from Breedene to Furnes they had only gained a few days' grace instead of securing her safety for a considerably longer period as he had hoped would be the case,

When it had become clear that no break-through was to be attempted Gregory had naturally assumed that the B.E.F. would dig in and hold the coast behind it until it could be reinforced from England. Its situation would then have been analogous to that of the Naval Division which Mr. Churchill as First Lord of the Admiralty had deliberately flung into Antwerp with great acumen and daring in the early weeks of the last Great War, only some twenty times stronger. That small force of almost untrained volunteers—the only land-force not under the control of the static Generals—had, under the personal leadership of the brilliant descendant of the Duke of Marlborough, played a not inconsiderable part in saving the Channel ports. The Germans, not knowing when it might be reinforced, had been compelled to detach three Army Corps to deal with it, as they dared not leave such a dangerous enemy bridge-head in their rear while they advanced into France. Now, one would have thought, this great Northern Allied Army could have constituted an infinitely graver threat if dug in round Dunkirk; but apparently it did not intend to threaten anybody; if it could get there, it was going home.

Whether it succeeded or whether the bulk of it was destroyed before it could be embarked, the thing that affected Gregory personally as a result of the strange and alarming new 'strategy' was that the Germans would enter Furnes at latest before the week-end was past. Once more he had to face the agonising problem—should he just hope for the best and allow Erika to continue the good progress she was making, or should he again risk her life by attempting to evacuate her with the B.E.F.?

Dunkirk was only about eleven miles away along the coast so that afternoon he decided to go there and see for himself what was going on.

After lunch he and Kuporovitch managed to get a lift on a lorry and joined the slow, apparently endless procession of British Army vehicles which was now meandering along at the best pace it could make towards the west. Great havoc was being made among the columns by the German planes but, as they neared Dunkirk, for the first time they saw British planes in action.

The German air-armada was so great that it was impossible to count even a portion of it. There were several hundred planes in the air all at one time, but for once they were not having it all their own way; the British fighters streaked out of the cloudless sky at them, flattened out, circled, zoomed up and dived again with their machine-guns spitting, and barely five minutes passed without a Nazi plane being brought down.

They arrived in Dunkirk at about half-past two but halted outside the town as bombs had reduced it to a complete ruin. Walking up on to the dunes to the right of the road, they saw an incredible spectacle. Scores of British destroyers and hundreds of small craft were standing in as near as they could to the long, sandy beaches. There were ferries, pleasure-steamers, private yachts, launches, fishing trawlers, life-boats and every conceivable type of vessel that could be driven by steam or oil, and snaky lines of khaki-clad figures were wading out through the shallow waters to be pulled on board them.

Yet for every man who was taken into a boat there were a dozen or more coming over the dunes from inland. Gunners, sappers, infantry, tank corps, A.S.C. drivers, officers, N.C.O.s and men were all inextricably muddled together in vast khaki crowds and it seemed utterly impossible that one-tenth of them could be saved by the little figures out in the boats who were working so desperately hard to prevent their falling into the hands of the enemy.

In the sky above a thousand planes turned and twisted in furious combat. Fleets of bombers came over escorted by fighter aircraft and were broken up by the pom-poms of the warships. The bombs were released haphazard and few hit their mark, but the Messerschmitts swooped to machine-gun the beaches until the Hurricanes and Spitfires chivvied them away or sent them reeling down in a smoky spiral. Gregory thought that it must be the greatest air-battle that had ever taken place and he was overjoyed to see that although the British planes were far fewer in numbers they were decidedly getting the best of it. The Navy too, was doing a magnificent and entirely impromptu job of work with the help of those hundreds of volunteer seamen, but it yet remained to be seen if those organising the rescue would prove up to the task of getting away more than a fraction of the helpless soldiers who were now mere mobs of men with neither arms to fight nor any further stretch of land over which to run.

Gregory and Kuporovitch agreed that no military evacuation on so great a scale could ever before have been attempted and the only thing which made its success even remotely possible was the unbeatable resource of the British Navy, in which Churchill had so clearly placed his confidence when faced with the collapse of the Army. They watched the astonishing, ever-changing scene for over an hour, then turned for home.

As there were no lorries going away from Dunkirk they had to trudge most of the way back to Furnes, but for the last few miles they got a lift in a Staff car. Gregory asked the officer who was in it how long he thought that the evacuation would take, and he replied: 'It only started last night and if we can get 100,000 a day off it will be doing marvels, so it's bound to be going on right over the week-end.'

It was clear now that if Erika was to be saved from the Germans the risk of moving her must be taken once more, but this piece of information decided Gregory to hang on for another day or two, so as to give her the maximum possible chance of regaining a little strength after her set-back.

All through the long, hot Saturday the B.E.F. staggered back through Belgium, many of them wounded and great numbers limping badly because they were so footsore from the terrific forced march that they had performed.

'At all events, they've got good boots,' remarked Kuporovitch, with the eye of a professional soldier, as he watched them from the garden gate.

'Yes,' sneered Gregory angrily; 'our Generals learnt that it was necessary to equip their men with good boots in the Boer War, so perhaps they'll equip them with tommy-guns when we have to fight the Germans again somewhere about 1960 and the Huns have armed themselves with something much more lethal.'

By Sunday afternoon Gregory felt that he dared delay no longer. The defences of Dunkirk had been reinforced by flooding, but at Furnes the stream of khaki had come down to a trickle of footsore soldiers. The ambulance was got out from the garage, and Erika was carried down to it; then, having taken leave of their kind Belgian hosts, they set off towards Dunkirk.

When they reached the outskirts of the town Gregory and Kuporovitch saw yet another fantastic sight. For miles and miles there stretched the baggage and the weapons of the once glorious British Army. Huge masses of supplies were being burnt and sabotage parties were putting tanks and guns out of action by removing their more delicate parts and smashing them with pick-axes; but not one-fiftieth of that vast sea of vehicles, which had cost Britain hundreds of millions of pounds and months of toil by her sweating factory-workers, could be rendered permanently useless.

There was no bombing now. The R.A.F. had won a magnificent victory against the terrific odds and driven the Nazis out of the sky. Even the gunfire to the east had slackened as Hitler, having inflicted on the British Army the most crushing defeat in its history, had swung the weight of his main attack south once more, contemptuously leaving the remnants of the B.E.F. to get home as best they could.

They drove the ambulance slowly up to the crest of the sand dunes. The spectacle beyond differed little from what it had been on Friday, except that instead of tens of thousands there were now only scattered thousands of men on the beaches, and that the foreshore was now black with countless thousands of rifles, tin hats, gas masks, haversacks, water-bottles and other items of the British soldiers' fighting kit. The destroyers and the gallant little boats, manned by every type of seaman and civilian, were still standing by hauling soldier after soldier up out of the sea as though they had never stopped during the whole of the forty-eight hours since Gregory had first seen them.

Taking out the stretcher, they carried Erika down to the water's edge, where every few hundred yards long strings of khaki-clad men were patiently queueing up and wading out chest-deep into the sea. Some were wounded, all were dirty and unshaven, but in spite of their plight their unquenchable spirit remained and they were still exchanging the typical witticisms which come from the British Tommy even in the grimmest circumstances; little cracks about 'free bathing' and 'bringing the wife to Dunkirk for a holiday next summer'.

There were no formalities, no customs or passport controls here, but some of the men turned to stare curiously as Gregory's party approached, for although there were quite a number of French and Belgian soldiers among the rabble, civilians were a rarity upon that hellish shore.

On that account Gregory felt that some difficulty might arise about his party being taken on board, so he waded in up to the knees and hailed a naval officer who was sitting in a small motor-boat near one of the queues, regulating its advance into the water.

The N.O. put in a little nearer to the shore to see what he

wanted, and lying with complete unscrupulousness, Gregory told him that his party consisted of an English lady who was hovering between life and death, a Russian who was attached to the British Secret Service, and four Belgians, a doctor, two nurses and an army chauffeur; and asked if they could be taken off.

His request was granted at once and the naval officer brought his own boat even closer in so that Erika's stretcher could be carried out to it.

Ploughing his way back through the gently-creaming foam, Gregory knelt for a minute beside the stretcher to see how Erika was. There could be no argument any more about her accepting the hospitality of Britain while the war continued but she did not even know what was going on, as her lungs pained her terribly and the doctor had forbidden her to talk in case she brought on another internal haemorrhage. Her face was dead-white and her eyes closed.

After a moment he stood up and said to Kuporovitch: 'You carry her out with the chauffeur, Stefan; I forgot to sabotage the car so I'm going back to wreck the engine, because I'm damned if I'm going to leave even an ambulance in running order for those blasted Nazis. Don't wait for me but get Erika on board as quickly as you can. I'll be seeing you later.' With a nod to the rest of them he turned and strode off up the beach towards the ambulance.

When he got there he did not lift the bonnet of the engine but sat down on the crest of the dunes to watch the embarkation. He saw Erika's stretcher lifted into the stern of the motor-boat and the two nurses, the doctor, Kuporovitch and the chauffeur hauled up out of the water after it. The motor-boat turned and sped out to a fishing-trawler that had the marks of German machine-gun bullets spattered all over its funnel. He saw the little party taken on board by bareheaded men in dark-blue sweaters. They were only little figures now and he could still make out Kuporovitch, who was standing at the rail in the stern of the ship, evidently anxiously waiting for him to join them; but he did not stir.

For over an hour the trawler remained there taking survivors of the routed Army on board, then puffs of smoke issued from its funnel. It slowly turned and headed for England.

The sun was sinking but the evacuation still went on; as some of the boats sailed for home, others arrived to take off yet more and more men. Gregory kept his eyes fixed upon the trawler until it became a little speck hidden by the gathering darkness, then at last he stood up and began to tramp through the heavy sand, towards the road. He would have given all that he possessed to be on that trawler with Erika, but the Black Baroness was still at large to wreak her evil will and he remembered Sir Pellinore's injunction.

It was *his* business to 'seek out and destroy the enemy',

21

The Road to Paris

Gregory slept in a shallow dip among the sand dunes. When he awoke dawn was just breaking. Seaward and to the west, where England lay, the scene was still obscured by semi-darkness, but to the east against the foreglow of the sunrise the silhouettes of little groups of troops already stood out upon the higher ground.

By the time he had roused himself daylight had come to reveal once more the remnants of the shattered Army. For four days now the B.E.F., once lauded as the finest land-force, for its size, in the world, had been evacuating and only its tail-end now remained to be taken off. The men were sitting glum and silent in little groups along the grassy dunes or were straggling down to the shore, where with the coming of dawn the armada of small craft had once more appeared. Gregory distributed half his cigarettes among a group of them and spent a few minutes listening to their stories.

There was nothing splendid about them, nothing heroic; they were just beaten—beaten by marching—marching for mile after mile through those grilling days and ghastly nights—while being chivied from pillar to post by the superior forces of a well-organised enemy. No blame to them. They had been game enough when they had marched into Belgium, and where they had met the enemy they had fought with stubborn courage. Gregory knew from those to whom he talked that if at any time on that retreat they had been ordered to stand they would have stood; but they had not been so ordered and they were only regimental officers or rank and file and they could do no more than obey the order to reach the coast somehow, destroy their equipment and get home.

The heroes of that chapter in British history were in the sky above, driving off Goering's air-armada, and on the sea, in all those little boats manned by old salts from Deal or Dover, by young boys from the Kent and Essex coasts, by week-end yachtsmen, by chaps who had just 'wanted to come too', and by the indomitable personnel of the Royal Navy, the R.N.V.R. and the Mercantile Marine.

Gregory knew perfectly well that had the rôles been reversed the scene would have been just the same. After days of marching and strafing without sleep the sailors and the volunteers would have sat with a woebegone expression, examining their blistered and bleeding feet, while had the soldiers been the men manning the little boats they would have proved just as gallant rescuers. Their tragedy was that they had lacked brilliant, or even distinguished, leadership.

The captain of *their* ship, General Lord Gort, had gone home two days before, when the evacuation was still in full swing, because, as one haggard, wounded subaltern put it to Gregory somewhat cynically, 'it was not considered that the men still remaining on the beaches constituted a command fitting for an officer of such senior rank'. He had been *ordered* home by the Government to report.

That report would doubtless appear years later in the history books, but Gregory did not feel that Mr. Churchill needed very much telling what had happened, and he *did* feel, remembering Nelson at Copenhagen, that there was a time to obey orders and a time to ignore them. He remembered, too, Marshal Ney, who had commanded the rearguard in the ghastly retreat of Napoleon's Army from Moscow, and that Ney, personally, had been the last man to fire the last musket on the bridge of Kovno, after he had conveyed the remaining stragglers of the *Grande Armée* on to the safety of Polish soil.

He also thought of the Old Contemptibles: the men of Mons, Le Cateau and the Marne. That B.E.F. of 1914 had been only one-third of the size of the B.E.F. of 1940. The German equipment had been just as much superior then as it was superior now. The odds in favour of the Germans had been just as heavy, in proportion, against General French as they had been against Lord Gort, but French had fought the Germans to a standstill; Gort had gone home to report.

Almost physically sick with bitterness and fury Gregory left the men to whom he had been talking and plodded across the sand dunes until he reached a rise from which he could see the scene of desolation inland. Tanks, guns, ambulances, lorries, cars, motor-cycles, searchlights, Bren-gun carriers, repair vans, aircraft tenders, listening apparatus, heavy howitzers, field cookers, petrol wagons, and every other conceivable type of army vehicle littered the scene in one vast higgledy-piggledy jumble for miles on either side of him and as far as he could see.

On reaching the road to Furnes he walked up to an abandoned tank, got the lid open and peered inside. Someone had evidently pitched two or three Mills bombs inside before leaving it, as the interior was just a mass of tangled and twisted machinery. He examined three or four others but they were all in the same state. At least the Germans would not be able to use them, but the number of tanks and guns abandoned there was so great that when they had the leisure the Nazis would be able to transport them home and present one to practically every town and village in Germany as an optical demonstration of the *Fuehrer's* complete and devastating victory over the hated British.

He walked on for about half a mile and came to another group of tanks, but these had had their tractors smashed so were also useless. A little further on, among a line of lorries which were half in and half out of the ditch, he saw another tank and had a look at that. At first sight it seemed to be all right, so he began a more thorough and very cautious investigation, as he thought it probable that some form of booby-trap might have been left inside it; but ten minutes' careful inspection satisfied him that nothing in or near the solitary tank was liable to go off and blow him up. Getting into the driver's seat, he proceeded to try to make it work.

He had never been inside a tank before and the mechanism looked horribly complicated, but he felt sure that a tank must function on the same principles as any other motor-driven vehicle. After experimenting for some time with the various switches and levers he gradually got the hang of the thing and, with a frightful jolting, succeeded in getting it out of the ditch on to the road.

The next thing was petrol, as the tank's supply was very low; but that presented no difficulty as there were thousands of reserve tins near at hand on the abandoned lorries. It took him three-quarters of an hour carting the tins before he had the tank filled to capacity and had also collected a good supply of iron rations. He then picked up a piece of chalk from the roadside, got into the tank, closed down the lid and set off.

At first he found the vehicle terrifyingly unwieldy. It had an odd habit of swerving suddenly and heading for the nearest ditch, as though it preferred ditches to a metalled surface. After a few miles he accustomed himself to its idiosyncrasies but found the heat inside it stifling, and by the time he had reached the outskirts of Furnes he was sweating like a pig; so he stopped, opened the lid and stripped himself to the waist.

His idea was to try to reach Paris, since he felt that he would stand a better chance there than anywhere else of getting on the track of the Black Baroness, but he had only a most rudimentary idea as to what was happening in his immediate vicinity. The officers with whom he had talked on the beach had told him that the French who had been cut off with them were covering the British evacuation by a rearguard action in the neighbourhood of the Mont des Cats, and he had no desire at all to run into the battle; so although it had meant going away from Paris he had thought it better to head for Furnes rather than inland, but at Furnes he felt that he could turn south-east towards Ypres without any great risk of becoming embroiled in the last desperate stand that was being made by the French.

The eighteen miles between Furnes and Ypres showed many traces of the British retreat. Here and there army vehicles which had been damaged by shell-fire had been left on the roadside. Once he passed a little group, a sergeant and seven men, wearily plodding towards the coast. Evidently they were the remnant of a party which had got cut off somewhere a few days before but had managed to make their way through the German lines under cover of night. A little further on a solitary officer came pedalling by on what was obviously a borrowed or stolen civilian push-bike, while every half-mile or so there were stragglers who from wounds or weariness had not been able to keep up with their units but were still doggedly endeavouring to escape from the Germans. By eleven o'clock, without any untoward incident, he entered Ypres.

A number of the houses had been wrecked by bombs or shell-fire, but by comparison with the tumbled heap of débris which Gregory remembered there in 1917 the town had hardly suffered at all. Turning south-west, out of the Cloth Hall,

Square, he took the road to Bailleul and, after a mile, seeing no more English or French, he knew that he was now coming into an area where at any time he might run up against the Germans. Pulling up, he got out and with the piece of chalk scrawled in large letters on the front of the tank: 'NACH PARIS. HEIL HITLER!' then got in again.

The Germans, he knew, would recognise the tank as of a British pattern but he had chosen it in preference to a car for the very simple reason that as long as he remained inside it nobody whom he passed would be able to see that it was driven by a man without a uniform, and he hoped that when the Germans saw the inscription they would assume that it was one of their own people driving a tank which had been captured from the British. It soon transpired that he had rightly judged his time in labelling the tank, as a few miles further on he came upon several parties of German infantry. Away to his right, beyond the higher ground, a battle was in progress. Out there towards Cassel the French were still making their last splendid stand and the Germans were moving fresh troops north-west, across the Ypres-Bailleul road, for the destruction or capture of this remnant of the great Allied Northern Armies which it had been decided to sacrifice in order to save Lord Gort's forces.

In Bailleul he found much greater numbers of Germans, as an armoured column was passing west, from Armentières towards Saint Omer, so he was held up in the square for some time. But nobody challenged him and by half-past twelve he was out of the little town, made immortal to the old B.E.F. by the presence at its *estaminet* of the glamorous Tina, sweetheart of ten thousand British officers, who, so it was said, in the last months of the War had been shot as a German spy.

From that point on the roads were rarely free of Germans and now and again parties of them were marching back groups of disconsolate-looking French prisoners. Between Bailleul and Arras he was twice halted by German military police who wanted to know what he was doing with a captured British tank, but shoving up the lid he popped out his head and naked, sweating shoulders to call a cheery greeting to them in his fluent German and laughingly declare that the tank was a personal war souvenir of his General, who had ordered him to bring it along for the victory celebrations.

Arras was in poor shape as the British had fought there about ten days before, when the Germans were still pushing troops towards the coast. There had been hand-to-hand fighting in the streets and the Germans had bombed the town severely. Not a pane of glass was left in any of the windows and many of the streets were half-blocked with rubble from the demolished houses; but that made Gregory more pleased with himself than ever that he had decided to journey to Paris—or as near as he could get to it—in a private tank, as the unwieldy old tin can could bump and clatter its way over all sorts of obstacles which would have been quite impossible for a car.

Even half-naked as he was, and with the lid up all the time, the heat in the tank was almost unbearable, so outside the town he drove off the road into a small wood and got out to have a rest. His trousers were wet through with perspiration and steaming from the heat, while he felt as limp and heady as though he had spent several hours in the hottest room of a Turkish bath. When he had recovered a little he made a meal off some of his iron rations then lay down in the shade of a tree. For over an hour he rested there out of the broiling sun and it was nearly four o'clock in the afternoon when he once more climbed into his sardine tin, got it back on the road and headed for Bapaume.

At Bapaume, where he again ran into many Germans, he could hear the guns, somewhere to the south; so it seemed as though the French were still holding the line of the Somme and he knew that his next job was to find a way of crossing it. The road to Paris lay through Peronne, which was actually on the Somme, and he hoped that if the Germans had already captured the town he might succeed in crossing the river there; but as he advanced with one of the German columns he found many indications that he was once more nearing a battle-front. The column gradually dissolved to deploy into positions to which each unit had been directed. Carefully-concealed heavy batteries boomed from the fringe of the woods on either side, many of the fields were occupied by infantry who were resting, and further on the sharp crack of field-guns came from the dips between the rolling downs, while German aircraft were again circling directly overhead.

By seven-thirty he had reached the outskirts of Peronne to find that it was in the hands of the Germans, but evidently they had not yet succeeded in establishing a bridge-head across the river and the French were pounding the town so heavily that it was out of the question to attempt to go through it.

Turning off the road Gregory headed west and went on for about two miles, keeping a small ridge between himself and the river, then ran the tank up to the crest of the ridge to see what he could make of the situation. He was not long left in doubt. A French ·75, concealed in a wood somewhere on the opposite bank, immediately blazed off at him. One shell screeched over and burst about ten yards to his rear; a second pitched thirty yards in front of him and dead on the line. He did not wait to make any further investigation but, heaving the tank round, rattled off back down the far side of the ridge again. Driving to the edge of a small coppice, he dressed himself and, having taken a good look round to see that there were no Germans about, got out.

He was loath to leave the tank which had proved such a good friend to him and which, in spite of his very rudimentary knowledge of its workings, was such an excellent piece of British craftsmanship that it had not once let him down during the whole of his ninety-mile jorney; but it was clear that he could not cross the river in it and so must take to his feet once more.

It was now past eight o'clock. With only about another hour of daylight to go and with his previous experience of crossing battle-fronts still fresh in his mind he felt that, dressed as a civilian, he would stand much more chance of making a safe crossing in the daytime, so having collected some of his iron rations he went through the trees to the far side of the coppice and sat down to make his evening meal.

No major action was in progress in the locality and such Germans as passed from time to time took him to be one of the innumerable homeless refugees who were wandering about the country, and after a bare glance in his direction went on. The night was warm and fine; as twilight fell he hunted round until he found a little dip in the ground which would provide a rough pillow for his head and, thoroughly tired out after his fatiguing day, soon fell into a sound sleep.

Shortly after dawn he was up again and making his way towards the river. He noticed that during the night the Germans had brought up a lot more troops and in one valley he saw a large concentration of tanks waiting to go into action, but he knew that before they could do so the German engineers would somehow have to fling a pontoon bridge over the river, which would not prove easy as the French had it under fire from the far bank.

At two points he was turned back by German sentries and, having decided against producing his German passport unless it proved absolutely necessary, he meekly submitted to their order, retracing his steps each time then making a wide semi-circle which brought him back towards the river again. At the third attempt he succeeded in slipping between the German outposts and reaching the river-bank at a place where it shelved steeply and where for several hundred yards the actual water of the stream was not under observation by the Germans in his rear. Slipping off his clothes, he tied them up in a bundle and entered the water for what proved to be a short and not unenjoyable swim, as a full four weeks of sunshine had warmed the Somme to a pleasant temperature.

On the far shore he scrambled out and, having dried himself as well as he could on his shirt, dressed again. No one challenged him and he crawled up the steep bank on his hands and knees. The second he put his head over the top a rifle cracked and a bullet whistled past his ear.

Ducking down, he lay there on the edge of the slope and began to call out as loudly as he could in French. A distant voice answered him saying that it was no good playing any of those tricks as he had better swim home to his friends; but now that he had made contact he was, for him, considering the earliness of the hour, in a most cheerful frame of mind. As he possessed a considerable mastery of French argot he told the troops ahead, in their own pet expressions, that he was not a German but a refugee from Lille; then he told them a dirty story which had been current during his last visit to Paris, and ended up his shouted monologue with the request that he might be allowed to come forward as he could tell them about the German dispositions on the other bank.

He was told to stay where he was and a few moments later a new voice called to him to advance with his open hands stretched up above his head. He promptly obeyed and walked forward into a landscape that did not appear to have a living soul in it, but when he had covered a hundred yards a *poilu,* who appeared to have grass growing out of his tin hat, raised his head a little and, covering him with a rifle, told him to jump down into a nearby ditch.

There were six men there in a cunningly-concealed machine-gun nest, and by a devious route one of them took him a few hundred yards further back, to Company Headquarters, where he was questioned by a morose-looking Captain.

Gregory told him what he had seen on the other side of the river and managed to convince his questioner that his slight accent was attributable to the fact that, although a Frenchman of Lille, he was of Belgian extraction. During the past fortnight there had been such an enormous number of civilians wandering about in the French battle-zone that the Army had long since given up arresting anyone against whom they had not definite grounds for suspicion, so after he had said his piece he was allowed to go, and set off across country in the direction of Nesle.

The Germans had begun their preparatory bombardment, which they were supporting with an aerial attack, so the first few miles proved dangerous going and—just as in Belgium—Gregory frequently had to take cover in the nearest ditch. At length, however, he got on to a side-road in a somewhat quieter area and was able to put his best foot forward; but by the time he was half-way to Nesle he was already regretting the loss of his tank. On him he had no credentials of any kind by which he might have persuaded the French Army to provide him with transport, neither could he use any form of personal touch such as he had employed with excellent effect when trying to induce the British General to lend him a Staff car to take him into Ostend; and apart from army vehicles the only traffic moving along the road consisted of an occasional farm-cart already appallingly overloaded with the belongings, women and children of some peasant family escaping from the battle-zone—and it was over ninety miles to Paris.

All through the long, hot morning he trudged on and it was after one o'clock before he reached Nesle. Although the little town was crowded with both troops and civilians he managed to secure a passable meal at a small restaurant, but soon found that there was no means of getting any form of transport which would help him on his journey. Nesle was on a branch line running between Amiens and Laon, which now formed the first line of lateral communications behind the new French front. The only trains working on it were packed with troops, and even if he could have secured standing-room on one it would not have carried him any nearer Paris; so at three o'clock in the afternoon he set off to walk to Roye.

It was nearly six o'clock when he got there but, when he did, he had better luck. The station was on the direct line for Paris and a booking-clerk informed him that although the trains were no longer running to schedule, one upon which civilians could travel would be leaving in the next hour or so. He had another snack and a bottle of red wine in the station buffet and at about half-past seven a train came in on which he managed to get a seat in a compartment that was crammed to capacity. All traffic had been entirely upset by the military requirements so the train was appallingly slow, but he stepped out on to a platform of the *Gare du Nord* a few minutes before ten o'clock. The journey from Dunkirk had taken him forty hours, but, all things considered, he thought that it had been remarkably good going.

He took a taxi straight to the Hotel Saint Regis in the Rue Jean Goujon, just off the Champs Elysées, where he always stayed when he was in the French capital; and when the English manager recognised his old patron in the dirty, dishevelled figure that came up to the desk to ask for a room he immediately took Gregory up to one of the delightful apartments which were so different from the ordinary hotel-bedrooms through being furnished with individual pieces many of which were antiques of considerable value.

Gregory's first necessity was to get news of Erika, so he put through a personal call to Sir Pellinore at Carlton House Terrace, knowing that Kuporovitch would have taken her there on landing. He then ordered a light meal and a bottle of champagne, and turned on a hot bath. In spite of his trying day he was not unduly exhausted, because he had had over nine hours' good sleep in the wood near Peronne the previous night, and although he would have much preferred to sink into the comfortable bed after his bath he felt that not a moment should be lost in getting on the track of *Madame la Baronne Noire*.

Although it was nearly eleven o'clock he thought that there was a good chance that in times like these Colonel Lacroix, the Chief of the famous *Deuxième Bureau*, would still be at work at that hour, so he rang up the *Sûreté-Générale*. The Colonel was there, and on Gregory's saying that the matter was urgent Lacroix told him to come round as soon as he liked.

He spent a quarter of an hour refreshing himself in the marble bath while the valet cleaned up his clothes as well as possible and found him a razor. Having dressed again he fortified himself with the bottle of bubbly and an *omelette aux champignons*.

307

Half-way through his meal the call came through. Erika had survived the journey but seasickness had caused a further haemorrhage, and she was very low. Sir Pellinore did his best to be optimistic but Gregory sensed his anxiety and decided that for himself only work could drug his acute distress and worry.

Ten minutes later he left the hotel. At a quarter to twelve he was taken up to the top floor of the big building on the south bank of the Seine and shown into the fine room which during the daytime had such a lovely view of the spires and domes of Paris.

At a big desk near the wide windows a tiny, grey-haired man, whose lined face resembled that of a monkey, was sitting. His hands were clasped over his stomach and his eyes were cast down in an attitude of Buddhistic contemplation. The desk was remarkable only for the fact that it had not a single paper on it and it seemed to Gregory almost as though the famous Chief of the French Secret Police had not even moved since he had last seen him.

'So you're back from Brussels?' said the Colonel in his gentle voice, suddenly glancing up.

Gregory smiled. 'And how did you know that I had been in Brussels, *mon Colonel*?'

Motioning Gregory to a chair the little man gave a faint sigh. 'I know so many things, *mon ami*, that sometimes I almost feel that I know too much, but agents of your ability and courage are not so common in the dark web at the centre of which I sit for me to lose track of one. Through the good Sir Pellinore I have followed your perilous journeys with the greatest interest.'

'I see. Then you'll know of the part I played in the November *Putsch* and how I succeeded in getting Goering to send me to Finland afterwards?'

'Yes. And I am happy at last to have the opportunity of felicitating you upon the many splendid services that you have rendered to the Allied cause.'

'That's kind of you, sir, and I shall never forget that when I fell down on my first big job it was you who gave me a second chance. A lot of water has flowed under the bridges of the Seine since then, though.'

Suddenly Lacroix's monkey-like little face changed from amiable passivity to black anger. '*Oui*. Much water has passed beneath the bridges of the Seine, also many British soldiers have crossed the Channel in the wrong direction.'

Gregory spread out his hands with a peculiarly French gesture that he often made when using that language. 'What would you, *mon Colonel*? He who fights and runs away lives to fight another day. Our men are still alive and free, which, after all, is very much better than if they were prisoners or dead. The B.E.F. will soon be reconstituted and sent back to France.'

'And in the meantime?' asked Lacroix angrily.

'In the meantime things don't look particularly rosy,' Gregory had to admit. 'Still, presumably you're bringing back from Africa every single man you've got, to form an army of manœuvre in Central France; and with Weygand at the helm I imagine that the people of Paris can still sleep soundly in their beds.'

'They may sleep, but not soundly. Did you know that between one-fifteen and two-fifteen today Paris was raided by two hundred and fifty Nazi planes?'

'The manager of the Saint Regis did mention that you'd had an air-raid but I got into Paris only at ten o'clock and I've seen no signs of any damage that may have been done.'

'They dropped 1,000 bombs, 254 people were killed and 652 injured. Now they have started this sort of thing it is likely to continue. From this point on we must anticipate that at least 1,000 Parisians will become casualties daily; which will lead to a great lowering in the morale and the war effort of the capital. And do you know why we must submit to this new blow? I will tell you. It is because the British Air Force was withdrawn to protect your Army during its evacuation from Dunkirk and will henceforth be occupied in defending England instead of being able to carry out its allotted task of defending Paris.'

Gregory shrugged. 'Really, sir, it's hardly fair to blame us because during the last few years your own Government has been so criminally slack that you haven't enough planes to protect yourselves.'

'But it was part of the agreement,' said the Colonel in a tired voice. 'France spent 70,000,000 of your pounds sterling upon her great Maginot Line. While Europe was still at peace 6,000,000 of her sons left their normal occupations which were productive to become non-productive for many months, but to fit themselves to defend their country in her hour of need. That was France's contribution. Britain refused to introduce conscription, but her part was to hold the seas and to create an Air

Force which should have been strong enough to balance that of Germany, while we held the great German Army at bay on land. Can you wonder that today in Paris everybody is saying that the English have let us down?'

'Surely, sir,' Gregory replied patiently, 'if we're going to hold an inquest we must go back to the beginning of the present trouble? There would have been no break-through towards the coast, and so no evacuation and no withdrawal of our Air Force, if your Generals Giraud and Huntziger had not made an incredible mess of things at Sedan and allowed the bridges across the Meuse to fall into the enemy's hands.'

Lacroix nodded. 'I give you that. But in spite of the German break-through there need have been no great military disaster had not the British lost their heads. They panicked and they ran.'

Gregory stood up. 'I'm sorry, but I can't remain here if you're going to say things like that. At Louvain, at Oudenarde, at Arras, they fought magnificently, but they were outflanked in the south entirely owing to the incompetence of your own General Staff and they were outflanked in the north through King Leopold throwing his hand in without even warning them. Finding themselves surrounded on three sides by German Armies which were enormously superior in both equipment and numbers, what else could they do but retreat?'

The little Colonel suddenly leapt to his feet; his black eyes flashed; he banged his small, brown fist on his empty desk and almost screamed:

'*Mon dieu, mon dieu, mon dieu!* What could they do? Why, cut their way through, of course. Gort had a quarter of a million men. With him were three French Armies and many Belgian units who refused to lay down their arms even when they were called upon to do so. The German corridor was only thirty miles in width for several days. Had the whole of that great army been flung against one fifty-mile sector of the corridor, how could the Germans in it possibly have failed to collapse under such a blow?'

'For the simple reason that the Germans had eight armoured divisions in the gap,' Gregory replied promptly.

'Eight divisions,' sneered the Colonel; 'and what is that? 150,000 men at most, even with Corps and Army troops. Do you suggest to me that 500,000 men could not have smashed them whether they were armoured or not? If Gort and the others had lost 100,000 men in casualties—one-fifth of the Anglo-

French force—they would have won a great victory by cutting off the Germans between Arras and the coast, and would still have come through with an Anglo-French Army of 400,000 men complete with tanks, guns and equipment. That force would then have been with us to hold the line of the Somme and defend Paris. But where is it now? Gone—vanished—dispersed—in confusion and disgrace, leaving behind it two-thirds of the peace-time output of your military armaments factories and leaving us naked to bear the whole brunt of the German onslaught.'

Gregory knew the whole sad story only too well himself and it sounded even worse when put by an indignant and bewildered Frenchman, yet he was not prepared to admit it. Instead, he said quietly:

'I'm sure that your information is much better than mine, but—without any information at all—it's quite apparent that your Generals were responsible for the break-through in the first place and that since then General Weygand has not signalised his appointment to the Supreme Command by initiating any counter-offensive which would have assisted the British move that you suggest. But surely no good can now come of mutual recrimination? Isn't it up to us to stop abusing our respective Generals and, instead, to strain every nerve to pull our countries out of the ghastly mess in which they have landed us?'

Lacroix suddenly sat down and Gregory was surprised to see an amiable smile dawn on his wrinkled, monkey-like features. 'I congratulate you, *mon ami*,' he said quietly. 'You stood up very well to my abuse of your countrymen; and now I will confess to you that I consider mine were every bit as much to blame.'

'Why, then,' said Gregory, also sitting down again, 'did you —er—turn on the heat?'

'Because it is important that you, as an Englishman who has many contacts, should fully appreciate what *my* countrymen are saying and feeling at the present time. Your people will be told one end of the story; mine are being told another. It is for both of us—we who can see the whole picture—to do our utmost to counteract this most unfortunate feeling of distrust which has now arisen. We have already sacked Gamelin and fifteen other Generals; it is to be hoped that your Government also will soon dismiss those of your military commanders who

311

were responsible for this most ignominious retreat. Then we must tell our peoples that under new leadership matters will be very different, because, unless we are to lose this war, mutual confidence between France and Britain *must be maintained at all costs.*'

Gregory beamed. 'How right you are, sir; I absolutely agree. But what is the present situation?'

Again folding his hands across his small stomach the Colonel said quietly: 'Owing to the stamina and the marching power of your soldiers, coupled with the brilliant performance of your Air Force and your sailors, your Army got away. They had nothing left but their shirts, but in due course the great majority of them will be able to take the field again. On the third day of the evacuation the Germans realised that their prey was slipping through their fingers so, like the military geniuses that they are, they expended no more effort in endeavouring to catch the British. Instead they proceeded, without the loss of a moment, to the huge task of rearranging their dispositions so that instead of facing west they faced south and east, with a view to launching another onslaught while the main French Army was still in a state of flux.

'It took them a few days to form new concentrations but they have now massed behind the Somme and as far south as Laon with the intention of attacking the Oise-Aisne Canal and seizing the road through Soissons to Paris. Many of our divisions must, of necessity, continue to hold the Maginot Line, if it is to remain effective, and the departure of the B.E.F. has left a most alarming gap in our line further west between Montmédy and the coast, which we are now doing our utmost to fill. I will reveal to you, because I know that you are trustworthy, that there is virtually no army of reserve.'

'Good God!' Gregory interjected. 'For days I've been living on the belief that you've been shipping over from Algiers and Morocco every man who can hold a rifle, to form behind Paris a great army of manœuvre which can be rushed up into the battle when the time is ripe.'

Lacroix shook his head. 'No. Every man, every gun that we can get hold of, is being thrown in upon the Somme to hold that portion of the line which the British should have held. According to my latest information the Germans will launch their attack tomorrow and the battle for Paris will be on.'

'What chance d'you think we've got?'

The Colonel hunched his shoulders eloquently. 'Fifty-fifty—not more. The British still have a few thousand men at their main depots in Le Havre and Rouen, but they are a mere bagatelle—they simply do not count. For all practical purposes Britain is just as much out of the game as Belgium or Holland. In this great land-battle, which may well prove decisive, France stands alone; and she has neither the numbers nor the weight of arms possessed by her enemies.'

'The situation is, then, absolutely critical?'

'Yes. All we can do now is to hope and pray. But tell me about yourself. What was it that you wished to see me about so urgently?'

'I have an account to settle with the Baroness de Porte. Having lost track of her I came to you, feeling sure that you would be able to inform me of her present whereabouts—or at least how I could get on her trail.'

'*Mon ami*, you are wasting your time,' said the Colonel gravely. 'There is nothing evil that you can tell me about *La Baronne Noire* which I am not prepared to believe. Had any ordinary person been responsible for one-tenth of her acts during the past few years I should have had her locked up in a fortress long ago. But she is not an ordinary person, and her protectors are so powerful that even I, with all my resources as the Supreme Chief of the *Deauxième Bureau,* cannot get under her guard. No warrant against her would ever be executed, because someone to whom there could be no answer would intervene. However much evidence might be collected against her, no charge could be substantiated; pressure would be exerted from above. If resignations were offered by way of protest they would be accepted; witnesses would be bribed, intimidated or eliminated; the case would never come into open court. That woman is above and beyond the law.'

'Above human law, perhaps,' murmured Gregory.

'Do you mean'—Lacroix leant forward ever so slightly—'that you are prepared to kill her?'

Gregory drew heavily on his cigarette. 'However black her record may have been when she was first mentioned to me, I would have much preferred that somebody else should be her executioner, but eight days ago she shot a woman who means more to me than anything else in the world.'

'Erika von Epp?'

'Yes—Erika. I managed to get her off at Dunkirk, but it's

still uncertain as to whether she'll live or die on account of her injuries; so, although she doesn't yet realise it, the Black Baroness has started a party out of which only one of us will emerge alive.'

Lacroix slowly nodded his head. 'Whatever may be said for or against her motives, it is Madame de Porte's avowed intention to destroy the French Republic as it is at present constituted, and she is utterly unscrupulous in the means she employs to further her end. I am the servant of the French Republic as it is at present constituted, therefore I will give you every assistance in my power; but great discretion must be used, otherwise I shall find myself dismissed, and then I should no longer be able to render any help either to you or to France.'

'*Merci, mon Colonel.* Do you know where she is at the moment?'

'She is in Italy; and you can guess what she is trying to do there.'

'To make Mussolini screw up his courage to the point of stabbing France in the back now that on land she has lost the aid of Britain and is fighting for her very existence?'

'*Sans doute!* Mussolini still wavers. He would never have dared to come out against us in the open, face to face, but now he is greedy to snatch a cheap triumph from us while our backs are turned; yet he knows how terribly vulnerable his new Empire is. Italy's African Colonies contain a considerable portion of her Army, which would be cut off from the homeland by the Mediterranean in the event of war; since, whatever may happen in France, Mussolini would still have to reckon with the British Navy. If wise counsels prevail there is still a chance that he may not come in, but if *La Baronne Noire* is left a free hand to pour her poison into the ears of all his satellites it is almost certain that Italy will enter the war against us. If you are prepared to kill the *Baronne* you may prevent that; therefore, such an act would be the highest service that you could render at the present time to both our countries.'

'All right.' Gregory smiled grimly. 'Time is obviously of immense importance. I'm game to start for Italy at the earliest possible moment.'

'Does the *Baronne* know you?'

'Hardly. She saw me face to face only for a few seconds, just after she shot Erika.'

'Even so, the odds are that she will recognise you again. You must adopt some form of disguise; otherwise immediately you enter her presence she will take alarm and, perhaps, shoot you first. Also, she guards herself very carefully so you will not find it by any means easy to approach her unless you can do so with special credentials which will cause her to believe that you are a friend.'

'What d'you propose?' Gregory asked.

After a moment's thought the little Colonel replied. 'I think it would be best if you assumed a new identity. Have you ever heard of the Reverend Eustace Arberson?'

'No.'

'He was a prominent member of the Nordic League and is one of Britain's most dangerous Fifth Columnists. He is about your height and age, and although there is no real resemblance between you I think you could be made up to look passably like him. As his hair is dark and he wears it *à la* Hitler that would hide the old scar on your forehead. A full, black moustache such as *Père* Arberson's would alter the appearance of your mouth, and if your eyebrows were plucked to resemble his they would no longer tend to turn up at the corners. To my certain knowledge the *Baronne* has not been in England for the past four years and, as far as I know, the Reverend Eustace has never travelled on the Continent, so it is most unlikely that the two have ever met, but they would almost certainly know of each other, and it is quite possible that if the Reverend Eustace were in Rome he would take the opportunity to meet her. Time, as you so rightly say, is now a vital factor, so during the course of the night I will have a letter forged which you can use by way of introduction, and the signature on the letter will be that of the ambitious Mayor of Bordeaux, one of *Madame la Baronne's* most trusted friends.'

Gregory nodded. 'Good. I shall be able to start for Rome tomorrow, then?'

'Yes. You will also require a passport in the Reverend Eustace's name, but I have a photograph of him which can be touched up to make it appear not unlike yourself, and I will then have it re-photographed for passport purposes. The Baroness's headquarters in Italy are the Villa Godolfo, in the Alban Hills, just outside Rome, and I expect you will find her there. In any case, you will first go to Antoine Collimard, in Rome. He is a barber and has a shop; *Numéro 25 Via Veneto*. Collimard is a master in the art of make-up and he is also one of my best agents, so you may safely leave yourself in his hands, and he will give you all the help he can. The passport, the forged letter of introduction and a line to Collimard will all be ready by midday. As the matter is urgent I shall place a pilot and a plane at your disposal to take you to Rome; and in view of the risk that you are running they had better wait there to get you out of the country immediately your job is done. Have an early lunch and your old friend Ribaud will call for you at one o'clock; he will deliver the papers to you personally and will run you out to the private aerodrome a few miles south of Paris from which you will start.'

The little Colonel stood up and, extending his hand, added: *'Bonne chance, mon ami,* and, should the qualms natural to a chivalrous man at the thought of killing a woman make you hesitate at the last moment, remember now that France has lost one Army through the defection—or shall we say indecision?—of your countrymen it may lie with you to prevent the Army of another great Power being added to her enemies.'

Gregory nodded gravely. 'I shall not forget.' And taking Lacroix's hand he shook it with the same earnestness as if he were signing a solemn pact.

As he went downstairs a few moments later he knew that on the following day he would be setting out upon the most horrible mission that he had ever undertaken. He was going to the country of assassins to become an assassin. In his heart of hearts during these last days he had doubted if even his urge to revenge Erika would ever bring him really to that point; but now, in order that the cause of justice, toleration and liberty should not have the weight of 50,000,000 Italians flung against it in its darkest hour, it was necessary that the Little Black Baroness should die

22

The Assassin

On the following morning, Wednesday, June the 5th, Gregory slept late and lunched early. At twelve-thirty he received a telegram from Sir Pellinore, which read: ERIKA NO WORSE NO BETTER DON'T PHONE WILL WIRE YOU IF SHE SHOWS ANY CHANGE:

and with this cold comfort he had to be content for the time being.

Punctually at one o'clock the porter at the Saint Regis rang up to say that a Monsieur Ribaud had called for him in a car, and on going down Gregory exchanged warm greetings with the fat little French detective who had arrested and later co-operated with him in the previous October.

As they drove through the sunny streets of the capital, which was much more crowded than when Gregory had last seen it, owing to the great influx of refugees, they exchanged views upon the war, but neither had anything very cheerful to say so Gregory was glad when they turned off the main road into the grounds of a small château outside Choisy and he saw a solitary aeroplane standing outside a hangar.

Ribaud introduced him to the pilot, Raoul Desaix, a lean, lantern-jawed, middle-aged man, and five minutes later he was waving good-bye to the detective as the plane took off.

It was a four-seater civil aircraft with a cruising speed of 160 miles an hour so Gregory knew that it would be about four o'clock before they reached the Mediterranean. There was little aerial activity south of Paris. The skies were a clear, bright blue and they were flying at no great height, so he was able to amuse himself by watching the landscape unfold beneath them.

From 2,000 feet there was no indication of war at all. The fields, villages and isolated châteaux looked very peaceful and it was an utterly different world from that other part of France through which he had passed by tank, on foot and in the train during the two preceding days. By half-past three the main colour of the patchwork quilt of fields and woods below had begun to change from a greenish hue to the greyish-brown of the olive orchards and myrtle scrub of Provence. They left Avignon, with its great Papal Palace and broken bridge across the Loire, on their left, and Nimes, with its Roman amphi-theatre on their right, to pass right over Arles, and a few moments later the plane came down on a private landing-ground just north of Marseilles. They refuelled there and went on, following the line of the coast until they passed over Hyères, with its islands, then, leaving the Côte d'Azur with its miles of famous pleasure-beaches on their left, they passed out over the Mediterranean.

The colouring of the scene—the deep blue sea creaming upon

the shore in a tiny white line, the gold of the beaches, the greens and the browns of the scrub, vineyards and woods, then far away to the north the mountains with the white-capped peaks of the Italian Alps standing out against a sapphire sky—was as vivid as that on a picture postcard. They had hardly left France behind when Corsica rose out of the sea ahead of them. It was perfect flying weather and the only bump they had was caused by the currents rushing up the ridge of mountains in the northern neck of the island, and as they passed over the sun-baked volcanic stone Gregory felt that he could have reached down and touched it with his hand. Five minutes later they could see Elba, a little island as flat as a pancake set in the wine-dark sea on their left, and Monte Cristo's Island, little more than a huge rock, right below them; then the coast of Italy loomed up, and a little before half-past six they came down on the airport outside Rome.

Gregory used his own English passport and Desaix having made arrangements for garaging the plane they drove to the Hotel Ambassador, where they both booked rooms, and Gregory then went at once to make contact with Monsieur Antoine Collimard. The shop was shut but he was fortunate enough to find the French hairdresser at home above it, which suited him much better than being seen entering the shop by a number of assistants when it was open.

Collimard proved to be a Basque. He was small, dark-complexioned, with a little hook nose and quick, intelligent brown eyes. Gregory presented Colonel Lacroix's chit which had attached to it the original photograph of the Reverend Eustace Arberson.

The Frenchman studied Gregory's face carefully for a moment and said: 'I think I can do it well enough for a casual acquaintance to mistake you for this man at a distance, at all events, and naturally the clergyman's clothes will help a lot. But you must appreciate that, while I could make your face into a mask which would be the image of his in semi-darkness it is impossible to use make-up which would alter the shape of your nose, chin and forehead in daylight.'

'I quite understand that,' Gregory smiled, 'but, to the best of our belief, the Baroness has never set eyes on the Reverend Eustace so a superficial resemblance is all that is required, and it's more a matter of altering my own face—which she has seen for just one moment—than of making it resemble his. Do you

318

know if she's still at the Villa Godolfo?'

'No. But I will find out. In any case, you can do nothing tonight as it will take me some hours to prepare the moustache and to study the matter of the eyebrows. There is also the question of clothes. You will see to that yourself, I take it?'

'Yes. Rome bristles with shops that sell clerical outfits, so I should have no difficulty in finding things to fit me tomorrow morning.'

'*Bon!* Come here a little after twelve, bringing your things in a suit-case, and by the time you leave I will have transformed you as far as lies in my power into the Reverend Eustace.'

Gregory thanked him and, returning to the Ambassador's, tried to put a telephone call through to London but he was told that there would be at least six hours' delay, so he booked one for the following morning. That night he had dinner with Desaix, whom he found to be an amiable though not particularly gifted man whose only grouse was that as he was over forty they would not let him fly a fighter plane in the service of his country.

Gregory endeavoured to console him by saying that he was doing every bit as good work by making secret trips like the present for Colonel Lacroix, and he explained that he did not know how long he would be in Rome but that he might have to leave in a great hurry. It was agreed that he should vacate his room the following morning and that they should see nothing of each other until the time came for a quick get-out to France; also that the airman should remain at the Ambassador's, going out only to places from which he could return in twenty minutes and leaving with the hall-porter the telephone number of the place at which he could be found.

Afterwards, up in his room, Gregory read the forged letter of introduction from the pro-Nazi Mayor of Bordeaux to the Baroness, together with the particulars of the Mayor and the Reverend Eustace which had been in the packet from Lacroix that Ribaud had handed him that morning. In an hour and a half he had committed to memory all the available data about the man he was to impersonate and went to bed.

Having spent a restless night, due to worry over Erika, Gregory took his London call only to learn that she was still in grave danger. He then paid his bill and went out to do his shopping. Since he had abandoned his suit-case in Ghent eleven days earlier his only luggage had consisted of shaving and washing gear which he carried slung around his shoulders in a small gas-mask container; so, after changing some of his English bank-notes for Italian *lira,* it was a joy to be able to re-equip himself with fresh underclothes, dressing-gown, brushes and pyjamas as well as the black suit, black slouch hat and clerical collars necessary to his new rôle. With the whole of his purchases packed into a large Revelation suit-case he arrived at Collimard's at a quarter-past twelve.

'I fear that I have some bad news for you,' was the Frenchman's greeting. *'La Baronne Noire* is in Rome no longer; she has left her villa out at Marino and gone north; one assumes to keep in touch with *Il Duce,* who is said now to be inspecting his troops in the Cottian Alps and other places on the French frontier.'

'Damnation!' muttered Gregory. 'Still, I suppose Mussolini is pretty certain to make his headquarters in Turin, so if I go there I ought to be able to get on her track.'

Collimard shrugged. 'Who can say? She left Rome only last night, but she may quite well be back here in a day or two. *Il Duce* is not a man to stay in one place for long and he moves very swiftly; if you go north you may pass her on her way south again.'

'That's true.'

'Also, you will find your disguise uncomfortable and worrying at first, so it is far better that you should wear it for forty-eight hours before putting it to the test.'

'But the matter is so frightfully urgent.'

'All right; go if you wish, but you would be far wiser to wait at least until I have been able to secure further news for you. By tomorrow I may have fresh information about *Il Duce's* intentions.'

'You're right,' Gregory admitted reluctantly. 'There's no sense in my setting off on a wild-goose chase without even knowing for certain where she is.'

Collimard then set about changing Gregory's appearance. He washed and set his hair *à la* Adolf Hitler so that it hid the scar over his eye, then he proceeded to pluck his eyebrows in one place and add single hairs, with minute particles of very strong gum, in another, until their shape was completely altered. He next opened a packet of false eyelashes and trimming them to half their length added them one by one to Gregory's own so that although his did not appear longer they became very much thicker. After that he placed more false hairs just in front of his ears, thereby giving him short side-whiskers, and, lastly, he attended to the moustache.

'There!' he exclaimed in triumph when he had done. 'You must use only a very soft brush each morning, and you are bound to moult a little as you turn in your sleep each night, so you must come to me to be touched up every two or three days, but I do not believe that your best friend would know you.' And when he looked in the mirror Gregory had to agree that his face had been changed beyond anything he would have believed possible.

Having dressed in his clergyman's clothes he thanked Collimard for his artistry and, going out, took a taxi to the station, where he mingled with the crowd, and a few minutes later took another one to the Hotel Excelsior, as though he had just arrived by train.

After registering there as the Reverend Eustace Arberson, and handing in his passport in that name for the usual police check-up, he wrote a note to the Baroness, on the hotel paper, saying that he was in Rome for some days and asking permission to call. Enclosing the letter of introduction with it, he posted it in the hall, then purchased the latest papers and sat down in the lounge to see how the war was going.

Lacroix's belief that the German preparations for the next stage of their offensive had been completed on the Tuesday night had proved correct. On Wednesday morning, June the 5th, the battle for France had opened at 9 a.m. On a hundred-and-twenty-mile front, from the Somme to the Aisne, the Germans had attacked with great masses of troops supported by over a thousand dive-bombers. Hitler's weather still held in France, but the paper said that the smoke of battle had been so thick that it had blotted out the bright June sun. The enemy had made no progress until the afternoon, but they had then succeeded in securing bridge-heads across the river and their tank columns had struck through Amiens, Peronne and Laon towards Paris. The French Cabinet had met to discuss the new crisis shortly before midnight.

That evening Churchill had made a statement in the House in which he had frankly referred to Dunkirk as a 'colossal military disaster' sustained by the British Army, which had enabled the enemy to acquire strategic bases of great importance and many of France's most valuable industrial areas. Britain had lost vast quantities of material and over 30,000 killed, wounded and missing, but 335,000 British, French and Belgians had been saved and the R.A.F. had covered themselves with glory. The B.E.F. was to be reconstituted and, said Mr. Churchill, Britain would never surrender.

Owing to the pro-German bias of the Italians the Government-controlled Press had printed Mr. Churchill's speech only in small type on the back page of the paper. The front page was devoted to that day's news; the announcement of a new French Cabinet in which Daladier, the sworn enemy of Italy, was out altogether, Reynaud's taking over Foreign Affairs as well as the Premiership; and a statement that although the French centre was reported to be holding for the moment it must soon give way, since the Germans had hurled 2,000 tanks into the battle.

Another headline on the front page announced Italy's declaration that a band of twelve miles round her coast and that of Albania must now be regarded as dangerous to shipping and that exit permits would be distributed to foreigners who guaranteed to leave Italy within two days.

Gregory's Italian was by no means as perfect as his German or French but he knew quite enough to read the paper with reasonable ease and its contents were extremely perturbing. The matter of issuing special exit permits might be only one more measure designed to scare the Allies and there was no suggestion that foreigners who did not take advantage of it would be interned; but the whole tone of the paper was openly threatening and it looked as though Mussolini was now very near the brink.

On the Friday morning, the third day of the battle, the news looked somewhat better. The French were reported to have destroyed at least four hundred German tanks and although at some points they had made withdrawals they had succeeded in throwing back the enemy forces which had reached the south bank of the Aisne.

Gregory rang up Collimard but the Frenchman had as yet no news and urged him to wait another day, as by that time either the Baroness would be on her way back to Rome or else he would have definite information of her whereabouts. He also tried to get through to London, but, owing to the crisis, the Exchange refused to take his call.

A small item in one of the afternoon papers caught Gregory's eye and he saw that Captain B. A. W. Warburton-Lee, of H.M. destroyer *Hardy,* had posthumously been awarded the first Victoria Cross of the war for his gallant attack on Narvik. The action had taken place barely eight weeks before, but Gregory thought sadly how far away Narvik seemed now and how utterly unimportant compared with the vast struggle which was at that moment taking place in Northern France.

The headline of the paper was to the effect that all Italian ships had been ordered to the nearest home or neutral port, which seemed to Gregory really sinister. Mussolini had been filling his money-bags by working his merchant fleet for all it was worth during the past nine months while his peace-time competitors were compelled to use theirs for war purposes. For him to have cancelled all future sailings was therefore showing the red light in earnest. That evening bands of excited young Fascists marched through the streets of Rome calling for war and hurling abuse at France and Britain.

On the Saturday morning Gregory telephoned Collimard again and learnt that both Mussolini and the Baroness were in Genoa, so he decided to go north at once. Having paid his bill he went to Collimard's, where he spent an hour having his disguise touched-up. At first its strangeness had irritated him exceedingly, particularly the moustache, which was the very devil while eating, but he was getting accustomed to it now and Collimard expressed his satisfaction at the way in which it had stood up to two days' wear and tear. Gregory then drove to the station and before catching his train bought all the papers— Italian, British, French and German—that he could lay his hands on to read during his journey.

The Germans had launched a new attack on a sixty-mile front, from Aumale to Noyon. To the forty divisions already engaged they had hurled in seven fresh armoured divisions and twenty new infantry divisions. The Nazis were now using 4,000 tanks, 2,500 planes and 1,000,000 men.

The British Admiralty had announced that after nine months of war the balance of naval strength in our favour was greater than ever before and that nearly a million tons of warships were building in British shipyards. That little paragraph made cheering reading, but the trouble was that it was of very little help to the French at the moment.

He arrived at Genoa at 6.30 in the evening and immediately bought fresh papers. The stop-press told him that the new enemy attack had sent the French reeling back from the Aumale-Noyon line and that the Germans had secured a small bridgehead over the Aisne but had not succeeded in actually breaking through; there was a rumour that Mussolini would speak on the following day.

He drove up the hill to the Hotel Miramar and, having secured a room, set about making tactful inquiries as to the whereabouts of Mussolini, representing himself as an American parson, since feeling was now running very high against the English. No one seemed to know anything for certain although the Italians—polite as ever—were willing enough to gratify the goggle-eyed foreigner's obvious desire to catch a glimpse of the great man. *Il Duce* had certainly been in Genoa that morning but he was living on his special train, which had moved out of its siding at half-past two in the afternoon; the probability was that he had gone up again to inspect other units on the potential battle-front. A little after midnight Gregory went to bed depressed and miserable. The awful uncertainty about Erika was preying on his mind, and he knew that it was hopeless to look for the Baroness until he had managed to locate *Il Duce*.

On the Sunday morning Gregory was up and out early. He found that the whole great city was alive with troops and pulsing with activity. Sailors, soldiers, airmen, Blackshirts, singly and in groups, crowded the hot pavements; aeroplanes hummed overhead, tanks, guns and lorries clattered through the streets or bounced along on their big balloon tyres. Genoa was the nearest Italian port of any size to the French Riviera so it was naturally a base of the first importance and it already had the appearance of a war-time city.

From the morning papers it seemed that the German war machine was at last losing its impetus and between Montdidier and Noyon the attack was certainly less incisive. It was not until after midday that he learnt definitely that Mussolini was now in Turin, so he took the afternoon train there and sat sweltering in his shirt-sleeves while the train wound its way up through the mountains and across the plain of Piedmont.

On arriving, he learned to his delight that *Il Duce's* train was actually on a siding just outside the town but he soon found that he could not get within half a mile of it; every approach was guarded by both Fascists in their black-and-silver and the picturesque Carabinieri with their comic-opera hats and fierce-looking black mostaccios. However, he thought it unlikely that

324

the Baroness was on the train and spent the evening combing every hotel in the city to try to get news of her.

Turin was also packed with troops and, if possible, even more of an armed camp than Genoa, Mussolini had not yet spoken, but it was thought that at any hour he might do so.

It was the fifth day of the battle for France, and for the Allies it might well have been termed Black Sunday. As Gregory listened to the last radio broadcast in his hotel that night he realised that for the French things were very black indeed. Near the coast a force of three hundred enemy tanks had penetrated the Bresle defences the day before. They had now reached the outskirts of Rouen and Pont de Larche, on the Seine. The Germans were within fifty miles of Paris and the French radio announced that all schools in the capital were to be closed and the children sent out of the city.

That morning at dawn a new attack had been launched on a wide front, from Château-Porcien to the Argonne. The French had stemmed it, but 2,000,000 men and 3,500 tanks were now storming their line along the entire front from the sea to Montmédy, and General Weygand, the hope of France, had spoken, saying: 'We have reached the last quarter of the vital hour.'

Italy's entry into the battle was unquestionably imminent, but Gregory felt that if only he could find and kill the Black Baroness there was just a chance that, with her evil influence removed from Mussolini's immediate followers, wiser counsels might yet prevail.

That night, therefore, he went back to the station for another endeavour to get near enough to *Il Duce's* train to question some of the people on it. He felt that, as the Italians are very open to bribery, if only he could get hold of one of the cooks or attendants they might be induced to tell him whether the Baroness had visited the train, or give him some fresh line to work on; but when he got to the station the train was no longer there. *Il Duce* was on his way back to Rome.

Weary, angry and despondent, Gregory inquired about the first train south by which he could follow and found that the next did not leave until 5.40 in the morning. For a moment he considered ringing up Desaix to ask him to fly north and take him back to Rome in his plane, but he abandoned the project almost as soon as it entered his head. Desaix was a Frenchman and he, as the Reverend Eustace, was travelling on an English passport. Turin was now a military area and it was certain that the Italian authorities would not allow aircraft belonging to their potential enemies to come and go freely from it any longer. The two of them might even be arrested on suspicion and detained. If that happened it might be days before they could get free again, or if Italy entered the war they might find themselves in a concentration-camp for good. He went back to the hotel, slept naked on account of the torrid heat, and caught the train south just as dawn was breaking.

He had come to loathe the sight of his thick, black clergyman's clothes and during the seemingly endless morning they proved almost unendurable. By mid-day the steel train was like a furnace and his clerical dog-collar had been reduced to a limp rag.

The papers that he bought in stations where the train stopped informed him that the French Army was still intact and that for the last few days fresh British forces which had been landed in France had been holding a sector on the French left flank. Churchill had sent a message to Reynaud promising that every available man should be rushed across from those units which still had arms and equipment, and calling upon the French to hold fast.

The Italian Press was now openly screaming for war. 'Nice, Corsica, Tunis!' they cried in union, aching to get their dirty fingers on the loot, like a sneak-thief who sees a householder at night already being bludgeoned by a powerful burglar. To add to the overflowing cup, the British aircraft-carrier *Glorious* and the destroyers *Asarta* and *Ardente* had been sunk while pulling the Army's chestnuts out of the fire in another 'skilfully conducted' evacuation. After all the shouting we had abandoned Narvik and left to their fate all that remained of the wretched Norwegians, who apparently had covered our withdrawal by a gallant action.

Arrived in Rome, Gregory drove straight to the Excelsior, and from there rang up the Villa Godolfo. A manservant answered him and he asked if *Madame la Baronne* was at home. To his immense relief he learned that she was, so he gave his name as the Reverend Eustace Arberson and asked the man to find out if the *Baronne* had received a letter of introduction which he had sent her some days before.

The man left the line and after being away some minutes returned to say that *Madame la Baronne* regretted her apparent discourtesy in not having acknowledged *Père* Arberson's letter, but that she had been away for several days and had got back only early that morning. Unfortunately she was leaving the Villa Godolfo again that evening so she could not ask him to lunch or dine, but if he cared to come out that afternoon she would be most happy to see him.

Gregory thanked the man, said that he would certainly come out that afternoon and hung up. He telephoned Collimard that he would be round in half an hour, had a quick bath to freshen himself up after his journey, and took a taxi to the *Via Veneto*. After having had the very minor ravages which had occurred in his numerous patches of false hair during his two days absence from Rome made good he rang up Desaix to warn him to go to the air-port, get ready to take off at once and stand by there until further orders. Collimard, whose part it was to take him to the Villa and get him away again swiftly, then led him round to a garage where a car was in readiness. Gregory got in the back and the Frenchman took the wheel as though he was the driver of a car that had been hired for the afternoon. Shortly before three they set off for the Villa Godolfo.

The sun was still grilling down and Gregory dared not mop his face except with the greatest care, for fear of deranging Collimard's excellent work; but in other respects the journey was a pleasant one, as it lay along the famous '*Via Appia*' for thirteen miles towards Alban, then round the shore of the Albano Lake to the little town of Marino. Half a mile past the town Collimard pointed out the Villa.

It was a lovely house set on the hill among terraced gardens and cypresses, looking right out over the lake. A short, private road led round to its entrance on the other side of the building. Gregory was hating with all his heart the thought of the task that lay before him; nevertheless he was determined to go through with it. As they pulled up he leant forward to Collimard and said in a low voice:

'I don't think I shall be long, as I mean to do the job immediately we're alone together. Be ready to start the second you see me coming out of the front door, and drive like blazes for the air-port.'

Collimard nodded. '*Bien, mon ami.* We may both be executed for this, but, *by God,* it will be worth it. *Bonne chance!*'

A black-clad servant had already appeared in the doorway,

and immediately Gregory gave the name of the Reverend Eustace Arberson he was led inside, through a wide hall to a fine room, the tall windows of which had a lovely view across the lake. The little Black Baroness was sitting there curled up on a sofa and she extended her hand to him with a charming smile.

As he took it his whole instinct was to get the terrible thing that he had to do over, whip away his hand and pull out his gun; but he knew that the servant was still standing in the doorway behind him. He must at least play the part of the Reverend Eustace long enough for the man to close the door and get away to his own quarters.

Half Gregory's mind was now obsessed with the murder he was about to commit. Was his gun loose enough in its shoulder-holster for a quick draw? Would the silencer on it work properly? Would he be able to make a quick, clean job of it and shoot her through the heart before she realised his purpose? Or would she leap up the second she saw him produce his gun and endeavour to escape so that he had to shoot her in the back, perhaps several times, before she died? If that happened, her screams might rouse the household and his escape would be seriously jeopardised. That must not occur if it could possibly be avoided. The only thing to do, then, to make quite certain that she did not scream before she died was to wait until her back was turned and shoot her through the heart from behind.

While those thoughts were racing through his brain she had been saying: '*Mon cher Pére Arberson,* how very nice to see you. I am desolated beyond words that you should have been in Rome for five days while I was in the north and that now I have to go again so soon I cannot entertain you properly, but I have heard so much about you from our mutual friends that even the opportunity of a brief meeting gives me the greatest pleasure. Come and sit down and tell me about the wonderful work which I hear you have been doing for us in that most difficult of all countries—England.'

Gregory felt his face crease into a smile and it was almost in surprise that he found himself saying in an unctuous voice well-suited to the part he was playing: 'It's most kind of you to receive me at all when you're here for only a few hours. I've been wanting to meet you simply for ages on account of the admiration I feel for one who has done so much for the cause that we all hold so dear.'

As he sat down he heard the manservant say: 'Shall I bring tea, *Madame la Baronne,* or would you prefer to wait until your usual hour?'

She glanced at her diamond wrist-watch and replied quickly: 'It is early yet—only half-past three. But wait. . . .' She suddenly broke off and smiled at Gregory. 'You will forgive me, I know, if I say that I did not expect that you would get out here quite so soon, although it is a compliment which I appreciate. I have one telephone-call that I must make before we settle down to enjoy a really interesting talk. Since it is a trunk-call it may take a little time, because the lines are so congested now that the crisis has reached its height, but I will be as quick as I possibly can. In the meantime, I am sure you would like to sit out in the garden, and as there is almost an hour to go until teatime you will have a glass of iced wine to refresh you after your journey.'

As she stood up, Gregory rose too, murmuring that he perfectly understood but inwardly cursing at the thought of this most inopportune telephone-call; which meant that for minutes that would seem hours he would have to sit contemplating in advance this ghastly thing that he had to do when she rejoined him.

The Baroness moved towards the door, a small, neat figure, and as Gregory stared at her back, through which he meant to put a bullet at the first suitable opportunity, it seemed impossible to believe that she was over fifty. When she reached the door she said to the manservant: 'Take *Père* Arberson down to the lower terrace and bring him some of the Lacrima Christi or any other refreshment that he may prefer.'

The man bowed her out and, turning to Gregory, murmured: 'Would you please to follow me, sir.'

With the feeling that he was acting in a play, or was the subject of some nightmare dream, Gregory followed the man through the french windows out on to the balustraded terrace, down some ancient stone steps at either side of which a fountain was playing, and along the sloping paths of the formal Italian garden until they reached a second terrace about fifty feet below the level of the house. They turned left along it until at its end they passed through an archway in a tall yew hedge and came out on a circular extension of the terrace which was shaded from the sun by tall cypresses and had a table and garden-chairs arranged upon it.

329

Gregory sat down and stared out over the placid blue waters of the lake below. It was very quiet there and cut off by the trees from the sight of any other house along the lake-shore. Not a thing was moving and the only evidence of the handi-work of man in the whole panorama was the lemon-yellow villas just discernible in the distance upon the further shore and the ancient moss-covered, stone balustrade immediately in front of him. It occurred to him that the scene must have been just the same nearly 2,000 years before when some Roman patrician had perhaps entertained his Caesar there.

The black-clad manservant had disappeared as Gregory sat down, but he returned with a large, flagon-shaped decanter which had a narrow spout rising out of one side of it like that of a teapot, and on the other a sausage-shaped hole which went right down into the centre of the flagon and was packed full of crushed ice so that the wine was cooled without the ice getting into and diluting it.

The man poured the golden wine into a cone-shaped crystal goblet and handed it on a salver to Gregory. With a nod of thanks he took the glass and drank. It was a light, dry Italian wine, deliciously cool and refreshing after his hot journey, but with a slight taste of sulphur about it which has prevented such Italian wines ever becoming popular in England.

He set the glass down and began to think again of the grim work before him. When the Baroness joined him where would she sit? Probably in that chair there, as it was beside his own and faced the view. How would he then be able to get behind her? How utterly revolting the whole business was, but it must be done—it *must* be done. The lives of thousands of soldiers, sailors and airmen, the happiness or misery of literally millions of families, the fate of two great nations perhaps hung upon it.

He drank some more of the refreshing wine and with a momentary flash of his old cynicism thought how fate had played into his hands in the matter of the Baroness's trunk-call. In this secluded spot which could not be seen from the house or observed from the roadway it would be infinitely easier for him to do the thing he had to do, without any risk of being caught in the act. No doubt there was a path leading round the house which would make it unnecessary for him to go back through it. With luck he would be able to slip away unobserved and the Baroness's body might not be discovered until he was well on his way back to Rome or perhaps hours later when

330

with Collimard and Desaix he was in the plane heading for Paris once more.

He suddenly realised that he was feeling very tired; the strain of the last two months, and particularly of the past four weeks, had been appalling. It was not only his own work which had taken it out of him so much, but the frightful mental stress of watching the world-tragedy unfold, with victory after victory going to Hitler. Norway seized, Holland overrun, Belgium smashed to her knees and now France in dire peril—yet there had seemed so little that one could do to halt the onward sweep of the mighty German war-machine.

He was sitting in the shadow, but the strong sunshine on the waters of the lake tired his eyes and he closed them for a moment. It was very pleasant there—so utterly peaceful and far removed from all the turmoil and the killing that was going on under the same sun far away to the north. For a little he remained between sleeping and waking; he did not hear her come, but when he opened his eyes again the Baroness was standing in front of him.

She was now dressed for travelling, in a light tweed coat-and-skirt. Her old-young face expressed none of the easy social charm with which she had greeted him on his arrival. Her dead-black eyes were staring down at him with a queer expression of mixed amusement and contempt.

'Well, Englishman?' A harsh note had crept into her soft voice as she addressed him. 'Are you the best thing that the British Government could find to send against me? Did you think for one moment that stupid clerical collar would deceive such eyes as mine?'

Gregory sat staring at her, his mouth a little open, as she went on mockingly: 'Your name is Sallust, isn't it? I think that was what Grauber said when I described you to him after that night when you tried to dissuade Leopold from surrendering and I had to shoot your little girl-friend who turned out to be the traitoress Erika von Epp.'

The moment Gregory had opened his eyes he had attempted to spring to his feet, but although his brain was still working perfectly clearly it seemed that it no longer controlled his body. All that happened was that after a slight jerk forward his feet slithered a little on the stones; but even by exerting all his will-power he could not lever himself up out of the chair. The awful truth came home to him with blinding suddenness—the wine had been drugged.

The Baroness lit a cigarette and went on calmly: 'I only caught a glimpse of you when we were with Leopold and the things someone has done to your face are very effective; but Grauber told me, too, that it was you who was the masked man that broke into my suite at the Hotel Weimar, and we stood within a few feet of each other for the best part of ten minutes then. It is useless to cover or alter your face unless you also do something about your hands—and you have very nice hands, Mr. Sallust; the moment you came into the room this afternoon I knew you by them for the man of Rotterdam.'

In vain Gregory wriggled, making superhuman efforts to get up, but it needed every ounce of concentration he had to move one limb at a time. He could raise either his hands or feet a few inches, but then it flopped back again and he was as fast in his chair as though he had been bound to it.

'Stop squirming!' she admonished him suddenly. 'It will do you no good. What you came here to do I don't know, but you have been caught by quicker wits than your own. Into the wine you drank I put an old and subtle Italian poison which is almost tasteless and leaves no trace. Its first symptoms you already know, the later ones you will learn in due course; I should think, judging by the amount you have drunk, in about two hours. No one will disturb you here; I sent a message out to your chauffeur that you had changed your plans and would not require him until ten o'clock, so he has gone back to Rome. My work in Italy is done and I am leaving now to hear Mussolini speak, before flying home. Count Ciano is already on his way to inform the French and British Ambassadors that Italy will enter the war on the side of Germany at midnight. Good-bye, Mr. Sallust; you will die quite peacefully and in no great pain.'

23

Poison

Having picked up the goblet and tossed its remaining contents into the bushes the Baroness had collected the decanter and gone; removing with her the only evidence as to the manner in which he might have met his death.

The partial paralysis which had Gregory in its grip had prevented his uttering a single word. He could move his lips and his tongue but only enough to mutter incoherently and, strive as he would, it was utterly impossible for him to emit a shout for help; yet he now knew that every moment that he remained there the poison would be working through his body, making less his chance of life.

If only he had not been so eager to make a quick get-away and had left the car out on the road a few hundred yards away from the Villa, Collimard would have become suspicious at his non-appearance after he had been in the house for over an hour, and when another hour had passed he would probably have made up his mind to come in and investigate; but by driving up to the front door in the car Gregory realised that he had made his own line of retreat extremely vulnerable.

Even had the Baroness sent out to tell Collimard that she was, herself, motoring her guest back to Rome, he would have smelt a rat; but on being told to return at ten o'clock he would assume that for some good reason, after having seen the layout for himself, Gregory had decided not to make his attempt upon her life until after dark. By squinting sideways Gregory could just see his watch. It was twelve minutes past four; the Baroness had given him two hours; by ten o'clock he would have been dead for over three hours.

He felt that if only he could have stood up there would have been some chance for him to counteract the toxin; because a subtle type that does not work quickly can nearly always be countered by an emetic if it is taken before the poison has had time to get right down into the system. Concentrating all his will-power, he first brought his head forward a few inches then raised his right hand to his mouth in an endeavour to put his finger down his throat to make himself sick, but, strive as he would, he could not make his finger do more than fumble at his lower lip. After what seemed an interminable time of agonising strain his arm suddenly relaxed and his hand dropped back into his lap.

He was sweating profusely and although his eyes were wide open and staring they no longer took in the placid scene before him. Every faculty he had remaining to him was concentrated in one awful struggle to think of some way in which he might save his life; yet each fresh thought seemed only to lead back to a nightmare circle. The poison was working in him, time was now his deadly enemy and with every second that ticked away his state of helplessness would increase.

After an interval of minutes that seemed like hours the sight of a little green lizard darting from side to side along the sun-warmed stone of the balustrade caused him to remember that when animals were ill or poisoned a natural instinct led them to a herb the eating of which provided an antidote to their complaint; yet, there again, he was stuck. As he could not get up he could not reach anything to eat even had he known of a plant in the garden which would have served as a remedy.

The golden-green lizard sat there now, basking in the sunshine and watching him with cautious curiosity from its little dark, beady eyes. Suddenly a small, crested bird dropped out of the sky. Fearing attack, the lizard instantly dived for cover, but as it shot along the stone its foreleg caught in a crevice, flinging it right over on its back so that for a second its pale-green tummy was exposed. In a single wriggle it was up again and had streaked away out of sight. Its tumble gave Gregory the germ of another idea. He could not stand up but he might be able to fall out of his chair.

Once more concentrating all his mental strength he got one foot up until it rested on the leg of the table in front of him; then, after pausing for a moment, he flung every ounce of will-power that he had into a sideways thrust. The chair tipped, hovered for an instant and crashed sideways, sending him rolling along the ground.

When he recovered from the fall he found that he was within a few inches of the yew hedge and, lifting his head, he began a titanic struggle to eat some of the sprigs of yew. He had no idea if they would serve his purpose but he felt that if he could get a few mouthfuls of the prickly herbage down they might upset him or irritate his throat to the point of causing him to vomit.

He seemed to have more strength in his jaws than in his lips and his teeth were good. The yew tasted horrible and when he strove to swallow the first mouthful it stuck in his gullet. With growing hope he tore some more sprigs from the hedge with his teeth and, filling his mouth, tried to force them down. Suddenly the muscles of his throat contracted, his stomach heaved and to his incredible relief the sprigs of yew came choking up with some of the liquid that he had drunk.

For a few moments he lay there panting and exhausted but he knew that he was as yet very far from having saved himself, as the great bulk of the poison must still be in his stomach. Sweating, straining, he forced himself to fresh exertions. Every time he opened and shut his mouth it was as though he was striving to shift a ton weight with his teeth, but such was his tenacity of purpose that three times more he filled his mouth with the prickly shoots of yew, tried to force them down and was sick in consequence, before he collapsed and passed into a stupor.

When he came round it was night, and from a faint jolting he knew that he was moving, but his mind was practically a blank; he was conscious only that he felt desperately ill without being able to remember how he had become so. After a time he realised that he was half-sitting, half-lying, on the back seat of a car, but he had no idea where he was being taken or even what country he was in. His eyes ached intolerably and his head seemed to split in half with every jolt of the vehicle, which was moving at high speed.

He lay there comatose until the car suddenly pulled up and he slid off the seat on to the floor. The door was flung open, hands seized and shook him, then as he pleaded to be left alone a voice addressed him urgently in French:

'It is I, Collimard—Collimard, the barber. I went back at ten and the butler said that you had left hours before but that he had not seen you go. I felt certain then that something had gone wrong so I held him up with my gun and forced him to tell me what had happened from the moment that you entered the house. He led me to the lower terrace and we found you there. What happened? You do not appear to be wounded. Did she suspect and give you a doped cigarette?'

'Poison,' Gregory moaned, as the whole series of events came back to him, 'poisoned wine.' Then the realisation that he had spoken, and all that it meant, dawned in his tortured brain. If he had got back the use of his facial muscles sufficiently to speak, the effects of the poison were wearing off, but, even so, he felt almost as though he were in *extremis* as he muttered: 'Doctor—get me to a doctor.'

'Listen,' said Collimard swiftly; 'Mussolini spoke at six o'clock. It is war. Italy will be at war with France and Britain on the stroke of midnight, and it is already nearly eleven o'clock. We are just outside the air-port. Desaix will be waiting

335

there. If you can make the effort to pass the officials we still have time to get away in the plane, but if we delay to try to find a doctor we shall be caught here and arrested as enemy aliens. How bad are you? Do you feel that you could survive the journey, or are you so bad that if you do not have proper attention in the next few hours you will die? It is for you to judge, and we will stay or go—whichever you decide.'

Gregory closed his eyes and tried to think. It was nearly eleven o'clock. Then, some seven hours had elapsed since he had drunk the poison. If he had survived so long, the odds were that a doctor could do little for him but ease his pain and it was now only a matter of time before the poison worked itself out of his system. He would have given a fortune, had he possessed one, to have had cool poultices placed round his aching head, with a soothing drink to ease his parched throat, and to have been able to relax his tortured limbs between clean sheets, but there were Collimard and Desaix to think of as well as himself; and even had they not been involved his every instinct would have been to face any agony rather than become the inmate of an Italian concentration-camp.

He nodded and gasped. 'I'll be all right; we must get off—at once.'

'Can you stand?' asked Collimard anxiously. 'The airport people may not let you through if they think that you are desperately ill or perhaps drugged, and that Desaix and I are taking you somewhere against your will.'

Gregory tested his limbs, knelt up and managed to struggle back on to the seat. 'I'm pretty groggy,' he muttered, 'but I'll manage somehow. Knees may give a bit, an'—difficult to hold up my head. Better tell them I've been on the binge—drunk.'

Collimard shut the door of the car, got back into the driver's seat and drove on for a few hundred yards until he reached the entrance to the airport. Getting down again, he opened the door to help Gregory out and, as he did so, he began to sing *The Marseillaise*.

Two Italian policemen came hurrying up with a small crowd of other people and one of the officers addressed Collimard indignantly, asking him how he dared to sing the national anthem of France when in little over an hour France and Italy would be at war.

Collimard hiccoughed and declared drunkenly: 'I sing because I am a Frenchman and I go home to fight for *la belle*

France. This'—he thumped Gregory hard on the chest—'is my gallant ally. He goes to fight by my side although he *is* a clergyman. But he is no ordinary clergyman—he is as drunk as I am. No; he is much more drunk than I am, because he can no longer sing. *Rule, Britannia! Britannia rule the waves.* Come! let us pass—lead me to my fiery steed—bring me my bow and my arrows tipped with gold—we'll show you—we'll show all of you.'

This extraordinary declamation was received in astonished silence by the group of Italians. It was a bold policy to declare oneself so openly, when groups of blackguardly young Fascists were lynching French and British subjects in the streets. But—war or no war—all the world has a slightly cynical but nevertheless soft spot for a drunken man providing that his drunkenness is neither beastly nor quarrelsome. Several of the bystanders began to laugh and pushing his way forward the Italian policeman said, not unkindly:

'I'm afraid you stayed too long in the bar, my friend. The last plane for France has gone.'

'Ah,' said Collimard, wagging his finger, 'that's where you're wrong; I have my own plane. Come and look at my plane; I will show it to you.' As he stumbled forward, supporting Gregory under one arm, the policeman said:

'Wait a minute; you can't leave your car here, you know.'

'My car—but why not? I cannot take my car with me in the plane and, if I could, my car could not fight for *la belle France* as my friend, the clergyman, is about to do; so why should I not leave my car here?'

'It's against regulations,' said the policeman. 'You should have sold it or given it away before leaving.'

'Ha, that's an idea!' Collimard exclaimed triumphantly. 'The war is one thing; personal feelings are another. I have worked in Italy for years, I have earned good money here. Although I go to fight for France I shall still love Italy. To Italy I give my car. You shall sell it for the Italian Red Cross.'

This generous announcement completed his drunken conquest of the crowd. Some good-hearted fellow said: 'Come on! There's no time to lose; we must get these fellows off or they'll be interned here. After all, we're not at war with them yet.'

With voluble offers of assistance the little crowd then surrounded Collimard and Gregory, talked to the airport officials on their behalf, found Desaix, who was in the waiting-room, and, to the airman's amazement, took them all out on to the flying-ground, where they were given a send-off as though they were national heroes instead of three potential enemies.

Owing to Collimard's aid Gregory had somehow managed to keep his feet while their passports were being examined and they were making their way across the landing-ground, but immediately he got into the plane he collapsed.

Hours later he learnt that when they had landed to refuel at Marseilles, Collimard and Desaix had held an agitated consultation as to whether they should take him to a hospital there or fly on with him to Paris; but both of them had to get to the capital, and as Gregory had appeared no worse they had decided to take him on with them. When he came-to on being lifted out of the plane he found that they were back at the private aerodrome at Choisy. Desaix asked him if he would like to be put to bed at once in the house, but as Choisy was only a little over five miles outside Paris he said that he would rather be taken to the Saint Regis, as the manager there knew him and would take all further responsibility for him off their hands. Collimard telephoned the Saint Regis to have a doctor there to meet them while Desaix got out a car, and by five o'clock Gregory was tucked up in bed in his old room at the hotel with a professional nurse in attendance.

When he awoke it was two o'clock in the afternoon. The first thing that struck him was that he could once more hear the rumble of guns, then he realised that he was back in Paris. He remembered little of the journey of the night before and nothing at all of having been examined by the doctor; but seeing that he was awake the nurse, a pretty, dark girl who told him that her name was Sister Madeleine, gave him something to drink which eased his throat, and gave him a telegram that had been waiting for him.

It had been handed in the previous Saturday and read:

ERIKA TOOK TURN FOR BETTER YESTERDAY STOP IN VIEW OF CRISIS CANNOT SUFFICIENTLY STRESS URGENCY OF YOUR COMPLETING JOB STOP GWAINE-CUST.

Gregory lay back and closed his eyes. Erika had turned the corner—Erika had turned the corner. That blessed throught kept playing like human music through his brain and he was still revelling in the marvellous relief of it twenty minutes later when the doctor arrived!

338

Apart from a certain haziness as to events after he had drunk the poison, Gregory could remember every detail of the events which had led up to his almost fatal experience and he knew enough about medicine to be quite certain that the professional skill could do nothing for him except keep him in bed until he had regained his health and strength; so he listened patiently to the doctor's humming and hawing while making his own mental reservations as to what he meant to do.

He felt very weak but the pains had left him and he could now use his limbs quite freely again. Sir Pellinore's telegram only confirmed his own feeling that for any man, however ill, who could stand on his own feet this was no time to lie abed, and the first step was to inform himself of what was going on; so when the doctor had gone he sent for the papers.

He saw with relief that Turkey had reaffirmed her obligations to the Allies on Italy's entry into the war the previous midnight and that President Roosevelt had made a great speech condemning Mussolini and implying that American neutrality was dead. Malta had that morning been bombed by the Italians, while the R.A.F. had carried out raids on Libya and Italian East Africa, but he knew that all these things could have little bearing on the titanic struggle which was taking place close at hand.

It was Tuesday, June the 11th, the seventh day of the battle for France, and the French had been forced to withdraw to new positions south of the Marne. Just eight nights before Lacroix had told him the awful secret that General Weygand had no army of reserve, as every available man had had to be thrown in on the line of the Somme; Gregory could only pray that during the past week that had been rectified. In seven days it should have been possible to have brought over large bodies of troops from France's North African possessions as well as many units which had not formed part of the original B.E.F.—and so still had their equipment—from Britain. If such a force was being concentrated somewhere south of Paris there was still hope, and Gregory felt that it must be so. Surely while France was in danger all other theatres of war entirely lost their significance. What did it matter if Mussolini invaded Tunisia or the Western Desert or the Sudan or Somaliland and gained a temporary foothold in any or all of these places, if only France could be saved? He could always be slung out afterwards.

It was now 14 days since the surrender of Belgium, 27 days

since the capitulation of Holland and 32 days since the opening of the *Blitzkrieg*; so for nearly five weeks the Germans had been sustaining their incredible offensive at maximum pressure. It was said that they had already lost half a million dead, with thousands of tanks and planes. It simply was not possible for them to continue that way for very much longer; they *must* be nearing exhaustion point. If only they could now be halted, and a counter-offensive launched, there was a real hope that the vast, overstrained machine might collapse upon itself and even that the war might be brought to a victorious conclusion by one well-planned counter-offensive.

At half-past four he got out of bed and told pretty Sister Madeleine that she must help him dress. The poor girl was horrified, but he smilingly told her that he knew perfectly well what he was up to and that it was no good sending for the doctor because the doctor was only his paid adviser and had no power whatever to restrain him from going out if he decided to do so on his own responsibility.

Seeing that nothing would dissuade him from his purpose, she helped him on with his clerical suit—the only clothes that he had with him—and once he was up he found that although he was a little shaky he was quite capable of walking about without assistance. She saw him downstairs and on the porter's securing him a taxi he drove to the *Sûreté Générale*. Having sent up his name to Lacroix he waited patiently in a room downstairs until nearly six o'clock, when at last a messenger came in to say that the Colonel would see him.

For once the little man was not seated behind his desk but was walking slowly up and down with his hands clasped behind his back. As Gregory was shown in he turned and, having stared at him for a moment, exclaimed:

'*Sacré Nom!* But what has happened to you, my poor friend? You look as though you have just got up out of your coffin. Sit down at once.'

'Thanks.' Gregory sank into a chair. 'You're right, sir; I *have* just got up out of my coffin—or near enough. I spent six days chasing that damned woman round Italy and when I at last ran her to earth she made a complete fool of me. Collimard's disguise was admirable, but my hands gave me away. She knew who I was from the word "go" and she put poison in my wine— the hell cat! This time last night I was as near death as makes no difference, out at her villa on Lake Albano, but I managed to save myself by the skin of my teeth, and Collimard behaved magnificently; he and Desaix managed to get me home.'

'But, *mon ami*, you ought to be in bed.'

'Of course,' Gregory shrugged. 'But how could anyone who has the strength to walk remain in bed at a time like this?' I had to know what's happening and I've come back to you again as a failure; but I mean to get that woman if I die for it. She's here in France again—at least, she was leaving for France when I last saw her.'

Lacroix nodded. 'She flew from Italy yesterday evening and arrived back at her château in the Forest of Fontainebleau just before midnight. Directly I heard that I knew that you must have failed, so I'm having her watched; but, as you know, there is nothing that I can do against her.'

Gregory laughed a little weakly. 'Maybe. But I'm still game to go after her. I'll drive out there tonight. I've a feeling that she's not going to be so lucky the third time that I get her on her own.'

'I forbid you to do so,' said the Colonel sharply. 'You are in no fit state to undertake any such venture.'

Gregory's chin came out in a stubborn line. 'Forgive me, but I'm not under your orders, *mon Colonel*. I'm a free man and I shall make my own decision as to how and when I tackle *Madame la Baronne*. Still, before I go I'd consider it a real kindness if you'd let me into how things are shaping. The papers say so little.'

Lacroix flung out his small brown hands. 'Matters could hardly be worse. It has been decided to declare Paris an open town, in order to save it from devastation. If it proves necessary our forces will be ordered to withdraw to fresh positions south of the city.'

'Good God!' Gregory exclaimed. 'But the moral effect on your troops will be positively appalling. Paris is now a great, natural bastion in the very centre of your line. If every building in the suburbs were made a machine-gun nest the Germans would never be able to take the city, short of starving it into surrender. You could hold it for months while the old B.E.F. is being re-equipped and a far greater one being shipped over week by week to your assistance.'

'And in the meantime?' asked Lacroix. 'We are no longer in 1870. The city suffered badly enough then from the German bombardments, but that is nothing compared to what the Germans could do today with both guns and aeroplanes.'

'But Paris covers a huge area. If the Germans bomb and shell it for weeks they may do quite a lot of damage but they couldn't destroy it beyond repair.'

'Would you, I wonder, take the same view if it were London that was threatened with destruction?'

'Yes,' cried Gregory angrily. 'I'm only saying what any Londoner would say when I tell you that I would rather die fighting among the ruins of Piccadilly than live to see the Germans march down it in triumph.'

'I believe you. And many Frenchmen—myself among them —would prefer to die crushed under the ruins of the Arc de Triomphe than allow the Germans to pass through it; but it is not to be.'

'Think what such a surrender means,' Gregory went on urgently. 'It's not only the moral uplift that the capture of the city will give to the whole German nation, and the disastrous effect that it will have on the mind of every Frenchman throughout the world, but if it is to be given up to save its buildings from destruction we won't be able to bomb it afterwards. A million Germans will be able to live here in perfect security, immune from all attack, and its great railway network will give the enemy an enormous advantage for future operations. In the Paris area there are great munition-plants and innumerable factories. All these will fall unharmed into the Nazis' hands and the loot that Hitler will collect is almost beyond imagination.'

The Colonel shrugged wearily. 'I know, my friend, I know; but that is the decision of the High Command and the Government is leaving Paris tonight.'

'Where for?'

'I do not yet know. I am now waiting to hear from de Gaulle.'

'Who is he?'

'You have not heard of him, eh? Well, he is one of our younger Generals and a man in whom I, personally, have great faith. He is Under-Secretary for War and Reynaud's general military adviser.'

'Is it he who has advised the abandonment of Paris?'

'On the contrary. He fought tooth and nail against it, but he was overruled. Today another great battle has been raging— a secret battle in which victory will go to those who succeed in influencing Reynaud to accept their policy. De Gaulle, Georges Mandel, who is the spiritual heir of Clemenceau, and their friends wish the Government to move to Quimpier, in Brittany, and to withdraw our forces to a line from Rouen to Orleans, and thence south-east along the Loire, so that we can make a last stand with our backs to the English Channel. His opponents wish the Government to retire to Bordeaux, where they would be further removed from the influence of the English should it become necessary to accept defeat and capitulate.'

'Capitulate?' cried Gregory. 'But this is ghastly!—unthinkable! What in God's name can Weygand be thinking of to permit even the suggestion of capitulation to be mentioned in the French War Cabinet?'

Lacroix looked up sadly. 'Mon ami, it is best that you should know the truth. It is Weygand who heads the party that is urging Reynaud to move to Bordeaux.'

Gregory mopped his forehead as he murmured: 'Weygand— France's hope; and Leopold warned me, yet I was fool enough to laugh at him. Is there nobody whom one can trust?'

'You may trust de Gaulle; but Weygand must from now on be counted among the enemy. Almost hourly, from Sunday last—Black Sunday—he has been telephoning Reynaud to say that there is no more than he can do and urging the Government to leave Paris. Today we reach the crisis. This morning Reynaud actually signed the order for the move to Bordeaux, but de Gaulle made him countermand it and preparations are still going forward for a move to Quimpier. But it was necessary for de Gaulle to remain with Reynaud in his office all day in order to ensure that he was not got at and that he did not change his mind once more. Then, an hour ago, your friend, the Baroness arrived there.'

'Oh hell! I thought you said she was at Fontainebleau?'

'She was. And it is virtually certain that she will return there tonight to collect her papers and valuables before moving south out of the new battle area, of which Fontainebleau will now automatically become a part; but this afternoon she did something which she has never done before—she came openly to the Ministry and demanded to see Reynaud in his office. At first de Gaulle made him refuse to see her, but no one dared to stop her and she forced her way into his room. She insisted on seeing Reynaud alone, but de Gaulle would not leave; and, as far as I know, they are still in conference. Those are the facts; I had them from de Gaulle's secretary, who left the room only after the Baroness had forced her way into it.'

343

Gregory had overestimated his strength when he left the hotel and he was now feeling desperately ill and weak again. 'I thought,' he said slowly, 'that the *Baronne's* affair with Reynaud was all over, long ago?'

'It is, I believe, many years since they were lovers but they have always remained close friends; and unfortunately she still has great influence with him.'

'God! That woman! How I wish I'd shot her in Rotterdam when I had the chance. If I can't manage to do something about it soon she'll hand us all over, bound hand and foot, to the Nazis. But can't you telephone—find out if there's anything fresh? To wait here like this is simply intolerable.'

Lacroix glanced at his watch. 'I should have been informed at once if any definite decision had been taken; but it's over an hour since I had the last report so I'll inquire how things are going.' He moved over to his telephone and asked for a number.

They waited in silence for a few moments while Gregory closed his eyes and mopped the perspiration from his forehead; then Lacroix made a series of meaningless ejaculations. Replacing the receiver he turned back to Gregory.

'They have just come out. De Gaulle remained in the room all the time but they persuaded him to stand by the window so that he was practically out of earshot. Five minutes ago Reynaud suddenly snatched up his hat and stick. He pushed the Baroness out of the room and exclaimed as he followed her: "De Gaulle, it will be the South after all—and this is final." '

Gregory roused himself and nodded. 'That, of course, means Bordeaux; so the Baroness wins once again. But I mean to see to it that she doesn't live to enjoy her triumph.'

'You are determined to go down to Fontainebleau tonight, then?'

'Yes. What's the name of her house?'

'It is the Pavillon de Chasse, Mirabeau, and you will find it deep in the forest, down a side-turning to the right of the main road, some three miles this side of Fontainebleau.'

The Colonel paused for a moment. Gregory felt positively deathly. There seemed to be a great weight on his chest and he could no longer see clearly, but he heard Lacroix go on:

'Since you are set on making this attempt let us derive all the benefit possible from it. Whatever may be the outcome of the present battle, you may take it that there are many men like General de Gaulle and myself who will fight on. Among the

Baroness's papers there must be many letters and other documents which will inform us whom we can, and whom we cannot, trust. Those papers must already be packed for removal; if you can secure them you will have rendered us a service of the utmost importance.'

Gregory mopped his head again. 'All right,' he said; 'I'll go now—I—I. . . .' As he stood up the room seemed to sway about him. He rocked unsteadily for a moment then crashed to the floor, unconscious.

24

Death in the Sunshine

As he knelt down beside the still body the little Colonel sadly shook his head. He knew that *Madame la Baronne Noire* was not destined to die by Gregory's hand *that* night and he felt that it might be many days—vital days—before Gregory was again fit to strike a blow at the enemy. Standing up, he rang his bell, and when it was answered, gave swift instructions for Gregory's removal in a police ambulance to his hotel.

Gregory came out of his faint before they reached the Saint Regis and by the time he was carried up to his room he had recovered sufficiently, in spite of his anger with himself at his own weakness, to be faintly amused at the reception accorded him by his pretty nurse.

'*Méchant, méchant!*' she upbraided him, wagging a slim finger in his face before proceeding to help him back to bed. 'What children men are! They think there is no limit to their strength, and that however ill they are the world will cease to turn if for one moment they must give up the new games with which they amuse themselves when they are too old any longer to play with their lead soldiers and their model aeroplanes. If women ruled the world your nasty dangerous toys would be taken from you for good and all, then there would be some peace and happiness for a change.'

For a moment Gregory wondered if there was not a great fundamental truth in what she said. Women ask very little of life except a mate and security in which to bring up their offspring. It is men who are the dreamers for good or ill, and for every outstanding male who lifts the human race by some great scientific or artistic achievement there is always an Attila, a Napoleon or a Hitler whose visions lead him to inflict untold misery upon his fellow-men. Perhaps, he thought, it would be better if, like the ants or bees, the human race were content to live under a matriarchy, where there was no progress, no ambition, but work and food for all; yet somehow he could not believe that, because if one rejected all hope of advancement as the price of permanent peace it meant the death of the spirit, by the possession of which alone man differs from the insects and the animals.

He slept well and woke the following morning still weak but better and with the knowledge that work lay before him which must be done.

Even with dissension rife among France's War Cabinet and a defeatist spirit in the very person of her Commander-in-Chief, that spirit had not yet spread to her junior Generals, her regimental officers or her soldiers, who were still fighting gamely; so France might yet be saved.

Reynaud had given in to the Baroness on the previous afternoon, but only after many days of constant pressure from her associates. It was quite on the cards that he might change his mind once again when the Government was removed from the atmosphere of Paris, which was now flooded with the defeatism brought by a million refugees from France's northern provinces. It needed only a slight weakening of the German effort --which by all reasoning was already overdue—a small counter-offensive launched with success in some sector by a Corps Commander, or even a Divisional General, to make the fighting spirit of de Gaulle once again paramount in the counsels of the wavering Premier; but as long as the Black Baroness lived she was a constant menace to any such last-moment recovery. She had to die, and it was Gregory's business to bring about her death.

After he had breakfasted he told Sister Madeleine quietly but firmly that his good night's rest had really given him the strength to carry on, this time, and that he meant to get up; but he was not destined to do so. With a superior air she lifted the receiver of his bedside telephone and asked for the *agent de ville* to be sent up.

'Come, come,' Gregory laughed. 'The law doesn't give you power to keep a sick man in bed against his will, so it's no good sending for the police.'

'They're here already,' she smiled, 'and what powers they have you will soon learn for yourself.'

When the *agent de ville* arrived he was very tactful, but it transpired that he was acting under the orders of Colonel Lacroix. He had been instructed to tell Gregory that the Colonel did not consider him in a fit state to operate for the time being and that if he attempted to leave his bed he was to be placed under arrest; also that Paris was in no immediate danger, but should the capture of the city become imminent the invalid would be evacuated before there was any risk of his becoming a prisoner. In the meantime, Lacroix sent his best wishes for Gregory's speedy recovery and a promise that he would be allowed his freedom the moment that the doctor's reports showed him well enough not to abuse it.

This was a state of things against which it was difficult to take counter-measures. Gregory knew Lacroix too well to believe that the Colonel would succumb to pleas or argument, and he realised that he was really not yet up to tackling the job of evading both Sister Madeleine and the *agent de ville*. In his heart of hearts he knew, too, that Lacroix's decision had been a wise one; so he resigned himself to accept it, but he sent for a war map and followed every fresh bulletin with the greatest anxiety.

It was known that the Germans were now within twenty miles of Paris. By mid-day news came in that their armoured divisions had smashed through on the Lower Oise to Persan and Beaumont. To the East they were now endeavouring to drive a spear-head behind the Maginot Line; around Rheims the pressure was increasing hourly, and they succeeded in forcing the Passage of the Marne at Château-Thierry. West of Paris the situation was equally critical; between Rouen and Vernon the Germans had established bridge-heads across the Lower Seine and by evening it was learnt that Le Havre was in peril.

This last piece of news seemed to Gregory especially grave. Le Havre was the main British war base and there stocks of millions of shells, thousands of lorries, hundreds of guns and colossal quantities of other equipment had been steadily built up during the whole nine months of the war. As long as Le Havre remained in our possession these could be used to re-equip fresh units sent from home; but their quantity was far too great for them to be moved, so if the Germans succeeded in forcing their way down the coast this incalculably valuable accumulation of brand new war material must be either destroyed or captured.

There had been little movement on France's Italian front, so it looked as though Mussolini was chary of testing out the valour of his Fascists, but the R.A.F. had bombed Turin, Genoa, Milan, Tobruk and Italy's Abyssinian bases, with good effect. Spain had made a formal announcement of non-belligerency in favour of the Axis, so evidently our new Ambassador, Sir Samuel Hoare, had cut little ice with General Franco as yet.

On the Thursday Gregory telephoned a store for some ready-made clothes on approval and from them selected an outfit to replace his clergyman's gear. The morning papers said that the French had made counter-attacks at Persan and Beaumont, winning back five miles of ground, but that further west, at Rouen, the situation was worsening hourly. The Germans were now throwing in their unarmoured infantry with utter recklessness and their troops were pouring over their bridge-heads across the lower Seine. East of Paris, Rheims had fallen and the new German thrust to outflank the Maginot Line was making rapid progress.

During that day the enemy were steadily closing in on the western, northern and eastern approaches to Paris, and General Weygand formally declared it an open city. At night Reynaud broadcast a last desperate appeal to President Roosevelt while the B.B.C. proclaimed that Britain's factories were now working night and day without cessation to equip a new army, the advance units of which were sailing hour by hour as rifles and gas-masks could be placed in the hands of the men who had been saved from Dunkirk.

On the Friday, Gregory had so far recovered that even Sister Madeleine agreed that he was sufficiently well to get up, and after breakfast he was just about to do so when, having left the room for a moment, she returned to announce a visitor. To Gregory's surprise and delight Kuporovitch walked in.

The Russian was in gigantic spirits. He had flown from England that morning and at last achieved his ambition of reaching Paris again after twenty-six years of exile from his beloved holiday resort.

Even the sound of the battle which was raging outside the city, and the sight of the streams of refugees passing through it,

348

could not altogether rob him of his joy. From his taxi he had seen many of the old familiar landmarks—the Opéra, the Madeleine, the Rue Royale, the Place de la Concorde, the Champs Elysées and the Petit Palais. Central Paris as yet had not suffered sufficient damage for the effect of the German air-raids to be apparent and the cafés, the crowded pavements and the gardens had seemed to him little altered, except for the change of fashion and the great increase in motor traffic, since he had seen them over a quarter of a century before.

To Gregory's anxious inquiry about Erika he replied at once: 'Be of good cheer. For some days after we reached London her state was again critical, but she turned the corner on the Friday after we left Dunkirk and this last week has made a vast difference. At last she is able to talk a little and she says that it was her will to live for you which brought her through the dark places when she so nearly died; so you may be certain that she will not slip back now.'

'Thank God!' Gregory sighed. 'And I'm eternally grateful to you, Stefan, for the way in which you looked after her.'

Kuporovitch shrugged. 'It was a joy, my friend. The good Sir Pellinore, to whom I took her immediately we reached London, has entertained me in a most princely fashion. To live in that great house of his is, except for some slight differences in national custom, to be back again in the mansion of a Russian nobleman as we lived before the Revolution. I had no idea that even in England such a state of things still survived outside the story-books, and London, too, is a revelation. In spite of everything the people lunch and dine in the crowded restaurants and go about their business as if there were no threat to their security at all; yet things are being done there now. Churchill, Beaverbrook, Bevin and some others are cutting the red tape at last and underneath the casualness one senses the iron will of the people to defeat Hitler whatever it may cost them.'

'I've never doubted that,' said Gregory. 'It seems always to take a frightful knocking about really to rouse the fighting spirit in us; but once it's there woe betide the enemy. Things are in a pretty bad way here, though.'

'So I have gathered. But who is to blame for that? The British were responsible for holding a great sector of the Allied line; instead of doing so they went home with little but their shirts. That left a great gap which the British could have filled again if they had broken through, or counterbalanced if they

349

had dug themselves in on the coast as a threat to the German rear. But they did neither, and the French were left to get out of the mess as best they could, alone.'

'I thought that too,' Gregory agreed, 'until I learned that the British had good reason for going home when they did. The French High Command is rotten, Stefan. Weygand is not the great man we thought him. There is treachery right up at the very top. I've now come to the conclusion that our Government must have known that and decided to get our men out alive, before the French ratted on them and they were left to face the whole weight of the German Army on their own, which would have meant absolute annihilation.'

Kuporovitch shook his head. 'No, Gregory; you are wrong there. The evacuation from Dunkirk was ordered on May the 29th and it is now June the 14th. As you and I sit here, the British Government is shipping troops back to France as hard as it can go. Do you believe for one moment that they would be doing that if they had already formed the conclusion sixteen days ago that the French meant to throw their hand in?'

'I suppose you're right,' Gregory sighed. 'If they brought the men off from Dunkirk because they feared the French were going to do a "Leopold" on us they could hardly be sending them back again while the situation remains so uncertain.'

'A "Leopold", eh?' Kuporovitch's dark eyebrows went up with a quizzical expression. 'I hope you realise, my friend, that when the history of this war comes to be written Leopold and the people responsible for Dunkirk are going to be lumped together. Whatever the English school-books may say, the school-books of the rest of the world will record that after seventeen days' fighting the Belgians ratted on the British and that after nineteen days' fighting the British ratted on the French. What other word can be applied to the fact that, while still whole and undefeated, one of the finest armies that your country has ever put into the field gave up any further attempt to wage war upon the enemy and abandoned its Ally?'

'I suppose one can't blame the French for looking at things that way,' Gregory admitted. 'The retreat and evacuation has certainly given Hitler's Fifth Column in France just the ammunition they required for their work of severing the Allies, and it's quite on the cards now that within a few days France may make a separate Peace.'

'True. But there is still hope that they may be induced to

350

carry on the fight. Even now our good Sir Pellinore is with Mr. Winston Churchill and Lord Beaverbrook, who are on their way to Bordeaux to see if they cannot bolster up the shaking edifice.'

'Is that what you came to tell me?'

Kuporovitch nodded. 'Now that Erika is out of danger I at last felt justified in appeasing my desire to see Paris again, and when I told Sir Pellinore that he said to me: "Find Gregory, if you can, and tell him how uncertain things are now with the French. If they decide to fight on—well and good; but if they surrender there is a risk that he might be caught in France. Tell him to make his way to Bordeaux and to join me at the Hotel Julius Caesar; then I shall be able to get him safely out of the country should France collapse." '

'And what view does Sir Pellinore take of things?'

The Russian hunched his shoulders. 'He is by no means optimistic. The loss of Paris will be a grave blow to France and he gave me the impression that he felt that only a miracle could save her now.'

Gregory frowned. 'I believe I might have pulled off that miracle three nights ago, but that little fiend, *La Baronne Noire*, poisoned me when I was in Italy and I've been laid by the heels ever since.'

'Poisoned you, eh? Tell me about that.'

Gregory gave a resumé of what had befallen him since he had parted from Kuporovitch on the beach at Dunkirk, and when he had finished, the Russian said:

'There is only one thing for it; we must get this woman, Gregory, and those papers of which Lacroix spoke. They are becoming of more importance every moment, now that with each hour there becomes more likelihood of France going out of the war.'

Gregory nodded. 'Lacroix can't keep me here much longer, because the Germans are at the gates, and I'm expecting to have a word from him at any time telling me that I can go. I'm quite fit enough again now to have another crack at the Black Lady and it will help a lot to have you with me; but it's rotten luck that you should have to leave Paris because the Germans are about to enter it the very day that you get here.'

Kuporovitch smiled ruefully. 'Yes; it is hard indeed. Perhaps now I shall never again see Montmartre, or the Luxemburg Gardens, or the Bois; but one thing I shall regret above all—

and that is, not to have taken my *apéritif* with a pretty girl on a sunny morning outside Wagner's on the pavements of the Rue Royale.'

'Well, that at least is not impossible,' Gregory laughed. 'It's eleven o'clock in the morning, you could hardly have a sunnier day, and I imagine that the cafés are still open. As for the pretty girl—why not ask my nurse, Sister Madeleine? You can get there in ten minutes in a taxi. Take her out and give her a drink while I telephone Lacroix and get dressed.'

The Russian beamed; Sister Madeleine smilingly accepted his invitation when she learned how far he had travelled for the pleasure of once more visiting her native city, and they set off together while Gregory got up to have his bath.

When he had finished he was just about to telephone Lacroix; but he had no need to do so as a messenger arrived for him at that moment with a letter from the Colonel, which read:

'I hear from your doctor that you are now fit enough to travel, which is good news indeed at such a time of grief. Our troops have now completed their withdrawal and only armed police to prevent looting are left in the capital. The salle Boche *will once again pollute the Champs Elysées by a formal entry at three o'clock this afternoon. Therefore, you should leave at once.*

'The lady of whom we spoke when I last saw you left Fontainebleau on Wednesday morning. Perhaps she feared that the sight of an expensive car might attract unwelcome attention from the more desperate of our refugees; or it may be that she had another reason. In any case, she left, with her chauffeur only, on the box of a blue Ford van lettered in gold "Maison Pasquette—Blanchisserie".

'It is virtually certain that she will have followed the Government to Tours and Bordeaux but she has a villa in the South of France. It is called Les Roches *and is at Pointe des Issambres between Saint Maxime and Saint Raphael, so later she may go there with her* baggage.

'May the good God have you in his keeping in these difficult hours and grant that in happier times we may meet again.'

The bare facts in the letter would have conveyed little to a casual reader, but to Gregory they conveyed a lot. The reason that the Black Baroness had elected to journey south by van instead of by car was plain enough. A Ford van could move just as quickly as a car on a road choked with refugees, and she had no intention of leaving her most valued possessions to be destroyed by shell-fire or looted in her absence. In the van there would be much more room to take pictures, furs, jewels and letter-files than in a car, and the underlining of the word 'baggage' clearly inferred that Lacroix hoped that now Gregory was fit again he would go after those letter-files; and that, quite definitely, was what he meant to do.

Leaving a message for Kuporovitch that he would be back by half-past one, he went out to make his arrangements. Paris was a sad sight that morning. Half the shops were already shut and those inhabitants who had decided to remain were pulling down their blinds in anticipation of the triumphant entry of the Germans that afternoon. All the main streets were crowded with sorrowing, gesticulating people packing bag and baggage on to their cars in preparation for making the journey, in most cases, into the unknown. Refugees had now been streaming south for many days, but there were still tens of thousands who had hung on until the last moment hoping against hope that they would not have to go after all, and these were now working at frantic speed lest they had left it too late and should be caught by the on-coming enemy.

He found it impossible to hire or buy a private car but at a garage with which he had done business in the past he managed to make what amounted to a hire-purchase arrangement with the owner-driver of a taxi-cab. The garage proprietor was no longer observing petrol restrictions as he was only too anxious to unload as much of his stock as he could before the Germans arrived; so Gregory was able to have the taxi's tank filled and to buy a dozen spare *bidons* in addition. He told the driver to run over the engine as thoroughly as possible in the short time available and to bring the cab round to the Saint Regis at half-past one: then he made a few purchases and, returning to the now almost empty hotel, ordered a large picnic basket to be made up.

At twenty to two he paid his bill, said good-bye to the sad-faced manager and went out on to the doorstep. The taxi was there but there was no sign of Kuporovitch. With considerable annoyance, Gregory assumed that the Russian amorist had found little Sister Madeleine so responsive to his blandishments that he had forgotten all about the time; but ten minutes later he had grave reason to regret his unworthy suspicions.

Sister Madeleine drove up in a taxi. As she jumped out he saw that tears were streaming down her face. Running down the steps he asked her with a sudden sense of alarm what had happened to bring her back in such a state.

Grasping his arm she sobbed out: 'It was an accident. Just as we were leaving he stepped off the pavement too soon and a car knocked him down. Oh, how tragic—how tragic! To think that for all these years he had longed for Paris and that he should come back only to die.'

Gregory moaned. For a moment he could hardly realise that the amiable Russian, who had been so full of life only that morning, would never laugh again. For over two months now he had been an almost constant witness of destruction and death in Norway, Holland, Belgium and France, so that the corpses he had seen in the blasted villages and on the roadsides in his recent journeys had come to mean little to him, but the thought that his friend had died in an ordinary street-accident had a peculiar bitterness all its own.

There was only one small consolation—Stefan Kuporovitch had at least achieved his ambition before he died. Just for an hour or so he had seen again the Paris with which he had fallen in love when he was young. He had even drunk his *Vermouth-Cassis* with a pretty *Parisienne* in the sunshine on the pavement of the Rue Royale. Then he had stepped off that pavement into oblivion as far as the things of this world were concerned. Gregory knew only too well that there were many less pleasant circumstances in which a man could die, and after a moment he pulled himself together to ask Sister Madeleine for particulars.

Although she was a nurse the tragedy had so upset her that she was bordering on hysteria, and it was only towards the end of her account that Gregory realised that Kuporovitch was not actually dead. His skull had been fractured in two places and she had no doubt at all that his injuries were fatal, but he had still been alive when they had taken him in an ambulance to the *Hôpital Saint Pierre*.

Gregory paid off her taxi and grabbing her by the arm led her towards his own, as he said: 'Quick! We must go there at once and hear the doctor's report.'

She warned him that the Russian's case was hopeless and when they reached the hospital a white-coated doctor confirmed her view. Kuporovitch had not regained consciousness but might last a few hours, though the doctor considered it most unlikely that he would live through the night.

Although he would have liked to stay, Gregory knew that it was of the utmost importance that he should go south after the Black Baroness with the least possible delay; so he asked Sister Madeleine if she intended to remain in Paris during the occupation.

'Yes,' she said with a sigh. 'I have an old mother who is too infirm to travel, and with the train-loads of wounded that are constantly arriving there will be plenty of work for me to do.'

Taking some bank-notes from his wallet he asked her if she would come to the hospital on the following day and make the necessary arrangements to provide Kuporovitch with a decent funeral. She took the money and agreed at once; then he thanked her for her care of him and, still half-dazed by the tragedy, sadly walked out into the sunny street.

April the 8th to June the 14th. It was just sixty-seven days since Hitler had swooped by night on unsuspecting Norway, and Gregory was thinking of the hideous chapters of history that had been made in that short time.

King Haakon and Queen Wilhelmina had been driven from their thrones. Leopold of Belgium was now branded for ever as a traitor. A million soldiers and civilians had died and another million lay wounded in the hospitals. Ten million people had been rendered homeless and another twenty million had fallen under the brutal domination of the Nazis. Paris had fallen and the enemy were in possession of the Channel ports, which brought their bombers within twenty-five miles of England. It had been one long nightmare tale of incompetent leadership, disaster, treachery and defeat.

Even in his own small world, Erika had only narrowly escaped death, Paula had died before his eyes. Lacroix had become virtually a fugitive. And now poor Kuporovitch was dead.

He, too, had suffered three major defeats at the hands of the woman who was his enemy, and one of them had very nearly cost him his life. He was very tired after these weeks of stress and now quite alone. But he knew that there could be no giving-up until he was dead or *his* battle was won.

Stepping into the taxi he said: 'Drive to Bordeaux.'

25

The Black Baroness

It was just on three o'clock; the hour at which the Germans were due to march in triumph down the Champs Elysées. The sounds of battle had receded to a distant rumble, so faint that it was hardly perceptible unless one deliberately listened for it; while in the city itself there was a strange and terrible silence. The last of those who meant to leave had gone; the streets were now deserted; bowed and weeping behind locked doors and shuttered windows, the people of Paris awaited in submission the coming of the conqueror.

As Gregory drove through the once gay streets he thought of the scenes which they were soon certain to witness. Thousands of German officers and Nazi officials would bring their families out of the bombed areas of Germany to live in the comfort and security of Paris now that it was a captive city yet must remain immune from aerial attack. In his imagination he could already see the crowds of fat, stupid, ugly, vulgar German women swarming in the Rue de la Paix, the Rue du Faubourg Saint Honoré, and the Rivoli, pushing and thrusting to get at the silk stockings, the hats, the frocks, the linens and the brocades; while their men jostled one another in the restaurants and bought up all the supplies in the tobacco and wine shops.

Their *Fuehrer* had denied them butter that they might have guns, and now they were to be given their reward. They would loot Paris of her vast store of the luxuries which they had not seen for years, and for which—if they paid at all—they would pay only in worthless paper.

Yet while those German hogs guzzled in the trough they would not realise that even this abundance must be absorbed in a few months and that the Parisian goose once having been cooked could lay no more golden eggs. The coming winter would find them cold and hungry once again, but for the time being the riches of the conquered territory would still their questioning and whet their appetites for further conquests. Dr. Goebbels would not fail to point the moral of the *Blitzkrieg*. He would say:

'In Germany for two generations we have scraped and

starved, but now you have seen for yourselves how the rich Dutch and Belgians and French have glutted themselves with good things through all those years. And why? Because they had Empire while Germany had not. It is our turn now, and once the final victory is won Germany's people will live in plenty for evermore. *Heil* Hitler! On with the war! Kill, crush, destroy!'

False premises, lying sophistry perhaps, but a subtle, poisonous doctrine which Gregory knew would find a ready hearing in the reddish, protruding ears of a host of blond, waxy-faced, pot-bellied Huns.

His driver was a dour, uncommunicative fellow, but the taxi was a good one and Gregory had promised the man a handsome bonus if he got the best mileage possible out of it, allowing for the conditions they met on the road; with the proviso that for any breakdown that might occur on the journey south twenty per cent was to be deducted from the promised reward. So the man had done his utmost during such time as he had had to ensure that his engine was in the best possible running order.

They ran smoothly through the deserted streets of Paris and out of the city through Mont Rouge and Bourg-la-Reine. A trickle of people was still moving along the road but not in sufficient numbers to prevent the taxi-man getting the maximum speed out of his car. As they reached the open country Gregory began to keep a good look-out for German patrols, since their advance units were reported already to be fifteen miles beyond the city; but the surrender of the whole Paris area had left a great vacuum in the battle-line so the country through which he was passing was for the moment no-man's-land. The first troops that he saw proved to be French detachments wearily marching south, so it seemed that the Germans, having been occupied all day in advancing through uncontested territory, had not yet caught up with their enemies.

Ten minutes after passing the first batch of French troops the taxi entered Etamps. The town was crowded with the retreating Army and Gregory thought that the men looked hopelessly beaten as they lay in groups on the pavements or stood drooping with weariness beside their vehicles. From that point on he was constantly passing units which were falling back to take up fresh positions behind the Loire, and he had also caught up with the tail-end of the vast civilian army that had left Paris on foot the preceding day or in the slower vehicles that morning. The refugees were inextricably mixed with the retreating troops, causing great delay and confusion. Nevertheless, the taxi-man managed to keep up a fairly good pace by winding his way in and out among the moving column and they reached Orleans at seven o'clock.

The town had been bombed and a large part of the main street lay in ruins so they had to circumvent it by taking side-turnings until they reached the great bridge over the Loire, which was badly choked by the retiring troops. It was three-quarters of an hour before Gregory could get across; and the road south of the bridge was little better. At any moment he expected an officer to order him off the road altogether as it was a matter of vital necessity that the troops should reach their new battle positions before dawn, but apparently the refugees were so numerous and the military so tired that the officers responsible for keeping some sort of order on the roads had long since abandoned the uneven struggle.

He who shouted and swore got through, while he who did not got pushed into the ditch. Fortunately for Gregory his driver possessed a fine flow of argot and, urged on by the thought of the promised reward, he cursed without discrimination the unfortunate civilians and the weary soldiers who got in his way.

Twenty miles south of Orleans the pressure eased a little, as the troops became less numerous, and now that night was falling many of the refugees had drawn off the road to snatch a few hours' sleep before proceeding further. From ten miles an hour they were able to increase their pace to fifteen, and at a little before midnight they entered Tours. In spite of their good start the first hundred and twenty miles of their journey had taken them nine hours.

Tours had been the headquarters of the French Government for a short time after it had left Paris and in consequence the town had suffered appallingly. Many fires were still burning and several streets in the centre of the town were now only a mass of ruins. Weaving a way through the columns of refugees had been tiring work, and although Gregory had been feeding his driver with some of the things in his picnic-basket, by pushing them through the front window of the cab, he felt that the man deserved a rest; so they pulled up at a small café that had remained undamaged and was still open.

It was crowded with refugees, rich and poor jostling together; haggard-eyed women in expensive fur-coats, pot-bellied bourgeois round-shouldered Jews, officers, soldiers, workmen in blue overalls and children of all classes and all ages; some pathetically silent and some angrily complaining of their woes. Among them Gregory saw a British R.A. Captain, so, having secured cups of hot coffee for his taciturn driver and himself, he asked the gunner if he had any news.

It transpired that he had heard the nine o'clock broadcast issued by the B.B.C. That morning the Germans had launched a fresh attack, west of the Saar, against the Maginot Line, but it had been repulsed with heavy losses. The 17,000-ton armed liner *Scotstoun* had been sunk by a U-boat, but a British airman had succeeded in getting a direct hit with a heavy bomb on the German battle-cruiser *Scharnhorst* while she was lying in Trondheim harbour. On balance it sounded not a bad day, if one ignored the fact that the Germans had that afternoon entered Paris.

However, the Gunner Captain was in a state of angry gloom or which he had good reason. He had been detached from the 51st Division some days previously, for special duties, and when he had endeavoured to rejoin his unit he had learnt that practically the whole Division had been scuppered.

British troops which had been re-landed early in the week had done their utmost to hold a line from Barentin, along the little River Saône, to the sea, in order to prevent the Germans reaching Le Havre; but the French on their right had let them down and, although the bulk of the British had been got off in a new evacuation, two brigades of the 51st Division had been cornered at Saint Valery. Some of Britain's most famous regiments had been there, including the Gordons and the Black Watch, and with the utmost valour they had fought unbroken in a desperate ring; but when at last their ammunition had run out their commander, Major-General V. M. Fortune, had been compelled to surrender, so six thousand of our best men had fallen into the hands of the enemy.

Gregory felt that this was a very different business from the ignominy of Dunkirk, where a quarter of a million men had been ordered to throw away their guns and baggage. In this case there had been tremendous odds against a few thousand infantry unsupported by tanks, heavy artillery or aircraft, and having fired their last shot before surrendering those splendid Highlanders had done all that was humanly possible, main-training untarnished the magnificent record of the Glorious 51st. Nevertheless, it was yet one more grim act in the colossal tragedy which had been unfolding before his very eyes day after day these past terrible weeks.

He offered the Gunner a lift in his taxi to Bordeaux, which was gladly accepted, and running again through side-streets they came out on the road to Poitiers. It was now one o'clock in the morning and Gregory thanked his gods that he was making this part of his journey at night, as he had reached the area where even greater numbers of the refugees who had left Paris ahead of him were making their way south.

The road was never entirely clear of that endless column which had its origins in all the desolated cities of Holland, Belgium and Northern France, to be swollen during more recent days by another two million evacuees from Paris; but thousands of them were now passing the night in the fields, as could be seen from the small 'bivie' fires and moving lights which from time to time threw up stationary cars, vans and carts piled with baggage and household belongings; and Gregory knew that had it been daytime their numbers would have rendered the roads absolutely impassable.

At dawn they passed through Poitiers and, halting south of the town, had some more food from Gregory's hamper to sustain themselves. Daylight now revealed the full tragedy that the last week of the war had brought about. The procession of luxury cars alternated with aged farm-carts; yet every few hundred yards vans, cars and lorries had been abandoned because they had run out of petrol, and on both sides of the road the endless ribbon of higgledy-piggledy makeshift camps continued.

All through the long, hot morning they stopped and started, stopped and started, but by mid-day they reached Angoulême, where during a short halt they picked up an R.A.F. sergeant-pilot and an A.S.C. private, both of whom had got themselves hopelessly lost.

In the café where they had found these two Gregory learnt that the new German thrust, directed at the western end of the Maginot Line on the previous day, had, after all, proved a success. The Huns were clean through, and their armoured columns were now racing east in an attempt to cut the whole Line off from the main French Army.

After leaving Angoulême the traffic became a little less congested and at a quarter to five in the afternoon the taxi pulled up outside the Hotel Julius Caesar on the outskirts of Bordeaux.

Taking leave of the three men to whom he had given a lift, Gregory handed the taxi-driver his bonus. They had accomplished the three-hundred-and-sixty-mile journey in just under twenty-six hours without a single breakdown and he felt that, considering the appalling conditions on the road, the man had well earned the money.

At the desk Gregory learnt, to his relief, that Sir Pellinore was in the hotel, and having sent up his name he was at once asked to go up to the Baronet's suite.

Sir Pellinore was delighted to see him, but he was not in one of his chaffing moods and was much too busy on a pile of papers spread out in front of him to enter upon long dissertations. After telling Gregory that Erika was now progressing well, and expressing his sorrow when he was told of Kuporovitch's death, he gave a bare outline of the state of things at the moment.

On this the eleventh day of the battle for France the situation had become absolutely desperate. After terrific fighting at Saarbruecken the Germans had gone clean through that ghastly white elephant, the Maginot Line, which had tied a great portion of the French Army to it during these last terrible weeks yet had failed in the end to fulfil its vaunted function as an impassable barrier. The German thrust had deepened alarmingly in the last twenty-four hours and their armoured units had penetrated as far east as Saint Dizier. They also claimed the capture of Verdun. That mighty fortress, the Glory of France, which in the last war had for months withstood the hammer-blows of the German Crown Prince's Army, had now fallen to Hitler's fanatical youth in a single day.

In the centre the French were giving way all along the line, and in the west Le Havre had fallen. Its huge stores of armaments and supplies, brand-new from the British factories, had been captured before there had been time to burn or destroy one-tenth of them. The only hope which now remained to France was that the German effort might at last peter out from utter exhaustion.

'And what of the political situation?' Gregory asked.

'God knows!' Sir Pellinore flung up his big hands in a weary gesture. 'We wrangled with them all last night and all this morning. Churchill and Beaverbrook have just left for home, but I understand that their intention is to discuss with the War Cabinet a last bid to keep the French from throwing their hand in. The suggestion is that we should offer them a solemn Act of Union by which all French citizens will in future enjoy the rights of British citizenship in addition to their own and *vice versa*; so that the two great Empires become insolubly united and each will benefit from the assets of the other.'

'By Jove!' murmured Gregory. 'Only a man like Churchill is capable of such great statesmanship. It may even be the beginning of a new world-order in which nation after nation unites to pool the whole world's resources.'

'Yes,' Sir Pellinore nodded. 'If it goes through, history will be made in the next few hours; but even if we make the offer, will the French accept it? The price is that they fight on, and it doesn't seem to me that they've got much fight left in them. But I can't stay gossiping with you. Tell me, as briefly as you can, what you've been up to.'

'I had a free trip to sunny Italy and afternoon-tea, consisting of poisoned wine, with that modern replica of Lucrezia Borgia, your little friend the Black Baroness.'

'The devil you did!'

'Two of Lacroix's men flew me back to Paris just in time to save me from being bottled up in an Italian concentration-camp and when I got back I was out of the game for three days owing to the effects of the poison.'

'Anything to show for it?'

'No; not a damned thing. I've even lost track now of the Baroness, but I'm hoping that she's here in Bordeaux.'

'She is. She's staying in this hotel.'

'Thank God for that! I've got a long score to settle with that little fiend, and I'll settle it tonight.'

'You'll do nothing of the kind,' boomed Sir Pellinore. 'She's already done all the damage that she can and, as a matter of fact, I happen to know that she's leaving Bordeaux this evening.'

'But since this is the centre of the whirlpool why on earth should she do that?'

'Because Pétain and Weygand have now openly taken over from her and are advocating surrender.'

'What, Pétain, too?'

'Yes. The old fool is absolutely gaga, and the others have persuaded him that he should fill the rôle of the white-headed martyr who saved his country from herself and further French *poilus* from being massacred by having the courage to face the obloquy of asking for an armistice. The Baroness is wise enough to know that any suggestion of petticoat influence now might be just the one thing that would swing matters the other way, so she's leaving matters in the hands of the men who actually sit at the Council table.'

'All the same, I tell you that I've got a score to settle with her.'

'Don't be a fool, Gregory. If you could have eliminated her somehow a month ago—a week ago—even yesterday—it would have been worth your while to run the risk of paying with your life for that pleasure; but not now. Her death cannot help us one iota, and since by the Grace of God you've come through these frightful weeks alive, I mean to take you home with me to Erika tomorrow.'

'I'm sorry,' said Gregory slowly, 'but I couldn't leave with a quiet conscience; because, quite apart from settling with her personally, there's still a job of work to be done.' He then told Sir Pellinore what Lacroix had said about the Baroness's letter-files and the Ford van which she had almost certainly used to remove them to Bordeaux.

'H'm; that alters matters,' grunted Sir Pellinore after a moment. 'Even if the Government give in, I've no doubt that many of the best elements among the French will elect to fight on with us, particularly in the French Colonies, and we can't afford to have untrustworthy men among them. Yes, you must get those files, Gregory, and if you find an opportunity to give that woman the works without being caught yourself, by all means do so; she deserves a bullet more than any criminal in the whole of Europe who still remains unhanged.'

'Have you any idea what time she's leaving?' Gregory asked.

'Yes. At seven o'clock. I actually heard her giving instructions to the head waiter for a picnic-basket to be ready for her at that hour.'

'D'you know where she's going?'

Sir Pellinore passed a hand over his white hair. 'No; I haven't the faintest notion.'

'She has a villa at Pointe des Issambres, so she's probably going there. At such short notice it would be almost suicidal for me to attempt to tackle her here in the hotel, so I think the best thing would be for me to try to hold her up at some lonely spot outside the town.'

'That's it,' Sir Pellinore nodded; but don't let her get too far, Gregory, because I'm sailing tomorrow at midnight and I want to take you home with me.'

'With luck,' said Gregory, 'I'll be back long before that. I know how busy you are, and as it's now nearly six o'clock I haven't any too much time to make my preparations; so I'll get along.'

When Sir Pellinore had gripped his hand and wished him luck he went downstairs and strolled out to the hotel garage.

Outside it were two mechanics and a little group of chauffeurs discussing the crisis with such animation that they were completely absorbed, and Gregory had no difficulty in slipping past without any of them noticing him.

There were several lines of cars inside the building but he soon found the Ford. It was the only commercial vehicle among the whole fleet of automobiles, and as he peered at it from between two other cars, he saw that a tough-looking fellow was sitting on the driver's seat with his head pillowed on his arms, drowsing at the wheel. This did not at all surprise him, as he had not for one moment imagined that *Madame la Baronne* would leave the pseudo laundry-van—which probably contained a fortune—unguarded.

Gregory's first intention, having identified the van, had been to go on ahead and choose some suitable spot for holding the Baroness up, but he was quick to realise that he had no guarantee whatever that she was actually going to Pointe des Issambres. She had a villa there but she might quite possibly be going somewhere else, in which case she would probably take a different road and he would then miss her altogether, It therefore seemed that his only safe course was to follow her when she set off until they reached a deserted stretch of road where he could puncture her back tyres by shooting at them and bring her to a standstill.

But a more careful scrutiny at the van showed him that, although it had the appearance of a Ford, it was not a Ford at all. The exhaust pipe was much too big, so evidently the Baroness had a far more powerful engine fitted under the Ford bonnet. That presented a nasty snag as, given clear roads— which were probable if she were crossing France from Bordeaux to the South through an area where few refugees would be moving—his taxi would never be able to keep up with her.

It then occurred to him that his best chance of achieving his end was, if he could, to conceal himself in the van and travel with her. As she was leaving at seven o'clock it was reasonable to suppose that she would put in only three or four hours' driving then pull up somewhere for the night. If that somewhere proved to be one of the many excellent wayside hostelries that line the roads of France he would have a much better opportunity of dealing with her and getting away afterwards than he could possibly have in Bordeaux, and he would still be back in plenty of time to sail with Sir Pellinore for England the following night.

Treading very cautiously, so as not to rouse the driver, he worked his way round behind several cars until he reached the back of the van; but, as he had feared, the doors had a good solid lock which it would have been quite impossible to force without alarming the man at the wheel.

For a few moments Gregory stood there deep in thought, then he tiptoed round to a car in front of and to the left of the van. The car had been left unlocked so that the garage men could move it. Opening the far door, Gregory crawled inside and gently lowered the opposite window. By squinting from it he could just see the driver without being seen himself. Taking out his automatic, he clicked a bullet up into the chamber, knelt down, rested the barrel on the ledge of the window and, aiming carefully so as not to hit the man, pressed the trigger.

Owing to its silencer the report of the pistol was no more than a cough, and, as Gregory had intended, the shot shattered the windscreen of the van just above the man's head. Ducking down so that he was completely hidden, he held his breath and waited.

The sound of tinkling glass was instantly followed by a yell of fright and rage, then louder shouts which brought the garage hands and chauffeurs running in from outside. In the excited conversation that followed Gregory gathered that the driver had no idea at all what had happened and was under the impression that somebody must have thrown a brickbat at the windscreen while he was dozing; but the others assured him that nobody had entered the garage, and Gregory soon learnt that his ruse had succeeded. The driver had been cut by the flying glass and was being led off by his companions to have his slight injuries doctored.

As soon as the coast was clear Gregory left his hiding-place, went straight to the back of the van and with two more shots from his pistol shattered its lock. Pulling open the doors he rapidly surveyed the van's contents. There were half a dozen medium-sized pictures in gilt frames, several packing-cases—doubtless containing other *objets d'art*—two Louis Vinton wardrobe-trunks, three suitcases, the rawhide dressing-case that he well remembered seeing in Rotterdam, six large japanned-steel deed boxes and five or six valuable fur coats thrown on the top of the pile.

It was the deed-boxes that he was after, but he could not possibly make off with all six of them, as he could distinctly catch the murmur of quick voices and knew that several of the chauffeurs must have remained outside the garage to discuss the extraordinary incident that had just occurred.

In ten seconds he had decided that he dared not attempt to burgle the van and must carry out his original idea of travelling in it; but the smashed lock, when discovered, would almost certainly lead to a search of the van's interior unless some explanation were offered for it, so the obvious thing was to make the whole episode appear like a carefully-planned theft.

Snatching up the fur coats, he hurried with them to an aged, semi-derelict Citroën that he had noticed at the back of the garage and pushed them into its boot, where it was unlikely that they would be discovered for some time; then, hurrying back to the van, he made a few rapid readjustments to its contents.

He did not alter the general layout of the various articles but drew them all a little nearer to the back of the van so that a space was left behind the driver's seat in which he could lie down without being observed by anyone who looked inside. Then, leaving the doors wide open, he took off his coat to form a pillow for his head and settled down to make himself as comfortable as he could.

He found that he was very tired now, and in spite of the hard boards upon which he was lying he dropped off to sleep; but he was soon roused by angry, excited voices. Evidently the driver had returned and discovered that the van had been broken into. There was silence for a time as the man went away, doubtless to report the theft of the fur coats, for when he returned Gregory could hear the Baroness talking to him.

At first her voice showed acute anxiety, but on ascertaining that only the furs had gone she quietened down and arranged with one of the garage hands to affix a padlock to replace the shattered lock, and a quarter of an hour later Gregory found himself a prisoner.

He did not mind that in the least. The great thing was that he had escaped observation. The Baroness would probably unlock the doors herself in due course, which would provide him with an excellent opportunity of coming face to face with her if he so wished; or, alternatively, if the van were left locked up for the night he felt confident that he would manage to break out of it. A few moments later the van began to jolt and drove out of the garage. They were on their way.

Apart from the fact that he suffered acute discomfort Gregory knew nothing of that strange journey. For a time they bumped over the pavé streets of the city, then evidently came out upon an open road, as the van began to run more smoothly and considerably increased its pace. Gregory then knew that he had been right about the engine, as on certain stretches the van appeared to develop the speed of a racing-car and was certainly doing well over eighty miles an hour.

Soon after they started he made himself more comfortable by sitting up and rearranging some of the things about him to prevent his being jolted quite so badly. A crack of light coming through the door was just enough for him to see by and he arranged matters so that although the contents of the van were to some extent altered around he was still hidden by the pictures, if at any time a halt was made without warning and the van doors suddenly opened.

Gradually, as night fell, the crack of light dimmed. When they had been on the road for two hours it was only a faint line, and after another hour the interior of the van was unrelieved Stygian blackness. Swaying a little from side to side as the van raced on into the night, Gregory thought of Erika and wondered if the gods who had so often favoured him would grant him one more slice of luck so that he might be finished with his business soon and in another few days be back with her in England. Then he slept.

He was wakened by the van jerking to a halt, and looking at the luminous dial of his watch he saw that it was five-past one. They had been on the road for over six hours so it seemed highly probable that the Baroness had accomplished the first stage of her journey and meant to remain for the rest of the night at whatever place they had reached; but Gregory was soon disillusioned in his hopes of this. Five minutes later the van started off again; evidently it had stopped only for petrol. Their pace, he noted, was now considerably slower but they were steadily eating up the miles and after drearily rocking from side to side, for what seemed a long time, he again dropped off to sleep.

When he next woke he could see the line of light again, but from the sounds around him he felt sure that they had pulled up in a street. His watch showed him that it was a quarter to six, but even at that early hour there was a considerable amount of traffic about. He could hear the hum of passing motor-cars and occasionally the hoot of horns, so, although the van remained stationary for some time, he did not feel that it was as yet advisable to attempt breaking out.

The fact that the Baroness had not stopped anywhere on the road to sleep considerably perturbed him, for it looked, now that morning was come, as if she intended to go straight through to her destination; and every mile that they covered meant another mile for him to traverse on his return journey to rejoin Sir Pellinore. They had now been nearly eleven hours on the road, so even if he had been in a position to turn back at once he could not have reached Bordeaux before five o'clock in the afternoon, and Sir Pellinore was sailing that night.

Gregory had a good memory for maps and distances, and assuming that the Baroness was heading for Pointe des Issambres he tried to work out how far they might have got. Taking into consideration the speed at which they had been going during the early part of the journey, he came to the conclusion that they had crossed from the Atlantic to the Mediterranean coast of France during the night and were now probably in Nimes or Avignon.

Evidently the Baroness had been refreshing herself with *petit déjeuner* at some hotel, as soon after seven o'clock the van jolted into motion again. Their pace was now much slower; he judged it to be not more than twenty miles an hour and could guess the reason. If, as he supposed, they were travelling east on the Route Nationale, which links Nimes and Avignon with Cannes and Monte Carlo, at the two former cities they would have come into the streams of refugees which for days had been heading towards the South of France.

As time went on the streak of light became quite dazzling against the surrounding darkness and the strong sunshine beat down relentlessly on the roof, making the interior of the van intolerably hot. Gregory would have given anything for an iced drink, but he had to content himself with a pull at the lukewarm brandy-and-water in his flask and a couple of bars of chocolate for his breakfast.

At ten o'clock the van stopped again, but only for a few minutes, evidently once more to fill up with petrol, and it seemed as though this interminable journey would never end. By that time they had been on the road for fifteen hours so Gregory had reluctantly had to give up any hope of getting back to Bordeaux in time to sail with Sir Pellinore. A little grimly he realised that if France went out of the war he would have to make his way back to England as best he could. By mid-day the van had obviously left the main road. Its pace was no quicker but it constantly twisted from side to side and went up and down steep hills, so Gregory felt certain that they must have reached the coast.

It was a little before three in the afternoon when, after a halt of only one minute, the golden streak of light suddenly went out as though it had been turned off by a switch, then came on again quite dimly as the van was brought to a standstill. With a sigh of relief Gregory felt convinced that they must have reached their journey's end, as the difference in the light indicated that the van had been driven into a garage.

Rousing himself at once, he got out his gun and crouched there behind the small stack of pictures. The van was unlocked; he could hear the Baroness and her man unloading and carrying away a portion of its contents. They made three trips, then the van was relocked without his presence in it having been discovered. Two sets of garage doors, one behind and one in front of the van, were slammed, and there was silence.

Standing up, he climbed over the intervening packages and set about breaking out of his prison. As the padlock was a temporary affair and its hinges had only been screwed on, he did not anticipate much difficulty in forcing it. The third time he threw his weight against the doors there was a tearing of wood and they flew open. He just managed to save himself from pitching out, and jumped down on to the garage floor. The doors were shut but there was plenty of light to see by, so he picked up the few screws that had fallen from the padlock staple and, closing the van doors, reinserted them in their holes so that if anyone entered the garage it would not be noticed, at a casual glance, that the temporary lock had been interfered with; then he tiptoed forward and, cautiously opening the door at the back of the garage, peered out.

The garage backed on to a garden. To his left, where the house lay, was a wide terrace with gaily-coloured sun-umbrellas and basket chairs. Below the terrace the garden paths twisted away among some dwarf pines, dropping steeply to a little cove which was lapped by the sparkling blue waters of the Mediterranean. To one side there was a promontory of huge green rocks, which was probably what gave the house its name, *Les Roches*.

Opening the door a little, he slipped out and warily made his way along to the terrace. Two wide french windows stood open there. Peering into the nearest he saw that they opened out of a large lounge-room that ran the full depth of the house and had other windows looking out on its far side. The room was empty, but at one side of it were stacked the six steel deed-boxes and other things that had been taken from the van. No sounds indicated the whereabouts of the Baroness or her man.

Gregory's brain was racing now that he had reached the end of the long chase, but he knew that he must act with caution or he might yet bungle matters. By now the man would almost certainly have gone to his room in the servants' quarters, which were on the far side of the house, to sleep after his nineteen-hour journey, and the Baroness had probably gone straight up to her room to tidy herself and rest. The problem was how to get at her, or lure her downstairs, without running into any other servants who might be about the place.

On consideration he decided that the best thing to do would be to go round to the front of the house, appear as an ordinary caller and ask to see her on the excuse that he had arrived with an urgent personal message from someone like Weygand or Reynaud. The probability was that he would be shown into the room which he had seen, and that she would then come downstairs. If she was alone—well and good; if a servant was with her—that could not be helped. This time Gregory was taking no chances and he meant to have his gun in his hand as she entered the room.

Tiptoeing back to the garage, he went through to its front entrance but found that the Baroness had locked that behind her, so he came out, and scrambling over a portion of the rock-garden that ran along the side of the garage he reached a low wall over which he could see that both the garage and the house

370

gave direct on to the coast road.

He was just about to climb over the wall when a car appeared round the bend, moving at a great speed, but it braked as it roared up the slope and in a swirl of dust pulled up outside the house. Gregory's heart almost missed a beat from the sudden stress of mixed emotions—surprise—delight—consternation. In it was his old enemy, *Herr Gruppenführer* Grauber.

His surprise was short-lived. There was, after all, nothing particularly extraordinary in the Chief of the Gestapo Foreign Department, U.A.—I, moving freely about in an enemy country in plain clothes, or that he should have had a rendezvous with his friend, *Die Schwartze Baronin,* to receive in person her report of the momentous conferences which had taken place in the last few days.

His delight came from this unexpected opportunity to settle accounts, once and for all, with this murderous pervert who had climbed to power over the tortured bodies of a thousand victims and was the living symbol of all that was most foul and loathsome about the Nazi tyranny.

His consternation was due to the fact that he knew the Baroness to be as subtle and poisonous as a female cobra and considered her quite enough to tackle single-handed without having to take on her equally redoubtable ally at the same time.

Gregory possessed immense self-confidence, but even he doubted his capability to overcome that ruthless pair in open daylight when there was at least one servant, and perhaps more, in the house who might come to their assistance. But just as the British destroyers had gone in against a superior force of Germans in the first battle of Narvik he also was determined to go in. Nevertheless, knowing that he would almost certainly be outgunned and that Grauber, at least, would get away, he decided to do his best to sabotage the Gestapo Chief's line of retreat.

Grauber had backed his car up to the front of the garage, where it was not visible from the house; then, getting out, he had gone to the front door where someone had let him in. Slipping over the wall and down into the roadway, Gregory opened the boot of the car, hunted round until he found a greasy leather tool-sack and took out a pair of pliers. Getting down on his hands and knees, he crawled under the car and partially cut through one of the wires of the steering gear. If Grauber did succeed in escaping a bullet he was not going to get very far on

371

that twisting coast road without having a nasty smash; and, with luck, he would go right over the precipice to meet his death on the rocks below.

Crawling out, Gregory replaced the pair of pliers, shut the boot, scrambled back over the low wall and through the shrubs at the side of the garage to its garden end. He paused for a moment to regain his breath, then once more crept with cat-like step along to the terrace, his pistol drawn ready in his hand.

Very, very cautiously he knelt down by the open French window, then gave one swift glance inside. Grauber was there, and Gregory's heart thrilled again. A merciful God had at last delivered his enemy, bound, into his hands.

Evidently the Gestapo Chief had asked for the Baroness and had been shown into the big lounge-room to wait until she came downstairs. He was sitting in a low armchair, facing the door and with his back to the window. His fleshy pink neck, which protruded in ugly rolls above his collar, was on a level with Gregory's head and only a few feet away.

There was not a second to be lost. At any moment the Baroness might appear, then Gregory would have lost his God-given opportunity. He had no scruples about what he was going to do. Grauber would have killed him or Erika without warning or compunction, just as he had already killed scores of other people. Reversing his pistol, Gregory took a firm grip of the barrel. Rising to his full height he took one step forward and brought the butt of the pistol crashing down on Grauber's skull.

Grauber slumped forward without a sound. Not even a moan issued from his lips as the blood began to ooze up through the broken skin of his cranium. Jamming his pistol back in its holster, Gregory seized the Gestapo Chief by the back of the collar and, hauling him out of the chair, dragged his body behind a nearby sofa where it could not be seen from the door of the room. Then he pulled out his gun again and tiptoed across the parquet to take up his position behind the door.

His hand that held the pistol was steady but his heart was thumping. For once the big cards in the pack had been dealt to him. Not only had he put one enemy out of the game already, but the coming of that enemy so unexpectedly had solved for him the tricky problem of getting the Baroness downstairs without her suspicions being aroused by the announcement that a stranger was asking to see her and without any of her servants yet being aware of his presence there.

He had hardly placed himself when the door opened and the Baroness came in. From his post of vantage Gregory was immediately behind her as she walked into the room. With his free hand he gave her a swift push in the back; with his foot he kicked-to the door. She gave a little cry, stumbled and swung round to find herself looking down the barrel of his automatic.

Her dead-white face, framed in its bell of jet-black hair, could go no whiter but he saw shock and dismay dawn in her dark eyes.

'I've got you now,' he said quietly; 'and don't imagine that the *Herr Gruppenführer* will come to your assistance this time. I've already dealt with him.'

She stared at him like a small, ferocious, trapped animal for a moment, then she murmured: 'I thought—I thought . . .'

'Yes,' Gregory went on for her, 'you thought that I was dead, but I survived your hospitality and I've come back from the gates of Death to claim you.'

'What—what d'you mean to do?' she breathed. 'Are you going to kill me?'

He nodded. 'As the price of your treachery you no doubt anticipate great rewards from your *Fuehrer*; but you're not going to get them. You are the woman who sold France to her enemies, and for that you are going to die.'

A new expression came into her face, neither resignation nor fear, nor determination to fight for her life, but a strange spiritual flame that lit up her whole countenance, as she cried in ringing protest: 'That's a lie! I did not sell France; and I shall go down in history not as the woman who betrayed France but as the woman who saved her.'

Gregory was so taken aback by this extraordinary declaration that he could only stammer: 'You—you've done your damnedest to ensure that France shall surrender and desert her Ally.'

'Her Ally!' she sneered. 'For nearly a thousand years England was our hereditary enemy, and the *Entente Cordiale* is a thing of yesterday, based on false premises. That unnatural alliance will pass as swiftly as it came and will soon be forgotten. Deep down in you the truth is as plain to you as it is to me. The French and the English neither like nor understand each other and their paths lie in opposite directions. For a few decades Britain has used France as the weaker partner to be her bulwark against

373

Germany. France suffered inconceivably more than Britain in the last war and, once again, she is being martyred in this one, while the English sit at home in their cities, safe and secure. But that is finished. Henceforth Britain must fight her own battles and France will go back as an integral part of the Continent to which she belongs.'

'I see,' snapped Gregory. 'It's not, after all, that you're pro-Hitler but that you're anti-British. Yet you worked on Leopold, who was just as much France's Ally as Britain's, to make him throw his hand in; and you helped to persuade Mussolini to stab France in the back. Your hatred of the English must have unbalanced your brain if just for the sake of making things difficult for us you've gone to the length of betraying France to the Nazis. Damn it, you must be crazy!'

'You fool!' she spat at him. 'I tell you I have saved France—saved her from herself—and if you knew the things that I know you would realise it.'

A sudden spate of words poured from her scarlet lips. 'France in our time has become decadent, vile, rotten to the core. Look at our great families—the aristocrats and the intelligentsia who should think for and lead the nation—how do they spend their lives? Money-grabbing at the expense of the workers so that Communism has become rife throughout the land. At all times in history the ruling caste has had its own code of morals, yet used a cloak of some decency to screen its love affairs. But not these people. They are not even content to sleep with one another openly, like dogs and bitches rutting in a field. Half of them are perverts, homosexuals, Lesbians, and they have so little shame that they proclaim their vices from the housetops. The other half are so degraded that they marry only as a matter of convenience, and their idea of amusement is to take their own wives to a brothel to witness every vile practice that the mind can conceive. A desire for children, the home, real love, have become things to snigger at. Dope, gambling, and the private cinema at which even bestiality is shown, have taken their place as the occupations of the rich. And what the rich do today the masses do tomorrow. That is why the ruling caste of France must die the death. It is to bring about their downfall that men like Weygand and Baudouin have striven with me. France must be purged for ever of this scum in order that the spirit of France which lives on in the common people may revivify her and make her once again a great nation.'

Hardly pausing for beath, she raced on: 'Communism could not do that; but National Socialism could. And however much you English may hate Hitler, I know him to be a great man. For a year—two years, perhaps—France will be occupied by a conqueror, but what is such a period in the hundreds of years of her history? Hitler will know how to deal with the real traitors; the wealthy parasites who have battened on the resources of the nation and paved the way for her downfall by the vile example they have set to her other classes. He will know, too, how to deal with the Communists and dangerous visionaries who preach their unworkable theories that all men are equal, which is fundamentally untrue.

'Out of chaos will come order. Under National Socialism we shall re-establish the ideal of the Family and reorganise our industrial resources so that the greatest good comes to the greatest number. For a time France must know the weight of a captive's chains in order that she may know how to utilise her freedom when she regains it once more. The people may suffer bitterness, humiliation, misery, but these things will pass, and when the time is ripe a new France will arise, reborn from the ashes of the old—a France clean in mind, strong in spirit and conscious of her glorious destiny.

'It is for this that I have lied and tricked and soiled my hands with blood, but you know that I speak the truth and you dare not call me a traitor now.'

For a moment Gregory did not reply. Her torrent of words had come crashing on to his brain, revealing her to be an utterly different personality from what he had thought her. Right or wrong, according to her own lights this small dark woman was a great patriot.

He knew that what she had said of the *Entente Cordiale* being an unnatural alliance was true. He knew that what she had said of the degeneracy of French society was true. He knew that any German occupation of France could not last indefinitely; and, however appalling it might sound, the Baroness's plan was, perhaps, the one and only way of restoring health and a new vitality to the moribund French nation. Yet he also knew that she had made one vital miscalculation.

'Do you realise,' he asked, 'that your vision of a new France will remain only a vision unless Hitler can secure Peace? For without Peace it will be impossible for him to reorganise Europe.'

She shrugged. 'With Hitler as master of Europe from northern Norway to the Pyrenees, Britain will not be able to carry on the war alone.'

Gregory shook his head. 'You're wrong there. Every man, woman and child in Britain knows that we dare not make a patched-up peace. Now that the war is on we are determined to fight it to a finish, because if we gave Hitler even a few months' breathing-space we should be completely at his mercy later on. You're much too clever a woman, Baroness, not to realise the truth of that.'

She shrugged again. 'Yes. You may fight on for a little, but what chance have you got? With the whole coast of France in his hands Hitler will be able to wear you down with intensive bombings until you are so weak that you will not be able to resist an invasion.'

'No, Baroness; there you're wrong again. He can bomb our cities but we shall stand up to the bombing somehow, even if we have to live in holes in the ground; and as long as the British Navy is paramount upon the seas he will never be able to land an invading force of sufficient strength to quell us. No threats, no terror, will be great enough to break the heart of Britain. And the worse things get the more determined we shall become to see matters through.'

As she stared at him he went on, speaking out of an unshakable conviction that radiated from him. 'I do not seek to belittle the gallantry of *your* people when I remind you that great areas of France have been conquered many times by the English and the Spaniards as well as by the Germans, and this would not be the first time if France is now compelled to accept the humiliation of a complete surrender; but in all their long history *my* people have never been conquered and have never surrendered. We broke the might of Spain; we fought your own King, Louis XIV, to a standstill. A Dutch fleet once entered the Thames, but we threw the Dutch out of the New World and broke their Sea Power for ever. Even when Britain stood alone against Napoleon she did not despair; she fought on until a British frigate took the former master of Europe into lonely exile.'

For the first time he saw a shadow of doubt enter the Baroness's dark eyes even as she protested. 'But this time it will be different. The English are effete; they've been pampered too long. They ran at Dunkirk. They'll give in—they'll give in.'

He smiled then, and he did not mean his smile to be patron-

376

ising, but there was something in it which drives all foreigners into a frenzy.

'Oh, no, they won't,' he said quietly. 'As a race we haven't altered. You mustn't allow yourself to be misled by what happened in Norway and Belgium. We're born muddlers, and in every war it takes us a little time to find our feet. You see, we're not like Continental countries; we're not organised for war, so our peace-time leaders are never any good when it comes to a scrap. But sooner or later we sift out the people at the top and things begin to happen. Last time we had Asquith, but he was replaced by Lloyd George, who, whatever may be said against him, was a great war leader. This time we had Chamberlain, but now Churchill has taken his place, and later on among the younger men we'll find some real live Generals.'

'Churchill!' she cried bitterly. 'Yes; he would still wish to fight if London were in ruins. But the people are not of the same metal; they'll revolt, throw Churchill overboard and sue for peace.'

'Don't you believe it!' His smile became a pitying grin. 'Churchill *is* England. He typifies the spirit of the Empire more than any other living man. He is what all of us would *like* to be, and ninety-nine per cent. of us are ready to fight with him to the last ditch. Yet even if a bomb or a bullet robbed us of him it would make no difference to the final outcome of the war, because other leaders would arise and we should fight on just the same. It was your own Napoleon who said that the British don't know when they're beaten; and that's the truth. It will be a long, hard road, but in the end the triumph of Britain is as certain as the rising of tomorrow's sun.'

'I don't believe it.' She nervously clasped and unclasped her hands, now openly doubting, but striving to resist any acceptance of the belief that he was forcing home on her.

'Oh, yes, you do,' he contradicted her. 'We've won the last battle in every war. That may be a cliché, but it's a fact; and it's going to be just the same this time. That is where you have made a terrible miscalculation, and, if you think for a moment, you will see how by Britain's refusal to accept a patched-up peace all your dreams must fall to pieces. Hitler may make himself lord of Europe; Goering may send his bombers to destroy our homes; Goebbels may lie and rage and threaten; but all the time the Blockade will go on, and sooner or later the Nazis will not know which way to turn for war materials and food. Then all those who have aided Hitler, and millions of innocent people as well, must pay the price of his damnable ambitions. And as long as France is Hitler's vassal she, too, must pay.'

'Stop!' cried the Baroness. 'Stop! I will not listen.' But he went on to point the moral with inexorable, relentless logic.

'Even if the Nazis destroyed our air-ports and our factories we should still fight on from Canada; and the United States are behind us now. All the vast resources of that great Democracy will be placed at our disposal to help us smash the Nazis. Our Navy and Air Force will render your ports useless for years to come; the shipping in them must lie idle because you will be cut off from your colonies and your world markets. Every industry in France will be ruined through lack of fuel and raw materials, and the machinery in your factories will rust. Your great Army will have to be disbanded, but there will be no work for the men to do. By next winter you will have ten million unemployed. Your herds and your livestock will die because there will not be enough cattle-food to feed them. To keep their own people from revolt the Germans will be forced to seize the bulk of your agricultural produce. The spectre of famine will enter every home from Calais to Marseilles, and disease will take its terrible toll from Strasbourg to Biarritz. There will be riots and street-fighting in the towns and cities; the starving crowds will wreck the food trains which are taking your crops into Germany and they will murder the Nazi officials who are set over them. Then there will be ghastly reprisals—huge fines—and your most spirited young men—those who should be your leaders of tomorrow—will be shot in batches against the wall of your German-occupied barracks. Whole towns may be given over to destruction in a ruthless attempt to keep you under, and the country will fall into the same state of lawlessness that made life so terrible in the Middle Ages. Bands of desperate, hungry men will roam the country, breaking into houses, killing people who oppose them and torturing others in the hope that they will give away the hiding-places of secret stores of food. The very children upon whom you are counting to grow up as the citizens of the new France that you have planned will die in their cradles, or only reach maturity warped in mind from the horrors that they have witnessed and crippled in body from malnutrition. That, *Madame la Baronne,* is what you will have done to France.'

She cowered away from him, her scarlet mouth a little open,

her black eyes wide, then she whispered: 'This is a ghastly picture that you paint, *Monsieur*.'

'Yet it is true,' Gregory insisted. 'All that I have said is absolutely inevitable if Britain fights on—and Britain *will* fight on.'

Suddenly her red mouth twitched and she cried: 'I hate you —I *hate* you! Never before have I been shaken in my belief, but you have made me doubt, and if I am wrong I deserve to die.'

Gregory put up his pistol and shook his head. 'No. I'm not going to shoot you now. Whatever you may have done in the past, you have convinced me today that you did it believing that it was for the good of your country. I only wish, though, that we had talked together months ago, because I believe that I could have shown you that you were wrong and persuaded you to use your great powers for good instead of ill; but it's too late now.'

'Too late,' she repeated. Then a new expression suddenly lit her dark eyes. 'I wonder. The military situation in France is now beyond repair, but if France could be kept in the war the Fleet could be saved—and the colonies.'

In a flash Gregory saw that he had achieved the seemingly impossible. The swift, cold brain of this extraordinary woman had not only analysed and accepted his arguments but had gone on to estimate future possibilities in the light of a new conviction. Without any telling she had grasped the fact that, although France was lost, if Britain fought on the only hope of saving her country from the horrors he had pictured lay in aiding Britain to smash Hitler as rapidly as possible so that France might be freed again before she fell into a state of anarchy.

Starting forward, he seized her by the arm. 'If there *is* the faintest hope still remaining we mustn't lose an instant.'

'Let me think.' She closed her eyes for a moment. 'What time is it?'

'It's getting on for four o'clock.'

'Four. Then Reynaud is overdue; he should have been here half an hour ago.'

'Here?' Gregory exclaimed. 'But the Government is still in Bordeaux. Surely he would never leave it at a time like this?'

'You don't understand,' she cried impatiently. 'It was part of the plan that he should resign and hand over to Pétain. He's been fighting against it for days but we've all been at him, and before I left Bordeaux yesterday his resignation had been assured.'

'Then, if he's no longer in power it's too late for him to do anything.'

'Not necessarily. Paul's instinct has always been to fight to the last ditch. I have only to say the word to him in order to reanimate him with the fighting spirit once again. When he arrives I could go with him to the local post-office, where we could get a priority call through to Bordeaux. If he could get in touch with de Gaulle and Mandel and the other leaders of the war party he could summon them to join him in Avignon. They could render the new Bordeaux Cabinet still-born by denouncing Pétain as a usurper, or at least proclaim an Independent Government from there, which would have Britain and at least half France behind it.'

Before Gregory had time to reply they both caught the sound of a motor horn, and ran to the window. One glance at the small, solitary figure getting out of the dust-covered car that had driven up in front of the house was enough for Gregory to recognise Paul Reynaud.

'Stand back,' said the Baroness quickly. 'Leave this to me. Your presence will only complicate matters.'

As Gregory stepped behind the curtains he heard Reynaud's voice calling up to the Baroness. 'It is finished. I resigned at eleven-thirty this morning and Pétain is forming a new Cabinet with Weygand as Vice-President. I took a plane to Toulon and hired a car from there. Thank God it is over!'

'Wait, Paul!' the Baroness called back. 'Don't come into the house—I am coming out to you. I have much to tell you but we can talk as we go. You must drive me down to the post-office at once.'

Turning from the window she said to Gregory: 'Stay where you are. Poor fellow, he looks so tired that he will be as putty in my hands. We may not be back for an hour or more, but wait here.'

She was already at the door before she had finished speaking and next moment she was running from the house. For a few minutes Gregory remained deep in thought, trying to assess the new possibilities which had arisen from that extraordinary interchange of views that had taken place between himself and the Baroness. Then he lit a cigarette and stepped out from behind the curtains. To his surprise he saw that Reynaud's car was still outside the house yet he could have sworn that he had heard it drive off. Next second he noticed that the rear off-wheel of Reynaud's car was deflated. He must have had a puncture and driven the last few miles on a flat tyre. Thrusting his head out of the window Gregory saw another car streaking down the hill. They had taken Grauber's.

'Stop! Stop!' he yelled at the top of his voice. 'For God's sake *stop*!' But at that very moment the steering-gear with which he had tampered gave way. The car suddenly swerved across the road. With a horrid clang of iron on brick and the sound of shattered glass it charged straight into the wall of a villa at the bottom of the hill.

Swinging round, Gregory dashed out of the house and ran at the top of his speed down the slope. When he reached the villa its occupants had already come out and were lifting two bleeding bodies from the wreckage. Reynaud was badly cut about the head and face, and unconscious but still alive. The little Black Baroness was dead.

After he had given what help he could he sadly retraced his steps. There would be no new fighting Government of France proclaimed from Avignon now.

     3   3   3   3   3

When he reached *Les Roches* the villa was still silent and apparently deserted. The servants were in the far wing of the house and none of them put in an appearance while Gregory was carrying the steel deed-boxes and other things round to the van. At twenty to five he set off on his long journey back to Bordeaux.

The whole of that lovely south coast of France which had been a joy to so many million holiday-makers was now a terrible spectacle. There had always been little camps, but gay affairs, with girls in beach-pyjamas and men in coloured shirts. Now the camps stretched through every wood adjacent to the beaches; but there were no beach-pyjamas and no gaily-coloured shirts. Five million homeless and foodless people had streamed into the area. They had reached the sea and they could go no further. The sun would warm them, but how they were to live and how many would survive the dark future no man could say.

But Gregory had no leisure now to speculate upon the awful fate that *La Baronne Noire* had brought upon her country and he had eyes only for the road ahead. Between ten to five and seven o'clock, when the post-offices shut, he made six halts at different points along his route and from each he sent a telegram, with the same message, to Sir Pellinore:

'GIVE ME UNTIL MIDDAY TOMORROW IF YOU POSSIBLY CAN.'

In the south and west communications had not been interrupted, apart from the congestion of the lines, and he could only hope that one of his wires might get through to Sir Pellinore before he left Bordeaux that night.

After that he made only two other stops, at Montpelier and Cahors, to fill up with petrol and to snatch a cup of coffee from a wayside buffet. All through the evening, all through the night, all through the early hours of the Monday morning, he drove on and on, crouched over his wheel, eating up the miles that lay between him and the Atlantic coast. If it had not been for the powerful Mercédès-Benz engine hidden beneath the bonnet of the van he could never have done it, but he pulled up in front of the Hotel Julius Caesar at twenty-five minutes to twelve.

Sir Pellinore was standing there on the steps, smoking a big cigar, in the bright sunshine. Beside him were two suitcases. The moment he saw Gregory he picked up the bags, ran down the steps and scrambled up beside him.

Gregory grinned wearily. 'So my telegrams got through?'

'Yes. I had two from you last night, and two more came in this morning. But we've got to get out of this place before it becomes too hot to hold us; we're in enemy territory now. Off you go! Straight to the docks. I'll direct you.'

As they drove through the streets Sir Pellinore gave Gregory the last grim bulletin. It was the seventeenth of June and the thirteenth day of the battle for France. The Army had collapsed and was now falling back in every sector, from its easternmost positions, near Dijon, to the sea. The last great German strategic operation, initiated five days before, had proved overwhelmingly successful. Hitler's iron columns had battered their way east, from Saint Dizier, through Chaumont, across the Plateau de Langres, to Gray and Besançon, on the Swiss frontier, thereby cutting the entire Maginot Line off from Central France. That morning Marshal Pétain had broadcast that on the previous night he had asked for an armistice. The mighty five-week drama had at last reached its terrible conclusion and the curtain was about to be rung down.

At the dock gates some petty French officials refused to allow the van to pass, but Sir Pellinore had already made arrangements to be met in case he had trouble in getting on board. A British naval lieutenant came out of the gates almost before the argument had got under way, and behind him was a squad of armed bluejackets. Unceremoniously they brushed the French aside, jumped on to the running-boards of the van and took it through to the dockside, where a small cargo ship, crowded with English refugees, was tied up.

The naval officer had not bargained for the van, but his orders were to do all in his power to render Sir Pellinore any assistance required. The French dockers refused to load the van so the British seamen hoisted it with a derrick; the fore-well of the ship was cleared and roped off, then the van was lowered into it. Ten minutes later the hawsers were cast off and the ship put to sea.

As they steamed out into the broad Gironde, Gregory said: 'Well, it looks as though we're in for pretty tough times ahead.'

Sir Pellinore drew slowly on his cigar. 'Yes; but there are always two sides to a question. You've read your history, Gregory, and you know a bit about military campaigns. Hasn't it often struck you that it's not so much numbers that win wars as singleness of purpose? When we fought Louis of France half Marlborough's trouble was getting the German princes and the Dutch—and all sorts of other people—to line up with him; and it was just the same when we fought Napoleon—one after another of our Allies let us down. Allies mean divided councils. The weakness of one hampers the war effort of the others, so I'm not at all certain that what has happened isn't for the best. We have no more Allies left to rat on us; but we have ourselves and the Empire. We can take all that's coming to us—you may be sure of that; then, when the time is ripe, we shall be able to strike *when, how and where we will*. But tell me,' he lowered his voice, 'did you get that woman?'

Gregory shook his head. 'No. I've an extraordinary story to tell you, but that will have to wait. Since I left Finland, thirteen weeks ago, I've travelled some seven thousand miles. That's well over five hundred miles a week on average, and fourteen hundred of it have been done in the last three days, over roads choked with French refugees; so I'm pretty well all in.'

'Of course, my boy,' Sir Pellinore nodded. 'I'll see that naval feller and, whoever else has to be turned out, he'll fix you a berth. But even if you didn't get her you haven't come away empty-handed; you got the van.'

'Yes; I got the van, with the letter-files that now mean so much to us, and a splendid fortune including a good hundred-thousand-pounds' worth of old masters. There's one there that I'd rather like you to have a look at before I turn in.'

They went down the ladder to the fore-well where the van had been chocked up, and wrenching away the broken padlock Gregory pulled open the doors. Its contents were exactly the same as when the van had left the garage of the Julius Caesar, but for one addition. A big, bloated, paunchy man, with his wrists and ankles tied, was lying on the floor, breathing stertorously in a half-conscious state.

'Hitler has won his battle,' smiled Gregory, 'but I've won mine. I don't think you've met my prisoner—*Herr Gruppenführer* Grauber.'

·   ⌘   ⌘   ⌘   ⌘

A little over eight hours later Sir Pellinore shook Gregory out of a deep sleep. 'I wouldn't have wakened you,' he said, 'but we've just had it over the radio that Churchill is going to broadcast at nine o'clock. It's an historic occasion that I felt you wouldn't want to miss and you can turn in again immediately afterwards.'

When Gregory came up the companionway he saw that the ship had passed the river-mouth and left the French coast behind. The stars of the summer night were coming out as dusk closed down upon the sea.

In the little saloon of the ship they sat with long glasses in their hands as the voice of the 'Lion of England' came clearly to them across the broad waters that are Britain's heritage.

'What has happened in France makes no difference to British faith and purpose. We have become the sole champion now in arms to defend the world cause. We shall defend our island and with the British Empire around us we shall fight on, unconquerable, until the curse of Hitler is lifted from the brows of men.'